Dream destinations...

Exotic pleasures...

The world's most eligible men!

Dreaming of a foreign affair? Then, look no further! We've brought together the best and sexiest men the world has to offer, the most exciting, exotic locations and the most powerful, passionate stories.

This month, in *Caribbean Caress*, we bring back two fantastic novels – by popular Modern Romance™ authors Catherine Spencer and Cathy Williams. In the hot Caribbean nights, one night is all it takes... Every month in **Foreign Affairs** you can be swept away to a new location – and indulge in a little passion in the sun!

There are millionaires with scorching sex appeal in
MEDITERRANEAN MOMENTS
by Sandra Marton & Josie Metcalfe
Out next month!

CATHERINE SPENCER

Catherine Spencer, once an English teacher, fell into writing through eavesdropping on a conversation about Mills & Boon® romances. Within two months she changed careers and sold her first book to Mills & Boon® in 1984. She moved to Canada from England thirty years ago and lives in Vancouver. She is married to a Canadian and has four grown children – two daughters and two sons – plus three dogs and a cat. In her spare time she plays the piano, collects antiques, and grows tropical shrubs.

Catherine Spencer's brand new book
The Doctor's Secret Child is available in
Modern Romance™ this month!

CATHY WILLIAMS

Cathy Williams is Trinidadian and was brought up on the twin islands of Trinidad and Tobago. She was awarded a scholarship to study in Britain, and came to Exeter University in 1975 to continue her studies into the great loves of her life: languages and literature. It was there that Cathy met her husband, Richard. Since they married Cathy has lived in England, originally in the Thames Valley but now in the Midlands. Cathy and Richard have three small daughters.

Riccardo's Secret Child is Cathy's exciting new novel,
available in Modern Romance™ next month!

caribbean caress

CATHERINE SPENCER & CATHY WILLIAMS

THE BILLIONAIRES' PLAYGROUND

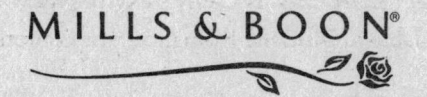

MILLS & BOON®

DID YOU PURCHASE THIS BOOK WITHOUT A COVER?
If you did, you should be aware it is **stolen property** as it was reported *unsold and destroyed* by a retailer. Neither the author nor the publisher has received any payment for this book.

All the characters in this book have no existence outside the imagination of the author, and have no relation whatsoever to anyone bearing the same name or names. They are not even distantly inspired by any individual known or unknown to the author, and all the incidents are pure invention.

All Rights Reserved including the right of reproduction in whole or in part in any form. This edition is published by arrangement with Harlequin Enterprises II B.V. The text of this publication or any part thereof may not be reproduced or transmitted in any form or by any means, electronic or mechanical, including photocopying, recording, storage in an information retrieval system, or otherwise, without the written permission of the publisher.

This book is sold subject to the condition that it shall not, by way of trade or otherwise, be lent, resold, hired out or otherwise circulated without the prior consent of the publisher in any form of binding or cover other than that in which it is published and without a similar condition including this condition being imposed on the subsequent purchaser.

MILLS & BOON and MILLS & BOON with the Rose Device are registered trademarks of the publisher.
Harlequin Mills & Boon Limited,
Eton House, 18-24 Paradise Road, Richmond, Surrey, TW9 1SR

Caribbean Caress © Harlequin Enterprises II B.V., 2002

Dominic's Child and *Accidental Mistress*
were first published in Great Britain by
Harlequin Mills & Boon Limited in separate, single volumes.

Dominic's Child © Kathy Garner 1996
Accidental Mistress © Cathy Williams 1997

ISBN 0 263 83189 2

126-0702

Printed and bound in Spain
by Litografia Rosés S.A., Barcelona

caribbean caress

DOMINIC'S CHILD

ACCIDENTAL MISTRESS

DOMINIC'S CHILD

CATHERINE SPENCER

For Grace Green
with love and gratitude for
her loyalty and support.

CHAPTER ONE

SOPHIE knew at once who it was rapping on her hotel room door in that imperious "Don't keep me waiting" manner, partly, of course, because the chief of police had forewarned her that Dominic Winter was en route to St. Julian, but also because there was in the summons nothing of the islanders' discreet *tap tap* that begged the favor of admittance.

Instead, this was the peremptory crack of bone on wood—the command of a superior being to one of lesser stature. If he'd bellowed, "Open the door, woman, and let me in!" his message could not have been clearer.

For all that she'd been expecting him, the proof of Dominic Winter's arrival had Sophie starting up out of the chair in a flurry of agitation. The sound of his knock seemed indecently loud somehow, and not at all fitting to the somber gravity of the occasion.

On her way to answer him, she made an unplanned stop before the mirror, though why she bothered escaped her. She knew her hair was perfectly in place, her attire as suitably subdued as could be achieved, given the sort of clothes she'd brought with her.

Perhaps it was because she needed to be sure that nothing in her face gave her away. Of course she was upset, saddened; under the circumstances, that was to be expected. But there was more. There'd always been something more where Dominic Winter was concerned, and that was what he must never suspect.

He strode into the room and, without the slightest concession to civil good manners, said in a tone as forbiddingly cold as his name, "Well, I hope you're happy with what you've done, Ms. Casson. My fiancée is dead and her parents are shattered."

"It was an accident," she heard herself reply defensively, and wondered why she didn't just set him straight and have done with it. Whatever other guilty secrets she harbored, culpability in Barbara's death was not among them. But one didn't launch into a diatribe about a dead woman's shortcomings, not to the man who'd hoped to marry her in another few months and certainly not within seconds of his arriving at the scene of her untimely demise. There would be opportunity enough for him to learn the details leading up to the accident later, when he'd recovered a little from the shock and from the draining exhaustion of travel.

If Sophie was prepared to show a little sensitivity, however, Dominic Winter was not. "You might call it an accident," he declared flatly, "but I've yet to be convinced that you aren't guilty of criminal negligence—in which case 'manslaughter' would be a more accurate term, or perhaps even 'murder'."

Sophie prided herself on being a capable, independent sort of woman. Going weak at the knees when someone tried to intimidate her simply wasn't her style. But she felt the blood drain from her face at his intimation. "Mr. Winter," she said, backing away from him unsteadily, "I was nowhere near Barbara when she died. In fact, I was completely unaware of her plans on Wednesday, and if you don't believe me then I suggest you check my alibi with Chief Inspector Montand, who is perfectly satisfied that I am in no way to blame for what happened to her."

"But I am not Chief Inspector Montand, Ms. Casson, and I do hold you to blame. You encouraged Barbara to come away with you. If you had not, she would be alive today."

What could she say that didn't sound like an excuse? Sophie bit her lip and turned toward the louvered doors that led to the balcony. Outside, the entire world seemed bent on the celebration of life. Everything, from the surf rolling rhythmically up the pale gold crescent of beach to the sultry sway of the coconut palms fringing the hotel grounds, seemed to echo the calypso beat of the ever-present steel band.

A scarlet hibiscus, shot full of burgundy fire from the sun, flamed next to an overpoweringly sweet-scented frangipani. Macaws perched on the backs of unoccupied sun chaises, brazenly flaunting their plumage.

But what she had found breathtakingly lovely only two days before struck Sophie now as obscene. How could there be death in the midst of such vibrant life? Tragedy did not marry easily with the carnival atmosphere that was St. Julian's stock-in-trade.

Closing her eyes, she struggled to find the words to ease Dominic Winter's pain. Because she knew he must be hurting, even though she'd noticed that he hadn't included himself among those shattered by Barbara's death. Or was that wishful thinking on her part? Would she have preferred him not to care?

Ashamed, she shut out the question just as, over the past ten weeks, she'd learned to shut out other inappropriate thoughts concerning this man. "I did not coerce Barbara into accompanying me, Mr. Winter," she said at last. "It was entirely her idea. In fact, she was so insistent she needed a change of scene to get her through the coming winter that if she hadn't come here with me, she'd undoubtedly have run off somewhere else."

"And you never thought to question the logic of that?"

"Why should I?" she cried, stung by his unremitting air of condemnation. "She was an adult, capable of making up her own mind, and I hardly knew her. If anyone should have recognized that she was...highly strung and wildly impetuous, it should have been you."

At that, the antagonism in his eyes faded somewhat and it occurred to Sophie that, for the only time in their acquaintance, he allowed her to see past the glower to the man inside. It also occurred to her how seldom she'd seen him smile, even in the early days of her association with Barbara when he'd presumably had every reason to be happy.

Sophie had met him in mid-September when she first began working at the Wexler estate, although perhaps "met" wasn't quite the word to describe his remote nod of acknowledgment when she had been introduced to him. Her first impression had been that he was a snob, the kind of man who found it beneath his dignity to treat an employee, whether his or someone else's, with the same respect he accorded to his own kind—even when, as in her case, the employee was a professional whose framed credentials attested to her expertise.

It was only later that she wondered if he made a particular point of maintaining a safe distance from her, a notion based more on feminine instinct than hard fact. Because, despite his apparent uninterest in her comings and goings, she'd several times caught him spying on her, even when she was at the far end of the property and about as far away from him as she could get. She'd look up and there he'd be at one of the long windows, or standing in the shade of the pergola that connected the

Wexlers' handsome Georgian-style mansion to the rose gardens below the terrace.

Tall and authoritative, with astonishingly beautiful eyes that, depending on his mood, changed from rich deep jade to brilliant emerald ice, he was a man of presence and impossible to ignore. She found him disturbingly attractive yet formidably remote. She'd had no more idea what went on in that head of his than she could have unraveled the mystery of the sphinx. He had remained an enigma, despite her clandestine fascination with him—until now, when tragedy fractured his reserve and rendered him marginally more human.

"Barbara was like a child," he said, pacing back and forth across the tiled floor, "incapable of recognizing her own mortality. If she had told me ahead of time that she planned to sneak off with you, I'd have done my level best to stop her. And if I had not been able to succeed, I would have warned you to keep an eye on her. What I don't understand is why, if, as you claim, you hardly knew her, you decided to share a holiday with her."

"It was a last-minute thing," Sophie explained. "Usually, I travel with my friend, Elaine, but she came down with the chicken pox three days before we were due to fly down here. I happened to mention it to Barbara and she immediately offered to buy Elaine's ticket. I saw no reason to quarrel with that, especially since Elaine hadn't bothered to take out cancellation insurance and stood to lose rather a lot of money. But I did make it clear to Barbara that, once we arrived here, we'd go our separate ways for most of the time."

In less than a blink of his remarkable eyes, Dominic Winter's antagonism rolled back into place again, swathed in biting sarcasm. "In other words, Barbara became an inconvenience once she'd served the purpose of averting a financial loss for your friend. Allow me to say, Ms. Casson, that I am overwhelmed by so commendable an attitude. You're obviously all heart!"

"This is a working vacation for me, Mr. Winter. I couldn't afford the luxury of whiling away the time the way Barbara did. She understood that. If you choose to put the worst possible interpretation on my actions, there's little I can do about it."

"And even less that you care."

Oh, she cared, more than he could begin to guess! But she'd be damned if she'd let it show.

"Exactly," she retorted, then made matters worse by compounding the lie with an even greater untruth. "Your opinion of me matters not one iota and if that offends you, Mr. Winter, perhaps the knowledge that I'm singularly unimpressed by you, too, will even the score between us. I don't know quite how I expected you to behave today but if you'd shown a glimmer of compassion, I might have felt more kindly disposed to tolerate your insults. As it is, I can't quite shake the feeling that perhaps it was the thought of spending the rest of her life with you that drove Barbara to behave so rashly last Wednesday."

He had the kind of skin that glowed with sun-kissed radiance regardless of the season, but at her words his face grew bleached with shock. Equally appalled, Sophie stared at him, her gaze fused with his. The man was clearly in pain. What was it about him that compelled her to add to his misery?

She knew. She'd always known, right from the start: she was afraid of him.

She'd never dared explore the reasons. It was enough that, from the first moment she'd set eyes on him, she'd felt a stirring of hunger for something—some*one*—who wasn't hers to have. And so, out of self-defense, she'd manufactured a dislike of him, and it had worked well enough until now when his chilly reserve slipped.

Perhaps it was as well that, at that moment, the phone rang and provided them both with a distraction. Certainly she was glad of the excuse to turn away from him and busy herself picking up the receiver.

She listened a moment, murmured assent, then hung up. "That was Chief Inspector Montand," she told Dominic. "He's downstairs in the hotel foyer and would like to speak to us."

"Why us and not just me? If you're as blamelessly detached from this tragedy as you claim to be, what more can he possibly have to say to you?"

She shrugged, calling up that old, contrived antipathy to arm herself against him. It was easy enough to do, given his miserable attitude. "Ask him. I don't make the rules around here."

Yet she hated the way she sounded, so hard and uncaring, as though the fact that a young woman had died didn't matter as long as that person wasn't Sophie Casson.

It was almost comforting to hark back to Wednesday evening when the wreckage of the Laser had been found and the awful truth of Barbara's fate had begun to take shape. Sophie hadn't been flippant then. Her initial reaction of paralyzed disbelief had given way to near hysteria. It had taken a sedative prescribed by the hotel doctor to calm her down. Not even Dominic Winter could have doubted the sincerity of her distress that night.

Today, however, was a different matter. Contempt curling his incredibly sexy mouth, he flung wide the door and with an extravagantly courteous flourish ushered her into the hall outside. "Well, let's not keep the good inspector waiting, Ms. Casson. I'm sure you have more interesting things planned for this afternoon than rehashing the tedious minutiae of Barbara's death."

He is suffering, Sophie intoned silently. *Remember that and refuse to enter into hurtful mind games with him, no matter how much he goads you.*

Spine straight, head high, she swept ahead of him. Her navy-and-white-striped skirt fluttered around her calves in concealing folds but her low-backed white blouse with its halter neckline left her feeling woefully underdressed. She could almost feel Dominic's glare branding her bare shoulders with the stigmata of his disapproval.

She had reached the top of the sweeping staircase before he caught up with her. His hand cupped her elbow, a cool, impersonal touch that stemmed less from concern for her safe descent than from the habit of inbred good manners. She was tall, almost five feet eight inches, but beside him she felt small. Small and defiant, like a child trying to match wits with a punitive uncle. But she would not give him the satisfaction of knowing that. There would be no more snide, insulting remarks, no insinuations of blame—at least not from her and not for the next several days.

And after that? Well, he'd no longer be even remotely involved in her life and she would be free to forget him—if she could.

At the far end of the foyer, St. Julian's chief of police, immaculate in white Bermudas and short-sleeved white shirt, tucked his pith helmet under one arm and snapped to attention at their approach. "Inspector Montand at your service, *monsieur*. I am sorry to welcome you to our island under such unhappy circumstances."

Dominic nodded and came straight to the point. "Have you found my fiancée's body yet, Montand?"

If the inspector was offended by so blunt an approach, he didn't allow it to show. Ebony features impassive, he replied in the melodious island accent that Sophie found enchanting, "Sadly, we have not. The ocean currents beyond the reef, you understand, and the sharks..." His shrug, half Gallic, half native Caribbean, would have been comical at any other time. "We do not expect to find her, *monsieur*."

"Her parents will find that very difficult to accept."

"I understand. *S'il vous plaît*..." He extended a pale palm in the direction of a trio of rattan chairs grouped beneath one of the many whirling ceiling fans. "Perhaps we could talk where it is cooler and more private?"

"How is it," Dominic asked when they were seated, "that no one thought to question my fiancée's ability to handle one of the hotel sailboats alone? It strikes me that the staff must bear some responsibility for her death."

Inspector Montand's gaze flickered beseechingly in Sophie's direction. She looked away and stared at an arrangement of tropical fruit on a side table, unwilling to help him out of what she knew to be a difficult spot.

The plain fact of the matter was that, practically from the moment she'd set foot on St. Julian, there had been any number of warnings leveled Barbara's way, and from more than one source, too.

It is not customary for unescorted ladies to behave so freely with employees, mademoiselle...

Barbara, you can't appear in public in that bikini! You'll offend the locals...

Mademoiselle, it is unwise to venture alone at night into the old section of town...

But Barbara had willfully ignored them all and instead seemed driven to excess in everything she'd done. She'd flirted outrageously with every male in sight; she'd partied with a frenzy that bordered on desperation. And, most recently, she'd taken to staying out all night, slinking back to the room she shared with Sophie just as the sun was rising. Her behavior had been downright embarrassing—not to mention downright odd for a woman supposedly in love and soon to be married.

Not that there hadn't been reason to question Barbara's devotion to her fiancé before then. "Dom's a wonderful catch," she'd boasted during one of her first conversations with Sophie. "Daddy says he's one of the few men who can afford me. Of course, he indulges my every whim, which is just as well because that's the sort of thing I've been used to all my life and I'm not about to settle for anything less just because I'm married."

Then she'd flashed her dazzling smile and shrugged as though to say she knew she sounded like a spoiled child but underneath she was really a charming, mature adult. As, indeed, she could be when it suited her. How else had she managed to wheedle Sophie into allowing her to tag along on the trip to the tiny island of St. Julian, a few hundred miles off the northeast coast of Venezuela?

Dominic's fingers rapping irritably on the glass-topped table brought Sophie back to the present with a start. "Well, Inspector, don't you agree? My fiancée didn't know one end of a boat from the other. As for raising a sail—the mere idea is absurd! She should never have been allowed—"

"As it happens, Monsieur Winter, Mademoiselle Wexler was not alone. According to hotel personnel who spoke with her on Wednesday morning and arranged for her to use the boat, she was accompanied by a member of the staff, a young man quite skilled at handling small craft such as the Laser."

"Then why the hell isn't he here now, answering my questions, instead of leaving you to do it?"

"Sad to say, he, too, was lost."

"Doesn't say much for his so-called skill, does it?" Dominic snapped.

The inspector shrugged apologetically. "The trouble appears to have been that they took the boat beyond the reef on the windward side of the island. Quite apart from the fact that a Laser is not meant to be sailed in the dangerous currents sweeping in from the Atlantic, it is also impossible for a person on shore to notice so small a vessel in distress. I am afraid that neither your fiancée nor the young man she hired as her crew showed very good sense when they chose to ignore the posted signs along that stretch of coast."

Dominic looked as if he might argue the point, then clamped his lips shut and glanced away. Sophie breathed a quiet sigh of relief. She would not have liked to be the one to corroborate what the chief inspector was trying so delicately to convey: that Barbara had invited her own disaster and was, perhaps, responsible for another person's death, too.

At length, Dominic turned back and this time leveled his bleak gaze on Sophie. "Where were you while all this was going on?"

"In the middle of town, photographing the water gardens outside the former governor's residence." Determined to let her better self prevail no matter how much he provoked her, she laid a sympathetic hand on his arm. "Mr. Winter—Dominic, I know it's hard not to want to lay blame on someone, but Barbara's death truly was an accident and the sooner you accept that, the sooner you'll begin to heal."

He shook her off as if she were an annoying little

lapdog begging for favors. "It was an accident that could and should have been avoided. What was this employee thinking of that he sailed outside the reef to begin with?"

"I imagine because Barbara insisted he do so," Sophie said, exasperation winning out over tact and lending a decided edge to her voice. "She could be very persuasive when she wanted something, as I think we both know."

He dismissed the observation with an impatient shrug and turned back to Inspector Montand. "Have you called off the search?"

"*Oui, monsieur.* There is little point in continuing. The windward coast is extremely treacherous."

"I'll reserve judgment on that until I've seen the place for myself. This afternoon."

The police chief nodded deferentially. "I will arrange for you to be taken there."

"No need." Dominic cut him off with an autocratic wave of the hand and favored Sophie with another inimical glare. "You're reasonably familiar with the island, I take it?"

"Yes, I—"

"Then you can come with me."

Not "will you?" or "would you mind?" and certainly not a hint of a "please". Just another order, rapped out and expected to be obeyed without any regard for the fact that, for reasons that almost made her blush, she might not wish to be thrust into his company like this.

But he was not a mind reader, praise the Lord, so as much to put a speedy end to this whole sad business as to accommodate him, she stifled a refusal and said instead, "Of course."

"Where can we rent a car?" He ran a finger inside the collar of his open-necked shirt. "Preferably one equipped with air-conditioning."

"We can't—at least not the sort you have in mind."

"What? Why not?"

"Except for a very few registered government vehicles, there are no cars allowed on the island."

"You mean that open contraption decked out in flowers that brought me from the airport—"

"It's called a jitney. And it's one of only two on St. Julian."

An exasperated breath puffed from between his lips. "Then what's the alternative? Riding bareback on a donkey and waving a straw hat in the air?"

Chief Inspector Montand's posture, which would have done credit to the French Foreign Legion at the best of times, stiffened perceptibly. Sophie flung him a commiserating glance before saying mildly, "There's no need to be offensive, Mr. Winter. St. Julian might lack the sort of sophistication you're used to at home, but its other charms more than make up for that. We can take one of the mini-mokes provided by the hotel. It'll be more than adequate. The island is quite small."

Except for the streets in the center of town and the route from the airport, there was only one other paved road on St. Julian. The Coast Road, as its name suggested, ribboned around the perimeter of the island, dipping down at times into secluded coves and at others climbing to offer dizzying views of turquoise sea and jungle-clad mountains. Because its passage was so narrow, island custom dictated that traffic move always in a clockwise direction, even though that meant that a five mile trip out involved a twenty-five mile trip back again.

The little buggy, the fringe on its striped canvas canopy fluttering in the breeze, swooped merrily along with a scowling Dominic at the wheel. "I've driven more sophisticated golf carts," he grumbled as they jolted over one particularly vicious bump in the road.

"Would you prefer walking?" Sophie inquired, unable to disguise the sarcasm as they approached the next steep incline.

"I'd prefer not to be here at all," he shot back without a moment's hesitation. "Nor would I be, if it weren't for you and your half-baked ideas of a holiday paradise."

"St. Julian doesn't pretend to be Rio or Monte Carlo, Mr. Winter. If it did, I wouldn't bother wasting my time visiting it. The sort of people who flock to places like that don't particularly appeal to me."

The merest hint of a grin touched his lips. "People like me, you mean?"

She pulled off her sunglasses and subjected him to a frank examination, wondering if the extraordinary conditions of their mission might offer a glimpse past the good looks to the man within.

She was doomed to disappointment. Black hair swept back from a wide, intelligent brow. His nose had been broken at some point but had suffered not the least for the misfortune and merely enhanced the strong, uncompromising line of his profile. His eyes were the deep still green of woodland pools and his lashes would have been laughable had not the set of his jaw promised dreadful retribution to anyone who dared to make light of their beauty. As for the rest of him, it was so formidably and sexily masculine that he'd probably had to beat women off since the onset of puberty. But as far as giving a clue to his inner self? Not a one!

"What are you staring at?" he inquired testily, swiveling a glance at her.

"You," she replied. "I'm trying to figure out if you're this irascible all the time or if it's a temporary by-product of grief and heartache. I'm inclined to believe the latter since Barbara didn't strike me as the type who'd willingly devote the rest of her life to a chronic grouch."

He flung her another outraged glare before turning his attention once again to the road. "How much farther?" he barked.

"About seven miles. Once we round the headland, we drop down to the weather side of the island. You'll notice the change in the coastline immediately. It's very wild."

That he grew progressively more withdrawn as they covered the distance was indication enough that he agreed with her assessment. "Good God!" he muttered at one point, as spray flying across the windswept beach and on to the road caused visibility to shrink to a few yards. "Is it always like this?"

"More or less, though during the hurricane season it gets much worse."

"I'll take your word for it," he replied dryly. "Barbara must have been mad to consider trying to sail in this."

They were approaching the wind-battered southeastern tip of St. Julian, the place where Atlantic fury met the point of most resistance from the land mass. The shore there was littered with easy pickings for the beachcomber: driftwood forged into fantastic shapes, and seashells by the thousand in every shade from dark pearlescent purple to palest satin pink.

"There's a lookout point right ahead," Sophie said. "If you pull over, we can walk across the dunes and you'll see the reef where..."

He nodded, sparing her the necessity of having to elaborate, and swung the mini-moke off the road.

They clambered down to the beach and waded through the fine, soft sand. Then stood shoulder to shoulder and leaned into the wind, together yet separated by the intensely private silence in which Dominic wrapped himself.

A jagged line of surf marked the hidden reef. Close into shore the water swirled and foamed, subdued but by no means tamed by the barrier over which it had hurled itself. But beyond, where the heaving green Atlantic rollers let loose their fury... Dear Lord, Barbara must have been bent on suicide to have tried to sail in that, because no sane person could have hoped to survive such unleashed violence!

Sophie couldn't quell her shudder and looked away. Small wonder no trace of bodies had been found. It was a miracle the splintered wreckage of the Laser had endured the sort of beating it had taken.

Dominic, however, stared impassively for so long at the scene before him that Sophie half wondered if he'd forgotten her presence. Then, without warning, he swung toward her, his features stark with misery. "Get me the hell away from here before I really lose it," he muttered savagely.

He saw the dismay she couldn't hide, saw how it softened to compassion, and didn't know how he contained himself. He wanted to howl his outrage to the heavens; to curse and revile the cruelty and waste he'd been helpless to prevent. But the shock Sophie Casson now felt would be nothing compared to how she'd react if he really let loose his emotions. They boiled inside him with the same destructive fury of the seas out there, clenching his jaw, his fists, the ridged muscles of his abdomen.

"Dominic," she said, so softly he could barely hear her above the roar of the seas, "what can I do to help you?"

How certain she was that she understood him, how

sure that she could assuage the misery. And how badly he wanted to smash her complacency! Out of the blue, a suggestion of the most outrageous magnitude sprang to mind, explicit, indecent.

Should he voice it? And would she accede to his wishes? Or would her wide gray eyes darken with horror as she backed away and began to run blindly as far from him as she could get?

He swiped at his hair with shaking fingers, appalled at the demons possessing him. Marshaling his features into a semblance of composure, he discarded the unconscionable and settled for the clichéd. "I think I would like to go back to the hotel and get thoroughly drunk. Would you care to join me?"

She was supposed to pucker up her sweet little mouth and simper that alcohol would merely add to his problems, not alleviate them. Instead, her eyes grew suspiciously bright and the next thing he knew, her tanned little hand with its short pink nails had tucked itself into the crook of his elbow. "Of course," she murmured sympathetically. "Anything you say."

And then she slipped her arm around his waist and led him back the way they'd come. Slowly, carefully, as if he were a very old, enfeebled man. The demons within itched to succumb to a black, unholy bellow of laughter. He could feel it pulsing deep in his chest and had one hell of a time suppressing it.

"Would you like me to drive?" she asked when they reached the toy that passed for transportation.

"No," he said, shrugging her off. Heaven forbid he should have a reason not to keep his eyes on the road!

Happy hour was well under way by the time they reached the hotel again. The sun hung just above the horizon, a great flaming ball far too large for its playground. Kerosene torches flickered palely among the trees in anticipation of the sudden rush of night typical of the tropics. Laughter and music combined to drown out the macaws' last screeching chorus of the day. It was party time. For everyone except Dominic Winter and Sophie Casson.

He decided it was in both their interests for him to ditch her and be alone to drown, if not his sorrows, then at least his guilt. "Look," he said, "I'm not fit company for a wolverine. What say we hold off on that drink until another time?"

She paused for as long as it took her to catch her lower lip between her teeth, then said, "Yes, of course. Actually, I'd just as soon go upstairs and take a shower before dinner." She rubbed at her bare arms and indicated the folds of her skirt. "The sea spray's—"

The last thing he needed was a guided tour on how the fabric clung damply to her long, slender thighs. "Whatever," he said rudely and, turning his back on her in a deliberate snub, headed straight for the bar and ordered a double brandy.

Let her think he was a sot. He didn't care, and the bottom line was he needed a little Dutch courage before he phoned the Wexlers. Not that anything he had to tell them would offer a grain of solace, but he'd promised he'd call and he would not willingly renege on a promise to them. If there was anything fine or good left within him after all that had happened, it was his genuine fondness for Barbara's parents.

Leaning both elbows on the bar, he stared down at the drink in his hand. What a hell of a mess—a no-win situation regardless of which way he looked at it! And those paying the heaviest price were two people who deserved something better in their old age than the heartbreak of outliving their only child. He downed the brandy in one gulp and raised a finger to the bartender for a refill.

Dutch courage be damned! He wanted to be numbed from the neck up. Maybe then he'd be able to banish the demons possessing him.

CHAPTER TWO

BY THE time Sophie had bathed and changed, another flower-scented night had fallen, the third since Barbara's death. The cocktail crowd had gathered around the outdoor bar. She could hear their laughter mingling with the clink of ice on crystal and the throbbing beat of the steel drums. Was Dominic Winter part of that group, his brain sufficiently desensitized by alcohol that the edges of his pain had blurred? Or was he holed up in his room, determinedly drinking himself into oblivion?

"It's not your business, Sophie," she muttered, slipping silver and amethyst hoops on her ears. "Let him deal with what's happened on his own. It's safer that way."

Still, she found herself scanning the crowd, looking for him, when she went downstairs. He was not in the dining room, nor, as far as she could tell, was he outside on the wide, tiled patio. But the table she'd shared with no one since Wednesday tonight was again set for two.

She had finished the chilled cucumber soup and was halfway through her conch salad when he appeared. He wore the same open-necked white shirt and ecru linen trousers that he'd worn that afternoon. His hair had been combed repeatedly—by very irritable fingers. There was the faintest shadow of beard on his determined jaw. He looked like a man who'd had one too many—a man looking for trouble and ready to take on the entire world.

Forcibly reminding herself that he had just lost the woman he loved and was more to be pitied than reviled,

Sophie forbore to point out that adding a monumental hangover to his troubles would not make them any easier to bear. Instead, she nodded pleasantly and waited for him to make social overtures if, and when, he felt so inclined.

He quickly made it clear he did not feel inclined. "Looks like the hotel is determined to throw us together every chance they get," he remarked caustically, flinging himself into the seat opposite with rather more grace than one might have expected from a drunk. "Or did your Mother Teresa complex prompt you to request my company so that you could keep an eye on me in case despair drove me to the same sad end that Barbara suffered? Because if it did, I wish to hell you'd just butt out of my affairs."

His deft handling of the cutlery and lack of slurred speech gave Sophie pause. Dominic Winter was not drunk, as she had first supposed. He was a powder keg ready to explode—*wanting* to explode—and searching futilely for an excuse to do so. And there wasn't enough alcohol on St. Julian to do the job. He could have imbibed all night and still remained painfully sober. It was there for anyone to see in his smoldering green eyes. The torment was eating him alive.

"I'm not trying to interfere in your affairs," she said quietly. "I just want to do whatever I can to help."

He picked up the scrolled sheet of parchment on which the dinner menu had been printed and slid off the silk tassel encircling it. "It would help me enormously if you'd get on with your meal without feeling the need to engage me in conversation. And it would help me even more if you'd do so quickly and then quietly disappear."

Normally, Sophie would have refused on principle to do any such thing, even given that his painstaking rudeness had robbed her of her appetite. But in his present mood, she had no more wish to spend time with him than he had with her. So why did she half rise from her seat, then pause uncertainly as if about to change her mind, thereby giving him opportunity to insult her further?

Sensing her hesitation, he glared out from behind the parchment. "I do not want your company, Ms. Casson, nor do I need it," he declared brusquely.

Cheeks flaming, she dropped her napkin beside her plate and, like the spineless ninny she undoubtedly must be, scuttled away.

She did not see him again until the following evening. "*Monsieur* has gone to police headquarters with Chief Inspector Montand, to take care of the necessary paperwork, you understand," the clerk at the front desk told her when she stopped by shortly after breakfast the next morning. "Such a shocking loss of a life can never be dismissed lightly, *mademoiselle*." He wrinkled his nose as though to imply that only someone as inconsiderate as Barbara would behave so boorishly in alien territory. "*Hélas*, that is especially true in the case of foreigners who die while they are here."

Sophie understood. Fellow guests who'd been friendly enough before the tragedy avoided her now as though afraid she'd somehow cast an evil spell on her friend and might do the same to them. If there'd been any way to cut her holiday short she'd have done so on the spot, but there were only two flights a week in and out of St. Julian, on Tuesdays and Fridays. Whether she liked it or not, she was prisoner there for another four days.

She spent the afternoon at an orchid farm and returned late to the hotel, leaving herself with barely enough time to shower and change for the evening meal. To her surprise, Dominic was already seated at the table when she went down to the dining room.

"Ah, Ms. Casson," he murmured, rising smoothly and pulling out her chair, "I was hoping you'd favor me with your presence again tonight."

He looked quite devastating in pale gray trousers and shirt. Urbane, sophisticated and thoroughly in control of himself and the situation.

Very much on her guard, Sophie said, "Were you? Well, I hate to add to your troubles, Mr. Winter, but if you're hoping to drive me off again by plying me with insults, I'm afraid you're in for a disappointment. I'm far too hungry to allow you to get away with it a second time."

Even after only one day of tropical sun, his olive skin was burnished with color, so it was difficult to be sure but she thought perhaps he blushed a little at that, an assumption that gained credence with his next words. "I'm afraid I behaved very badly last night," he said contritely. "I must beg your pardon. I wasn't at my best."

You don't have a best! she felt like informing him. Except she didn't really believe that. She'd thought for a long time that he was far too good for Barbara. She'd even gone so far as to wish....

Conscience-stricken, she picked up the menu and pretended to read it. Bad enough she'd allowed herself to fantasize when Barbara was alive. To do so now was tantamount to dancing on her grave!

Glancing up, Sophie found his gaze trained on her face. He was different tonight. The rage in his eyes had been replaced by a clouded emptiness as though the reality of Barbara's death had at last sunk in and he realized no amount of ranting or blaming was going to bring her back.

Sophie almost preferred the other Dominic, the one breathing fire and condemnation. That one moved her to anger despite her better nature; this one moved her to pity—dangerous territory at the best of times.

"I really do apologize," he said.

"Apology accepted." She shrugged and searched for another subject, one that would draw her attention away from his broad shoulders and the burden they carried. He was a Samson of a man not intended to be broken, but Barbara's death had brought him perilously close to the edge. "What looks good for dinner, do you think?"

After some discussion, he ordered turtle steak and she the fish caught fresh that morning. "And wine," he decided, adding with a faint inflection of humor, "Don't worry, I'll behave. I'm a man of fairly temperate habits and don't, as a rule, choose to drown my sorrows in drink."

He was trying to be charming and succeeding, and she wished he'd stop. It made too great an assault on her defenses, leaving her vulnerable to the most preposterous urge to comfort him. It was a relief when their food arrived. It gave her something else to do with hands that ached to reach out and touch his long, restless fingers; to cup his cheek and stroke the severe line of his mouth. To pillow his head against her breast...

He'd probably deck her! He wanted glamorous Barbara Wexler, not unremarkable Sophie Casson, and would almost certainly view any attempt on the latter's part to share his grief as unforgivably presumptuous.

"What did you do today?" he asked, interrupting her line of thought and, when she told him, said, "Do you get many ideas from your travels abroad? For your work, I mean?"

He was no more interested in her answer than was she in his question, but meaningless small talk was safer than silence that allowed her mind to stray to thoughts better left unexplored.

"I remember the first time we met," he remarked later, staring absently into his glass of wine. "You were halfway up a tree on the Wexler estate, wearing dungarees covered in mud and with a camera slung around your neck."

"And you thought I was trespassing. You were ready to throw me off the property."

He nodded. "Yes. I knew they'd hired a landscape architect to design a waterfall and lily pond, but you hardly fitted the description. I'd expected—"

"What?" she snapped, welcoming the surge of annoyance his words inspired. "A man?"

"Not necessarily. Just someone more...professional-looking."

"Tell me, Mr. Winter," Sophie shot back, "when you first started out in the construction business, did you show up on the job wearing a three-piece suit?"

He smiled, such a rare and pleasant change from his usual gravity. "As a matter of fact, I did. I'd decided to buy five adjacent properties, all very run-down, and wanted to impress my bank manager into lending me the money to complete the sale. And I think we should drop the Mr. Winter–Ms. Casson thing. It seems to breed hostility between us and we've got enough to deal with, without that."

"If there's hostility," Sophie couldn't help retorting, "it's of your making, not mine, and has been ever since we met."

She expected he'd argue the point but he didn't. He merely raised his elegant black brows and shrugged. "I daresay you're right," he admitted. "But that was then and this is now. Things have changed."

His habitually somber expression was firmly back in place. It was hard to imagine him succumbing to flighty Barbara's charms; harder still to picture him lowering his icy reserves and making love to her.

The audacity of such speculation sent a wash of color over Sophie's cheeks. "Um..." she said, nearly choking on a morsel of fish, "I wonder if the Wexlers will still want me about the place after this. Have you spoken with them since...?"

His manner became even more guarded than usual. "I called them last night."

"They must be—"

"They're devastated."

Sophie sighed, thinking of the gentle elderly couple whose entire existence had revolved around the daughter who'd arrived on the scene so late in their lives. "Yes," she said softly. "To outlive your children is completely contrary to the proper order of nature. I can only imagine how difficult they must be finding it."

"Try 'impossible'," he suggested shortly. "Nothing you imagine can begin to equate with what they're going through. At this point, I doubt they're fully able to comprehend it themselves." The animosity that, fleetingly, had faded from his eyes, resurfaced. "And I'm quite sure they won't want you around to remind them of what they've lost. At the very least, stay away until you hear from them—or better yet, from me. In fact, it might be best for everyone if you were to delegate someone else from your company to complete your share of the landscape project."

Sophie stared at him over the rim of her glass. "It really doesn't come as much of a surprise that you'd assume I'm too lacking in tact or respect to show any sensitivity toward the Wexlers, so I won't waste my breath trying to counteract your opinion," she said, nothing in her demeanor betraying the hurt his remark had inflicted. "I can live with the fact that you don't much like me, Mr. Winter, but I will not tolerate your repeated insinuations that Barbara's death was in any way my fault, and I will not allow you to drive me into hiding. If and when the Wexlers are ready to have me finish the job *they* hired me to do, I shall make myself available."

"It would be better for all of us if you stayed away," he maintained obstinately, and for all that she tried to stem it, another blast of hurt shafted through her at the unbending accusation in his voice. She could protest until the world stopped turning but, just as it was clear nothing could alter his initial antipathy toward her, so it was equally clear that he still held her accountable for the pain he was now suffering.

She was sorely tempted to get up and leave, but pride wouldn't let her be put to rout two nights in a row. So, willing her voice not to betray her by trembling, she said, "In that case, why don't you ask to sit somewhere else for the duration of your stay here? Because heaven forbid I should cause you indigestion on top of all my other manifest sins."

Sophie didn't know whether or not he'd taken her suggestion to heart because she walked into town for breakfast on Sunday, spent the rest of the morning in the botanical gardens and stopped at a roadside stand for a lunch consisting of a sandwich and freshly squeezed fruit juice cocktail.

It was after two when she got back to the hotel and

the breeze that normally made the heat tolerable had died completely. Out of respect for Barbara, she'd abandoned her habit of skin diving in the lagoon beyond the palm-fringed beach each afternoon, and spent the time instead with a book under an umbrella on the patio. But that day, fatigued as much by the fact that she hadn't slept well the night before as by the hot Caribbean sun, she slipped into a bikini and stretched out on a wicker chaise in the restful shade of her balcony. That she was also going out of her way to avoid Dominic Winter and his cold, disapproving gaze was something she preferred not to acknowledge.

The murmur of the ocean, in concert with the musical splash of the fountains in the gardens below, soothed like a lullaby. All the hard-edged events of the past few days softened, their colors paling to dreamy pastels. Lassitude spread through Sophie's arms, her legs, and she welcomed it, happy to drift in the no-man's-land between waking and sleeping.

She didn't notice when the colors faded to black or the languor took complete possession of her mind as well as her body. She knew nothing until she became suddenly and alarmingly conscious of someone moving about in her room.

There were discreet signs posted throughout the hotel, warning guests to keep their bedroom doors locked and all valuables stored in the safe at the front desk. Sophie had no valuables worth worrying about except for her camera equipment, and she was reasonably certain she'd locked her door, but there was no doubt someone had managed to gain access. Slewing her gaze sideways, she could see through the slats of the louvered balcony doors the shadow of a man moving back and forth within the room.

A glance at her watch showed that more than an hour had passed since she'd apparently fallen asleep. Time enough for a seasoned burglar to pick the lock and go about his business. His mistake, however, lay in choosing a victim who'd already been on the receiving end of Dominic Winter's unabashed displeasure. She was in no mood to take further abuse from anyone else.

Without stopping to consider the wisdom of such a move, she slid off the chaise and moved swiftly around the half-open door. But the outrage she'd been about to vent at the intruder dwindled to wordless shock at the sight before her.

Dominic was naked from the waist up, his torso in all its sleekly muscled beauty narrowing to fit snugly into the waist of khaki linen shorts. And yet, that was not quite accurate. Although invisible, desolation hung about him like a second presence.

He stood before the low dresser that still contained Barbara's things, his broad shoulders paralleling the bowed despair of his dark head. In the palm of his hand lay the diamond ring he'd given her, even its bright fire temporarily dimmed.

Sophie's breath escaped in a soft exhalation of protest at being too long trapped in her throat. The sound looped across the mourning hush that filled the room and wound itself around him, bringing his head up and swinging around to face her. His eyes were the deep dark green of moss clothing ancient gravestones. And his mouth...!

Her heart contracted with pity, leaving no room for the anger and hurt she'd nurtured from the night before. "Dominic," she breathed, and cupped her hands in front of her as if they held the magic formula guaranteed to wipe away his hurt.

He blinked and focused his gaze on her slowly, the

way a person does when emerging from deep sleep. "They told me you were gone for the day," he said, his voice a husky echo of its usual rich baritone. "I thought it would be a good time to take care of...this."

His fingers closed around the ring, his other hand gesturing at the contents of the open drawer. Little bits of silk and ribbon-trimmed lingerie frothed in disorder, just the way Barbara had left them. Her suitcase lay open on Sophie's bed, one half already filled with items from her share of the closet.

Still poised near the balcony doors, Sophie nodded understanding. "I would have done it myself, except I didn't feel it was my place."

"It wasn't your responsibility." Impatiently, Dominic tossed the ring on top of the articles of clothing remaining in the drawer and, scooping everything up in both hands, turned to stuff it in the suitcase.

As he did so, something slid out from between the folds of fabric and slipped to the floor despite Sophie's attempt to catch it. It was the tooled-leather picture frame that, for the first few days of the holiday, had sat on the bedside table next to Barbara's bed. Hinged in the middle, it contained two photographs, one of Dominic and one of Barbara.

Stooping, Sophie retrieved it and passed it to him. He sank to the edge of Barbara's bed and for the longest time stared at the image of his dead fiancée.

Not a trace of emotion showed on his face. The seconds slowed, tightening the already-tense atmosphere so painfully that Sophie wished she'd ignored her scruples and simply taken charge of packing Barbara's things herself.

At last, Dominic slapped the frame closed the way a man does a book that, regretfully, he's finished reading for all that he never wanted it to end. But instead of completing packing Barbara's things, he remained where he was, hands idle, with the photograph frame clasped between them.

Yet another goodbye, Sophie thought, sympathy welling within her. *He must wonder if they'll ever end.*

Covering the small distance that separated them, she perched next to him and gently removed the frame from his hands. Unwillingly, he looked at her, the expression in his eyes veiled by the thick fringe of his lashes.

He did not want her to see his grieving, as though there was something shameful in allowing himself to succumb to it. She knew because her brother, Paul, was just the same.

What was it about men that what they accepted as healthy and normal in a woman they saw as weakness in themselves? Didn't they know the healing took longer if it was denied? That only by accepting it and dealing with it could they validate eventual recovery from it?

Seeing Dominic closing in on himself and refusing to let go, Sophie could only suppose they didn't, and so she offered comfort exactly as she'd have extended it to anyone, man, woman or child, in the same state of grief. With one hand she reached up and brought his head down to her shoulder, and with the other raised his fingertips to her mouth and kissed them.

For an instant, he resisted. She felt his opposition in the sudden rigidity of his arm, heard it in the hissing intake of his breath. And then, like a house of cards caught in a sudden draft of air, he collapsed against her, the weight of him catching her off guard and pushing her backward on the bed. He followed, his face buried at her neck, his hands tangling in her hair, his legs entwined with hers.

He smelled of soap and clear blue skies and sun-drenched ocean, all bound together by lemon blossoms. His skin, more bronzed than ever, scalded where it touched, the heat of him a strange elixir that penetrated her pores to coil within her bloodstream.

At least, she thought it did—as much as she was capable of thought. Because what had begun as a reaching out in commiseration changed course dramatically, though exactly how and when escaped her. One minute she and Dominic were behaving with the decorum of two people sitting side by side in church, and the next they were rolling around on the brightly patterned bedspread with the hungry abandon of lovers.

Somehow, his mouth found hers and fastened to it, seeking comfort wherever it was to be found. How could she have known the shape it would take, how have avoided what happened next?

Without volition, her lips opened. She felt the heat of his breath, the moisture of his tongue accepting the invitation so flagrantly offered. There was no use pretending it was an accidental and utterly chaste collision of two mouths intent on other things, because it was not. It was a wrong and unprincipled and utterly, irresistibly erotic prelude to even greater sin.

Without warning, the cool and distant Dominic Winter she'd known metamorphosed into a lover as swiftly as night fell on St. Julian.

Of course, *he* could be excused. He was not himself. He was ripped apart with anguish, lost, lonely...oh, there was any number of reasons for *him* to behave irrationally. But what was her justification? Why did she wind her arms around his neck as if she never wanted to let him go, then kiss him back and let him touch her near naked body in its pitifully brief little bikini that she'd never have countenanced wearing in public?

Why, when he pushed aside the spaghetti straps holding up the bra, did she shift to accommodate him? And when he stroked her breasts, then lowered his head to kiss them, why did she arch toward him with about as much restraint as a drowning woman reaching for a lifeline? How could she explain the rush of damp heat between her thighs or the aching drumroll of desire building within her womb?

She knew why. This wasn't some sudden tropical fever robbing her of propriety or decency; it was a slow-growing affliction that had begun months ago. That day in the Wexlers' garden, it had been the impact of his cool green inspection, and not her rapid descent from the tree, that had sent her practically sprawling at his feet. He'd stood there like some beautiful avenging angel, and despite the disapproval manifest in his gaze and in his voice, something inside her had responded to him in a very primal way. He'd ignited a spark that had been waiting for a chance to burst into flame.

She'd tried to ignore it, heaven knew. It had been the only sane course to follow, given that, in addition to his overt disaffection for her, he was also engaged to marry Barbara. A woman would have to be blind as well as stupid to think for a moment that a man—*any* man— would look twice at ordinary Sophie Casson if fascinating Barbara Wexler was his for the taking.

But that was then and this was now. Barbara had gone, and for whatever reason, Dominic had turned to her, Sophie. Even in the midst of passion, she knew he was trying to lose himself, to forget, if only for a little while, his pain. And if it was shameful to welcome the chance to assuage his need, then she was guilty. Because wild dogs would not have deterred her at that moment.

He stripped away her bikini bottom, fumbled with the belt at his waist, and she helped him, her fingers nimble at the buttoned fly of his khaki shorts. He rolled to one side, shrugged himself free of the confinement of clothing, and then he was covering her again. Covering her, and entering her, hot, frenzied, reckless.

She took him into herself. Absorbed his pain, his loss, and made it hers. Did whatever she had to do, gave everything he silently begged of her, to make things more bearable for him. If it had been within her power, she'd have brought Barbara back, even though doing so would have made her own loneliness more acute.

And why? Never mind why. The reason wasn't to be entertained. To allow it even momentary lodging in her mind would be to invite misery into her heart as a permanent guest. Instead, she shut out her own needs and catered to his.

He drove himself as if the hounds of hell were in pursuit and he was desperate to outrace them. Willingly, Sophie raced with him, her peripheral awareness shrinking as a great roaring flood gathered inside her. There was not a force in this world or any other that could have stopped either of them.

And then it was over as suddenly as it had begun and there was nothing but the sound of sudden rain splashing on the tropical shrubs outside and dimpling the surface of the pool. As if the sun couldn't bear to witness such wanton conduct and had ordered the rain to wash away the shame of it all.

Looking anywhere but at her, Dominic rolled into a sitting position, reached for his clothes and climbed into them even more speedily than he'd shed them. She thought he'd simply walk out of the room and that would be that, but he didn't. Instead, he stood at the open balcony doors and stared out.

Unable to bear his silence a moment longer, Sophie slid to her feet, wrapping herself in the flowered bedspread as she did so, and went to stand beside him. "Say something, Dominic," she begged.

His shoulders rose in a great sigh. An unguarded sorrow formed in the curve of his mouth, then in his eyes as they focused on the distance beyond the windows. As if he was watching a ship bearing a loved one disappear over the horizon. "What in God's name can I say?"

A slow trembling began inside her, gathering force as it spread until she shook from head to foot. She was the one who'd started everything when she'd reached out and touched him. It was all her fault.

"Tell me that you don't hate me for what I allowed to happen," she whispered. "That you don't think it was something I planned. I feel guilty enough without that."

He swung his head toward her and she thought she had never looked into such emptiness as she found in his eyes. When he spoke, his voice was raw with...what? Rage, pain, regret?

"Right now," he said, "I don't give a rat's rear how you're feeling. I'm too busy despising myself."

Once again, he reduced her to such shock that her knees almost buckled beneath her as the blood rushed from her face. But he didn't notice, nor would he probably have cared. Snatching up Barbara's suitcase, he rammed it shut. Then he stalked across the room to the door, opened it, stepped through and closed it quietly behind him. And just to add salt to Sophie's wounds, the rain passed as suddenly as it had begun and the sun came out again.

* * *

She did not go down for dinner that night. She took a long, too-hot bath and tried to scrub away the shame and the hurt. And then, while people laughed and danced on the patio below, she lay in her bed and tried to ignore its twin standing empty only a few feet away.

But even though the night was moonless, the hurricane lamps in the garden flung up enough of a glow for her to see the other bed's outline quite clearly. Its pillows sat not quite straight and one corner of the flowered cover trailed on the floor. As though whoever had thrown it back in place had done so carelessly. Or furtively, because its disarray had been caused by people who had no business lying on it in the first place, let alone making unseemly imitation love there.

Shame flowed over Sophie again, more invasive even than Dominic's hands, licking over every inch of her skin, into every secret curve and fold until she burned from its onslaught. How *could* she have allowed herself?

If only Elaine hadn't fallen victim to the chicken pox. If only she hadn't agreed to let Barbara take Elaine's place! Why had she when, of all people, Barbara Wexler was a woman with whom she shared nothing in common?

She knew why. For the sadistic pleasure of listening to Barbara talk about her fiancé. For vicarious thrills. Because, from the outset, Sophie had wanted him.

Well, now she'd had him, however briefly. And she felt like the lowest form of life ever to slither across the face of the earth.

CHAPTER THREE

IN THE hours following, Sophie learned that it didn't take sleep for a person to find herself trapped in a nightmare. Much though she would have liked to divert them, disturbing questions raced through her mind. Had he known to whom he'd just made such desperate love? Was it Sophie Casson with her conscience, like her mind, clouded by a raging hunger, who'd filled him with passion—or Barbara's ghost taking up temporary residence for one last farewell?

Worn out with anguish, Sophie fell asleep just before dawn and awoke a short time later to a day luminous with sun and that special clarity of light indigenous to the Caribbean. Her immediate reaction was to bury her head under the pillows and remain there well into the next century, but a thump on her door put an end to such wishful thinking.

Probably the maid, she thought drearily. But it was Dominic, the very last person in the world she wanted to face with her hair standing on end and her eyes red ringed from hours of on-again, off-again crying.

He stared at her, the turmoil he was suffering plain to see. From the beginning of their association, he'd struck her as a man of many layers, all of them designed to keep her at a distance. He wore pride over arrogance, distaste over reserve, hauteur over grief, drawing each one around himself like a cloak. And now, on top of them all, his raging disgust for having allowed her to glimpse that vulnerable side of himself that she suspected he seldom acknowledged even to himself.

Without invitation, he stepped into the room and shouldered the door closed. Too dismayed to ask what he thought he was doing barging in on her like that, she backed away from him, cringing inwardly at the bars of sunlight slanting through the louvered windows to reveal her in all her disheveled glory.

"I expected you'd be awake already," he said, following her.

She tugged furtively on the hem of her nightshirt, which came only midway down her thighs. "I am—now."

His beautiful brows shot upward as though he thought only the most dissolute of creatures would still be in bed at such an hour, but at least he had the good grace not to voice the opinion aloud. "I just came back from a meeting with Inspector Montand. All the red tape's taken care of finally, so I'm free to leave. I'll be on my way within a couple of hours."

That's all he knew! "There isn't another flight out until tomorrow afternoon," Sophie informed him, a certain malicious satisfaction at being one step ahead of him for a change coloring her tone.

His gaze slewed past her as if he found the sight of her singularly offensive. "For other people, perhaps, but I'm not prepared to wait that long, so I've chartered a private jet. If you care to, you're welcome to come with me. I can't imagine you're still in a holiday mood after everything that's happened."

He was right. More than anything, she wanted to escape from this island and all its painful memories. But the thought of spending ten or more hours in the undiluted company of a man who clearly viewed her with a combination of embarrassment and disgust was even less appealing. "Thanks anyway, but I think I should stick to my original travel plans."

His gaze flickered to Barbara's bed and away again. "Yes," he conceded. "Perhaps that would be best."

His attitude, and the way he abruptly turned and left, reminded her of another time earlier that fall. Sophie had started work at the Wexlers' about nine on a morning so damp and dreary that Mrs. Wexler had insisted she come in out of the cold and have lunch with them.

She hadn't found it a particularly relaxed meal. The Wexlers were kind and called her "Sophie" and "dear". Barbara, who seemed compelled to abbreviate everyone's name but her own, called her "Sophe". But Dominic had steadfastly stuck to "Ms. Casson"—on those few occasions that he called her anything at all.

"So you're still here, Ms. Casson," he'd said when he came upon her still hard at it later that afternoon. "Does that mean you'll be joining us for dinner, too?"

From his tone, one would have thought she made a habit of cadging free meals! "No," she'd assured him, aware as always of the undeclared currents of war flowing between them. "I'm an employee, not a friend of the family, and hardly belong at the dinner table."

"It might be a good idea for us all to remember that," he'd replied enigmatically, then stalked away, just as he did now, without bothering to say goodbye. An adversarial, uncivil man, she'd decided at the time, his exquisitely tailored suits and elegant black Jaguar with its pale gray leather upholstery notwithstanding.

Well, the war had been waged at last, and Barbara's bed had been the battlefield. The question was, had anyone emerged a winner?

She didn't see him again. By the time she came downstairs he'd already left, and her last day on St. Julian was uneventful. The next afternoon, she left, too, and slept that night in her own bed, comforted by the knowledge that once she'd sent flowers and a note of condolence to the Wexlers, it would be over, all of it.

But it wasn't. The following week, she got a call from Barbara's mother. "I wonder, my dear, if you'd come to see us and tell us, if you will, what you know...?" Gail Wexler's voice broke, and a stifled sob punctuated the brief silence before she was able to continue. "Please, will you come, Sophie? You were the last person to see our daughter alive, and if we could talk to you, it might help us to...accept what's happened."

It required a colder heart than Sophie possessed to refuse. Nothing would be over for any of them, she realized then, until all the rituals of grieving had been observed. "When would you like to see me?"

They settled on the following evening at eight o'clock. When Sophie pulled up in her car, she found Dominic's Jaguar already parked in the driveway outside the house. She'd half expected he'd be in attendance, too, since the Wexlers clearly regarded him as a son, and she had thought herself prepared to cope with the eventuality. Still, when he opened the mansion's front door to her, the sight of his unsmiling face unsettled her badly.

I let him make love to me, she thought, appalled all over again. *I shared the ultimate intimacy with a man whom I knew to be in love with someone else at the time.*

Something of her dismay must have showed on her face because as soon as she'd greeted the Wexlers in the drawing room, Dominic took her by the elbow and steered her to a side table where a silver coffee service waited.

Under the pretext of filling a cup for her, he said in a

low tone, "Please try to hide your aversion to being here. It isn't pleasant for any of us, but you don't have to make it any harder on the Wexlers than it already is."

"I'm fully aware of that," she said softly, annoyance at his choosing once again to interpret her actions in the most unfavorable light diminished by her shock at the change in Barbara's parents. They had aged dreadfully over the past few weeks and seemed terribly fragile.

But Dominic wasn't done harassing her. "Furthermore," he decreed in that bossy way of his, "although I gathered from Montand that you pretty well agreed with him when he intimated that Barbara asked for trouble down on St. Julian, her parents don't need to be told that."

It was the verbal slap in the face needed to restore Sophie. "I wouldn't dream of it," she muttered indignantly. "What sort of person do you take me for?"

"You don't want to know," he shot back, lowering his lashes to hide the scorn flaring in his eyes.

Mrs. Wexler patted the cushion beside her on the brocade sofa. "Bring your cup and sit here with me, Sophie. We're so grateful to you for coming tonight and I know we'll both feel better for your visit. Won't we, John?"

If anything, Barbara's father looked even frailer than his wife. "She was only twenty-four," he murmured plaintively. "I don't understand how someone so young and full of life could be snuffed out like that. Why did it happen?"

"I think perhaps because she *was* so full of life, just as you say, Mr. Wexler," Sophie suggested, trying hard to tread the fine path between honesty and tact. "She was impatient…"

Apparently, she hadn't tried hard enough. From his

post at the corner of the fireplace, Dominic frowned a caution. "'Eager' might be a better word, Ms. Casson."

So might "rebellious", Sophie thought, *not to mention "selfish" and "willful" and "downright cheap".* But of course, he didn't want to hear that sort of thing, any more than the Wexlers did, and who was she to belittle anyone else's morals in light of her own fall from grace?

"But was she having fun...until...?"

The pathetic hope in Mrs Wexler's next question broke Sophie's heart. It was a relief to be able to say quite truthfully that, until the accident, Barbara had been busy having a wonderful time on St. Julian. Fortunately, neither parent asked Sophie to elaborate on the remark.

"There'll be a service next week in the Palmerstown Memorial Chapel, and a plaque placed in the gardens," Dominic informed her when he saw her out. "The Wexlers would appreciate your being there."

"Of course." Resigned, Sophie nodded. Just this one last observance out of respect to the Wexlers and then it truly would be over, all of it. She could go back to her own life, her own friends, and there'd be nothing to remind her of the senseless tragedy that had taken place on a tiny island just off the coast of South America.

Nothing, that was, except for the lingering memory of Dominic Winter's kiss, the inexcusable longing to feel his touch again—and, as the following days turned into weeks and two months slid quietly by, the horrifying suspicion that the past was not going to fade quietly away after all.

By the time February howled in on a blizzard, she was terribly afraid that she was to be left with the most permanent reminder possible, in the shape of Dominic's child.

* * *

What with Christmas and the painful emptiness it brought to the Wexlers, then the chore of organizing the mess of paperwork on his desk that always accumulated at the end of the fiscal year, Dominic found it easy enough to put off what he knew, sooner or later, had to be done. Not that he wouldn't have preferred to act as if nothing had happened. Hell, he'd spent most of his waking hours since regretting the single moment of weakness that had undermined everything he prided himself on possessing: integrity, decency, loyalty, fidelity.

Of course, there were some who'd say he deserved to be cut down to size. He'd stepped on more than a few toes in his drive to reach the top and been called a lot of unflattering things on the way. "Cutthroat" and "ruthless" didn't begin to do justice to some of the adjectives that had been applied to Dominic Winter, the man who'd built a fortune on hard work and a willingness to take chances, and who now owned half the real estate in Palmerstown as proof that the gamble had paid off.

But other people's opinions had never struck him as worth losing sleep over as long as his own sense of self-respect remained intact. He supported worthy causes, donated his share and then some to make sure that mothers, children and old people didn't wind up homeless on the streets of Palmerstown. Neither did he play fast and loose with married women or investors' money.

He paid an honest day's wage for an honest day's work, no employee of Winter Development Corporation ever had to worry that ill health would cost him his job, and every person on his payroll found a fat bonus included in his December paycheck. Given all that, looking in the mirror every morning and seeing an unprincipled schmuck of thirty-five staring back at him was a bit more than Dominic could stomach.

He didn't bother to phone her ahead of time. She'd probably hang up on him or else suggest he take his belated concern and perform some anatomically impossible act with it. Instead, late on the eighth Sunday after Barbara's memorial service, he looked up Sophie Casson's address and drove to the outskirts of town where she lived to pay her a surprise visit. Why go about it any differently? It seemed to be the story of their whole association after all, her tripping over him when she least expected it. No point in breaking the mold now.

It was another bitter night, but at least the snow had stopped and a ragged moon shed enough light for him to see the lopsided little house where she lived and, beyond it, the wind-ruffled surface of Jewel Lake. A well-situated piece of property, he surmised, and one which, at any other time, he'd have been itching to see put to more attractive use. But he wasn't ringing her doorbell as a developer; he was coming, metaphorical hat in hand, to make overdue apology for taking sexual advantage of her and to make sure there weren't any unwelcome surprises lurking on the horizon as a result of his rash behavior.

It took her a moment or two to answer. He heard her footsteps as she ran down the stairs, saw her shadow loom closer through the frosted-glass panes on either side of the entrance, and then the front door opened and light spilled out into the night to show her the face of her visitor.

To say she was surprised to see him was an understatement. In fact, he was across the threshold before it seemed to register with her that her eyes were not deceiving her.

Her reaction then was out of all proportion to the situation and scarcely flattering. She'd obviously not been home long herself. She wore high-topped leather boots, and had left her coat slung over the newel at the foot of the stairs. From the small empty bag stamped with the name of the local drugstore, which she held in one hand, it would appear she'd been shopping.

When she realized that he was not simply an unpleasant figment of her imagination, she clutched the bag to her as if it contained the crown jewels of England and stared at him, her gray eyes huge in the sudden pallor of her face. "Have you been following me?" she demanded, her voice unnaturally shrill.

He stared at her, genuinely perplexed. "Why the hell would I be doing that?"

She opened her mouth to tell him, then seemed to think better of the idea and clamped it shut again.

"Look, Ms. Casson..." he began forcefully, until the absurdity of calling her Ms. after the intimacy they'd shared stopped him dead. He raked a hand through his hair and started again. "Sophie, please! I'm here because I'm concerned."

"Concerned?" she repeated in that same high, brittle voice. "Concerned about what? I'm perfectly all right. Why on earth wouldn't I be?"

This was not the same woman who'd dealt so calmly with events on St. Julian. This was a woman on the verge of falling apart and he wasn't sure he wanted to know why. "No reason," he said offhandedly. "I just wanted to make sure, that's all. If nothing else, I feel I owe you an apology, even if I can't offer an explanation for what happened down in the Caribbean."

"Nothing happened," she said, her face flushing. "You don't owe me anything."

He sighed, a strange disappointment overtaking him. "I suppose it's too much to expect that we might just once sit down and talk like normal, civilized people?"

At that, it seemed to occur to her that her behavior was not entirely rational and she made an effort to gather herself together a bit. "No, of course not." She gestured toward an open doorway. "There's a fire set in the living room, if you'd like to go in. I'll join you as soon as I've hung up my coat."

It was a tiny, late 1920s house, he'd guess, and not particularly well built by today's standards. The fire she'd mentioned had not been started, leaving the room at the mercy of drafts creeping in through the cracks around the windows.

Squatting down before the grate, he piled a little more kindling atop the pyramid she'd built, then felt inside the chimney to make sure the damper was open. He was rewarded with a shower of soot speckling his hand and the cuff of his shirt.

"Oh dear!" she exclaimed from the doorway. "I should have warned you not to touch that. It sticks."

"So I gather," he said dryly. "How do you ever manage to get a decent fire going?"

She grimaced, pursing her lips and wrinkling her nose in a way that he found rather charming. "Actually, I seldom do."

"Small wonder. Will it offend your notions of feminine emancipation if I offer to fix it for you?" He surveyed his filthy hands ruefully. "I'd hate to think I ended up looking like a chimney sweep for nothing."

Her smile more than made up for the antagonism she'd shown earlier. "I'd be very grateful. On really cold days I have to bring in an electric heater to make the room bearable."

"Do you rent this place? Because if you do, it's your landlord's—"

"I own it," she said. "If you discount the rather hefty mortgage, that is."

"Ever think of selling?" He wrenched hard on the lever that controlled the damper and received another liberal dousing of soot.

"No. The house might not amount to much, but the garden...!" She sighed and hugged her arms. "It's lovely and more than makes up for any other shortcomings."

"I should have expected an answer like that. I remember how you drooled over the Wexlers' arboretum."

Bad move! he realized at once. By alluding to the Wexlers, he'd brought back reminders of a time he and Sophie both preferred to forget. Her expression, which moments before had become more open and relaxed, closed like a limpet.

"Well," he said hastily, ramming the damper lever more securely into a niche inside the brick-lined chimney, "that's about the best I can do for now, but if you like, I'll send over one of my workers to fix it permanently. Is there some place I can clean up a bit?"

"The bathroom's at the top of the stairs," she told him. "First door on the right."

She left him to find his own way and disappeared into the kitchen.

Before he reached the upper landing, he heard the whir of some small kitchen appliance, followed almost immediately by the aroma of freshly ground coffee.

At the top of the stairs, a small brass lamp set on an old military trunk illuminated the photograph of a mustachioed man in uniform standing next to it. A swag of dried flowers tied with a cream silk ribbon hung above a small oriel window. Cosy little touches that played no part in the austere decor of Dominic's penthouse, and which he'd never missed until now, when, somewhat to his surprise, he found himself envying the leggy blonde in the kitchen downstairs.

She might not enjoy the sort of luxury with which he'd surrounded himself, but she'd found something else, something rarer: a sense of home, of belonging, that he'd never known. It showed in the ambience she'd created in her funny little house. It showed in her smile when she allowed it to emerge, and in her eyes when she talked about her garden and the work she loved.

Bending his head to avoid cracking his skull on the sloping ceiling, he nudged open the door to the bathroom, glad he'd decided to pay her this overdue visit. He was almost enjoying himself and, for the first time in a very long time, began to think it might be possible to put the past behind him and make a fresh start.

And then she was racing up the stairs after him, calling to him to stop. But she wasn't quite fast enough. He'd already flicked on the light, walked to the old-fashioned sink and seen what it was she'd left on the glass shelf above it.

And he realized it was too late after all. Too late to turn back as she was begging him to do, and too late to plan a future that was free of the past.

Breathless with dismay, Sophie leaned against the doorjamb, one fist pressed to her speeding heart. Her gaze locked with his and she knew without his having to say a word that he'd seen.

No more than a couple of yards separated him from her, yet when he spoke, his words seemed to swim across miles, reaching her ears with that same rushing sense of distance that transmits the human voice halfway around the globe. "This is yours?"

Courage, bravado, defiance—where were they when

she most needed them? Huddling in a corner of her mind and leaving her with nothing to speak but the truth! "Yes."

He picked up the package, turned it over in his grimy hand. "It hasn't been opened."

"No. I brought it home only a little while ago, just before you arrived, as a matter of fact." As if that made any difference to the appalling state of affairs!

He nodded and dropped the box back on the shelf, then turned on the hot water and proceeded to scrub his hands, paying particular attention to his short-trimmed nails. When he was done and had hung the towel on the rack, he rebuttoned the cuffs of his shirt.

"Well," he said, impaling her with his cool green gaze, "I imagine you'd like to be alone while you do what has to be done."

"Done?" She felt her face flare with color. Surely he didn't expect...?

His reply made it clear that he did. "Take the test."

"*Now*?"

"Why not now?"

"*You're* here."

The rigid set of his shoulders, the shuttered expression on his face, told her how loath he was to admit the truth of that. "Indeed I am," he said, "and I intend to remain here until we learn the results. I'll be downstairs when you're finished."

She floundered for a reason—any reason—to get rid of him. "What if this...procedure...has to take place first thing in the morning?"

He picked up the box and read the directions printed on the back. "It doesn't," he said flatly. "It states quite clearly that the test can be administered at any time. So quit stalling and get on with it."

"We're not talking about some mundane matter like—like whether or not a cake's finished baking," she spluttered, embarrassed beyond measure at the situation in which she found herself. "This is something intensely personal and private, and doesn't involve you."

"If your believing you might be pregnant is the result of our having had sex on St. Julian, then it certainly does involve me, Sophie, so take the damn test and put us both out of our misery."

The door clicked shut behind him, cutting off any response she might have felt inclined to make, which was just as well, since realistically, there was nothing she could offer to refute the logic of what he'd said. If she'd thought she had a ghost of a chance of pulling it off, she'd lie to him, tell him the test came out negative. But she'd never been able to look anyone in the eye and tell a barefaced lie. It simply wasn't in her nature. In any case, he was the type who'd ask to see the proof.

She came downstairs fifteen minutes later, but instead of going to where he waited for her, she finished the job she'd started in the kitchen, brewing the coffee and setting mugs, sugar and a jug of cream on a tray, searching out napkins—anything to keep her hands busy and give her mind time to compose itself.

He stood at one of the windows in the living room, staring out at the snow-draped night, but when he heard her come in, he pulled the drapes closed and fastened his attention on her. Acutely conscious of his scrutiny, she set the tray on a low table in front of the fire, which by then was burning brightly.

It was a warm, cosy scene, the kind seen on Christmas cards, with the faded burgundies in her prized antique Turkish carpet echoing the rich red of the velvet curtains.

All that was missing was a cat on the hearth and perhaps a smile on the face of the man standing across from her.

"How do you take your coffee?" she asked, trying for a voice that didn't tremble and a smile that didn't waver. Neither quite worked.

"Black," he said. "Did you take the test?"

So much for polite small talk! Abandoning any pretense at gracious hostessing, she replied in the same unadorned vein that he'd asked the question. "Yes."

"And?"

"I'm pregnant." She hadn't expected him to whoop with joy at the news, but his silence bespoke a condemnation that she found insupportable. To end it, she said with a pitiful attempt at irony, "My goodness, is it possible that I've rendered you speechless? Is there nothing you'd like to say to me?"

"Just one thing," he said. "Is the child mine?"

Under different, less strained circumstances, she might have found the question reasonable enough. He was hardly privy to her sexual liaisons after all, and was not to know that, except for a brief affair a long time ago, she'd been intimate with no one until that night on St. Julian. But the way he looked at her when he spoke, as if he'd somehow found himself entangled with a woman of questionable morals, was one thing too much on top of everything else.

Too distraught to hold them back, she let the tears spurt from her eyes and splash down her face. "Yes, it's yours!" she cried. "What do you take me for?"

"Not a virgin, certainly, so please don't try pulling that old chestnut out of the fire."

Already regretting that she hadn't had the wit to answer him with scorching dignity, she drew in a great breath and tried to collect herself. But just when she thought she had the tears under control, she looked at him again and a fresh spate of misery erupted at the empty despair she saw in his eyes. "I've only ever been with one other man and that was when I was twenty-four," she wailed. "Even you can't seriously believe I've been carrying his child for the past three years."

He let fly with a bark of laughter at her response, an incongruous sound in that tension-filled room. "Not quite, no."

Somewhat restored, she swiped at the tears. "I would no more think of trying to pass off another man's child than I would—"

"There's no need to belabor the point, Sophie. I believed you the first time you said the child was mine." Finally abandoning his post by the window, he came over and dropped into the chair opposite hers. Elbows braced on his knees and hands dangling limply, he went on, "What we must now decide is how to proceed from here."

He was going to offer her money, put forth options that she'd find unacceptable. She could sense it in the way he hesitated as though anxious to phrase his idea as delicately as possible. "I will not have an abortion," she said flatly, forestalling the suggestion before he aired it.

He raised his eyebrows reproachfully. "Have I suggested you should?"

"Not yet, but you were about to. I can tell."

"It would be as well if you didn't try to second-guess me, Sophie, particularly since you do it so badly. An abortion is the last thing I have in mind." He picked up his mug of coffee and took a mouthful. "The way I see it, there's only one course of action open to us. We'll get married as soon as it can be arranged."

"*Married?*"

He misunderstood the dismay she couldn't hide. "I know your career is important to you and that having a child right now is probably at the bottom of your list of priorities." He shrugged and stared into the fire. "For what it's worth, it's not exactly number one on mine, either."

Should she tell him that her dearest ambition was not to go down in history as the most illustrious water-garden artist of the modern world, but to settle down with a good man and have babies? But that not in her worst nightmare had she imagined it happening like this, with a coldly proposed merger between the future parents of a child carelessly conceived while the father was in grief for his true, lost love?

"If the idea of marrying me is so very repulsive to you, Sophie," he said, breaking into her reverie, "think of it as a temporary solution. We'll stay together for two years and then evaluate the situation. By then, the difficult early months of late-night feedings and colic and all those other things that babies apparently thrive on, will be over. We'll both have had time to adjust to the idea of parenthood and at least we'll know we gave our child the best possible start in life, with two parents who put his welfare before their own."

He smiled, a wry, sad curving of his sexy mouth, as though he knew very well that what he was about to say next was highly unlikely. "And who knows, maybe we'll find we manage rather well together, and a divorce won't be worth the inconvenience and upheaval it will create. Stranger things have been known to happen, you know, and perhaps our chances are better than average since neither of us is dazzled by notions of romantic happily-ever-after. This is a match made in bed, not heaven, and I think we're both too intelligent not to recognize that."

In her secret heart, Sophie knew that, had they met under other circumstances, their relationship might have evolved differently and they might have found happiness together. Now he'd flung the opportunity into her lap and she knew only an overwhelming sadness because clearly he expected no such outcome.

"You seem to have thought of every angle except one," she said bleakly. "What are people going to think of our getting married so soon after Barbara's death?"

"I stopped caring what other people think a long time ago."

"I didn't. And whether you want to admit it or not, there are some who would be hurt if we were to go ahead as you suggest. The Wexlers, for instance. They're finding it difficult enough to cope with losing a daughter without finding they're losing the son they almost had, as well."

He stared into the fire again and she thought how hard he looked at times, how much like one of his bulldozers flattening everything standing in its way. "That part of my life is over as Gail and John Wexler will be the first to understand," he said. "Any other obstacles you'd like to throw up?"

Just one, but she wasn't fool enough to invite his scorn by giving voice to it. Of all the reasons he'd listed for them to marry, he hadn't once mentioned love, and if she was idiot enough to want gilt on her gingerbread, he didn't have to be made aware of the fact.

"I can't think of any, not at the moment."

"Well, then?" He fixed her in his laser-sharp gaze. "What's your answer? Are we engaged, or not?"

CHAPTER FOUR

OF COURSE she and Dominic Winter weren't engaged! The question was preposterous. They were on the brink of the twenty-first century, for heaven's sake, and shotgun weddings had gone out of fashion a long time ago, along with marriages of convenience.

On top of that, he didn't much like her. No man who proposed marriage in such cut-and-dried terms could possibly harbor any fondness for his intended bride. And although she might find him scandalously appealing, Sophie wasn't so far in thrall to the attraction that she was willing to sacrifice herself on the altar of conventionality because she happened to be carrying his baby.

"Well, Sophie? What's your answer? Are you going to marry me?"

She studied his well-shaped head with its sweep of thick black hair, and the equally dark parentheses of his brows. She hazarded a glance into those still green eyes, found it a thoroughly unnerving experience and quickly passed on to his very sexy mouth.

A terrible mistake! Desire, plain and simple, stabbed her, laying waste to what was left of her meager supply of common sense. If she'd dared close her own eyes, she knew her mind would have been filled with memories of St. Julian. Of the heady perfume of flowers and the rhythmic roll of the surf. And of Dominic lying naked beside her, all smooth, firm muscle and sleek, silken strength. The possibility, however slim, of that same sweet rush of passion consuming her again, of its weaving an indelible thread through the fabric of her life, seduced her into what she could only assume constituted temporary insanity.

Her mouth formed a reply without any regard for the frantic message from her brain. "All right, we'll give it a try."

He rubbed his hands together with the brisk satisfaction of a man who'd just effected a contract so full of loopholes through which he could extricate himself that he didn't have to worry about the problems inherent in its execution. "Good. What sort of wedding would you like? A traditional affair with all the trappings—" he let his glance slide fleetingly to her still-slender waist "—or something more discreet?"

Scrambling to gather her scattered wits, she said, "Right now, I'm more concerned about our reaching a clear understanding of the kind of marriage we're entering into than I am about the social correctness of my having a white wedding."

"I'm not sure I know what you mean."

"Well, this isn't exactly the customary way to go about things."

He inclined his head in assent. "I thought we'd already agreed that it's not."

"Yes," she said, "we have."

"Then what is it you don't understand?"

She might have known he'd make her spell it out. "What do you want of me in all this, Dominic? What sort of living arrangements do you have in mind?"

"Are you talking about sex, Sophie?"

A blush chased all the way up from her feet to her face. "I'm trying to discuss a delicate subject without causing either of us unnecessary embarrassment, something which you're obviously incapable of appreciating."

"You *are* talking about sex." A hint of glee touched his mouth but was gone before it had time to reach his eyes. "If I was not prepared to honor my obligations to you, I would not have proposed marriage. The same code of decency forbids my demanding conjugal rights from an unwilling wife. Whether or not we share the same bed is entirely up to you, Sophie. I am perfectly willing to follow your lead."

"You—you're making this very difficult," she stammered.

"Not at all. I'm not made of stone, nor am I immune to your considerable charms—witness the fact that you conceived my baby in a thoroughly orthodox fashion. If you want me again—for whatever reason—all you have to do is let me know. We're both normal, healthy people, subject to normal, healthy urges, and I can't imagine that either of us will jump to any farfetched conclusions in the event that we choose to satisfy them. Does that clarify matters for you?"

Dear Lord, yes! In spades! He would marry her and even enjoy sex with her, but he would not love her.

"I see that I have." He stood up and flexed his shoulders, a gesture Sophie found herself watching with morbid fascination. "It's been a long day. Why don't we table further discussion until tomorrow?"

It was probably the only smart suggestion he'd made all night. Sophie needed to be alone. More than anything, she needed to climb into bed and sleep the clock around, and hope that that would be enough to restore her sanity.

And then she could do what she should have done tonight: say "Thank you very much, Dominic, but I won't marry you although I do appreciate your having asked." She'd do it now if she wasn't so desperately tired and he wasn't so hard to say no to.

He touched her face, running the back of his fingers from her jaw to her cheekbone. "I have a meeting with my architect at nine in the morning, and another with my project manager right after," he said, "but I should be finished by noon. What say we get together for lunch some time after that, and you can tell me what you've decided on in the way of a wedding? And then, perhaps, we should break the news to your family. I imagine they'd like to hear it before it becomes common knowledge around town."

The mere thought of her parents' shock and surprise at learning their daughter was rushing headlong into marriage with a stranger almost had Sophie doing the brave and decent thing and saying right there and then that she couldn't continue playing this charade a moment longer. But there was something so invincible in the set of Dominic's spectacular shoulders, in the unwavering gaze of his long-lashed green eyes, that she took refuge in cowardice once again.

"I suppose so," she hedged, disgusted by the pitifully indecisive creature she'd become.

Her tone, or perhaps the way she fairly drooped with exhaustion, had Dominic subjecting her to an even more thorough scrutiny. "You look worn out," he said, the concern in his words seriously eroding her composure.

"I feel worn out," she practically whimpered.

"Then go to bed and get some rest." He leaned forward and surprised her with a kiss full on her mouth. It was brief and hard and dismayingly arousing. "Good night, Sophie. Sleep well and I'll see you tomorrow."

She had an early appointment herself the next morning, a consultation for a fountain garden in the atrium of one of Palmerstown's grand old houses, which was being turned into apartments. Although she always made a point of looking her best for such meetings, Sophie spent extra time that day, applying more makeup than she usually wore, in an attempt to camouflage the ravages of fatigue. Because, Dominic's exhortation notwithstanding, she had not slept the previous night, let alone slept well. Her mind had been too full of the man whose impact on her life had her swinging repeatedly from resentment to desire, from simple logic to wild fantasy.

What if she married him and things did work out between them? she'd wondered as midnight crept past. What if they fell in love after the fact instead of before? It wasn't unheard of after all, and their one experience of intimacy had been breathtaking, at least for her. Why couldn't it always be that way? Why couldn't something strong and enduring grow out of the passion and closeness that came from lovemaking?

But then the pendulum swung the other way, stripping her dreams of their magic and revealing them for the foolish delusions they were. A man like Dominic Winter wasn't the type to switch allegiance so quickly. He had loved Barbara and was still grieving her death. Sophie was merely an inconvenience he'd brought upon himself during a moment of weakness, one for which he was paying the price.

For him, it had been sex, careless sex: something that never would have happened had he not been so tormented by his loss. But happen it had, and since he no longer had a future with Barbara, he was doing the honorable thing by the woman who had briefly brought him surcease from his pain. If truth be known, he probably had to think twice to remember Sophie's name.

And so it went, back and forth, until the cold light of reason, coinciding with that of morning, finally won out.

She was twenty-seven, not seventeen, and had too much pride to run second best with any man, even if he was the father of her child.

She chose her wardrobe with care: a wool dress with a dropped waist and flared skirt, simple gold jewelry and plain black leather accessories. The ensemble boosted her confidence just an extra notch because she didn't delude herself. Rejecting Dominic wasn't going to be easy.

She did briefly entertain the thought that he, too, might have had second thoughts and decided to call the whole affair off. It seemed unlikely, however, especially when she checked her answering service about ten-thirty and learned that he'd made a one o'clock lunch reservation in the Lakeside Room at the Royal Hotel. A person didn't need to go to such lavish lengths to end things, especially not when a simple phone call would do the job just as well. She very much feared that, as far as Dominic was concerned, the engagement was still on.

Being kept waiting left Dominic in a very testy frame of mind. Admittedly, it wasn't her fault that he got to the hotel ten minutes early, but that didn't prevent his irritation from growing when she still hadn't shown up at five past one.

He dismissed the notion that her nonappearance might be an indication that she'd had second thoughts about marrying him. If she thought that by standing him up she'd so easily slither off the matrimonial hook, she sadly underestimated him. At the very least, he expected the courtesy of a face-to-face refusal. And in this case, a refusal wasn't an option he was prepared to accept.

Forcing himself not to look at his watch again, he thumbed through the morning paper to the business section and immersed himself in the stock market report. Too bad women weren't as easy to analyze!

Granted, she'd looked a bit thunderstruck last night when he'd come out with his proposal and he supposed, to be fair, that he might have employed a little more finesse, but hell, she wasn't the only one reeling with shock. Just when, if ever, she'd planned to let him in on her little secret, had he not shown up when he did, was something he'd never know. The point was, as soon as he'd found out she was pregnant, there'd only ever been one outcome for the two of them and that was marriage.

It might not be the ideal solution but, the way he saw it, they could both do worse. He was going on thirty-six, experienced enough to know women weren't repelled by him, and smart enough to know that it took a lot more than illusions of love to make a marriage work. Furthermore, he'd meant what he said about a child needing two full-time parents. Weekend daddy was not a role he'd willingly adopt.

And she?

He flipped the page irritably. Hell, by her own admission she was no sexual ingenue. She knew how babies were made and if she hadn't wanted to be saddled with a child, she should have kept her distance, instead of seducing him with sympathy.

Her familiar white car screeching to a stop outside the hotel's front entrance diverted his attention. The driver's door swung wide on its hinges, a daintily shod foot emerged, a flare of teal blue fabric swirled around a well-turned ankle. Pale gold hair spilled over the collar of a winter white cape, a head turned, a smile captivated the doorman into whistling for the parking attendant.

She smiled again and, gathering the collar of her cape close at her throat, hooked a black handbag over her wrist and reached out a gloved hand to set the hotel's revolving brass doors in motion.

To his intense annoyance, Dominic felt his mouth go dry.

The Royal was the most splendid among Palmerstown's admittedly few hotels, but that was not to say it lagged behind its big-city counterparts. Its old-world opulence and dignity rendered it beyond question the only place in town with the glamour and panache to host special occasions. Weddings, anniversaries, charity balls, it knew them all.

Sophie, though, had always found its Austrian chandeliers and extravagantly molded ceilings rather formidable. Even the views of Jewel Lake from its tall, elegant windows were overwhelming. However, it was the sort of place that suited Dominic Winter to a T—big, impressive, invincible.

The minute she entered the foyer shortly before a quarter past one, she saw him. He leaned against one of the ornately carved library tables, scanning the morning paper and looking as he always did: well dressed and supremely at ease with himself and his place in the greater scheme of things. No one would have guessed he'd found out, just the night before, that he had fathered a child with a woman he barely knew.

"Sorry I'm a bit late," she said, slightly out of breath more from nerves than exertion. "I had rather a full morning."

He pushed away from the table and cast a pointed glance at the grandfather clock in the corner. "Did you? Well, the next time you decide to keep me waiting, do me the courtesy of phoning and letting me know in advance."

She refrained from telling him there and then that there wasn't going to be a "next time", at least not in the way he thought, and said only, "Sorry, it couldn't be helped."

Of course, he couldn't just leave well enough alone. He looked down at her from his lofty height and said patronizingly, "Time is money in the business world, you know, and I have little patience with people unwilling to appreciate that."

"I'll keep that in mind," she retorted, her own hackles only too ready to rise in retaliation, "provided you do me the courtesy of remembering that I'm in business, too, and it just so happens I had a previously scheduled appointment across town that took up most of my morning. As it is, I had to cut things short to get here when I did."

"Humph," he snorted. "Well, now that you are here, let's get a move on. We have a great deal to discuss."

Slapping the newspaper down on the table, he relieved her of her cape and deposited it in the coat-check booth. At about the same time, a burst of laughter erupted from the Lakeside Room, followed seconds later by a group of women who streamed across the carpeted foyer toward the revolving doors.

Striding back toward her, Dominic took Sophie by the elbow and drew her aside to let them pass unimpeded. Perhaps if he hadn't, they might have flowed around her, too involved in their animated conversation to take note of the rather ordinary woman busy scooping her hair free of her dress collar.

But no matter what their age, Dominic Winter was too arresting a man for women to overlook, especially when they were a little giddy from a celebration lunch. And most especially when they belatedly recognized the person he was escorting and saw the way he held on to her as if he had the right, as if, like a parcel of land, she was something he owned.

"Why, look, Anne!" one of them caroled. "Here's Sophie, come to check up on her mother!"

Sophie stood rooted to the spot, appalled to find herself and Dominic the object of mass curiosity. Eight pairs of eyes darted birdlike from her face to his and back again as the chatter, which moments before had filled the lobby, sank into expectant silence.

Her mother was the one to break it. "Hello, dear!" she exclaimed. "What a nice surprise running into you like this!"

She didn't add, *With this interesting, handsome man and when are you going to remember your manners and introduce us?* but she might as well have done. Neither her attention nor that of her friends faltered by so much as a blink.

"Um..." Sophie muttered inarticulately. "Um... Mom...?"

Anne Casson's gaze flitted to Dominic again. "That's right, dear," she said encouragingly. "What brings you here in the middle of the working day?"

"I'm...um, we're...having lunch."

"Oh, so were we," her mother chirped. "Our annual Valentine's Day lunch. You know the ladies from my bridge club, don't you?"

"Yes," Sophie mumbled, continuing to behave like a socially arrested teenager. Miserably aware of Dominic looming at her side, she faced up to the unavoidable. "And this...um, this is..."

"Dominic Winter." The scowl provoked by Sophie's late arrival melted beneath the warmth of the smile he turned on her mother. "How do you do, Mrs. Casson? I'm delighted to meet you."

Anne Casson never had had much of a head for wine. One glass stretched her tolerance practically to the limit. Sophie could only suppose she'd had two that day. How else to account for the outrageous liberties she proceeded to take?

Simpering at Dominic, who was busy doling out more charm than he'd ever spared Sophie in all the weeks she'd sort of known him, her mother said, "I'm very pleased to meet you, too, Mr. Winter," then had the nerve to add coyly, "Have you and my daughter been friends for very long?"

"Long enough for me to ask her to marry me and for her to accept," he announced baldly.

The mingled gasps and squeals *that* elicited from his audience quite swallowed up Sophie's groan of dismay.

"Marry? Oh, my dear, what wonderful news!" Wreathed in smiles, Anne folded Sophie in a hug. "When did all this happen?"

"Last night, which is why you weren't informed sooner," Dominic said, speaking for both of them as if Sophie's tongue had taken a walk. "We're hoping to fine-tune the arrangements over lunch."

Sophie's mother dimpled disgustingly. "Then I won't detain you, but won't you both please come for dinner this evening? I know my husband is going to be as thrilled with your news as I am, and he'll certainly want to meet the man his daughter's agreed to marry."

"We'd be delighted, wouldn't we, Sophie?" Dominic said, his perfunctory invitation for her opinion nothing more than token acknowledgment that she understood English.

"Well, actually—"

"Shall we say around seven?" her mother cut in, apparently no more concerned with her daughter's views than he was.

Placing his hand in the small of Sophie's back and steering her firmly toward the dining room, Dominic nodded. "Perfect," he allowed.

Resisting the urge to drag her feet like a reluctant child, Sophie followed the hostess to the best table in the room. Set in a vaulted alcove overlooking the lake and secluded from other diners by marble pillars and a screen of tropical plants, it was the ideal spot to bill and coo—or engage in outright warfare.

Sophie chose the latter. "What did you do that for?" she demanded crossly as soon as they were alone.

Dominic picked up the menu and perused it at leisure before deigning to inquire, "Do what?"

"You know perfectly well what! Going on about our being engaged, as if it was a fait accompli."

"But it is, Sophie," he said flatly, regarding her over the top of the menu. "Make no mistake about that."

"Don't be ridiculous! You don't really want to marry me. The only reason you even suggested it is because you feel responsible for me and—"

"That's not why," he said.

The remark, dropped so coolly in the face of her simmering outrage, threw her into total confusion. "It's *not*?"

"Not in the slightest."

Offended despite herself, Sophie glared at him. "Then what is?"

"The child, of course. I thought we agreed last night that you and I—what we want, what we had planned—aren't what matter here," he said, his voice chill with reproof. "I am marrying you to give our child a name."

"It will have a name," she said. "Mine."

"And a few others, too, if you have your way, including 'bastard'."

"Dominic, people don't think like that anymore. In this day and age, it doesn't make any difference if a child has only one parent."

He ignored her. Or at least, he ignored her for a moment and turned his attention to the waiter discreetly hovering beyond the pillars. Only after he'd ordered a scotch for himself and a Perrier with lime for her did he resume the conversation.

"A child never has only one parent," he pronounced, leaning back in his chair and pinning her in his sharp, intelligent gaze, "although some unfortunate children might never know more than one. Mine, however, will not be among that number."

"I wasn't suggesting cutting you out of our baby's life," Sophie exclaimed, wondering why on earth she was arguing the point with him when, logic and wisdom notwithstanding, part of her yearned simply to give in. It had always been like that where he was concerned: balancing precariously on the knife-edge of emotion, with pulsing attraction ready to engulf her on one side, and on the other its antidote, hostility.

Even at his most imperious, he was still attractive, and she wished he'd found something in his undoubtedly extensive wardrobe other than the tailored camel-hair jacket and ivory shirt that set off his tanned skin and dark hair to such advantage.

She sighed, last night's inner war breaking out anew and raging as fiercely as ever without either side showing signs of gaining the upper hand. "We don't have to get married for you to play a part in his or her upbringing," she said, clinging to reason despite the insidious little voice within trying to sabotage her efforts.

Dominic continued to regard her impassively. At length, he said, "All right. We won't."

The most dreadful, contrary disappointment welled up and struck her solidly in the solar plexus. "We won't?" she echoed.

He shook his head and smiled with suspect affability. "No. Since you find the idea so offensive, I'm perfectly willing to bring up the child by myself."

"*Without me*?" Outrage combined with astonishment to send her voice soaring.

"Of course not. To quote you, I'm not suggesting cutting you out of our baby's life, but we don't have to be married for you to play a part in his or her upbringing."

"But it's my baby! I'm its mother!"

"It's my baby, too," he countered with irrefutable logic. "I'm its father."

"What are you hinting at, Dominic?"

"Hinting?" He laughed scornfully. "I'm not hinting, Sophie. I'm *telling* you that I'll assume full custody of our child and accord you generous visitation rights."

She hadn't expected he'd make things easy for her but never in her wildest imaginings had she anticipated this! "A man alone bringing up a baby?" she scoffed, sounding a lot more certain than she really felt. "It'll never happen!"

"You're wrong." He spoke calmly and with utter, inflexible finality. "It's a not uncommon arrangement these days. As you've pointed out, we're living in the nineties. Single fathers are finally receiving their due and being acknowledged as having the same rights as single mothers to the full pleasures of parenthood. They no longer have to assume the role of powerless spectators in the raising of their children."

"You'll never persuade the courts to see things that

way. You won't be able to coerce a judge the way you're trying to pressure me."

"I won't have to. I'll simply provide an excellent home, hire a nanny of unimpeachable reputation and a housekeeper and, if necessary, the best possible legal representation to be had—none of which you can afford to do. I'm sure, given all that, that a judge would be quite happy to award me custody."

"This isn't about money, Dominic!" she whispered furiously. "You can't buy a child."

"Of course you can, Sophie," he purred with a shameful lack of guilt. "Anything can be bought for a price, including a judge, provided a person has enough money—and I do."

"You're bluffing."

He leaned forward as though what he had to impart next was of the utmost confidentiality. "You don't know me very well. If you did, you'd recognize that I'm very single-minded once I decide to go after something. I don't give up and I don't back down as more than a few people in this town who've tried to cross me can attest. I can count on one hand those who've succeeded, Sophie, and still have five fingers left at the end of the exercise."

He was the most despicable man she'd ever known. Yet although the blood raced through her veins at twice its normal speed, heating her cheeks and sending perspiration prickling down her spine, something cold and fearful lodged in Sophie's heart. "I will never give up my baby."

"Then you'll have to marry me because those are the only two choices you have."

It was what some aberrant streak in her had wanted all along, to be left with no alternative but to marry him. That way she wouldn't have to deal with all the uncertainties that nagged at her. Instead, she could consign herself to destiny in the shape of Dominic Winter. "Go with the flow", as Elaine was fond of saying. And bend all her energies to creating something wonderful out of something improbable, love and happiness out of carelessness and inconvenience.

But not this way. Not because he was blackmailing or intimidating her.

Suddenly, she hated him. Hated his imperturbable confidence, his certainty that he would win no matter what obstacles she threw in his path. Hated his smoldering sex appeal, the graceful fingers curled so casually around his glass, the long, dark lashes drawn down to cover the expression in his eyes. The empty, beautiful smile on his cruel, beautiful mouth.

"Then I will marry you, and I will make your life a living hell," she promised rashly, tears trembling in her voice.

He stretched out both his hands and pried apart her clenched fists, stroking each finger with a tenderness that, at any previous time in their association, would have reduced her to putty. But not now. Never again, after today.

"Will you?" he asked softly.

"Yes," she said, wrenching her fingers free. "I will. *I will*, Dominic."

He raised his lashes and bathed her in the cool green depths of his gaze. "No, you won't, my darling. Because that will not be a healthy environment for our child and you will want the very best for him."

"Her," she said mutinously. She didn't want a son. Sons grew up into power-hungry men with no heart.

"Her," he conceded, waxing magnanimous. "So, are there any more objections, or are we once again agreed that marriage is the best resolution of our situation?"

"What if I try hard to make it work and despite that you're dreadfully unhappy with me?" she said, snatching to find straws and finding them pathetically thin on the ground.

His laughter rang out, a rich blend of amusement and exasperation. "Don't you know that if you go looking for trouble, you're certain to find it?"

"But we're not in love," she said, finally finding the courage to bare what to her was the fatal flaw in their arrangement.

He sobered. "No, we're not. And as I pointed out last night, that improves our chances of making a success of things. When you have few expectations, you're less likely to be disappointed."

Oh, she really did hate him! At this rate, she'd probably murder him before the ink was dry on the marriage license!

She cast about for something with which to puncture his self-confidence, to make him question, just a little, his invincibility. "Is this the way you went about things with Barbara, railroading her into a marriage she didn't want? Is that why she felt she had to get away from you?" she asked flippantly. And immediately regretted having done so.

His face wiped itself clean of all expression. Only his eyes glowed with a light that was almost feral. "My relationship with Barbara is none of your business and I have no intention of discussing it or her with you."

The pain Sophie had sought to inflict turned itself on her with brutal force. How foolish of her to have thought she could hurt him! There was nothing she could do that would matter to him, neither love him nor hate him, because he didn't care. He was too numb to feel anything she leveled his way.

Everything sweet he had to give to a woman, he'd given to Barbara. All that he had left for Sophie was his bitterness at having lost the real love of his life.

If she were truly vindictive, she would increase his misery a thousandfold. She would tell him how his fiancée had betrayed him during her fling on St. Julian. She would reduce him to the same despair that he'd invoked in her.

But she could never hurt him like that no matter how richly he deserved it. Because, of course, she could never really hate him no matter how much she wished she could.

CHAPTER FIVE

HE HAD to know he'd won. Even a fool could have interpreted the body language so clearly trumpeted by the slump in her spine, the trembling in her hands, the way she bent her head so that her hair fell forward to hide the distress on her face. And whatever else he might be, Dominic was no fool.

"You'll feel better when you've eaten," he announced blandly, nudging the menu toward her.

She would be sick all over the table if she took so much as a mouthful of food. And it would serve him right! "I'm not hungry."

"Well, I didn't say you were, Sophie," he replied, all sunny equanimity now that he'd wrung surrender out of her. "I said—"

"I heard what you said! Every last, extorting word!"

"*Extorting*?" Laughter untouched by anything but genuine entertainment came weaving across the table to filter its way through the strands of her hair.

"Enjoy your amusement, Dominic," she snapped, staring at the carpet and refusing to be coaxed into forgiving him. "It won't last long."

"Ahem," the waiter said, and Sophie saw his well-polished black shoes come to a halt beside her.

"My fiancée will have the cream of asparagus soup, followed by a small portion of sole," Dominic decreed, laughter still shimmering in his voice, "but I'll settle for something a bit more fortifying. Bring me a spinach salad and the oyster stew."

When it was placed in front of her, Sophie wanted to throw the soup all over him. It would have afforded her delicious pleasure to watch the rich green cream drooling down his expensive camel-hair jacket. But the aroma of delicate herbs and fresh asparagus was too tempting and she wished she'd not told him she wasn't hungry. Doing her best to pretend he wasn't there, she spooned a little of the soup into her mouth.

"How is it?" he asked.

She touched her napkin to her lips. "Excellent, thank you."

"Good. You need to look after yourself."

One word about my eating for two, she thought savagely, *and he really will be wearing this*! "I'm not in the habit of doing otherwise."

"Have you been bothered by morning sickness?"

"A little, when I first get out of bed, but it doesn't last long."

"Have you seen a doctor?"

"No, Dominic," she said, staring at her soup because anything was preferable to looking at him in his present solicitous mood. "I just told you, I'm feeling very well."

"Nevertheless, pregnant women shouldn't take any chances. I know a very good obstetrician—"

"So do I," she said shortly.

"Then make an appointment, Sophie, and let me know the date and time."

"Whatever for?"

"Because I intend to go with you for the first visit."

Her spoon fell into her soup with a decided clatter. "Absolutely not!" she said flatly, abandoning her study of the tabletop and favoring him with a glare. "If you think I'm about to have you...let you..."

"What?" He raised quizzical brows.

Witness me flat on my back, with my ankles hoisted into stirrups and heaven only knows how much of me on display...! Her face flamed, giving her away.

Of course, he noticed. He noticed everything he wasn't supposed to see, from pregnancy tests to the precise number of seconds he'd been kept waiting for his blasted lunch.

"Oh, for Pete's sake, Sophie, I'm not suggesting I accompany you into the examining room!" he snorted. "I'm no voyeur. If I'm going to see you naked, I'd just as soon do so in private. All I want is to talk to the doctor and find out what I can do to make the pregnancy as pleasant as possible for you."

Just when she'd decided he lacked a single redeeming quality, he came out with something that left her feeling smutty-minded and immature. Grudgingly, she muttered, "Well...thank you."

"You're welcome," he said. "Now can we call a truce and concentrate on enjoying this excellent lunch?"

Somehow she managed, resorting to monosyllabic answers to his attempts at general conversation. But there was one subject she felt obliged to discuss more thoroughly before they went their separate ways for the afternoon.

"About our having dinner this evening with my parents," she said. "You might as well be prepared for the fact that you won't bamboozle my father as easily as you did my mother. She's been itching to be mother of the bride ever since my brother got married and all she got to do was cry at the ceremony. My father's a different proposition altogether. He's likely to ask some very awkward questions."

"I'll be happy to answer them," Dominic said calmly.

"No doubt. The point is, I'm not sure how much we should tell them—about the baby, that is."

"I'm not afraid to come out with the truth, if that's what's worrying you. On the other hand, our reasons aren't anyone else's business but our own, so if you'd rather your parents didn't know about the pregnancy, that's how we'll handle it."

"I hate deceiving them but in this case I think it might be best if we don't share everything with them, not yet at least. I'm afraid they'll jump to all the right conclusions if we do, and that would worry them terribly."

"What conclusions are you referring to, Sophie?"

"The fact that we barely know each other and aren't the least bit in love."

He smiled wryly. "I see. Then we'll keep quiet and put on an act that will convince them otherwise."

"What about your parents?"

"Parent," he corrected her. "And he isn't interested in my doings."

Curiosity begged to be satisfied but it was clear from the way that mask of privacy suddenly descended over Dominic's features that the subject of his family, like that of Barbara, was closed.

"If I don't know anything about you," Sophie ventured, "how am I ever going to convince anyone that I want to marry you? It isn't normal for people not to talk about their families. For instance, have I mentioned that I'm a twin, or that my brother is seventeen minutes older than I am and presently living with his wife in England, completing a research fellowship in Roman history?"

"Good God!" Dominic exclaimed, for the first time looking faintly rattled. "Does that mean you might give birth to twins, as well?"

"Not necessarily. At least, I don't think so. But that's not the point."

He shot back his cuff and checked the time on his watch. "You're quite right, it's not," he agreed, scribbling his signature on the bill and pocketing his credit card. "Unfortunately, I can't take the time to exchange personal histories right now. I have a meeting with the land development office at city hall, so I'm afraid the sordid story of my life will have to wait."

She barely had the chance to collect her purse and gloves before he was ushering her out of the dining room and into the foyer. He retrieved her cape and sent the parking valet scurrying for their cars.

"Where shall we meet tonight?" she asked as he hustled her toward the revolving doors.

"We won't," he said. "I'll pick you up at six-thirty. That should give us enough time, shouldn't it?"

To get to her parents' home by seven, perhaps, but not to fill in all the biographical blanks. She grabbed at his sleeve in an attempt to slow him down. "Dominic, I think we need a bit longer than that. Can you make it half past five instead, so that we can talk about...well, things we need to learn about each other?"

Impatiently, he swung back to face her. "No. I hear what you're saying, and once again I admit you're right, but it's something that will have to wait."

"I see." She blew out a sigh. "Well, I can't very well force you to tell me things you don't want me to know. But sooner or later, you're going to have to make a few concessions, or this marriage we're contemplating really will be pure hell whether you like it or not. You can't expect me to be the one who always backs down. I'm not cut out to be any man's doormat."

"It never occurred to me that you were. On the other

hand, if you hadn't been so bloody-minded about trying to wriggle out of marrying me, we could have spent the past hour discussing the very things you're harping on about. Now I really have to get a move on. Have a nice afternoon."

Talk about being summarily dismissed! Resentfully, Sophie watched his long-legged stride carry him outside and into the black Jaguar, and decided that they were in for a very rough ride indeed if this was how he intended to approach their marriage.

Her mother had gone to considerable trouble to make the evening festive. She'd put champagne on ice, and candles and bowls of flowers were everywhere in the apartment: tulips and freesia on the living room coffee table, roses in the dining alcove, and even a little crystal vase of Devon violets in the powder room.

Her father, although warm enough in his greeting, seemed a little more reserved in his pleasure. "So this is the man who's swept my daughter off her feet," he remarked, sizing Dominic up. "Well, although I must congratulate you on your good taste, I admit I'm a bit bowled over. It strikes me you've arrived at this decision rather suddenly."

The beginnings of a blush warmed Sophie's cheeks. Aware of her father's glance swinging toward her, she busied herself helping her mother pass around slender flutes of champagne.

"I think I took Sophie by surprise, too," Dominic agreed, neatly evading any sort of explanation for the unexpectedness of his proposal. "But when the time is right, there's not much point in postponing, is there?"

"As long as you're both sure you know what you're doing, I suppose not," her father admitted doubtfully.

"Sophie's old enough to make up her own mind, and it's not as if there's any big rush to set a wedding date."

The flush that Sophie had just about brought under control flared up again. Noticing, Dominic relieved her of the glass she was about to offer him and slid an arm around her shoulders. "Call me an anxious bridegroom if you like, Mr. Casson, but I don't want to wait a day longer than I have to to make Sophie my wife," he said, gazing with every appearance of besotted adoration into her eyes.

"I see," her father said, plainly not seeing at all. "So when's it going to be, Sophie?"

She would have loved to land Dominic in the thick of things and say, *Don't ask me. I'm only the bride and haven't been told yet*, but all that would have done was worry her parents. "Well," she hedged, "we...um, we thought some time around...um..."

"The first Saturday in March," Dominic supplied.

Her mother gasped. "But that's less than four weeks away!"

Sophie saw the sharpened speculation in her father's eyes and her cheeks burned. She swallowed twice, knowing full well she looked like a guilty child found with her fingers in the cookie jar.

Dominic noticed and immediately took steps to effect a little damage control. Shielding her with his body, he bent his head and brought his mouth down on hers. It was a very calculated kiss, not too long, not too short, and appropriately enthusiastic.

It might have been tolerable if he'd closed his eyes for the duration, but he didn't. He kept them wide open and stared at her. She knew because she stared right back. It was her only defense against the disconcerting urge to melt into his embrace and pretend the kiss was for real.

With the possible exception of Sophie's father, no one could have guessed that the prospective bride and groom were anything but panting to exchange their vows and plunge into happily-ever-after.

Her mother burst into tears. "I'm so happy for the two of you," she sobbed cheerfully.

But her father, still plainly suspicious of the whole endeavor, said, "I thought weddings took a long time to plan. Is there anything else you'd like to tell us while you're at it?"

Keeping Sophie firmly within the protection of his arm, Dominic shook his head. "Not at this time, sir," he replied with a firmness that brooked no further interrogation.

"Well," Doug Casson conceded, backing down, "as long as you're happy, Sophie."

"I am," Sophie muttered, doing her damnedest to look radiant.

Mercifully, her mother produced a notepad and shifted the focus to the practical arrangements of putting together a wedding on such short notice. Over the course of dinner, it was settled that the church ceremony would be followed by a small but elegant wedding breakfast in the Crystal Room at the Royal, followed by a brief honeymoon whose destination had yet to be decided.

"Spring's a busy time of year in my business," Dominic explained. "I'm afraid I can't afford to take off more than a few days."

For the first time since they'd arrived, Sophie's father showed some real enthusiasm for the topic under discussion. "I've read about your company and understand you run an impressive operation, Dominic. Residential construction, isn't it?"

Dominic nodded. "With the emphasis on low-density

housing. I'm not one of those developers whose first priority is to chop up a piece of land into as many building lots as is legally possible."

At last a safe subject, Sophie thought gratefully, but her relief faded as quickly as it had arisen when her father remarked, "Well, Sophie only just got back from a holiday in the Caribbean, so I don't suppose she'll mind postponing the honeymoon."

"Oh, let's not talk about that," her mother said. "Every time I think of that poor young woman drowning...! Of course, you must know all about that, Dominic. It was in all the papers and—"

Not daring to cast a glance in Dominic's direction, Sophie braced herself for the worst.

Dear heaven, it was all going to come out, she thought in horror. Her father, whose memory would put an elephant's to shame, would recall every last detail that was printed or aired about Barbara Wexler's death. He'd put two and two together and come up with a big, fat four, and this supposed engagement celebration would be exposed for the shabby little deception it really was.

But she had not counted on Dominic, who cut her mother off before she could elaborate further. "Yes, it was tragic," he said impassively. "Have we covered everything to do with the wedding, do you think?"

"The dress!" Instantly diverted, Anne Casson scribbled frantically on her notepad. "If you're thinking of white, we'll have to get going on it immediately, Sophie, although you could probably find something from the sample rack that could be altered to fit if you had to." She eyed Sophie assessingly. "You're still a size eight, dear, aren't you?"

Sophie shot a beseeching glance at Dominic. "She was

when we met," he said, for once seeming to be at a loss for the right answer.

"And when was that?" her father wanted to know.

While Dominic skated over the thin ice of judicious truth, Sophie tried not to choke on her mother's excellent chicken Marsala. By the time the evening dragged to a close, she was a nervous wreck.

"That," she groaned, the minute they drove away from her parents' building, "was a nightmare. I don't know how I managed to get through it. When the subject of Bar—um, the Caribbean came up, I was horribly afraid they'd connect you with...the whole thing."

"That was over two months ago," Dominic said. "People soon forget—at least, most do."

But not you, Sophie thought bleakly. *You'll never forget.*

"It was a bit like tap-dancing through a mine field, though," he went on. "Lies of omission require some pretty fancy footwork."

She stared at the dim outline of his profile illuminated in the lights from the dashboard. "Yet you managed very well."

"That came out sounding like an accusation, Sophie, as if you think I make a career out of withholding the truth from people."

"Do you?"

"Only when it's absolutely necessary."

"Does that mean that you'll lie to me if I persist with questions you don't want to answer?"

"I'd prefer to be completely straightforward with you, but there are some things I'd prefer not to share with you at this time."

"Like your family history?"

He shifted gear as the car approached a hairpin bend

on the lakeshore road. "No. It's not my favorite subject, but if it's all that important to you, I'll tell you what there is to know."

"It's that important, Dominic. You're my baby's father."

"Okay." Steering skillfully through the curve, he shifted again into high gear. "My mother gave birth to me when she was twenty. My father, who was thirty-eight, was her college professor, had a Ph.D. in literature and fancied himself a poet. He believed in love, especially if it was free, but wasn't big on follow-through. When my mother told him she was pregnant, he suddenly remembered he was married and due for a year's sabbatical leave. He gave her a thousand dollars to buy an abortion if that's what she wanted, packed up his wife and personal possessions and was busy spouting iambic pentameters at some campus in Kentucky when I was born six months later in Vancouver."

He spoke lightly, as if what he had to say was of little consequence, but the set of his jaw and his grip on the steering wheel told Sophie that it was what he left unsaid that counted.

"Did your mother tell your father that she'd decided to go through with the pregnancy?"

"No. He'd already made it plain he wasn't interested in what she did."

"How sad."

"The only sad part," Dominic said, his words forged from steel, "is that my mother actually loved the jerk and continued to do so for the rest of her life. She died of acute cirrhosis when she was thirty-eight."

"Oh!" Sophie couldn't contain a small gasp of dismay as the implication of his disclosure struck home.

Without taking his eyes off the road, he nodded.

"That's right, she was a drunk. A two-bottle-a-day woman by the time her liver gave out."

Sophie would have liked to touch his arm, to do something that would convey her sympathy. But he had walled himself off so thoroughly that there might as well have been a pane of glass separating her from him. So she said the conventional, hopelessly inadequate thing. "I'm very sorry, Dominic."

"Don't be. She was a lost, unhappy woman, abandoned by my father and disowned by her family. She didn't give a tinker's damn about her life. It just took her a long time to end it, that's all."

"But she had you. Surely that must have brought her some comfort?"

"I'm afraid not. Being saddled with a child and forced to support him by taking on whatever menial job she could find fell a long way short of postgraduate studies in Paris and love in the afternoon with my father."

"So you're not close to your grandparents?"

His laughter ricocheted around the interior of the car. "Grandparents?" he inquired mockingly. "Don't they belong to the same make-believe world as Santa Claus and tooth fairies?"

"But what about your father? Did he never change his mind and decide he wanted to get to know his son after all?"

"My *father* and I," Dominic said, referring to his other parent so scathingly that she flinched, "have spent the grand total of forty-five minutes in each other's company at the end of which time we parted in mutual relief. I went looking for him, convinced I could make him see the error of his having walked out on us, and he made it clear he harbored not a single regret for his decision. I was sixteen at the time, which is the only excuse I can offer for being such a bloody fool, but after, I vowed that no one would ever shove me aside again as if I was of no account. I'd be in control. And damn it, I have been.''

"Do you have any half brothers or sisters?"

"No. Children, the good professor informed me, were a scourge not to be tolerated, and I can quite see how they would have cramped his style. Imagine trying to preserve the image of dashing lover if you have to cut short the big seduction to take your kid to football practice!"

"I cannot imagine anyone turning his back on his only child," Sophie said softly.

"Good. Then you should have no trouble understanding why I'm not about to stand back and let you raise our son or daughter alone. I intend to be a very immediate presence in my child's life. And one other thing you can count on, Sophie, is that I'm not cut from the same cloth as my old man. One woman at a time is quite enough for me."

There was no reason for the little flame of optimism that warmed her at that, but it flared up anyway.

He turned down the lane that led to her house. On the right, a pewter swath of moonlight dappled the surface of Jewel Lake.

"Will you let me come in for a minute?" he asked, drawing the car to a stop at her front door. "There's one thing we haven't discussed that needs to be taken care of right away."

In light of his revelation of past rejections, it seemed unfeeling to refuse. Once inside the house, he stalked uninvited through the main floor, ending up in the kitchen. There he paused for a moment, surveying its cramped dimensions, then pushed aside the curtain covering the window in the door and stared through the darkened panes to the garden outside. Puzzled, she trailed after him.

"How much land do you have here, Sophie?" he asked.

"Just over an acre."

"With how much lakefront?"

"About a hundred and fifty feet."

"And you hold clear title?"

"I have a mortgage, as I told you last night."

"Oh, that!" He snapped his fingers dismissively, as if the matter of thousands of dollars owed to the bank was small potatoes to a man of his means. "No, I'm talking about freehold title. You're not on leased land, are you?"

"No."

"Excellent. Given the state of this building..." He thumped the door frame, which set the glass to rattling alarmingly. "Hell, it's about ready to fall down on its own without any help from me."

"I'm not sure I'm following you, Dominic."

He waved an airy hand around the kitchen, embracing its old-fashioned cabinets and temperamental plumbing. "I'm going to knock down your house, Sophie, and build you something better."

"What if I don't want my house knocked down?" she said, less because of her attachment to the drafty old thing than because she resented the way he dismissed it.

It seemed to occur to him that he was pushing his luck a little in taking so much for granted. Bathing her in one of those rare and charming smiles normally reserved for other people, he asked, "Wouldn't you like something more convenient? Something with fewer stairs and higher ceilings?" With both hands, he painted broad, sweeping strokes across an imaginary canvas. "Think of a house with wide hallways and French doors that open onto patios that face the lake. Picture a breakfast nook flooded with morning sunshine, a formal dining room for parties. His-and-her en suite bathrooms with jetted tubs. Nanny's quarters next to a bright, airy nursery. Hardwood floors and marble countertops, modern appliances and light fixtures. Space to move without bumping into things."

The dinosaur of a furnace chose that moment to clank into operation.

"And six-zone hot-water heating that neither makes a noise nor fills the air with the accumulated dust of the past fifty years," Dominic said, swooping in for the kill.

If he thought he could bulldoze her the way he planned to bulldoze her house, he was in for a big surprise. "This house is good enough for me," she said, knowing it was a lie and that she'd give her eyeteeth for the kind of house he'd described.

"Well, it's not good enough for my baby—or my wife, come to that," he informed her. "You're already concerned about the conclusions your parents will reach about our marriage when they find out you're pregnant, and I'm not about to add fuel to their speculation by allowing you to remain in a hovel like this."

He would not *allow*? "You—you have no right to belittle the way I live," she spluttered, incensed.

"Don't I have the right to want to give my child the best I can afford?"

Unaccountably depressed by his reply, she turned away and stroked an affectionate hand over the worn Formica counter. Granted, the house wasn't a palace, but she'd been happy here and she couldn't shake the feeling that, all its modern luxuries notwithstanding, the home he planned would be sadly lacking in that one commodity.

"You think money can buy anything you want, Dominic, don't you? You think, because you've got money and I haven't, that you can just barge into my life and take it over." She swung back to face him. "Well, I won't stand for it."

"In case you've forgotten, there's a line in the marriage ceremony that goes something like 'with all my worldly goods I thee endow'," he shot back. "And if there's one vow I can keep, it's that."

He was glaring at her, his eyes shooting green sparks of anger. His beautiful mobile mouth that, even without trying or really meaning to, could turn out kisses sweet enough to soften any woman's resistance was pressed into a hard, uncompromising line. And suddenly, Sophie knew she wanted more from him than just the promise of his worldly goods. She wanted things that had nothing to do with money, things that he wouldn't dream of giving to any other woman, that he would save for her alone.

She wanted to see him look at her across a room full of people, his eyes molten with desire—for her. Wanted his fists to uncurl now and close over her shoulders in persuasion. Wanted him to reach out in unadorned hunger and pull her so close that she could feel the proof of his arousal pressing against her, then sweep her into his arms and carry her upstairs to bed.

She had every reason in the world to despise him. He'd shown himself to be cold, bitter, judgmental, not to mention unnaturally controlled in the face of Barbara's death. Yet he made Sophie's heart flutter and stall and filled her wicked mind with images of his face hovering over hers, his mouth closing on hers, his body...

Dear heaven, she had the moral fiber of an alley cat in heat! Was this what the hormonal upheaval of pregnancy did for a woman—turn her into a raving nymphomaniac? She blinked and gave herself a mental shake. "I'm not for sale, Dominic."

Surprisingly, his shoulders slumped. "I never thought you were," he said tiredly, "and if that's the impression I've given you then I'm sorry."

So am I, she thought, *because the real problem here is that you and I have never been able to communicate except for one memorable time when, although we shared our bodies, we never bared our hearts or souls to each other.* "What I've already got is good enough for me," she said, the hollow untruth of her statement ringing in her ears.

Did he hear it, too? Or was it possible that he also regretted the dearth of emotional closeness between them? Was that what made him ask so gently that he verged on tenderness, "But wouldn't you like something better for the baby?"

Small wonder he was so successful in business if he always pinpointed his opponent's weak spot so accurately! "And if I do, where am I supposed to live while all these miracles occur?" she whispered, her resistance crumbling into dust.

"With me, naturally. I have a place downtown and it'll only be for a month or two. We'll be well settled in the new house before the baby arrives."

In a flash, her opposition resurfaced. "Did it ever occur to you that I might not be the type who believes in living with a man before marriage?"

The silent scorn with which he countered that feeble argument spoke for itself: *Where were your lofty moral principles the day you fell into bed with a stranger?*

And he was right. Her layers of deceit were building faster than even she could count. When had she slipped from attraction so covertly disguised that she could pretend it didn't really exist, to this contagious madness?

When had he gone from shadowing her waking fantasies to possessing her nighttime dreams?

She couldn't bear the gnawing hunger ripping at her, the feeling that she'd lost control of her life and been tossed into an emotional whirlpool.

"Would you really feel more comfortable staying with your parents until after the wedding?" he asked, his voice as neutral as his expression.

And try to hide from their observant eyes her morning sickness and her heartsickness, and heaven only knew what else?

She shook her head. "No. They have only one bedroom in the apartment and a pull-out sofa in the den for overnight guests. We'd be falling all over one another."

"Then you don't have much choice. It's my place or a hotel, and if you think your father's suspicious now, wait until he discovers you're camping out in a rented room."

He'd won again, the way he always did, Sophie thought wearily.

"So that's where we're at," she said, blowing a strand of hair out of her eyes and grimacing at Elaine, who was helping her empty her kitchen cupboards into cardboard boxes. "The wheels have been set in motion and all of a sudden not only am I pregnant and engaged, I'm about to become homeless."

"Hardly that! You're moving into a pretty plush apartment with Dominic Winter, Palmerstown's most eligible bachelor." Elaine breathed his name on the same awestruck breath that other people mentioned sightings of Elvis.

"You're beginning to sound like a broken record, Elaine," Sophie said irritably. "Yes, with Dominic Winter, and it's all your fault. If you'd had the chicken pox when you were a child like the rest of us, instead of waiting until you were pushing thirty, Barbara Wexler would be alive today, probably married to him herself, and I'd feel less like a woman heading down a mountain in a car whose brakes have failed."

Not in the least perturbed by the implication that she'd brought about one woman's death and condemned another to life imprisonment, Elaine continued to go about her work, saying only, "Don't blame me if you've fallen in love out of your league. I didn't twist your arm and force you to leap into bed with the man the first chance you got! You managed that all on your own."

"Fall in love?" Sophie's voice rose to a near shriek. "Don't be ridiculous! How could any right-minded woman fall in love with a man who's arrogant and overbearing and secretive—not to mention in mourning? He's giving me his name, but Barbara Wexler's the one who has his heart and she took it to the grave with her."

Elaine sat back on her heels, a smug grin inching over her face. "Deny it all you like, old friend, but the signs are unmistakable. You're definitely well on the way to falling in love with him."

"Elaine, I don't even *like* the man!"

"And I can quite understand why you don't. From everything you tell me, he's not a very nice person. So why don't you just call his bluff and invite him to take a hike? Why assume a lifetime punishment for one little sin?"

Sophie was spared having to answer by the sound of the front door opening and the clump of several pairs of heavy boots coming down the hall. "That'll be him," she whispered. "He said he'd stop by with a couple of his workmen to go over the demolition plan."

"You mean I get to meet him?" Elaine could barely contain her delight. "Oh, be still my heart!"

"Shut up and behave yourself," Sophie hissed. "Things are bad enough without your making them any worse. Do you realize we'll be living together after today and I don't even know his birthday?"

"Try asking him. I'm sure he'd be only too glad to tell you."

"Tell you what?" he inquired, appearing in the doorway. "What do you want to know, Sophie?"

"Nothing," she mumbled. "I don't believe you've met my friend, Elaine."

"Hi, nice to meet you." He grinned with that special other-people charm. "How's the packing going?"

"As well as can be expected," Sophie announced primly.

The grin faded and he made the kind of face a man might make if he bit unexpectedly into a lemon. "I see. Do you think you'll be finished fairly soon?"

"Probably," she said, aware of Elaine rocking with silent laughter at her side. "Why?"

"Because I've got the truck outside and a couple of my men to help move things. Once I'm done going over next week's work schedule with them, I thought we'd load up all your stuff and haul it away to storage for you."

"I'm quite capable of taking care of it myself, Dominic," Sophie said.

"No doubt. However, those cartons are pretty heavy and I don't want you lifting them," he told her flatly. "We'll be ready to load up in about half an hour, so try to have everything ready to go by then, okay?"

Sophie glared after his retreating back. "See what I

mean?" she said through clenched teeth as the door swung closed.

"Oh, yes," Elaine murmured dreamily. "I see very well. No wonder you're in over your head. Sophie, he's gorgeous! He can impregnate me *any* time!"

She wasn't serious, of course, but that didn't prevent a totally irrational flash of jealousy streaking through Sophie. "Hardly gorgeous!" she scoffed. "He's too tall and lanky."

"Sleek and muscular," Elaine insisted.

"Bossy," Sophie snapped.

Elaine subsided into giggles again. "Masterful."

"Coldly impersonal."

"Sexy."

"Hateful."

"Irresistible," Elaine said, sobering. "Admit it, Sophie. We've been friends too long for me to let you get away with fooling yourself a minute longer."

Sophie looked away, appalled as the truth of Elaine's words found its mark with the deadly accuracy of an arrow. For weeks there had been such a yearning inside her, such an ache. One born of wanting and dreaming. And loving. Long before those few days on St. Julian, she'd been fighting the attraction, telling herself it was wrong, immoral, unhealthy.

Like an oyster, she'd learned to live with the irritation and been so busy hoping it would simply go away that she hadn't noticed when it turned into a pearl. But now, with her soul stripped bare like her house, she saw it for what it really was.

Her agreeing to marry Dominic had nothing to do with his threats to claim custody of the baby, nothing to do with coercion. And everything to do with her wanting to be the woman he called his wife.

Once she'd admitted it, there was no going back, no more deluding or denying. Hopelessly, she recognized it for the kind of love that perhaps only a woman could know, something that transcended time or logic. It simply *was*, and like a pervasive and thoroughly hypnotic disease, it had taken control of her.

"Irresistible," she admitted, and burst into tears. "Elaine, what in the world am I going to do?"

CHAPTER SIX

"Marry him, of course," Elaine said, as if that would solve all the problems.

"You seem to be forgetting he's still in love with Barbara," Sophie wailed. "How can I compete with a ghost?"

"Just because you can't make him forget her completely doesn't mean you can't have a good time trying. And you might even succeed, if you'd stop treating him as if he's something that crawled out from under the nearest rock."

"I don't!" Sophie protested, swabbing indignantly at her tears.

"If what I just witnessed is any indication, you certainly do. Good grief, Sophie, he's doing the best he can. He hasn't disowned the baby, he hasn't walked away from you, he's trying to do the decent thing. What more would you like?"

"For him to want me for who I am, not for what I'm bringing to his life and not because he feels responsible or guilty or anything like that."

"Then I suggest you change your tactics," Elaine replied, adding sagely, "Ever hear about catching more flies with honey than with vinegar?"

"If you think I'm going to grovel for his affections…!"

"Who said anything about groveling—although it strikes me that's exactly what you'd like *him* to do." Elaine heaved the last box onto the counter and dusted off her hands. "No, I think a bit of simple honesty might work wonders."

Sophie stared at her in horror. "I couldn't possibly tell him I'm in love with him!"

"Perhaps not, but you could stop behaving as if you find him repulsive."

"Lie down and play dead, you mean? Fat chance!"

Elaine sighed, pure exasperation written all over her face. "What's with you, Sophie? What's happened to the nice, reasonable woman I used to know, the one who always tried to see the other person's point of view?"

"She got buried under the mess her life's turned into."

"So start sorting it out, and do it soon, before the other half of this proposed partnership decides he hasn't struck quite the bargain he first thought. And while I'm dishing out home truths, here's another for you to chew on. Stop laying all the blame for this pregnancy on him. It took two, kiddo."

"I don't blame him."

"Not consciously, perhaps, but you're looking for someone to lambaste for what you call 'the mess her life's turned into', and he makes a convenient whipping boy."

Sophie bristled. "Well, I'm human, too, you know. And I don't like finding myself up to my ears in deceit—having to lie to my parents, to him, to myself. It's just not my style, Elaine."

"Then put an end to it. Stop letting yourself be manipulated by circumstances it's too late to change. He's willing to take a chance on marriage. Do your part to improve the odds in your favor."

"I hate you, Elaine Harrison," Sophie muttered, subsiding into a reluctant laugh. "Will you be my bridesmaid?"

"I'd already planned on it *and* on being the baby's godmother. They're two things you don't have any choice about," Elaine said, giving her a hug. "Now go and find that man of yours and invite him to take you out for dinner tonight. It might make going home to his place afterward a bit less strained if you both relax first over a meal and a bottle of good wine."

Things grew hectic shortly after that, what with a couple of the work crew loading all the furniture and boxes littering different rooms, and Elaine directing traffic, but Sophie took advantage of the activity to track down Dominic and try to make a fresh start.

She came across him in the dining room, where he was poring over blueprints spread across the table. "I'll get out of your way," he said politely when he noticed her hovering in the doorway, and started to roll up the sheets of paper.

He looked tired and more than a little discouraged. Enough to make Sophie wonder if she'd left it too late to adopt a less adversarial approach to their relationship. Daunted, she forced herself to stand beside him and rest a hand on his arm. "Are they the plans for the new house?"

He grew very still at the physical contact. "Yes."

She swallowed the nervousness clogging her throat. "May I see them?"

There was no reading the expression in his eyes. "If you wish, but there are still a few final details to be worked out."

"Still, I'd like to see, though I'll probably need you to explain things to me." It wasn't easy, offering the olive branch after all this time. His arm beneath her touch was iron hard, unresponsive. Dismayed, she tried to let her fingers slide unobtrusively to the sheaf of drawings on the table. "Is this how it'll look from the outside?"

His hand came down hard on hers, sandwiching it against the blueprint. "Drop the act, Sophie," he said stonily. "You're not so dense that you can't recognize the front elevation of a house when you see it, so what's this really all about?"

"Nothing," she said, coming as close to stammering as she had since she was about four. "I'm just... interested...."

"Really? Since when?"

Her throat ached with trepidation. He had never spoken to her so coldly, not even in the early days when he'd made no secret of his dislike of her. She swallowed and scraped together the dregs of her courage. "Since I came to see that you've been right all along and that we do need something bigger. My house really doesn't lend itself to raising a family."

"Is that all?"

"Well, I was thinking that..." She raised her chin and looked him in the eye, determined not to take the coward's way out. But his gaze, burning into her, shrivelled her confidence to ashes. "Oh, never mind, it doesn't matter."

"It matters, Sophie," he said, and this time there was a hint of velvet underlying the reserve in his voice. "What is it you were thinking?"

Was it possible that, with goodwill and effort, each might discover in the other a soul mate? Could they work together to put aside everything that had gone before? And even if they couldn't, didn't they have a moral obligation to try, for the baby's sake?

...a bit of simple honesty might work wonders, Elaine had said. *Do your part to improve the odds in your favor.*

Sophie blew out a long breath and jumped in with both feet. "I thought we might start over again, try to get along. Work together. Make the...best of...things."

His attention remained firmly fixed on her face, driving her to recklessness.

"I mean," she babbled, "I know this isn't what either of us planned, and if we had things to do over again we'd almost certainly do them differently. Not that I'm saying I don't want the baby or anything, you understand, but having it sprung on me—well, not sprung on me exactly. I mean, you weren't expecting it, either, and I'm not saying it was all your fault but...but... Damn it, Dominic, say something, even if it's only to tell me to shut up!"

"Shut up," he said.

She glared at him, stung. "Is that the best response you can come up with?"

"What else would you like me to do?"

She would never listen to Elaine's advice again. Never. "You could be gracious enough to accept my apology."

"Is that what you were offering, Sophie? An apology?"

No, she thought miserably, *I was offering a whole lot more than that, but you're not interested in accepting it.* That was dangerous thinking, though, especially with his continuing to pin her in a gaze that she feared saw far more than she intended to reveal.

Drawing what was left of her dignity around her like a shield, she said, "Yes. I know I've been a bit unreasonable of late. Put it down to hormones if you like, because I don't think I'm normally so hard to get along with. The thing is, I'm willing to make more effort if you are, particularly since we'll be living under the same roof as of tonight."

"Very well, it's a deal. How would you like to seal it?"

"Seal it?"

He nodded and folded his arms across his chest. If his voice was a little less hostile, the expression in his green eyes remained unabashedly suspicious. "That's right," he said. "It's customary in business to sign a contract when a deal is closed. What had you in mind in this instance? Some sort of prenuptial agreement?"

He really must despise her if he figured she was the type to demand that sort of material security, she thought, stunned at how much it hurt to acknowledge the fact. "No," she said, turning away before he caught the sparkle of tears in her eyes. "Your word is good enough for me and I'm sorry if my behaviour of late gives you reason to doubt mine."

She was almost at the door before he spoke again. "How about something simple, then, like a handshake?"

How could she refuse without losing credibility? And how could she pretend a handshake would suffice when what she wanted was so much more?

She heard the floor creak as he moved, felt his presence at her back, and thought he must surely sense the desolation possessing her. "If that's not enough, Sophie," he said, his voice rolling over her like syrup, "all you have to do is say so."

The tears were threatening to splash down her face and all she could think, foolish, vain creature that she was, was that she looked like hell when she cried. Her nose ran and her face contorted into what her twin, Paul, had once informed her reminded him of a pickled red cabbage. Pride would not allow her to present Dominic with such a sight. She was at enough of a disadvantage as it was.

"It's enough," she managed, struggling past the lump in her throat and, averting her face, thrust out her hand.

His fingers closed over hers and didn't let go. "Then look at me, Sophie," he commanded softly, drawing her round toward him, "and tell me why you're choking back the tears. Is it something I've done—or not done?"

"It's got to be the pregnancy," she said on a pathetic little sob. "I never cry as a rule, but lately I'm an emotional mess."

"How so?" he asked, his voice a murmuring caress.

She dashed the tears away. "I don't know! If I did, I'd do something about it. I hate these wild emotional outbursts."

She hated the aching need to be close to him, too—the vicious, ceaseless hungering that nothing but his touch, his kiss, could assuage. But she couldn't control it, so when he opened his arms to her, she flung herself into them with an abandon quite foreign to her normal nature.

It didn't matter, though. All that counted was that at last she was exactly where she wanted to be. She pressed her face against the soft flannel of his shirt and closed her eyes, drowning in the safe, masculine strength of him. He held her close, stroking his hands up and down her spine in long, sensuous sweeps and she thought that perhaps his heart started to drum just a little faster and his breath to emerge more raggedly.

She even went so far as to allow herself the luxury of believing that perhaps, one day, he might fall a little bit in love with her, too. Enough for her to dare say, "There's so much that still has to be arranged, so much we haven't yet talked about. I wondered if tonight—?"

Then the door opened and one of his workmen stuck his head into the room. "Call for you, boss," he announced, holding out a cellular telephone. "It's Mrs. Wexler. Thought I'd better let you know since you mentioned you were waiting to hear from her."

"Yes, thanks." Disengaging himself from Sophie, Dominic took the phone. "Hello, Gail, how are you?...No, of course I hadn't forgotten.... Oh, sure, six-thirty's fine.... Yes, looking forward to it...."

Sophie felt a chill where seconds earlier she'd absorbed warmth. Felt a mere yard stretch a mile of distance between her and Dominic. She saw the smile that turned up the corners of his mouth as he listened to Gail Wexler; heard the softening in his voice, the affection. And knew that nothing he'd ever offered her came even close to what he gave so freely to Barbara's mother.

This evening she was moving into his apartment. They would be sharing breakfast, the morning paper, even a bed if that was what she wanted. Their wedding might still be two weeks away, but to all intents and purposes they were starting their marriage today. And tonight, when she'd hoped they might bridge the awkwardness of the transition with a quiet dinner for two, she found he'd already made plans to spend the evening with his late fiancée's parents.

The message was clear. It would take a lot more than Sophie could offer to relegate Barbara to second place in his life.

As unobtrusively as possible, she edged toward the open door. When he noticed anyway and, without breaking the thread of his conversation with Mrs. Wexler, raised his hand and mouthed, "Hold on a minute," Sophie pretended she hadn't seen and kept on going.

Although the snow had gone from town, traces of it still remained under the trees bordering the paths of Heron

Hill Provincial Park on the far shores of Jewel Lake. It was deserted that February afternoon, a bleak and lonely sort of place that echoed Sophie's mood.

Down near the beach, she found a picnic bench sheltered from the wind playing briskly over the waves. Wrapping her arms around her knees, she huddled inside her coat and stared across the water to Palmerstown's skyline squatting at the foot of the inland hills.

Dominic's penthouse apartment crowned one of those buildings just coming alight as day faded into dusk. She had seen its spacious rooms: the self-contained guest suite that was to be hers for the next several months, the streamlined kitchen, the comfortable living area with its deep leather couches, the dining room austerely furnished in smoked glass and teak.

Those things she'd need in the immediate future, her clothing and personal items, waited to be unpacked from the suitcases and neatly labeled boxes stacked at the foot of the bed. In separate, sturdier cartons were a few special pieces intended to make her feel more at home: her favorite painting, a couple of lamps, Paul and Jenny's wedding portrait.

Tomorrow her desk would be delivered, along with her houseplants. The key Dominic had given her a few days ago lay coldly in her palm. Everything she needed to take up residence was ready and waiting. Except her courage.

That was why she'd come out to this place of solitude: to try to drum up the fortitude to deal with the bald reality of her future. It wasn't the fact that Dominic had made other arrangements for an evening she'd wanted to spend with him that had driven her to find this windswept, barren spot more than sixty miles away from town; it was the dull certainty that he would repeat the pattern.

There would be many other evenings and days—and

perhaps even nights—when she would find herself not a part of his plans. If she hadn't been so busy hiding from her real feelings, she might have seen that such an arrangement was probably part and parcel of every marriage of inconvenience and prepared herself for it.

A month ago, when self-deception had all been part of the game, she might have said it didn't matter if they went their separate ways much of the time. She might have argued it was better that way and that the less they saw of each other, the easier it would be on both of them. But then, a month ago she hadn't bargained on the jealousy and pain that came of unrequited love, any more than she had on finding herself its prisoner.

Only now, when it was much too late to change anything, did she discover that what bound her to Dominic was not the right he'd demanded to share fully in the upbringing of their baby, but the utter claim he'd staked on her heart.

What made matters worse was knowing that, even though nothing but empty rooms awaited her, she would eventually drive back over the winding road to Palmerstown, past the turnoff to her once-and-future home, and all the way along Lakeshore Drive to the elegant white condominium building that Dominic had built and owned. And she would do so not because he would be waiting to welcome her to his luxurious top-floor apartment, but because she could not live without him and would take whatever crumbs he tossed her way as long as she could be near him.

She would let herself in with her borrowed key, unpack her suitcases, arrange her clothes in the mirrored closet, bathe in the deep marble tub and climb into the wide, empty bed. When tomorrow came, she would smile to cover her heartache and pretend that she didn't care if he preferred to cling to the past by spending time with the Wexlers.

Instead, she would concentrate on the future and the baby. *Their* baby, hers and Dominic's. Because a baby was the one thing Barbara had not given to him.

A sudden gust of wind sent the skeletons of last year's leaves swirling around the picnic bench and drove the chill of late afternoon inside the folds of her coat. It was time to go.

About forty miles from the outskirts of Palmerstown, she stopped at a roadside inn for a meal. She had eaten nothing since breakfast, and although it was easy enough to ignore her own hunger pangs, she would do nothing to endanger her baby's health. Apart from any other consideration, the baby was her passport to a future with Dominic.

The penthouse was dim and quiet when she stepped through the front door. Beyond the foyer, the floor-to-ceiling windows that lined one wall of the living room glimmered with light from nearby buildings, enough for her to find her way to the hall that led to the bedroom wing.

She was perhaps halfway past the open archway leading to the living room when the entire place was flooded with sudden light. From the depths of a wing chair that matched the leather couches, a voice demanded rawly, "Do you know what time it is?"

Badly shaken, she spun around, shading her eyes against the glare. "Dominic, you scared me! I thought you weren't home."

He rose to his feet, lithe and lethal in the rage he made no effort to hide. "I asked you, do you know what the hell time it is?"

"Ah...about eight o'clock?" she managed over her thundering heart.

"Try closer to nine-thirty," he said, advancing on her with such deadly intent that she found herself backing away until, abruptly, she came up against the wall. "And what I want to know is where the f— have you been until now?"

"Dominic!" Shocked, she stared at him and saw a black-clad stranger, a man so close to not being in control that she almost cringed.

The breath hissed between his lips as he fought for composure. "I'm waiting, Sophie. Where were you?"

"Out," she said with a bravado that crumbled when she saw his fingers curl into fists. She swallowed and added hurriedly, "I drove out to Heron Hill Park."

"At this time of year?" he sneered, skepticism blazing in his eyes. "You can do better than that, Sophie."

She inched to the left, trying for a little distance between them. "Believe it or not as you choose, but that's where I was. I stopped for dinner the other side of Beaver Creek."

"I have been waiting for you to come home for the past two hours," he said, the menace in his tone only slightly contained.

"No, you haven't," she replied, too outraged by his lie to weigh the wisdom of attacking him in his present mood. "You dined with your erstwhile future in-laws, the Wexlers, so don't pretend you've been hanging around here waiting for me. I'm sure I was the last thing on your mind!"

Very briefly, he showed surprise at her outburst, although he hid it rather better than she had managed hers when he'd accosted her so suddenly. His shoulders stiffened beneath the black sweater, his brows drew together, his mouth assumed a grim line, and it occurred to her, in a flash of mental irrelevance, that he was all dark parallel bars of displeasure.

"The Wexlers returned today from a six-week cruise to the Orient—" he began in measured tones.

Her voice rang out, shrill with accusation, and not for the life of her could she silence it. "And you couldn't wait to rush over and welcome them home, could you? I understand perfectly, Dominic. You don't have to explain. Although it does strike me that all your talk about wanting to make a go of marriage with me amounts to a load of rubbish as long as your real allegiance lies with the parents of your late fiancée."

"For your information," he cut in, so icily that goose bumps prickled over her skin despite her heavy winter coat, "I spent precisely three-quarters of an hour with Barbara's parents and that only because I thought it fair that I be the one to tell them I was shortly getting married to you."

Dismay flooded through her. "Oh," she moaned, covering her face with both hands.

"They send you their very best wishes and their love. Unlike you, my dear Sophie, they are able to separate the past from the present."

"I'm so sorry! I'm afraid that once again I jumped to the wrong—"

"And then," he continued remorselessly, "I came back here, assuming I'd find you and intending to act on your suggestion this afternoon that we make a fresh start. I thought perhaps dinner at Le Coq D'Or might be in order. I did not know you had taken offense because we were interrupted by a phone call. I had, after all, indicated to you that our conversation was not finished, that there still were things we had to say to each other."

A spate of excuses bubbled up, but in the end all she could mutter again was, "I'm sorry," because, pitifully inadequate though they were, they were the only words to express her remorse.

"So am I." He sighed and turned away, leaving her blind with regret.

She wished for so many things. That she could go back to that moment just before she'd fallen in love with him—that time of utter self-containment. That just once he'd look at her with desire smoking in his eyes and let his smile warm her...secret, knowing.

To her shame, that familiar flush of jealousy attacked again at the thought that Barbara, for however short a time, had known Dominic's love and the outpouring of his passion. It lessened the tragedy of her death somehow, and left Sophie numb with horror at her own mean-spirited, unfeeling envy.

Dominic swung back toward her. "We seem to spend a great deal of time apologizing to one another, Sophie, and yet somehow there's never a sense of real regret. We don't change, we don't make things better. You continue to resent me, blame me—"

Why couldn't she tell him that wasn't true, instead of aiming the accusation back at him and insisting, "No, it's the other way around. *You* feel trapped, and if you could, you'd find a way to get free of me. I know it, here—" she clutched a fistful of coat in front of her heart "—and that's why I thought you'd chosen to spend the evening with people you associate with..." She wanted to speak Barbara's name, to spit it out like the bad taste it was in her mouth, but she didn't. She'd done enough already, leaping to false conclusions and hurling accusations. "...happier times," she finished lamely.

He strode to the bar at the far end of the living room

and poured a dollop of whiskey into a heavy crystal glass. "I asked you once before not to try to second-guess how I feel or what I'm thinking. I have many faults, as a lot of people in this town will be only too glad to tell you, but I like to think that moral dishonesty of the kind you describe is not among them, so let me spell it out for you one last time. Barbara is dead and you are not. *You*, not she, will be my wife. As such, you will never have cause to question my loyalty."

He made her feel small and unworthy and so lacking in generosity that she wanted to curl up and die. If ever there was a time to call forth that simple honesty Elaine had prescribed, it was now. But not with words. All words had ever done was create barriers between the two of them.

Swirling the whiskey in his glass, he paced restlessly back and forth in front of the fireplace. She hovered just within the room's entrance, despair a leaden weight rooting her to the spot.

It wasn't the silence stretching unbroken between them that daunted her; it was the invisible shield of aloofness separating her from him. Either she broke through it now or she looked into a future bereft of any sort of closeness between them.

Whoever had decreed that the first step was always the hardest forgot to add that it went beyond difficult to sheer torture. The way was not straight and easy but a tightrope of uncertainty swinging without benefit of safety net above a chasm of fear.

Sophie lifted one foot, and then the other. Prayed for endurance and fortitude. Fought the temptation to turn tail and run to the safety of her solitary room. If only he'd reach out and draw her past the obstacles and into the haven of his arms! If only she could read the thoughts inside his dark, handsome head, see beyond the unsmiling dispassion that carved his beautiful face!

His gaze raked over her, deep and mysterious as a forest pool. She paused, hoping for some sign from him—even rejection—because nothing could be worse than this, with her teetering midway between heaven and hell.

He heaved a great sigh and, as though he couldn't bear the sight of her, swung away to face the mantelpiece.

His dismissal broke her heart. Blinded by tears, she stumbled toward him and pressed her cheek against the unyielding line of his spine. "Dominic!" she begged, naked yearning tearing at her voice, and for once it was the right thing to say.

She heard the groan deep in his throat, the crack of Baccarat on marble as he slammed down his glass on the mantelpiece and swung toward her. A string of words escaped him, four-lettered every one and laced with frustration.

They sang in her ears like music and her heart lifted just a little. A man didn't curse like that, did he, unless something...someone had slipped past his guard and found the sweet, vulnerable soul he kept so well protected?

She felt his hands in her hair, his lips at her temples, at her tear-streaked eyes. And then, at last, at her mouth, demanding, asking and finally begging.

She wrapped her arms around his waist and clung to him. At his urging, she sank with him to the carpet. She stretched beside him and, without saying another word, told him in a thousand different ways that this was what she wanted: to be here, with him, and that if he wanted her, all he had to do was take her.

He wanted her. Too badly to try to hide it. His kisses

trailed fire down her throat. He wreaked havoc with her clothing, shoving aside her coat, pulling her free of its confinement and flinging it behind him. She heard buttons wrench free from the fabric securing them; felt sudden coolness on her skin as her blouse fell away, swiftly followed by the warmth of his mouth at her breast.

Her skirt rode to her hips. His palm stroked up her calf, swept along her thighs, nudged them apart. She knew the instant he encroached beyond the frail barrier of her panties to reduce her to searing, flooding delirium, but had no idea when audacity guided her to exact a similar revenge and take the silken weight and vigor of him in her hands.

Somewhere from the back roads of memory, she recalled that first time on St. Julian and the hurried, furtive coupling that had taken place. Even then, there had been magic of a kind. But this time it was intensified a thousand times because, whereas then they had not acknowledged each other except in the most primal way, this time the connection was more complete, a physical union cemented by shared hope for the future. Along with their clothes, so many layers of fear and misunderstanding melted away.

"I had no idea you had changed so much," he muttered hoarsely, his eyes devouring the lush contours conferred on her by pregnancy. "Do you know how beautiful I find you?"

He made her heart sing. She—slight, unremarkable Sophie Casson—felt voluptuous. Desirable.

A short time later, when she pressed herself to him, reveling in the close tangling of his limbs with hers and the proud thrust of his erection at the juncture of her thighs, he muttered, "I want you so badly, Sophie, I'm afraid. What if I hurt you or the baby?"

And she felt cherished, treasured.

"You won't," she whispered, opening herself to him. "Hurry, Dominic, please. I need you. Let me feel you inside me."

Loving him with her eyes, her hands, her soul, she wrapped her legs around his waist, tilted up her hips and captured him. She saw the sweat break out on his forehead, felt his tension as he fought to exercise restraint. And felt whole for the first time in months when he lost the battle and buried himself deep within her.

She had known desire before. At least, she thought she had. But it was only then, in Dominic's arms, with the fires of passion raging between them and creating such turmoil in her blood, that she realized she'd known nothing.

Less than nothing. Because this was passion that went beyond mortal cognizance to approach the sublime. He could take whatever he wanted of her and she would give until she had nothing left to give. And then she would give some more.

"Wow!" he breathed when the clenching shudders subsided. Lifting his head, he grinned at her, a marvelous shining joy curving his mouth. "Would you like to do that again some time?"

Simple truth. "Yes," she said. "Often."

"Here?" The smile crept past the thick sweep of his lashes to his eyes. "I can light the fire to make it more romantic."

"I'd miss you," she said.

"You wouldn't have time. All I need to do is reach up and press the switch that turns on the gas." He lifted himself and leaned on one elbow. "Or we could behave like the decorously married couple we'll soon be and retire to the bedroom."

"Yours?" she inquired pertly, raking a fingernail through the dusting of dark hair on his chest. "Or mine?"

He sobered and cupped her face in his palm. "How about ours?"

He told her he loved her all night long, if not with words then in the ardor with which he possessed her more than once as the hours slid by, and in the way he held her during the times in between.

When she awoke, he was beside her still, pushing the hair away from her face and kissing her. He promised her breakfast in bed but made love to her instead. And she couldn't keep the feelings to herself. She had to try to seal them with words.

"I wish it could always be like this, Dominic," she breathed, rippling around him as ecstasy took hold.

"Just keep this moment," he panted, fighting to stave off completion. "Hold it to you and remember it tomorrow, next year—whenever you feel unsure."

She held him close and rode with him, too consumed with the fire to say what she really wanted to say, which was that she had loved him for a long time and would do so for the rest of her life.

There would be time enough for that. There might even be a time when he would say the same thing to her.

"I'm not going into the office today," he told her after breakfast. "I've got a load of paperwork to wade through but I can do it here. That way I'm handy if you need help with any of those boxes."

"It's mostly clothes," she said, suddenly unsure of herself again. Did he expect her to share his room now, or would that be an occasional thing only? Deeming it wiser not to push too hard, too soon, she continued, "I guess I'll get started hanging them in the guest room."

He combed his fingers through his hair and laughed. "That's probably best. My closet's a mess. You'll have to take me in hand and cure me of my bachelor ways when we move into the house."

For the first time, she dared to believe they could break free of the past. The future shone full of bright optimism, with no premonition of disaster to darken it.

Humming to herself, she lifted lingerie from her open suitcase and folded it neatly in the paper-lined drawers of the triple dresser running along one wall of the guest room. The ringing of the doorbell didn't rouse her to alarm; it didn't even interrupt her singing. There was nothing in the world that could spoil her happiness.

She was marginally conscious of Dominic crossing the marble-tiled foyer to the front door and of the nanosecond of silence that followed. And still that famed intuition with which all women were supposedly blessed failed to alert her. She was blithely, utterly caught up in her fantasy of happily-ever-after, which perhaps accounted for her taking so long to register the reality of what happened next.

The laugh penetrated first, rippling through the penthouse like quicksilver, followed almost immediately by the unforgettable voice. "No, Dom darling, you're not seeing a ghost! It's me, Barbara! I'm alive after all!"

The words hit Sophie like a body blow. Recoiling, she clutched the edge of the dresser. But the carnage had only just begun.

Not content with the pain it had already inflicted, the lilting, confident voice dealt the ultimate coup de grace to Sophie's pitiful little dreams. "And guess what, darling. Miracle of miracles, I'm pregnant! We're going to have a baby, Dom! Isn't it wonderful?"

CHAPTER SEVEN

PAUL and Jenny were living in Bath, in England's West Country. Not far away was Wells, ancient and imperturbable, a place blessed with a timeless serenity that might, in time, heal her. Sophie knew the minute she walked in the shadow of its cathedral that she'd found a haven.

"But why not stay with us?" Jenny asked that night over dinner. "There's enough room here and we won't intrude on your privacy."

Not intentionally, perhaps, but they knew her whole pathetic story, and, well-meaning though Jenny was, Sophie couldn't take the inevitable flood of sympathy, the constant reminders of Dominic and the fact that she was pregnant and alone. As if she was likely to forget! "No," she said, "but I love you for asking."

"But you don't know anyone in Wells and you shouldn't be by yourself right now."

"I *need* to be by myself, Jenny."

"It isn't right!" Jenny's brown eyes filled with sympathetic tears. "You should be with the father of your child. I hope the rat fries for the hell he's putting you through!"

"He didn't ask me to leave," Sophie pointed out. "It was my decision to put distance between us by catching the first flight over here."

Jenny threw up her hands in frustration and turned to Paul. "Can't you talk her out of this? She doesn't know a soul in Wells. What if she needs us? What if she becomes ill, or has an accident? Who'll let us know?"

Paul leaned back in his tufted leather chair, the smile he directed at Sophie telling her she didn't have to explain. He understood, just as he always had; neither time nor distance had weakened the bond between them. "Twin telepathy", Jenny had once called it. "We're a phone call away. Leave it, honey," he told his wife, then asked Sophie, "You want to borrow our car to go house hunting?"

"I don't think so, thanks. Driving on the left takes a bit of getting used to, especially on these narrow country roads. I'll take the bus into Wells in the morning and let the estate agent who's showing me properties be the chauffeur."

Two mornings later, Sophie signed a short-term lease on a tiny furnished house fronted by a flagstone courtyard. At the back, enclosed by a stone wall, was a long, narrow garden, a secluded, tranquil place that trapped the gentle warmth of spring and promised refuge from the brisk winds of autumn. Yew trees grew along the bottom along with a willow, and there was a sheltered sunny spot outside the paned glass doors of the living room.

If she decided to extend her stay until after the baby was born, he'd sleep there, safe in his sleek English baby carriage, and awake to the sound of cathedral bells. He would grow up happy and healthy, with rosy cheeks and chubby little fists. He would smile when he saw his mother's face, and even though he wouldn't understand the words, she would read and sing to him and he would never guess the heartache surrounding his conception and birth.

Her determination to bring those things to her baby's life made Sophie's own unhappiness a little more bearable. Most of the time. Except for those nights when she awoke and felt her child stir within her, as though he knew that it was then, with the moonlight shining through the tiny paned windows of the bedroom, that the misery crept past her guard.

That last scene in the penthouse would flash to life, each detail as sharp and shocking as ever. She would see again Barbara launching herself into Dominic's arms—and of them closing securely around her. She would see Dominic's shell-shocked expression, the sudden widening of his eyes when he noticed Sophie watching from the end of the hall and the swift, unmistakable jerk of his head ordering her back into the bedroom, out of sight.

How long had she huddled like a refugee on the clothes-strewn bed, hearing muffled voices, Barbara's peal of laughter? How long after the front door closed again before she realized she was alone in the penthouse, both out of sight and out of mind?

It hadn't taken Sophie long to cram her things back into the suitcases, to scribble the note that gave away nothing of her misery or rage and expressed only the very rational opinion that, from the beginning, she and Dominic had rushed things. "I need time to come to terms with everything that's happened, even if you don't," she'd finished, "so please accept my decision to spend the next few weeks alone."

She had done the right thing, of course, but that didn't lessen the sadness. She would turn on her side on the thick feather mattress in her little English house and watch winter ease toward spring. Outside, the stark branches of a plum tree gradually grew fat with buds ready to burst into blossom. At the bottom of the garden, the willow turned green almost overnight.

The loneliness was a wound that never healed, the

wanting—the sight, the scent, the touch of him—always aching even in sleep. But waking was the worst. Knowing the memory of him was a little more faded by the passing of another day, his loving, such as it had been, that much more removed.

She wrote to her parents and told them that things hadn't worked out with Dominic but that she was well and would come home in a month or two. She did not tell them about the baby because they would have been frantic with worry. And just in case Dominic felt obliged to try to track her down, she gave them Paul's address because she knew she could trust him to keep her whereabouts secret.

She became friendly with her next-door neighbor, Violet Barclay, a spry little widow of seventy. When Violet found out that Sophie was expecting a baby in September, she started to make a layette of exquisite hand-sewn garments with smocked yokes and embroidered hems.

The bonds of affection between the two women grew quickly, perhaps because they were both alone. On what should have been her wedding day, Sophie confided the whole story of her relationship with Dominic. It was such a relief to be able to talk openly about it to someone of Violet's objectivity and wisdom.

"You will survive, lass," she promised Sophie. "We women always survive, no matter how crushing the tragedies or disappointments imposed upon us. A part of this man will always be with you in the shape of his son or daughter. Look to that and the future you will make for your child."

With the onset of warmer weather in April, Sophie bought a little car and ventured farther afield, visiting such legendary places as Winchester and Cheddar Gorge and Stonehenge. Other days, she discovered tiny market towns with quaint names like Shepton Mallet and Yeovil.

Of them all, though, her favorite spot was Glastonbury. She found a sort of enchantment in the shade of its ancient ruins that countered that dreadful sense of loss brought on as the days since she'd left Dominic became weeks.

"It nourishes me somehow," she told Violet, "as if everything that happens to us here is part of some greater cosmic plan. I'm not explaining it very well, I guess, but I come away with a sense of—" she spread her hands, palms raised upward "—destiny at work."

Violet nodded. "It renews your soul and gives you the strength to go on," she said. "I understand perfectly."

Slowly, the hurting places inside began to heal a little, giving Sophie the stamina to accept the reality of her situation. If proof that she had never amounted to anything other than a stand-in for the real thing was what she wanted, the fact that almost eight weeks had passed and Dominic hadn't come looking for her was testimony enough. Even her baby, which he'd sworn he'd never abandon, had been relegated to a bit part once he'd learned he'd fathered a child with his true love. By now, he and Barbara were probably married.

"But we'll manage without him," Sophie told the baby. "We'll never be really alone. We'll always have each other and someday soon we'll go home again and you'll get to know the rest of your family. It'll be enough, I promise."

Dominic was tired of being thwarted, first by the parents, then the brother. Discovering that Sophie wasn't home when he finally tracked her down to the address he'd weaseled out of her sister-in-law was the last straw.

"You are disturbing the peace, young man," a refined English voice informed him. "Miss Casson is away for the day and I take great exception to your banging on her door like that. It will not bring her home any sooner."

He turned to find himself impaled by the stern gaze of a venerable old woman, who either stood about seven feet tall in her stockinged feet or else was perched on a stepladder on the other side of the wall from Sophie's garden. "Sorry," he said brusquely. "Do you know when she's expected back?"

Disapproving blue eyes peered over the rims of wire-framed glasses. "And if I do?"

Realizing belligerence would do nothing to advance his cause, Dominic adopted a more mannerly approach. "Pardon me, ma'am. I don't mean to be rude, but I've traveled a long way and I'm rather anxious to see her."

"You are the father of her child," the woman determined, eyeing him as if he was something scraped from the bottom of her shoe. "The man who, it appears, would like to have his cake and eat it, too. Am I not right?"

Taken aback, Dominic stared at her and wondered what the hell Sophie had said about him to instill such a bad impression on the old biddy. It wasn't often that he found himself at a loss for words, nor did he care for the experience. "Well, I'm not sure what you mean about the cake, but yes, I'm the father of her child," he finally managed.

The woman disappeared so suddenly that he half feared she'd fallen from her perch. A minute later, however, she reappeared in the gateway to Sophie's courtyard, all her five-foot-two-inch frame apparently intact.

"It's taken you long enough to get here," she scolded.

"It's taken me long enough to find out where she's been hiding."

"Well, now that you have, what are you going to do about her?"

He'd watched television sitcoms from Britain that featured people like this woman and had found them hilarious. In the flesh, though, such individuals weren't quite so funny. "With all due respect, ma'am, that's hardly any of your business."

"Then neither are Miss Casson's whereabouts any of yours," the old dame retorted, and marched back the way she'd come.

Grinding his teeth in frustration, Dominic steeled himself to patience. He'd waited this long to have things out with Sophie; he could wait a few hours more. One thing he did know: he wasn't about to be run off by her self-appointed watchdog next door.

Stretching out on the sun-warmed stone bench under the window next to her front door, he shaded his eyes with an up-flung arm and settled in for the duration. She'd decided that running away was the solution to their problems and had asked him not to come after her, but he was not by nature a patient man and he'd played along with her vanishing act for long enough.

The sun had disappeared behind the trees, leaving the garden full of purple shadows, when the creak of the iron gate leading to her courtyard alerted him to her homecoming. Lowering his arm, he turned his head so that he could watch her as she made her way along the flagstone path to the front door.

She did not notice him, and he seized the small advantage to study her. She wasn't glamorous like Barbara, not exotic. But she was lovely in a classical sense, a delicate molding of bone caressed by skin of exquisite texture and fragility. A sun goddess, all light and sunshine, where Barbara had been storm and gales.

And yet, she'd changed. Most obviously, she'd let her hair grow longer and wore it caught in a band at her nape. Then, halfway to the house, she reached up to pick a few flowers from the creeper hanging over the wall, and he noticed the swell of her abdomen beneath the loose sweater, the fullness of her breasts. Intellectually, he'd known that by now the physical evidence of her pregnancy would be fully apparent, but he hadn't expected the emotional realization to pack quite such a wallop.

Still unaware of her audience, she pressed a hand to her ribs, let it trail unselfconsciously over one breast to her throat, then ran a finger inside the cowl collar of her sweater and flicked free the tendrils of hair caught there. Dominic stared, captivated by the insidious seduction of her womanliness, its separate parts made all the more irresistible by her utter unawareness of the impact of the whole.

Just looking at her made him ache. He wanted nothing more than to limn the sweet dimensions of her in his two hands, to taste her mouth, inhale the scent of her hair, test the fragility of her pale and lovely skin.

He had thought himself braced to deal with any eventuality when he saw her again, had been prepared to use whatever means presented themselves to bend her to his will and bring her back to him. He had thought he'd be the one in control, that his surprise appearance would afford him the advantage. But he had not counted on the aroused stirring of his flesh or the tide of pure hunger that swept over him at the sight of her, and he did not like the way it undermined his purpose.

Discomfited, he swung his feet to the ground.

Aware of movement to her right, Sophie swung around in time to see a figure unfolding from the bench beneath the window box outside her living room. Even in the dusk of early evening, she recognized him. There were conceivably several hundred thousand men in the world possessed of a similar long-legged, lean-hipped, masculine grace, but only one who could make her heart sprint so unevenly that she felt as if the earth was falling away beneath her feet, taking with it every last particle of her hard-won peace and acceptance.

Dominic picked up his jacket, which he'd used as a pillow, and looping it over his thumb, slung it over his shoulder. "So," he drawled in the same honey-rich voice that had haunted her dreams, "you're finally home. I was beginning to think I was going to have to sleep out here."

As a lover's greeting, it fell distinctly short of romantic. Dark, provocative tone notwithstanding, he sounded peeved rather than relieved. That alone should have been enough to send up red-alert flags and remind Sophie that, with him, disenchantment always followed brief euphoria.

To her dismay, however, the old molten hunger surged up within her, all the more ravaging for its hiatus. The urge to run to him, to know just one more time the feel of his arms around her, the beat of his heart beneath her cheek, tore at her.

Forcibly restraining herself from any such action, she asked frigidly, "What do you want, Dominic?"

"Isn't it obvious?"

"If it were, I wouldn't have asked."

He swore long and colorfully.

When he stopped to draw breath, she said with a marvelous facsimile of composure, "How charming! You've obviously lost none of your skill at profanity since the last occasion I elected to distance myself from you when, as I recall, you were equally vulgar."

"Perhaps," he replied, thunderheads roiling through his voice, "because then, as now, you saw fit to try my patience beyond human endurance. This disappearing act you're so fond of pulling when you decide things aren't going quite the way you think they should is wearing thin, Sophie, particularly when there's no reason for it."

If he'd hoped to prick the fragile balloon of her self-control, he'd chosen the right way to go about it. "The way I see it, I had reasons to spare when Barbara Wexler came waltzing in your front door, crowing about carrying your baby," Sophie exploded. "With your prodigious capabilities, you could start your own sperm bank!"

After a moment's stunned silence, he burst out laughing, great hooting guffaws that had him doubled over. Sophie wanted very badly to scratch out his eyes, to kick him where it would do the most damage. But he'd made her feel foolish enough already; she wouldn't allow him to goad her into diminishing herself further.

"I'm so glad I've afforded you a little entertainment," she said, marching past him and thrusting open the front door. "I would hate to think you'd come all this way for nothing."

A gentleman would have taken the hint and left, but all the trappings to the contrary, Dominic Winter clearly was no gentleman. Before she could slam the door closed in his face, he'd shouldered his way into her tiny living room. "I came all this way to bring you home, Sophie," he declared, "and I have no intention of leaving without you."

"Then you really have wasted your time because I have no intention of going anywhere with you. I like it here. I am happy here. And I intend to stay here for as long as it pleases me."

He rolled his shoulders in a shrug and lowered his

lashes to a sultry half-mast. "Hope you've got room enough in the bed for me, then," he purred.

Tamping down the unconscionable flash of delight that remark produced, Sophie snapped, "Stop playing games, Dominic! I'm serious."

His amusement vanished. "For once we're on the same plane, then, because I'm serious, too. We were supposed to be married over a month ago and instead what do you do? Sneak off the minute my back's turned and leave behind a two-line note that more or less tells me to kiss off and have a nice life."

Baffled, she stared at him. If she didn't know better, she'd almost be persuaded that he'd missed her. "I thought you'd be grateful I'd gone so quietly without making a fuss. After all, we both know I have no place in your life now that Barbara's back."

Shaking his head from side to side and rolling his eyes, he expelled a long, frustrated breath. "You're turning out to be one pack of trouble with your propensity for jumping to wrong conclusions, do you know that? You had no reason to run off, no reason at all."

She had thought herself resigned to losing him, had mapped out a future that, of necessity, didn't include him. Yet, at his words, a tiny flame of hope flickered to life. Doing her best to snuff it out before it brought her more pain than she could possibly bear, she affected a nonchalance she was far from feeling and said, "Well, it beat being asked to leave. Or did you expect me to sit quietly in my room and wait to be formally dismissed?" She laughed, a ragged, miserable effort that proved nothing except that her control was teetering on the brink of annihilation. "Sorry, Dominic, that's just not my style!"

"Are you so certain that's how things would have turned out, Sophie?"

"Oh, yes," she sighed, sudden weariness swamping her. "Just as I'm certain the only reason you're here now is to tell me that since you've got your hands full with Barbara and the baby she's expecting, I can come out of hiding and do what I wanted from the first without fear of interference from you."

"And what is it that you wanted?" he inquired softly.

"To be free to bring up my child without having to sell my soul first."

"I see. Well, if by that you think I'm about to simply turn my back—"

"Oh, I'm sure you'll try to sweeten rejection by offering to compensate the understudy."

"You're pushing your luck, Sophie," he warned, his tone soft and dangerous.

"Really?" Ignoring the inner voice of caution, she stared him in the eye and plowed on rashly, "Are you or are you not the man who once pointed out to me that money could buy anything? And what's a little payoff between...?"

"Friends?" he suggested when she floundered to a halt. "Enemies?" He moved closer, trapping her between the fireplace and the overstuffed armchair next to it. "Or were you thinking more along the lines of 'lovers'?"

"You and Barbara were lovers," she said, wincing at the pain of the admission. "You never really wanted me."

She'd touched a nerve, no doubt about it. Anger tinted his eyes, sharpening their sultry jade to emerald fire, and for a brief instant she thought he might shake her. "Then what in the blue blazes did you think I had in mind when I asked you to marry me?" he roared, looming over her and dwarfing the room with his sheer presence.

The effort of pretending she didn't care a rap about

him, when just seeing him again was tearing her apart, defeated her. If the only way she could be rid of him was to tell him the truth, then so be it.

"You didn't ask me," she said dully. "You suggested it was the right and logical thing to do, which led me to understand that your principles were involved but not your heart. And I wanted your heart. All of it. After all, I gave you mine."

The thundering silence of his response to that insane disclosure seemed to last a small eternity and was so much worse than anything else he could have offered. Disbelief, amusement, scorn—those she could have defined and dealt with, but not his tacit agreement that, indeed, he had never pledged himself to her for any but the most expedient of reasons.

Abruptly, she slipped past him. "Excuse me, please," she muttered, tossing the words over her shoulder as she disappeared into the sanctuary of her kitchen. "I left a casserole in the oven and I think I smell it burning."

He did not at first follow her, for which she was grateful. If he had a single sensitive bone in his body, he'd leave while her back was turned and spare them both the embarrassment of trying to gloss over her unforgivable lapse.

Wrenching open the oven door, she hauled out the casserole and discovered she hadn't told a complete lie in order to escape him. The beef ribs she'd put in to bake that morning badly needed basting if they were to be edible. Yet all the time that she busied herself with the task, her attention remained focused on the man she could hear wandering around her living room, and she knew to the second when he came to lean in the kitchen doorway and watch her at work.

Suddenly clumsy, she burned herself on the ovenproof

dish. "Damn," she muttered, snatching back her hand and sucking at the painful spot on her thumb.

He was beside her in a flash. "That's not going to do much good." He reached over her shoulder to the sink and turned on the cold water. "Hold your hand under here instead. It'll reduce the burning."

But only in her thumb, she thought, and that was the least disturbing thing that ailed her. The fire in her cheeks and that other, more subtle heat that had flickered into life at his touch flared with renewed savagery. The kitchen was small enough at the best of times, but with him at her back, it verged on the claustrophobic.

"I can manage," she insisted, and attempted to fend him off with a backward thrust of her elbow.

But he was as solidly immovable as the proverbial mountain. Holding her hand firmly under the stream of water, he brought his mouth close to her ear and said softly, "Did you really give me your heart, Sophie?"

"I suppose so—temporarily. But I soon realized I'd made a dreadful mistake, so I took it back again."

He turned off the water and reached for the towel hanging from a hook on the wall. Turning her around, he very carefully dried her hand, then tipped up her chin so that she had no choice but to meet his gaze. "Are you sure?" he asked.

Quickly, before he saw in them the pain she couldn't hide, she closed her eyes. "Please, Dominic," she begged, her defenses crumbling into ruins, "don't do this. Please, say what you came to say and then just go. I really am very tired and don't think I can take much more today."

She felt his fingertips at her jaw, tracing its length from her earlobe to her lower lip. "And tomorrow, and the day after, and the day after that? What about them, Sophie? What about the future you and I had planned?"

"It died," she said dully, the tears seeping between her lashes, "the day Barbara showed up alive. And if you don't want to spell it all out for me because you think it's too cruel, then I'll say it for you. I was only ever second best and you had no reason to settle for that when the real love of your life came back. So go home, Dominic. Go back to your wife and leave me alone."

He caught the tears and swept them aside with the ball of his thumb. "Listen to me, you blind, willful creature," he commanded softly. "Barbara is not my wife, nor will she ever be. She and I are finished. We have been finished for quite some time."

They should have been the most reassuring words in the world. A month ago, a week even, Sophie would have sold her soul to hear them, yet now that they were hers to treasure, she looked for the conditions attached, the ones that would dash her hopes to pieces and send her spiraling back into the darkness from which she'd only recently begun to emerge.

"Because you thought she was dead," she said. "Now that you know she's alive, though—"

"It makes no difference, Sophie. Even if she was the same woman I once asked to marry me, I'm not the same man."

"But you loved her."

"I thought I did. I realize now I was mistaken."

Of all the questions to which she sought answers, the only one she ached to ask at that moment was, *Why? Because you love me?* But she was teetering again on that emotional tightrope, with despair on the one side waiting to engulf her, and she dared not take the chance of falling the wrong way. "And how does Barbara—?"

With fatal tenderness, he cupped her face in his two hands and pressed his thumbs to her mouth, sealing it closed. "Tomorrow, sweet Sophie, I'll explain everything," he whispered fiercely. "But for tonight, will you please just trust me enough to believe that I will never again allow anything or anyone to come between us? I flew halfway around the world and badgered your family into telling me where to find you because what I most want to do is set things right between us. And I'd like to begin with this."

His thumbs slid away to make room for his mouth. Threading his fingers through her hair and imprisoning her head so that she couldn't turn aside, he kissed one corner of her mouth and then the other. He kissed her eyelids and her nose, and then came back to her mouth. He drew his tongue in a sweet, damp line over her lower lip, banishing all the long, empty hours of missing him.

Yet it was her fault, not his, that things quickly escalated to a raging wildfire. He didn't push for more than she was prepared to give; he showed her every way he knew how that he was content to savor each delicious second without rushing ahead to the next. But his touch triggered an explosion within her that decimated every instinct for self-preservation she'd ever harbored.

She melted against him, ignoring the reasons for their estrangement, past caring that the higher she flew toward paradise, the harder she'd fall if it eluded her. Yes, she'd been hurt, and angry, and disappointed, but that was yesterday and this...oh, this was now, and closer to heaven than she'd ever thought to find herself again!

She closed her eyes, luxuriating in the scent and warmth of him. Her mouth softened in tacit connivance, letting him know that she would give anything and everything he chose to ask of her.

Shamelessly, she angled against him, wedging her thigh between both of his, there where he was most vulnerable to seduction. Her hands tugged his shirt free of his trousers and burrowed beneath it to search out the smooth planes of his back.

The consequences were instantaneous and irrevocable. A tremor shook him as though a thousand demons battered at him, urging him simply to take her there and then, between stove and sink, and to hell with the finer points of protocol.

He deepened the kiss, clouding her mind to any other perception but the certain knowledge that she needed him, hard and imperative inside her, claiming her body just as he'd long ago claimed her soul.

"What about the casserole?" he murmured on a strangled breath.

"To hell with the casserole," she said, then felt her heart spill over with all the love she'd tried so hard to contain when, with unwavering purpose, he swept her up in his arms and swung toward the narrow staircase opposite the front door.

Apart from a small bathroom, the upper story of the house consisted of only one room with a windowed alcove at the far end that she'd planned to turn into a nursery, and a floor that sloped unevenly toward the east.

The bed, an ancient, carved affair never designed to accommodate more than one person at a time, groaned audibly beneath the combined weight of two. But it served the purpose. With desire raging at fever pitch between them, a canvas army cot would have served the purpose.

He shed his clothes with impressive speed, but for the first time, he undressed her at delicious leisure, stripping away each item with dedicated control. Sophie felt the air of the April night cool on her naked flesh, then Dominic's hands charting her contours in mute fascination at the changes he found there.

"Wait," he begged when she tried to pull him down on top of her and reached out an arm to the bedside lamp. "Let me see you first." Rose-tinted light flooded the room, illuminating every inch of her to his absorbed gaze. "You are beautiful," he marveled, tracing a line from her breast to her softly rounded abdomen and resting his palm there.

The baby rolled over accommodatingly and kicked an acknowledgment. The pupils of Dominic's eyes flared, narrowing the irises to bands of dark, opaque green.

"Well, I'll be damned!" he breathed. "The little devil knows me! I had no idea—" he shook his head wonderingly "—no idea what to expect. I've never...this is all new to me."

Helpless to prevent it, Sophie found her memory rewinding with chilling accuracy to another time two months before. *Guess what, darling. Miracle of miracles, I'm pregnant! We're going to have a baby, Dom!*

New? How could it all be new?

"Sophie?" Dominic touched her cheek. "Where have you gone?"

It was unfair to let the same old ghost displace her once again. Unfair and unthinkable. He had said Barbara was out of his life, that it was she, Sophie, who mattered.

"Nowhere," she whispered, sliding her hand from his ribs to his navel. Made bold by the rasping intake of his breath, she touched him, closing her fingers possessively around him in sultry emulation of intimacy. "I'm right here where I most want to be."

Sweat beaded his brow. "Just once," he said, holding

himself very still, "I wanted to make love to you slowly...all night long...and kiss every inch of you...."

She tilted up her hips, nudging at his flesh with her own.

He slipped his finger between her thighs. "I wanted to watch the flush steal over your skin when I touched you here...like this...and told you things I should have told you long before now...."

She looked at him, all dusky in the lamplight, with the sheen of vitality that marked everything about him glowing in his eyes, and the need that had started to build from the minute he first touched her overflowed in a pool of molten heat, driven by hunger and the superstitious certainty that they'd be tempting fate to delay things any longer. As if only by joining their bodies in glorious defiance could they deflect any mischief the gods rained down on them.

"Dominic, please," she begged on a fractured cry. "The talking can wait...but I can't!"

CHAPTER EIGHT

His passion had never been more unreserved, his tenderness more profound, nor her response more intense. They achieved a harmony that night that surpassed the mortal and joined ranks with the divine. As if all those obstacles that once had seemed so insurmountable had been wiped away.

After, however, when Dominic had fallen into deep, jet-lagged sleep, the misgivings Sophie had repressed rose up again, threading along her nerve endings to sound distant chimes of alarm deep in her heart. Everything was falling into place too smoothly, too easily, and it wasn't meant to be this uncomplicated. Those things that really mattered never were.

When, in the murky light of dawn, he turned to her again, his mind still fogged with exhaustion but his body hungry, she snatched at borrowed happiness, riding passion's crest over and over again with a voracity whose aftermath left her weak and trembling. Because instinct warned her it might not last.

She crept from the bed just as the sun filtered through the plum blossoms to glint on the topmost windowpanes. In the remaining hour before Dominic awoke, she had time to shower and dress, plug in the coffeemaker and walk down to the bakery to pick up fresh rolls for breakfast.

"Something smells good," he said not long after she returned, and she looked up from setting a vase of forget-me-nots on the table to find him leaning over the banister watching her.

"Sweet rolls," she said, her heart lurching at the sight and sound of him. "And homemade cherry preserves."

"Cherry preserves, hmm? How'd you know they were my favorite?" He ambled across the room and, looping one hand around her neck, aimed a lingering kiss at her mouth as if he surely loved her, just a little bit.

If only he'd say so, perhaps the nagging anxiety would stop dogging her and she'd feel secure enough to tell him that she'd lied when she'd said she'd taken back her heart, that it was his to keep for the rest of time. But he'd never come close to such an admission, not even last night when, in the midst of scorching passion, he'd cried out her name and begged her never to leave him again. Why not? What hindrance deterred him from making that ultimate acknowledgment?

She slipped out of his embrace. "I didn't know they were your favorite. My next-door neighbor gave them to me as a housewarming gift when I moved in here."

"Ah, yes, the next-door neighbor! We met yesterday and were mutually unimpressed." He passed a rueful hand over his unshaven chin and broke into a grin. "Exactly how much does she know about me?"

So relaxed, so charming, so...*un*-Dominic! After the first time they'd made love, that afternoon on the island, he'd hardly been able to stand the sight of her. The second time, in his penthouse, he'd dropped her like a hot coal the minute Barbara showed up at the door. The ax was surely going to fall this time, too. The only question was, when.

"I told her everything I know, and it isn't very much—which brings us to the promise you made last night. I think I've lived with the questions long enough, Dominic. Now I'd like some answers.''

The accusation in her voice sobered him. He sat down and gestured to the coffeepot. "Okay. Top me up with a quart of that, then fire away. Ask me anything at all."

Sophie filled his cup and began with the simplest. "How did you find me?"

"It wasn't difficult," he said, eyes narrowing slightly when she chose to sit in the chair opposite rather than the one beside him. "I went to see your parents. I was reluctant to do that at first in case you hadn't told them you'd gone missing, but it was obvious that they already knew and that they blamed me."

"That hardly explains how you tracked me down."

"Their attitude underwent a change when I told them you were pregnant and that I was not about to renege on my responsibilities to you or our child."

"You told my parents I'm expecting a baby?" Her other concerns overshadowed by this disclosure, Sophie stared at him, appalled. "Oh, you shouldn't have, Dominic! That's something they deserved to hear from me first."

He took a mouthful of coffee, then set down his cup very deliberately before replying, and she realized that the steel was still there beneath the engaging charm. "So why did you choose to leave them in ignorance, Sophie? It's not as if you didn't have plenty of time to fill them in on the facts."

She wriggled uncomfortably under his prolonged scrutiny. "I could hardly come out and say, 'I'm expecting and I've run off to lick my wounds because complications have arisen that make it seem unlikely that marrying the father is going to work out quite as simply as I'd hoped'."

"Why not? That's more or less how I put it to them, and they seemed to understand very well what I meant."

"They'd have been worried sick all these weeks!"

"They were anyway when you just upped and disappeared. Enough that it took very little persuasion on my part for them to tell me that your brother knew how to find you and for them to encourage me to come after you. Which," he added forcefully, "I had by then decided to do in any case, even if it meant hiring a private investigator to find you. Your folks weren't the only ones who were worried. Since speaking to them, I've had a few sleepless nights myself, wondering why you'd go to such lengths to keep the pregnancy secret, and I don't mind telling you, Sophie, I didn't much care for some of the reasons that occurred to me."

She didn't know what he meant by the latter part of his remark, nor did she much care just then. It seemed more to the point to inquire rather acidly, "Really? Is that why you waited over six weeks to come looking for me?"

He raised his eyebrows in mock confusion. "Your note stated quite emphatically that I'd rushed you into too many decisions since the start of the new year and that you needed time-out from all the pressure. If you didn't mean that, Sophie, why did you say it?"

"If you were all that worried about me, why didn't you ignore what I said and start searching for me sooner?"

"Because unlike you, my darling, I don't profess to know what's going on inside another person's head unless it's spelled out for me." There was no mistaking the exasperation creeping into his voice. "I'm told it's a common failing among men."

Sophie's intuition clicked into high gear. "Why do I

get the feeling Barbara suddenly entered this conversation?"

"Because I apparently failed to 'understand' her, too." He slapped a generous spoonful of Violet's cherry preserve on his roll. "And I'm surprised it's taken you so long to bring up her name. I'd have thought you'd be more interested in clearing up the mystery of her disappearance more than four and a half months ago than in quibbling over petty details of the past few weeks. Don't you want to know the story behind her miraculous resurrection from the dead?"

Suddenly losing what little appetite she'd mustered, Sophie pushed away her plate with her sweet roll barely touched. The truth was, she wished they never had to mention Barbara's name again. She wished they could forget she'd ever existed. But her reappearance made it plain enough that she wasn't about to be so easily dismissed. "Not really," she admitted, "but not knowing is worse. So tell me, where did she spend the time and why did she let everyone think she'd drowned?"

"With the help of her boyfriend, she set the scene of her apparent demise, then disappeared with him to some neighboring island in order to 'discover' herself. Spouted a lot of rubbish about 'needing to make contact with her deep inner self before settling down', but the bottom line is, running barefoot through the sand with a lusty young lover promised to be a lot more exciting than marrying me. Until she realized how dependent she was on Visa, American Express, and all the comforts of home, that is. At which point she decided that life as a latter-day flower child in some third world speck of a country in the Caribbean wasn't quite her speed after all."

"I see," Sophie said. And she did, very clearly, although she might have had trouble believing anyone could be so callously irresponsible if she hadn't witnessed firsthand Barbara's utter disregard for anyone's interests but her own.

Dominic eyed her curiously. "You don't sound surprised by what I've told you. Care to explain why?"

"No."

His gazed sharpened. "Don't tell me you knew all along what she was up to!"

"Of course I didn't!" she exclaimed indignantly. "It's just that her behavior before her disappearance was rather...well, unusual."

"*Unusual*?"

"Yes."

"In that case," he said when she volunteered nothing further, "don't you think you should have passed along that information to the police at the time of her presumed death? It might have triggered a more thorough search, which in turn might have spared all of us, particularly the Wexlers, untold misery."

"The police knew. Everyone on St. Julian knew—except you."

"Knew *what*?"

She sighed unhappily. "Don't make me spell it out for you, Dominic. It—"

He'd been resting his chin on his fist, but at her obvious reluctance he slapped the flat of his hand on the table with such force that the cups danced in their saucers, slopping coffee everywhere. "Damn it, Sophie, stop beating around the bush! I've got a right to know. I was engaged to her."

"Precisely. And I don't want to be the one to shatter your illusions."

"Do you really think I've got any left where she's concerned?" he asked scornfully. "Come on, Sophie, spit it out. Obviously there were other men, but what else? Parties? Booze? Wild, antisocial behavior?"

She crumbled her roll into little pieces and pushed them around her plate with the tip of her forefinger. "That just about sums it up, yes."

"Why didn't you tell me at the time?"

She looked up from the mess she'd made. "You can't be serious! Good heavens, Dominic, you were so beside yourself with grief that you blamed me for her death. You certainly wouldn't have believed any attempt of mine to shift responsibility to her."

"Damn!" Abruptly, he shoved back his chair and paced the short distance to the window. For a while, he stood with his hands rammed in the back pockets of his pants and stared out at the clouds wheeling in from the west to obliterate great stretches of blue sky. She watched in silence. Finally, the unyielding line of his shoulders relaxed and he passed a weary hand down his face. "What the hell," he muttered, swinging back toward her, "this is crazy! I didn't come here to fight with you. I came to clear away all the garbage from the past that's driving a wedge between us and I guess the only way I can do that is to start at the beginning."

"I saw the beginning," Sophie reminded him tartly. "When I first started working on the Wexler project, I watched you with her, and even then I hated it. I don't think I want to relive it now."

"What did you see, Sophie?" Dominic asked, coming back to the table and snagging her fingers in his.

"A man in love."

He laughed dryly. "Funny how appearances can be deceiving, isn't it?"

She pulled her hand away. "If you're going to tell me

you weren't smitten with her, Dominic, save your breath! It was obvious to anyone with eyes to see."

"You're right," he said bluntly. "I was in love with the whole idea of her. If I was the commoner who'd pulled himself up by the bootstraps, she was the princess. Where I'd had to claw my way to the top, she'd just floated. I was drawn to her glamour and energy and vitality, and by the time all that started to wear thin, other facets had come into play. I'd become one of the family, a son to the Wexlers, and I liked the feeling of belonging, of being needed. They knew Barbara was highly strung and saw in me a continuity of the stability they'd always provided. And without quite realizing when or how, I found myself taking over the role of protector. If it wasn't quite what I'd had in mind when I first proposed, other things that I hadn't expected made up for it."

"Are you saying you'd have married her just to please her parents and be accepted by them?" Sophie asked skeptically.

"I don't think I'd have recognized that was what I'd be doing." He reached for the coffeepot and refilled both their cups. "It's very easy to get comfortable enough in a situation to put up with its shortcomings, especially if, down the line, other things might come along to compensate."

"Like children, you mean?"

"Yes." He made no effort to dissemble. "I've always wanted children. That would have been a major factor in my decision to go through with the marriage, except..."

He paused and let his gaze roam over her face.

"Except what?"

"Except this leggy blond woman came to work on the estate. *Woman*, Sophie. Called herself a landscape architect but was really just a frustrated gardener who roamed around the place in dungarees, grubbing in dirt up to her elbows half the time, alongside her hired hands. She was hardworking and conscientious, and oh, Lord, was she kind to those old folks! Never too busy to stop and chat, never so full of herself that she couldn't spare the time to listen to their concerns."

He pinched the bridge of his nose. "Trouble was, the more I saw of her, the more I realized that Barbara was just a little girl playing at being grown-up, and no more cut out for marriage or motherhood than a boy is meant to shoulder a man's responsibilities."

Sophie fought against the flood of pleasure induced by his confession. "But you detested me on sight."

"I certainly tried hard enough. You made me question everything I was doing with my life. I found myself wondering what would have happened if I'd met you first." He raked the hair back from his forehead. "Crazy thoughts! Hell, you could have been married for all I knew."

"I'd never have guessed you felt that way. I found you so cold, so...suspicious. You acted as if you thought I might blow the place up when no one was looking. Every time I turned around, you were watching me."

A faint grin touched the corners of his mouth. "You'd better believe I was watching you! Do you know how delectable your backside is when you're bent over a flower bed?"

"You never even hinted—"

"I was scared spitless! Bad enough I was having serious second thoughts about sticking with my engagement without trying to start something with a woman I'd met through my future in-laws." He sighed. "Is any of this making sense to you?"

This was the man who'd once said with unshakable

confidence, "I'm very single-minded...I don't give up and I don't back down..." but for the first time he sounded unsure of himself. Yet although what he'd told her was unexpected, it made a certain sense and it definitely made him more human. She nodded. "More or less."

"Barbara must have guessed I was having doubts. She became edgy, more temperamental. Started testing me, picking fights over trifles, making scenes. Her folks were afraid she was headed for a breakdown of some sort. Apparently, she'd gone through some kind of emotional crisis the year before I met her and had threatened suicide. I felt like a jerk knowing that while they worried, all I cared about was finding a way to end things gracefully with the least amount of damage to everyone concerned. And then, as if she guessed what I had in mind, she took off to the Caribbean with you. And the next thing I knew, she was dead."

Sophie's heart filled with sympathy. She remembered the tortured expression on his face the day they'd driven out to the scene of the boat wreck, the agony she'd witnessed the afternoon he'd come to her hotel room to pack up Barbara's things, and for the first time she understood. If only he'd told her the truth then, how much pain they could have spared each other. But he was so good at presenting that cold, controlled front to the world, so very good at hiding his real feelings. "You felt guilty. Anyone would have."

"Guilty and, in a sick sort of way, relieved. The problem had been removed. I was free. And to make matters worse," he said, smothering a sigh, "there you were, very much alive. All sun-kissed apricot skin and warm, unselfish concern, worrying about me, trying to comfort me."

"You looked so torn up."

"I was! The idiot in me wanted to confess and throw himself on your mercy, the gentleman in me forbade it, and the lecher..." He shoved his fingers into his hair and ground the heels of his palms against his closed eyes. "Oh, the lecher drooled and fantasized and waited for the chance to cash in on a good thing, which happened sooner than I dared expect when you touched me that afternoon in the hotel room—"

"I couldn't help myself," Sophie cried. "You were so alone, so unhappy. And after, I thought how much you must despise me."

"Despise *you*?" He shook his head. "Hardly! All I could think was that the apple never falls far from the tree and that I had behaved no better than my father, a man for whom I had nothing but contempt. Yet even under those imperfect circumstances, making love to you exceeded anything I'd known with Barbara. That I was unlikely ever to have the pleasure of a repeat experience seemed fitting punishment."

"If you had only told me!" Sophie mourned.

"If you had only told me what had been going on before I arrived on the island!"

"What sort of woman would I be to have done a thing like that? You'd just lost your fiancée and were suffering enough. I wasn't about to make you feel any worse."

"No," he said wretchedly. "Your sort of woman would open her heart and her arms and give everything she had to make a man feel whole again. Which just brought home to me what I'd suspected all along—that you were my kind of woman."

"Did it never occur to you that you might be my kind of man?"

"No. What would someone like you want with a morally bankrupt jerk like me?"

She got up and went to stand behind him. She leaned down and rested her chin against his thick, dark hair. He smelled of her soap, her shampoo. French lilac and mimosa, all mixed up with the scent of sheer masculine vitality. She loved him so much at that moment that she trembled from the force of it. It consumed her, body, mind and soul.

"You're not morally bankrupt, Dominic," she whispered, sliding her arms around his neck.

"Oh, yes, I am," he said, tilting back his head and trapping her in his clear green gaze. "When I found out you were pregnant, I saw my chance to nab you and I did, without a moment's hesitation. I'd been given a second chance and I wasn't about to blow it. The baby was the means, but you were the end."

Pregnant. The baby. Barbara.

They had yet to deal with the most serious issue of all. The realization slid into Sophie's consciousness just about the same time that Dominic reached up to draw her around his chair and onto his lap.

"I've covered up the truth for a long time, Sophie," he murmured in her ear, "but no more. I'll never lie to you again. You're everything I've ever wanted and I'll never let you go."

"Dominic," she said quickly, before the imperative quiver of her thigh beneath his hand erased the more urgent question in her mind, "what are we going to do about...?"

He was kissing her, delicate, feathery kisses that stole up the side of her neck until they found her mouth. And his wicked, clever hand...oh, it had no scruples whatsoever, inching up her skirt in full view of anyone who might look in the window. "You're going to make an honest man of me as soon as possible," he informed her, misinterpreting her question, and kissed her again, deeply, erotically.

She snatched a shallow breath and fought against allowing her knees to fall slackly apart at the sweeping invasion of his hand. "Before I do," she said, "there's one very important point we've yet to discuss."

He nibbled at her ear, traced its inner curve with the tip of his tongue. His eyelashes flickered seductively against her cheek. "Can't it wait?"

"No." She pushed away his hand, straightened her skirt. "Dominic, what are you going to do about Barbara?"

His eyes snapped wide open, simmering with wry exasperation. "For crying out loud, sweetheart, not Barbara again—not now!"

"I have to know. We can't go on pretending she doesn't exist, especially not considering the circumstances."

He looked genuinely perplexed. "What circumstances? I told you, she and I are through. Finished. Done. She's probably got some other guy on her hook by now."

"But what about the baby?"

The amusement in his eyes died, extinguished by an emptiness that chilled Sophie to the bone. "There is no baby," he said.

"You mean she lied? She wasn't really pregnant?"

His expression turned hard, cold, cruel. "Oh, she was pregnant, all right. She had an abortion."

There it was at last, the thing Sophie had feared all along: the fatal flaw that would mar this new, too-perfect happiness. It hovered between them, a wicked, destructive thing made all the more ugly by Dominic's bald explanation.

With blinding hindsight, his offbeat remark about not caring for some of the ideas that had occurred to him when he learned that she hadn't told her parents about the baby, made sickening sense. That was what had prompted him to come looking for her: the fear that she'd run away to terminate her pregnancy, too, and that he stood to lose both his investments.

Sophie sprang to her feet, instinctively wrapping her arms around her middle in mute possession of her own child. "An abortion?"

"Yes. Sweetheart, you look as if you're going to pass out. Come back here and sit down."

"No!" Still clutching herself, she reeled away from him, around to the other side of the table, away from his beguiling, lying mouth.

Make an honest man of him?

It was enough to make her laugh!

He hadn't changed and he never would. He wanted a child, and once again, Barbara had outwitted him. So here he was, laying claim to his other investment. And because Sophie was so desperate for his love, she'd chosen to listen only to those things he said that fed her need when, in reality, he'd spent a far greater proportion of the relationship telling her things that denied it.

She doubled over, trying to contain the hysteria bubbling up.

He sprang from the chair, his face a mask of solicitous concern. "What's the matter, sweetheart? Is something wrong with the baby?"

She heard the sound of her own unlovely laughter. "Oh, *my* baby's just fine, thank you," she howled, clutching the back of a chair for support. "We both are.

So why don't you get the hell out of my house and go home? Because neither of us needs you."

He rounded the table and made a grab for her. "What the devil's gotten into you, Sophie?"

Blindly, she lashed out. Caught him squarely on the jaw with one flailing fist, curved her fingers and went for his eyes with the other. And didn't care that in submitting to such behavior, she was violating one of her most dearly held principles. At that moment, she could have killed him.

He swung her around so that her back was to the table and bundled her unceremoniously against him, pinning her hands behind her back, plastering her breasts against his chest, trapping her legs between his. He subdued her with all the same moves he'd used to seduce her. Sexy, masculine. Deceitful, heartless.

"I don't know what you think I've done or said," he informed her flatly, "nor do I particularly care, but I'm damned if I'll stand idly by and let you use me as your personal punching bag."

She glared at him through the tears coursing down her face. He stared steadily back, his eyes at close range so utterly beautiful that she could hardly bear it. Why couldn't he have been as flawed on the outside as he was on the inside? It would have made him so much easier to resist in the first place.

Anguish swept through her, dissolving her rage. She sagged against him, not the way she had the night before, full of sensual entreaty, but in complete, crippling dejection. "Let me go," she said, her voice a pale echo of the apathy laying waste to her soul.

He released her. "Now what was all that about, Sophie?"

She turned away, amazed that the hollowness invading

her hadn't robbed her of mobility. "I know why you're here, Dominic. Pretending to care about *me*, to want *me*."

"For crying out loud, if this is still about Barbara, I don't know how else to tell you that I *don't want her*."

"You don't want either of us," she said. "You want what we can give you. The difference is, she was smart enough to realize it a lot sooner than I was, and tough enough to know exactly how to thwart you."

"Exactly what are you saying, Sophie?" The question emerged loaded with warning.

She paid no heed. "You're a liar. Every word you say, every move you make, they're all calculated beforehand. You use them the same way you use money—as a disposable commodity to get you what you want."

"And just how did you reach that scintillating conclusion?"

"I took a long, hard look at the facts." She swiped at her tears, at the undignified dribbling of her nose. "You said it yourself not half an hour ago. You've been covering up ever since you met me, and you still are. No wonder you were so thrilled at how thoroughly pregnant I look! It would have been a real blow to discover you'd been robbed twice, wouldn't it? Because you didn't come after me. You came after your child. Well, enjoy the visit, Dominic, because I'll see you in hell before I let you get within a mile of him or me ever again."

With unruffled calm, he snapped one finger under the band of his watch so that the dial sat squarely in the center of his strong, elegant wrist. "You feel quite sure, do you, that you have sufficient evidence to make that decision?"

The inscrutability of his expression almost unnerved her. He had never seemed more remote, never more thoroughly veiled in that hauteur he was able to adopt with the flick of an eyelid. Then she remembered that this was all part of the disguise and that it was designed to set her off balance; to make her question her own judgment so that she'd more easily fall prey to his.

Marshaling herself to give an equally compelling performance, she said stonily, "Quite sure."

But she turned her back on him before she spoke, because otherwise her face would have betrayed her. The tears were welling up afresh, the grief contorting her features. How she held it all in check she didn't know.

He remained rooted to the spot, making no attempt to argue, to cajole her with a touch, an entreaty. At last, with the silence threatening to crack her composure to pieces, he moved.

He went up to the bedroom. She heard the creak of the floor above as he moved around. He came downstairs and opened the front door. She felt the brisk April breeze dance around her ankles.

"I hope you change your mind, Sophie," he said coldly. "I also hope you don't take too long to do it because I've just about run out of patience, and believe me, my darling, you'll like me even less when I play really dirty than you do when you just think I'm being a perfect bastard."

His measured stride rang out on the flagstone path of the courtyard. She heard the iron gate clang shut.

The emptiness that overflowed her heart exploded then, filling the room, the house, the rest of time.

He had gone from her life just as he'd come into it. With quiet, complete devastation. And the knowledge nearly killed her.

CHAPTER NINE

DOMINIC had known Grant Kaplan since high school. They'd played on the same football team and won identical scholarships to the same university. Circumstance had brought them together; shared ideals had made them friends.

When Grant got married the week after graduating from law school, Dominic had been his best man. Three years later, when the Kaplans outgrew the tiny apartment they'd rented shortly after the wedding, and no other landlord in town was interested in leasing to a couple with a fourteen-month-old toddler and another baby on the way, it never occurred to them to turn to anyone but Dominic to build them a house they could afford.

Five weeks after Dominic came back from England with steam pouring out of his ears and decided to set in motion the wheels of justice as they pertained to custody of his child, he naturally went to his old college buddy, Grant Kaplan, who by then had earned the deserved reputation of being one of the hottest lawyers in town.

When Dominic learned there wasn't much he could do to enforce his paternal rights until after the baby was born and that, even then, Sophie still had the upper hand as long as she remained abroad, he did exactly what he'd promised her he would do if she didn't change her attitude. In true bastard fashion, he instructed Grant to put the squeeze on her.

Grant chewed the end of his pen, the same disposable plastic type he'd always favored, and subjected Dominic to what he probably thought was an insightful stare. "Are you sure this is the route you want to take, pal? It's not the sort of action likely to improve your relationship, no matter what the motivation, and what good is victory if you can't take any pride in the way you went about achieving it?"

"Draw up the papers and stop playing pop psychologist," Dominic snarled.

"Have you tried talking to her? Explaining—"

Dominic swore colorfully.

"Very good," Grant commended him when the expletives finally ran dry. "Now, to repeat the question—"

"How do I talk to someone who consistently refuses to hear what I'm saying and whose sole reaction to the slightest hint of trouble is to freeze me out and put as many goddamned miles between us as possible? So don't bother repeating that she's legally free to live wherever she chooses and that if I want to exercise my parental rights I'll have to wait until after the baby's born and then go through the British court system, because I've no intention of sitting around on my butt waiting for her to disappear again. I want her brought back here before she gives birth, and if playing dirty is the only way I can do it, I'll play dirty. It'll come as no great surprise to her, believe me."

"She could end up hating you."

"She already hates me. I hate her. Hell, we hate each other!"

"Yes. Well, that certainly explains how the two of you ended up in the sack together and why you've tried so hard to coerce her into marriage."

"Draw up the papers," Dominic advised him darkly, "and save the funny stuff for someone who appreciates it."

* * *

"You look like a pregnant Joan of Arc waving the rebel flag," Paul said when Sophie paid a visit early in July. "Sit down and take a load off your swollen ankles. Screaming at me isn't going to change anything."

"I thought you'd be on my side," Sophie raged. "I expected it."

Paul, who'd taken to smoking a pipe and affecting all sorts of other donnish British customs, tamped down his tobacco and replied placidly, "It's not a matter of taking sides, Sophie. It's a matter of what's best for you and ultimately for the baby. And rampaging around the West Country in your little Mini-Minor hardly fits the bill. Anyway, I rather liked your Dominic."

Jenny beamed. "So did I."

"He's not my Dominic," Sophie fumed. "I wouldn't take him if he was the last man on earth."

"Just as well," Paul said, "because the way you're going about things, you aren't going to get him. What did you do, for crying out loud, to bring out the savage in him like this?"

"I called him a liar to his face. Which he is."

"Are you sure?"

"Of course I'm sure! He followed me over here and tried to convince me he wanted to take me home and marry me!"

Paul nodded through clouds of pungent smoke. "I can see why you'd find that very hard to believe," he remarked cheerfully.

Sophie could have strangled him. It was shocking, in fact, how frequently her thoughts had turned to violence since the letter had arrived, although she supposed it was preferable to the dreadful apathy that had hounded her ever since Dominic Winter walked out on her.

She'd known that a person couldn't go on indefinitely

skipping meals and taking refuge in sleep, but she'd certainly given it a royal try. Anything had been better than trailing through the long summer days, reliving useless regrets.

Violet had been very worried. "You don't look well, lass," she'd said. "Are you going in for regular checkups at the clinic?"

She had been. Sort of. But the lineups were often long, and occasionally she got a peculiar sensation low down in her womb, a sort of pressure that, while it wasn't painful, was rather disquieting. So, depending on how she was feeling, she sometimes stayed home and lay on a chaise in the back garden, reading books that were just as good as prenatal classes at preparing her for childbirth.

Besides, it was very hard being around happy expectant mothers who more often than not had doting husbands in tow. Sophie didn't need the reminder that she was alone. She never forgot it even for a moment, and she never stopped hurting over it.

"What am I going to do about this?" she demanded, waving the letter under Paul's nose again. "You've read what's in it. What do you think?"

"That either you go home and call a cease-fire while the pair of you sort out your differences, or you'll wind up flat broke. And in view of your condition, the latter seems a trifle inconvenient."

He'd mastered the British art of understatement, too. He'd be wearing academic robes and keeping an old English sheepdog next! "It just goes to prove that Dominic Winter's every bit as rotten as I thought," she spat. "What kind of man would deliberately reduce the mother of his child to insolvency?"

"The kind you're in love with, obviously," Paul said to Jenny's tittering approval. "Good Lord, Sophie, why don't you stop working yourself into a lather and just go and talk to the guy? He didn't strike me as all that unreasonable.''

The fact was, she'd known in her heart that she'd reacted hastily and perhaps even unfairly to Dominic. She'd been ready to cave in and try to make amends, if not for her own sake then for their child's. Until this, his latest attempt to bend her to his will, had been delivered to her door. Now she'd rather die than give him the satisfaction!

"I should have taken his money and run with it when I had the chance," she lamented. "He's the one who wanted to pay off my mortgage at the bank, but I thought it'd make me feel less as if I was being bought if he became the lender of record instead. I insisted we have an official agreement drawn up—and look where it's landed me!"

"Up the creek without a paddle," Paul concluded wittily. "Or, more accurately, hugely in debt and divested of your home, because there's no doubt he can sell off the property to recover his losses on the house he custom-built for you."

"And this is the man who swore he'd never renege on his fatherly obligations!"

"He's not. All he's asking—"

"Demanding! He never *asks* for anything."

Briefly, Paul forgot he fancied himself as a sober academic and sniggered into his teacup.

Jenny rushed to keep the peace. "All he wants is for you to show up in person, Sophie, and sign an agreement spelling out his visitation rights and the child support payments he's prepared to make."

"He's blackmailing me."

"And managing to keep his integrity intact while he

does it," Paul said, recovering himself. "I must admit I rather admire him."

Sophie stared at him, dumbfounded. "You're not going to help me, are you?"

He fiddled around with his damnable pipe again. "If by that you mean am I going to meddle in something that's none of my affair, the answer is no, I'm not. I do not relish ending up in the cross fire between a man and a woman who are being kept apart by something that, to my mind, might be easily and quickly resolved if you, my dear sister, would swallow your pride long enough to ask Dominic one very simple question."

"Oh, really," she said, dangerously miffed. If it hadn't been for Jenny, who kept stroking her back as if she were an overbred cat refusing fresh cream, she'd walk out. It was the one thing she'd practiced rather often of late and she was becoming quite good at it. "And what question is that, my dear brother?"

"You know that this Barbara person was pregnant. You know she had an abortion."

"So?"

"Did you ever bother to determine if the child she carried was Dominic's?"

Sophie felt her jaw drop, and just for a fleeting, glorious moment, hope soared. Then reality returned with a thud. "I was there when she made the announcement. I heard her say, '*We're* going to have a baby'."

"And you believed her?"

"Why wouldn't I?"

"Considering that you now know the lengths to which she'll go to have her way, why would you? She lied about everything else, didn't she? What's to say she didn't try to pass off her lifeguard lover's child as Dominic's? And what if Dominic knew from the outset that there was no way the child could be his? What if it never entered his mind that *you'd* believe it, either?''

What if, indeed! It provided considerable and provoking food for thought, especially since not a hint that she might be pregnant had once passed Barbara's lips. In view of how free she'd been with her other confidences, it hardly seemed likely she'd have kept quiet about something as momentous as a baby in the making.

"If the baby had been Dominic's," Jenny put in thoughtfully, "that would mean she was already pregnant when she went down to the Caribbean with you at the end of November, and she'd be at least fourteen weeks along by the time she showed up again in Palmerstown. You saw her, Sophie. Did she look pregnant to you?"

"She looked the way she always did, skinny as a reed."

"It all adds up if you ask me," Paul said, puffing complacently on his damned pipe.

"Yes," Sophie said meekly. "Now that you mention it, I suppose it does."

Paul shrugged. "Then instead of spinning your wheels over here, book the next possible flight to Vancouver and find out, Sophie. And don't take too long to do it. It's the height of the tourist season, seat space is at a premium, and you've only got until August the fifteenth to sign on the dotted line if you don't want to lose your house."

She must have looked even more churned up than she felt. The flight attendant swept a keen, professional eye over her, tucked her ticket stub to one side and, as soon as the Air Canada jet had reached cruising altitude, moved her to business class where, in addition to being wider and reclining farther, the seats came equipped with little footrests that afforded divine relief to Sophie's swollen, eight-month-pregnant ankles.

She was plied with extra pillows, another blanket, an early lunch. After, while the rest of the passengers watched a movie, she tried to sleep. But every time she closed her eyes, the same unlikely scenario played itself out: what if Paul had alerted Dominic to the fact that she was coming home, and when she cleared customs in Vancouver, he was waiting to sweep her into his arms? What if, in between breathtaking kisses, he confirmed what she now suspected, that the other baby hadn't been his, and Barbara's decision to end the pregnancy had had nothing to do with him?

Just like before, though, it was too easy a solution to bear up under pressure. Problems didn't solve themselves so neatly. The difference was that this time Sophie was prepared for disappointment and therefore not overly surprised to find no one waiting to greet her amid the mob of people waiting to meet the flight.

Within the hour, she was on the road in the car she'd rented for the last leg of her journey, the long and arduous drive into the southern interior. She drove until early evening, then stopped for the night in a motel. It seemed a smart idea, especially as she was again conscious of that low abdominal pressure.

Once this latest mess was sorted out—if it ever was— she really would have to devote more time to taking better care of herself and the baby. She had exactly four weeks in which to conclude her business with Dominic and find a place to live. Unless...

She shook her head impatiently. It was too late for unlesses and what ifs. She and Dominic might have begun their relationship in the bedroom, but it was ending in a courtroom. Not a very auspicious sign!

The temperature was hovering around ninety the next afternoon when she drove over the mountain pass and down into the blistering heat of the valley. The dry, semi-desert air hit like a blast furnace, scorching her lungs and turning the steering wheel tacky beneath her hands.

She could have pared fifteen minutes off the final lap of her journey if she'd taken the upper highway from there, but she turned the other way, along the narrower, quieter lakeshore route, past the place that had once been home. It was cooler down by the water and it wasn't as if anyone was expecting her. She was coming home the same way she'd left—unexpectedly.

The road unrolled in front her, distorted by heat waves. In the orchards on either side, the last of the peach crop hung ripe and golden from the trees. Up on the hills, the vineyards were heavy with fruit.

Even with all the windows rolled down, the car was still unbearably hot. It was another typical August day in the southern interior: somnolent, windless and glaringly bright. She could taste the dust in her throat, feel her clothes sticking to the leather upholstery of the car.

She hadn't intended to slow down at the turnoff to the rutted driveway that led to the site of her old house. It was more as if the car had a will of its own and wasn't about to take direction from her.

There was no sign of life about the place; nothing new or different at all, in fact. The grove of fruit trees remained undisturbed by all the supposed changes while the broad leaves of the huge old maple drooped listlessly in the blistering heat. Everything looked just the same. Until she rounded the last bend and saw the house he'd built for her.

It didn't sprawl exactly; it was much too elegant. Instead, it reclined on the long, grassy slope above the lake as if, when God made the earth, He'd had this particular spot in mind for just such a dwelling.

Killing the engine, Sophie remained behind the wheel of her car and simply stared through the windshield, dry-mouthed with admiration. Whatever else he didn't do right, Dominic knew how to design and build a house. Sunshine dazzled its white stucco walls and blue tiled roof. Tall, gleaming windows soared to deep, protective eaves. A flight of shallow, curving steps led up to double front doors with etched-glass inserts.

She couldn't resist a closer investigation. Nudging the car door closed with her hip, she walked up the steps, pressed her nose to the nearest window and knew right away she wouldn't be satisfied simply to look.

She tried the front doors, found they were unlocked and, like Alice, stepped into a wonderland of pale hardwood floors, twelve-foot ceilings and deep moldings. There was a kitchen with granite countertops and a breakfast bar; a dining room big enough to entertain royalty; a nursery with a built-in intercom. Entranced, she walked quietly down the hall, passing spacious rooms flooded with sunshine and shimmering reflections from the lake.

French doors stretching the width of the back of the house gave access to a brick-paved patio. From there, a path wound down to the water. To either side, mounds of topsoil waited for the landscaper to restore the flower beds that had been disturbed by all the construction. Sophie itched to get down on her knees, bury her hands in the rich loam and bring the garden back to brilliant life.

At the foot of the property, the lake lapped indolently against the shore. Farther out, the surface of the water lay smooth as glass. Picking her way carefully, Sophie crossed the rock-strewn strip of beach and, without bothering to remove her sandals, waded up to her ankles in the relatively cool shallows.

It felt so good to be home again.

And then she heard it floating across the somnolent air of midafternoon: the unmistakable growl of a vehicle cruising up the driveway from the road. If it was Dominic returning...oh, she couldn't face the indignity of his catching her snooping around and looking like an oversize pumpkin in a travel-creased tent!

Splashing ashore, she cut across the beach at an angle to avoid being seen from the patio, intending to sneak away up the side of the property. But her eyes were dazzled from the glare of the water, her leather-soled sandals slick on the sunbaked rocks. She blundered forward, her mind fixed on escape at any price, and felt her ankle twist out from under her.

Clutching at thin air, she skidded, lost her footing and landed hard astride a huge boulder. She blinked at the moment of jarring pain, seemed to hear each vertebra crunch against its neighbor. Slithering to the sand, she rotated her ankle and gingerly tested her weight on it.

Miraculously, no bones appeared to be broken. And yet...something wasn't quite right. Something had torn loose inside, where her baby was supposed to remain safely cocooned for another four weeks. That feeling of pressure was back, more persistent, more ominous than ever. Every instinct urged her to remain still in order to minimize whatever problem was manifesting itself.

"Help!" she cried, her throat aching and her heart unraveling with fear.

Her voice floated up into the thick, hot air and was met by drowsing silence. The sun beat down mercilessly. A flicker of pain stabbed the small of her back. And in the distance she heard the sound of the Jaguar's engine fading down the driveway, heard it slow down as it met the junction with the road, then take off with a roar of power in the direction of town.

Forgetting all the things she'd read about, she tensed, helpless to control either her body or her mind. No one had answered her cry for help and she didn't need a book to tell her that her baby was coming, uncaring that it was too early and that his mother was alone on a deserted stretch of beach.

The pain had subsided to a persistent ache, but a sense of urgency gripped her. She was in labor and she had to make it back to the house while she still had the strength, to the kitchen where she remembered seeing a phone on the breakfast bar.

Cradling her belly in her hands, she stumbled forward and tried not to think of the number of steps she'd have to take to reach her objective. She was only halfway home when the first contraction hit.

With a monumental effort at control, she breathed deeply. She must not panic, even though she was helpless to govern the order of events or the speed at which they were occurring. Emptying her mind of all but the urgency of dragging her reluctant body up to the house, she navigated the last of the rocky shore with excruciating care and determination.

Rough-hewn cedar steps with a single railing spanned the drop from garden to beach. She hauled herself up the first two well enough, but as she attempted the third, another contraction clamped hold and something flooded warm and thick between her thighs.

She knew instinctively that what was happening to her was not a normal part of labor. Things were happening too quickly and in the wrong order. This was not the beginning of birth but a slow sort of death for her baby.

"Dominic!" she wailed softly, tears filming her eyes.

She had threatened never to let him know his child, but she hadn't meant it. She would never have punished him like that. She loved him. She loved him and she needed him. But she'd left it too late to let him know. Because if their baby died, he would neither believe her nor forgive her.

Their baby would not die. She would not allow it.

Gritting her teeth, she pressed on, shutting out the dizzying pain, the blinding sun, the endless, endless path, and at last the French doors that looked out on the patio were a hand's grasp away. From somewhere beyond the fear, she scraped up the energy to wrestle them open, to drag herself over the threshold and across the floor to the breakfast bar.

She'd made it. She was home.

Her hand reached for the phone, closed around the cord, pulled it toward her. Then the last of her strength gave out, and with a sigh she sagged against the side of the bar and slid all the way down to the smooth oak floor, taking the receiver with her.

Dominic jumped down from the truck to check on the unfamiliar car parked at the foot of the steps, saw the purse lying on the front seat with a ticket stub tucked into the side pocket and knew at once who the unexpected visitor was.

"Don't bother waiting," he told his foreman. "I'll lock the place up and hitch a ride back into town with my guest."

As soon as the truck disappeared down the driveway, he leaped up the steps and into the house because he'd thought at first that that was where she'd be, especially when he noticed the front door standing open.

When he didn't find her there and there was no answer when he called out her name, he raced back outside again, struck suddenly by the thought that she could drive away while his back was turned. It would be just like her to sneak off before they had a chance to straighten out the ridiculous mess they'd managed to get themselves into.

Her car was exactly where she'd left it and he was running in circles, so bloody exhilarated that she was back that he wasn't thinking straight! She was probably hiding somewhere in the garden, enjoying watching him make an ass of himself. Well, he'd fix her wagon. Literally!

Sauntering over to the car, he reached inside, removed the key from the ignition and tossed it into the bushes. Then he strolled up the steps and went back into the house. He'd wait and let her come to him for a change because neither of them was going anywhere until she did.

It wasn't easy to be patient. He'd missed her badly. As the days had passed, all the aggression he'd nurtured had faded into one long, aching need that flared wild and unruly through his veins.

He didn't care anymore that she'd hurt him with her accusations, or angered him with her threats. All he wanted was to hold her, feel the reality of her in his arms, the substance of her close to his heart. He wanted to touch her and tell her that he loved her and that if he had his way they'd never spend another night apart.

He ambled down the long hall, looking into each room as he passed, just in case he'd missed her the first time around. Had she liked the nursery? The master suite? The nanny's quarters?

He passed by the dining room and pushed open the

swinging door to the kitchen, the heart of every house he built. And felt his own heart stammer to an agonizing halt when he saw her crumpled in a heap next to the breakfast bar.

The universe narrowed to her closed eyes, the sharp angle of her cheekbones. Dropping to his knees beside her, he scooped her into his arms, shocked at her pallor and appalled at her fragility.

"Sophie," he whispered brokenly, rocking her to and fro. "Sophie...my darling, my love, what have you done to yourself?"

When he saw the stain on her hyacinth blue dress, he at first refused to acknowledge what it had to be and tried to pretend his eyes were deceiving him. But nothing changed, no matter how fiercely he blinked. Sophie was hemorrhaging.

"Hold on, sweetheart," he told her. "I'll get you to Palmerstown General before you know it."

Except that he had no means of taking her there. The key to the car was buried in waist-high shrubbery because he had been so anxious, once again, to show her who wielded the power.

Cursing, he secured the phone in the angle of his shoulder and dialed the emergency number. Heard himself barking out directions to find the house. But all that really registered were Sophie's pale, drawn features and the terrible dread that in pushing for what he wanted, he'd finally gone too far.

This was not the way to write their ending, with her dying in his arms. They had too much loving to share.

Emergency vehicles arrived within half an hour, their various sirens splintering the stillness of the afternoon. Swift, efficient men in white poured into the kitchen and took charge. They bundled her onto a gurney, wheeled her outside to a waiting ambulance and took her away. Dominic sat beside her, holding her limp hand to his cheek, willing her to hold on, to take all his strength and use it for herself.

They hung tubes from her arms, pierced the softness of her skin with needles, fed her oxygen. A young paramedic bent over her, an intent stranger with his alien hand on her stomach, listening through a stethoscope to the baby's heart.

"Never mind the child," Dominic snarled, beside himself at being reduced to the role of helpless spectator. "Listen to *her* heart—save *her* life."

"Calm down, buddy," the paramedic advised laconically. "We don't aim to lose either one."

Murderous rage rose up in Dominic. What did this cocky young bastard know?

Enough to keep his attention where it belonged.

Chagrined, Dominic followed suit. "Sweetheart," he whispered, kissing the hand he held in his. "Sweetheart..."

Miraculously, she opened her eyes. He lifted his head and saw she was looking at him, that she was radiant. "Dominic," she murmured, smiling like an angel through the pain. "I needed you and you came."

"Of course I did," he replied huskily, the emotion almost choking him. "Where do you get off trying to cheat me out of being here for my son's birth?"

"What if she's a girl?"

"Not a chance," he said. "We're starting our own football team. Anyhow, girls are always late. She wouldn't have finished packing yet."

Her smile faltered and beads of sweat popped out on her forehead. She gripped his hand with bone-crushing force. "Ohhh," she gasped, drawing in a great breath. "Are we nearly there?"

The paramedic caught Dominic's eye and nodded. "Just about," he said, "and we've radioed ahead. They're expecting us."

He sounded calm. But he looked anxious.

CHAPTER TEN

THE worst thing about hospitals, Dominic concluded savagely, as the congregation of personnel attending Sophie huddled for another whispered conference, was that everyone from the most junior clerk in admissions to the head nurse on the maternity floor seemed part of one great conspiracy to keep people like himself firmly on the outside.

"No, I'm not her husband," he snarled when they tried to shoo him out of the cubicle where they had Sophie cloistered. "I'm her lover and that's my baby she's about to deliver. So don't tell me that what goes on here is none of my business because I'm making it my business, damn it!"

"You don't make the rules around here," the iron-faced head nurse informed him severely. "In fact, you don't have any clout at all. So unless you want to find yourself booted out of this unit, please lower your voice."

Only Sophie, clutching his hand and whimpering softly, kept him from firing back a retort that would likely have landed him behind bars.

"That's better." The nurse nodded approvingly. "Now, I need to get some consent forms signed. Feel up to doing that for me, Sophie? Time is of the essence since that baby of yours is in such a hurry to make an appearance."

"Give them to me," Dominic said, reaching for the clipboard. "She's got enough to deal with."

Old Hatchet-face slapped his hand away. "You're not eligible. If the patient isn't able to sign, we'll have to send for the next of kin."

"Please don't do that," Sophie begged. "I can sign."

"Wonderful. Dr. Overby just arrived and will be in to see you as soon as we've finished the paperwork."

"This man Overby," Dominic said, chasing the nurse out of the cubicle, "how good is he?"

She favored him with a fishy-eyed glare. "Count your blessings, Mr. Winter. From the looks of it, Ms. Casson's going to need the best and fortunately that's what she'll be getting."

Dominic didn't like the sound of that. He liked even less the sober expression on the specialist's face when he came out to the waiting area after completing his examination of Sophie.

"You're the father of Ms. Casson's baby, I understand," he said, approaching Dominic.

"Yes. And her fiancé."

"I see. Well, I'm afraid we're looking at surgery, Mr. Winter."

The words rang with a foreboding that made Dominic's skin crawl. "What sort of surgery?"

"A cesarean section—something I normally try to avoid."

Dominic couldn't get used to the idea of not being in charge. It went against the grain to be at the mercy of someone else's judgment, especially a stranger's. "Then avoid it now."

"That's not possible," the doctor said firmly. "I'm sorry."

Suddenly, Dominic wasn't a thirty-five-year-old man; he was a kid again, standing in another hospital like this and listening to another doctor tell him that his mother was dying and there was nothing anyone could do about it. "Why not?" he'd asked, his seventeen-year-old heart aching, because he'd known that, if she hadn't been saddled with him, her life might have turned out differently. "Why not?" he asked now, his heart nearly breaking. "Is it my fault?"

The doctor's gaze softened. "No one's to blame, son. She's very narrow through the pelvis and you..." He indicated Dominic's breadth of shoulder. "Well," he said dryly, "it wouldn't have been easy under the best of circumstances. But there are unforeseen complications."

Dominic felt the ground rock under him. "Complications?"

"Unless we intervene, I'm afraid that she'll deliver the placenta first and that could cost us the baby."

"How dangerous is this surgery?"

"All surgery's serious, but..." The doctor shrugged. "It's routine procedure."

There was nothing routine about someone taking a knife to his Sophie! "Listen," he said, "Sophie comes first. Do whatever you must, but if it comes down to a choice, save her and let the baby go. There'll be other children but..." He stopped, almost choking in the effort not to break down. "But there'll never be another Sophie."

They had given her something that filled her with rainbows. She floated just out of reach, aware of what was happening around her but not a part of it.

She smiled. From beyond the thin wall of the cubicle, Dominic's voice rose in frustration. He was having such a hard time taking orders for a change, instead of dishing them out....

"...her fiancé," he said. She liked the sound of that.

"...my fault," he said, and she heard the agony in his voice and wished they'd give him something for his pain, too. "...Sophie comes first...save her and let the baby go."

Let the baby go?

Never, she thought hazily. The baby is my gift to you, my darling.

The curtains rustled and she knew he was beside her again. She felt his strong fingers close around hers, felt his lips against her cheek. "They're taking you upstairs in a minute, but I'll be down here waiting, sweetheart," he said. "I'll always be here, no matter what."

The rainbows spread, swirling through her mind and taking her away.

"Look at it this way," Old Hatchet-face had told him when they wheeled Sophie into the elevator. "You'll be spared all that pacing up and down the halls. It'll be over before you know it."

Not so. Distracted, Dominic glanced at the wall clock for the fortieth time in as many minutes. He'd paced miles, waited centuries, and still there was no word. Her room was ready, the high, narrow bed with its stark linens mocking him with its emptiness.

As empty as his life would be without her, he thought, his heart swelling painfully. She eased his most vital hunger, answered his most quiet need. She was his whole world.

Behind him, the elevator doors whispered open. "You have a son, Mr. Winter."

It was like a television drama. The doctor stood there wearing his silly green hat, a mask dangling around his neck, his shapeless green suit and boots making him look like one of the seven dwarfs after a hard day in the gold mine.

"A son?" Was that his voice cracking? And why, for Pete's sake, were the geometrical proportions of the hall blurring? He hadn't cried when his mother died, and he'd been only a kid then. "A son...!" And he a father with the tears running down his face for all the world to see. "What about my fiancée, my Sophie?"

"Take a look for yourself."

Rubber wheels swished from behind. Swiping at his face with the cuff of his sleeve, he looked down and saw she was smiling in her sleep, the lightest flush staining the hollows of her cheeks, and so delicate under the sheets that she looked little more than a child herself.

"Sophie?" he whispered, and miracle of miracles, she heard him. Her eyes opened and focused on him.

"It's going to be a football team, Dominic," she murmured drowsily. "They were all out of little girls."

Of course, it would have been easy to wallow in the euphoria and forget there'd ever been a cross word exchanged between them.

"After all, Sophie," her mother had said, beaming down at her new grandson the next afternoon, "you and Dominic are together again. He stayed with you all last night, despite everything the hospital staff did to try to evict him, and look at the beautiful flowers he sent. Obviously, whatever the problems were, this little fellow's banished them. So why don't you put the past behind you and enjoy your little son?"

"Problems don't go away because you ignore them, Mother. Dominic and I still need to sort out a few things."

"They can wait until you're home and settled down again."

But where was home?

"I'd make it clear it's wherever he hangs his hat—not to mention his pants," Elaine declared when she stopped by that afternoon after work to meet her godson. "For heaven's sake, don't keep adding to your misery! The most gorgeous guy this side of heaven's built you a mansion, he's the father of this adorable, wrinkled creature, and you love him. I should be half as lucky!"

The baby stretched, waved a tiny fist in the air and let out a screech of protest. "Just like his daddy." Sophie smiled. "Less than twenty-four hours old and already expecting to run the show."

"Ganging up on me already?" Dominic inquired from the doorway.

"Oops! Time I was out of here." Elaine scooped up her bag and planted a kiss on the baby's head. "Nice seeing you again, Dominic," she said in passing, "and congratulations."

Even after she'd gone, Dominic continued to hover on the threshold as though unsure of his welcome. "Come on in and say hello to your son," Sophie suggested.

He half shrugged and deposited a huge bunch of white lilies on the foot of her bed before going to stand over the bassinet. Sophie watched him reach out a long, tanned finger and saw the look on his face when the baby grabbed ahold.

"Wouldn't you like to hold him, Dominic?" she asked softly.

He shuffled his feet uneasily and closed big awkward hands around the tiny bundle. "I'm not sure I know how."

"Then you'd better learn," she said. "Unless, of

course, you plan to leave me to do all the work of caring for him."

He lifted the baby clear and cradled him against his chest. "Isn't that what you said you wanted, Sophie?"

"Oh, Dominic," she sighed, wishing he'd just come and put his arms around her, as well, instead of keeping such a safe distance between them, "we've managed to say so many things to each other that we didn't mean. What I accused you of when you came to see me in Wells, what I said about Barbara..."

He looked at her over the top of his son's head. "It wasn't my baby, Sophie. There was no way it could have been and I knew that right away."

She dipped her head. "I guessed as much."

"I shouldn't have left you guessing. I shouldn't have pressured you into coming home." He heaved a great sigh and tucked the baby back in the bassinet. "I've done and said nothing but the wrong thing ever since I met you and I never meant things to be like that."

"Did you mean it last night when I heard you say, 'let the baby go'?"

He looked down at their child again, his eyes full of pain. "Yes. But that was last night and I thought I might lose you. Now, today, I have a son and I can't unwish him. We hardly know each other, yet already I love him."

And what about me? Sophie longed to ask. *Do you love me, too?*

Outside the window, the sunbaked hills rose above Palmerstown. The waters of Jewel Lake shone blue and aquamarine beneath another cloudless sky. And across the room, Dominic looked at her with eyes the color of jade. "I'll never try to take him away from you, Sophie,

I promise. I'll do whatever you ask, but please, let me see him once in a while. Let me know my boy."

"Is that all, Dominic?" she asked, her voice breaking. "Is there nothing else you'd like to say to me?"

"There's nothing else I can say, except I'm sorry."

That wasn't all he could say! It would be so easy to set everything right between them if only he could tell her the one thing she most needed to hear. But he had turned away and was staring out of the window at the melon-colored tones of early sunset tinting the western sky.

"I'm sorry, too," she said quietly, "because I don't know where to go from here."

He pivoted toward her, looking as close to shamefaced as she ever expected to see him. "All my talk about repossessing the house was just so much hot air, another example of my not knowing when to keep my mouth shut. The house is yours if you want it, you know that."

"And what do you want, Dominic?"

He shook his head and the expression in his beautiful eyes undid her. He had never looked more vulnerable or uncertain. "I want you," he said. "You're all I've ever wanted. I love you."

Just that. The simplicity of it knocked everything else—the hurt, the loneliness, the doubt—clean out of her head and into the past where it belonged. "Oh, Dominic, then that's all that matters because I love you, too."

He stared at her unbelievingly. "But how can you? After everything—the way I am, the business with the house—"

"I don't care about the house!" she cried, holding out her arms to him. "Don't you know that I could live in a shoe box and be happy as long as you're there to share it with me?"

"I'll try to change, to be a better person—"

"No. I love *you*, Dominic."

"Enough to marry me?"

"More than enough."

The beginnings of a smile illuminated his eyes and softened the sober line of his mouth.

"Thank God!" he breathed, and finally took the first step in the last two yards that separated them. "*Thank God!*"

The baby let out a squawk of annoyance just then, as though to remind them that he was supposed to be the star of the show.

Midway between the bed and the bassinet, Dominic stopped and looked at Sophie uncertainly. "Do I have to pick him up again?"

She laughed. "You might as well get used to it, Dominic. I have the feeling he's going to be just as demanding as his daddy."

"Maybe he's hungry." Dominic made a face. "Or wet. Listen, Sophie, I'm not sure I'm going to be much help when it comes to diapers and that sort of thing."

"You'll learn," she said. "We'll learn together, about all sorts of things. Bring our son here, Dominic, and let's get started."

He carried the baby to her and perched beside her on the bed. "I want to hold you, but I'm afraid of hurting you," he said, sliding a tentative arm around her shoulders.

She lifted her face to his. "I could stand being kissed without experiencing too much discomfort."

His lips hovered over hers. "I will never disappoint you again," he murmured against her mouth.

"Oh, Dominic," she sighed, leaning into his embrace,

"all that matters is that we love each other and our son, don't you know that?"

He kissed her then, a deep, possessive kiss. It might have lasted the rest of the night if the baby hadn't let out another outraged squawk.

"He's got quite a set of lungs," his father observed.

"He needs to be fed," his mother replied. "He also needs a name."

"How about Tiger?"

"How about Screecher?"

"Do you want to name him after your family?"

"I want to name him for ours, yours and mine. Let's choose something fresh to mark our brand-new beginning."

"Before we do that," Dominic said, running a loving hand through her hair as she settled the baby at her breast, "let's choose a wedding date. He might as well understand from the beginning that sometimes we come first."

EPILOGUE

THEY decided on a Christmas wedding.

"Business is pretty quiet in December," Dominic said when they put the idea to Sophie's parents. "We'll be able to take a nice, long honeymoon."

"And by then the baby won't need to be fed quite as often," Sophie said, referring to the fact that in the weeks immediately following his birth, Ryan demanded meals at regular two-hour intervals.

Sophie's mother was ecstatic. "It's the perfect time! Paul and Jenny are coming home for Christmas anyway, and we'll have a full three months to organize something lavish."

"Lavish?" Sophie's father echoed. "I'd have thought discreet was a better choice, considering they've both done everything backward. In my day, a man usually married a woman before he got her pregnant and, in the event that he couldn't manage *that*, definitely before the child was born."

"Oh, Doug, how can you be such a hypocrite?" his wife admonished with a coy little smile. "Why, as I recall—"

"Never mind," he interjected hastily. "Anything you decide is fine with me."

They chose a late-afternoon ceremony at St. Jude's church, and a dinner reception at the Royal. Elaine agreed to be maid of honor and in early September the three women went shopping for Sophie's wedding dress.

Given the circumstances, Sophie refused to wear white

but compromised with a long gown of heavy blush pink satin embroidered with pearls. "Because I know you've been looking forward to this from the minute I was born, Mom," she said.

"And a veil," Anne begged. "Please, Sophie! The gown cries out for a veil, even if it's just one of those short affairs."

"All right, but no train or it'll still be coming in the door when I arrive at the altar. St. Jude's is a very small church, you know."

"Stuffed quail," Anne and Sophie suggested when it came time to choose the dinner menu.

"Roast beef," Doug insisted, and Dominic concurred.

"Actually," he confessed that night, climbing between the sheets and leaning on one elbow to watch Sophie giving the baby his last feeding of the day, "I'd have agreed to stewed truck tires if that's what he'd wanted. Anything to earn a few brownie points with my future father-in-law!"

"He's mellowing by the minute, sweetheart," Sophie said placidly. "After all, you fell in love with me, so you can't be all bad."

"Speaking of which," Dominic said, tracing a possessive fingertip over her lush breast as she propped the baby on her shoulder and patted him on the back, "how much longer do we have to wait before we can make love again?"

She cast a quick glance at the clock on the bedside table. "About five minutes, I'd say—or as long as it takes me to coax a burp out of your son."

For once, Ryan cooperated.

In the weeks that followed, everyone cooperated. Plans meshed with the ease of well-oiled machine parts slipping into place. The long, hot days of summer were forgotten as autumn slipped into winter. By the end of the first week in December, Jewel Lake sparkled under a thin coating of ice.

The Saturday before the wedding, Dominic brought home a nine-foot-tall Noble fir Christmas tree. That evening, he draped it in colored lights while Sophie hung spun-glass balls from its branches. Ryan supervised the entire operation from his swing by the fire, gurgling approval the whole time. Later, with the baby fast asleep in his nursery, they toasted their first Christmas in their new home with champagne and made love on the rug before the fire.

In a passing nod to tradition, Dominic moved back to his penthouse two nights before he was to meet Sophie at the altar. And instead of Sophie going to stay with her parents, they came to stay with her because their place was so small and it was much more convenient.

"I'll miss you," she whispered, snuggling up to Dominic at the front door of their house just before he left. "This'll be the first time we've slept apart since Ryan was born."

He kissed her long and hard. "And the last, if I have my way."

And then, early on the morning of the day before the wedding, it started to snow. At first, it was nothing more than a dusting that settled lightly on the naked branches of the trees, but by midafternoon the view across the lake was obscured behind swirling flakes as big as dimes.

"What if the cars can't make it up the hill to the church?" Sophie's mother fretted, patrolling back and forth in front of the French doors with Ryan in her arms. "What if the airport has to close and Paul and Jenny miss the whole thing?"

"What if the baby throws up in the middle of the service or the groom doesn't show?" Sophie's father replied, dropping a sly wink at his daughter behind her mother's back. "If it's trouble you're looking for, Anne, there's always plenty to be found."

"Sometimes, Doug," Anne snapped, "I wonder why I married you!"

"Because you had to," he said wryly. "As you're so fond of recalling at the most inappropriate times, you were already expecting the twins and I didn't like the way your father's shotgun was aimed at my backside. Hand my grandson to me, for Pete's sake, before you drop him."

"Don't worry about a thing, honey," Dominic told Sophie when he phoned to say good-night. "I picked up Paul and Jenny at the airport half an hour ago, and I've got a crew on standby to clear the roads tomorrow, if necessary. One way or another, I'll get you to the church on time. You're not slipping through my fingers again."

Sophie didn't lose sleep over any of it. She believed in that old adage about the sun shining on happy brides, and her faith was rewarded. By her wedding morning, the skies arched blue and brilliant over Jewel Lake, showing off Palmerstown in all its dazzling glory. Ryan surveyed the world in wide-eyed wonder from his grandfather's arms while Sophie, her mother and Elaine gave each other manicures.

At four o'clock, two long white limousines drew up outside the front door. There was plenty of room in one for all the trappings a baby might need at his first wedding, and for his grandmother and the maid of honor.

Sophie rode in the other with her father. "You know," he said, clasping her hand in both of his, "I wasn't sure Dominic was good enough for you when all this started. But seeing how happy he makes you, and the way you look at each other, well, I have to say I think you've both done pretty well for yourselves, and that grandson of mine is a lucky little guy."

Sophie hadn't thought it was possible for the day to get any better, but this kudo from her hard-to-please father added the finishing touch. "Don't make me cry, Daddy," she said shakily. "You'll ruin my mascara."

St. Jude's, all dressed up for the season, was packed. Scarlet poinsettias lined the steps leading to the altar. In the narthex, where the wedding party took their places to begin the processional, stood a softly backlit Nativity scene with painted figures of the Holy Family kneeling amid straw brought in from one of the nearby farms.

"They're ready for us," Anne said, straightening the collar of Ryan's blue velvet outfit. "I'll take the baby and go to the pew now."

"And here's your bouquet, Sophie," Elaine whispered.

But beautiful though the white lilies were that Dominic had ordered for his bride, Sophie couldn't draw her gaze away from the crèche. It was simple and unpretentious, but it moved her so profoundly that she feared her mascara was going to be washed away before she took one step down the aisle and past the guests waiting with such an expectant hush for her to appear.

"Sophe?" Elaine gave her a little nudge. "What's up? You're not getting cold feet at this stage, are you?"

"No, but there's been a last-minute change of plan," she said. "Here, Mom, you take my flowers and walk in with Daddy."

"What? Sophie, you can't come down the aisle empty-handed and alone."

"I know," Sophie said, holding out her arms for her son and pressing a kiss to his downy head.

If the guests at the Casson-Winter wedding happened to notice that the mother of the bride carried the bouquet intended for her daughter, they appeared not to care. They were too delighted by the sight of the bride carrying her infant son down the aisle to meet his father at the altar.

"It seemed the right thing to do," Sophie whispered when she reached Dominic's side. "Ryan should be part of this, not just an onlooker. We're a family after all. Do you mind?"

"Mind?" Dominic's voice was suspiciously hoarse. "How could I mind when you look like an angel and a Madonna all rolled into one? Anything you choose to do is fine by me if it makes you happy."

"Knowing you love me and Ryan is all it takes to do that, Dominic," she said.

Dominic reached over and settled his son on his right arm, then placed his left hand firmly around Sophie's sweetly slender waist. "I will love you both for the rest of time, my darling," he promised huskily. "You can count on that."

ACCIDENTAL MISTRESS

CATHY WILLIAMS

CHAPTER ONE

IT WAS raining very hard. Lisa Freeman pulled her coat tightly around her, wishing that she had had the sense to wear something waterproof instead of her thick navy blue coat which now seemed to be soaking up every wretched drop of water and growing heavier by the minute.

She also wished that she had had the sense to take a taxi to the airport instead of foolishly counting her pennies and deciding in favour of the bus, because the bus had been running late, so that she had spent the entire journey agonisingly looking at her watch every five minutes to make sure that she wouldn't miss the plane. It had also deposited her further away from the terminal than she had expected, which had meant braving the rain with no hat, no raincoat, one suitcase and her hand luggage.

She dumped the suitcase on the pavement so that she could consult her watch for the millionth time and also give her arm a rest, and comforted herself with the thought that soon she would be flying away from all this appalling weather. Flying to sunny climes—or at least it would be sunny if the newspaper weather listings were anything to go by. Spain, she had read the day before, was warm. Not hot, because it was, after all, January, but warmer than wretched England with its never-ending clouds and wind and sleet and rain and depressing promises of more to come.

Through the driving rain, the airport terminal loomed

in front of her, and she began to feel a little panicky. It was the first time she had ever been overseas. It was difficult to try and think back to exactly when she had started contemplating a holiday abroad. Certainly, as a child, she never had. Her time had been spent on the road, traipsing behind her parents as her father went from one job to another, settling down in cheap rented accommodation, only to be uprooted just when their lives appeared to be taking shape.

It wasn't something that she had resented—at least not until she was old enough to realise that friends would never be a permanent fixture and that the only company she could rely on was her own.

Both her parents were now dead, but the legacy of the nomadic childhood they had subjected her to must have been more tenacious than she would ever have believed possible, because only within the last three years had that ferocious desire to be in one place, to be safe and secure, eased up sufficiently to allow daydreams of other countries to enter her head.

And until now, at the ripe old age of twenty-four, and in an era of cheap foreign travel, she had still never managed to get around to going anywhere out of the country because there had always seemed to be something better to spend her hard-earned money on.

Every year, for the past three years, she'd told herself that she would treat herself, every year she'd religiously collected a mouth-watering pile of brochures on places ranging from the Mediterranean to the Seychelles, every year she'd given herself a long, persuasive lecture on how much she would dearly love a break abroad, and every year she'd worked out the costs.

It had never been feasible. Anywhere like the Seychelles was out of the question. She'd only got the brochures because the pictures were so alluring. And the Mediterranean, while within the scope of her finances—just—had always been so carefully considered, each pro and con meticulously worked out, that in the end she'd always abandoned the idea. The spot of decorating in the living room surely needed doing before a two-week fling on the Costa del Sol. Then there was her car.

Her car, for the past three years, had always seemed to need some expensive repair work just when her savings had reached their optimum in the building society. She had begun to suspect that the heap of slowly disintegrating machinery had a mind of its own and the mind was telling it to make sure that its driver did not vacation abroad and leave it unused for two weeks.

But this time things had worked out for her.

She heaved the suitcase off the pavement, realising that it felt even heavier now that she had rested her arm for a few minutes, and thought about that envelope that had slipped into her letterbox three months before.

Never having won anything in her life before, and then suddenly winning a trip abroad had made it doubly exciting.

She smiled at the memory of it, stepped off the pavement with her eyes firmly focused on the terminal building ahead of her, which, through the driving rain, was only a blurred outline, and then what happened next became a somewhat confused sequence of events.

Had she slipped on the wet road? Had she stupidly not looked where she was going? Or had the driver of the car been as blinded by the rain as she had?

She just knew that she saw the car bearing down on her, moving quite slowly, although from where she was standing it seemed like a hundred miles an hour, at precisely the same time as the driver saw her step in front of it. There was a horrendous squeal of brakes and she felt a sharp burst of pain as the car swerved, but not enough to stop it from glancing against her leg.

She lay on the ground, unable to move, and all she could think was that she was going to miss her holiday. She had spent every waking hour looking forward to it and now she was going to miss it. She didn't even stop to think that she was lucky—that things could have been worse.

Her leg was hurting badly, with a red-hot pain that made her grit her teeth, and in between the pain she had images of the plane taking off and merrily winging its way to sunny climes without her, and depositing all of its passengers onto the tarmac at the other end, less one, because here she was, lying on the ground, with what felt very much like a broken leg. Or at any rate a leg that wasn't going to do much walking for a little while yet.

She moaned heavily, noticing that quite a crowd appeared to have gathered around her and also that her suitcase had thoughtfully split open and was revealing its cargo of sodden clothes to whoever cared to look.

'I've called an ambulance from my car phone,' a voice said from next to her and she turned her head slowly towards it. 'It will be here any minute.'

The onlookers were crowding in to hear what was said, and the man, whoever he was, made a swift, authoritative movement with his hand. They shuffled back and within a few minutes most of them had dispersed.

Lisa looked at him. He had black hair, plastered against his face because of the rain, although that didn't appear to bother him unduly, and the lines of his face were harsh and aggressive. Aggressive enough to have sent the circle of bystanders skittering away.

He looked down at her and the fuzzy, fleeting impression of someone quite good-looking crystallised into the most amazingly masculine face she had ever seen in her life. His features were hard, his eyes startingly blue, the face of a man born to give orders.

'Are you an airport official?' she asked faintly, and a glimmer of a smile curved his mouth.

'Do I resemble an airport official?' he asked. He had a nice voice, she thought, deep, lazy, with an undertone of amusement running through it that lent it a certain indefinable charm.

She heard the wail of the ambulance pelting towards them.

'I hope it stops in time,' she said with weak humour, no longer thinking of the missed holiday, simply relieved that she would soon be able to have some wonderful, numbing injection to take the pain away, 'or else there will be a few more broken bodies lying around than they'd bargained for.'

The man, who was still bending over her and was not an airport official—stupid question really since she could see his expensive grey suit underneath the flaps of his overcoat and since when did airport officials wear expensive grey suits?—laughed. He had, she thought, closing her eyes and feeling rather light-headed and faint, a rather nice laugh as well. Warm and rich and vaguely unsettling. Or maybe the pain was just making her hallucinate slightly.

Then, through the swimming haze, she heard voices and the sounds of things happening and she felt someone carefully examining her, feeling her leg—but so skilfully that it didn't hurt—and then everything moved quickly.

Painkillers were administered, she was carried by stretcher into the back of the ambulance, still with her eyes closed, and that was all she remembered.

The next time she opened her eyes she was on a small bed, in a small room, with a doctor bending over her and a thermometer sticking sideways out of her mouth.

'I'm Dr Sullivan,' the man said, smiling, while the nurse who was standing next to the bed whipped the thermometer out of her mouth, looked at it, and then shook it so vigorously that Lisa, staring, felt quite faint. 'Do you remember how you got here?'

She dragged her attention away from the nurse, now writing up some notes. 'Hit by a car,' she said with a faint smile. While clutching my battered suitcase, she could have added, and feeling terribly thrilled at the prospect of a holiday abroad.

'You've suffered a fracture to your leg,' the doctor said, 'and quite a few bruises which will look far worse than they feel. I need not tell you that you were very lucky indeed.'

'I would feel luckier if it hadn't happened in the first place,' Lisa said seriously, and the young doctor threw her a bemused look before smiling politely.

'Of course you would, my dear,' he said kindly, straightening up and consulting his watch. 'But unfortunately these things happen. It does mean, however, that you'll be with us for a couple of weeks, while everything knits back together. Nurse will show you where everything is, and I shall be back to have a look at you later on today.'

Nurse was smiling efficiently and as soon as the doctor had left she fussed around the bed, pointing out where the alarm call was, the light switch, the television switch, and then she said, as she was leaving, 'You have a visitor, by the way.'

'A visitor? What visitor?'

The nurse smiled coyly, which only served to deepen Lisa's bewilderment.

'I thought he was your young man, actually. He travelled behind the ambulance to the hospital and he's been waiting here ever since.'

Lisa would have liked to ask a few more questions, including what had happened to her suitcase, last seen baring its contents to all and sundry, but the nurse was already leaving and in her place walked the man who had been bending over her on the road. Her visitor. The man with no name who had taken control of everything until the ambulance had arrived.

She looked at him as he shut the door quietly behind him and felt a quiver of pleasure surge through her. She also felt quite surprisingly shy and tongue-tied and she had to make a huge effort to tell herself that she was being silly.

She was a grown woman now. No longer the child trailing behind her parents, no longer the gauche adolescent with no experience of the opposite sex, no longer the young girl deprived of that network of giggling contemporaries who dropped her eyes and pulled away the minute a boy started taking an interest in her. Those years were behind her now. She told herself that quite firmly and felt better.

She furtively eyed her visitor as he pulled the one and only chair over to her bed, sat down, and proceeded to give her the full benefit of his attention.

'I believe the last time we spoke no introductions were made,' he said, and his voice was precisely as she remembered. Dark and somehow inviting you to give all your attention back to him. Willing it, in fact. 'How are you feeling?'

He had dried out. His hair, she saw now, was thick and black, as were his eyelashes, and he had removed his coat and jacket and rolled the sleeves of his white shirt up to the elbows, so that she could see his forearms, with their sprinkling of fine dark hair.

'Fine,' she said. 'A bit restricted, but I suppose I'll get used to that in due course.'

'I'm Angus Hamilton, by the way,' he said with a smile, stretching out his hand to her and then grasping hers so that she felt her skin tingle, and she hurriedly shoved it away under the starched sheet as soon as she could.

'Lisa Freeman,' she said, blushing slightly. 'Nurse said that you came here after the accident. There was no need, really.'

'Oh, but there was every need.' He sat back in the chair, which seemed far too small to accommodate him. 'You see, it was my driver who knocked you over. I'm afraid he didn't see you soon enough. You stepped out in front of the car and he tried to brake in time. The rest is history.' He was looking at her intently as he said all this, his blue eyes fixed on her face.

'Oh.' She paused. 'I should have used the pedestrian crossing,' she said frankly. 'I was in a dreadful rush, though.' She thought about the wonderful holiday and her frantic preparations and felt a lump of regret swell in her throat. 'What happened to my suitcase?'

'I collected the lot and gave it to the nurse. Were you on your way to catch a plane?'

'Lanzarote.' She was normally quite a self-contained person but right now she felt emotional, with tears brimming up behind her eyes.

'I'm really very sorry,' he said, and to her embarrassment he reached into his pocket and extracted a fresh white handkerchief which he handed to her. 'I have no idea what happens in a situation like this, but I'm sure that some compensation can be reached. I've sorted out this room for you and naturally I shall make sure that whatever money has been lost on your holiday is forwarded to you.'

'Y-you sorted out this room?' Lisa repeated, stammering.

'Your stay here will be private.'

'There was no need.' She looked at him, aghast. It had crossed her mind that being the sole occupant in a room in a very busy hospital was a bit peculiar, but it had never occurred to her that someone else might have paid for it.

'It was the least I could do,' he said, frowning.

'Well, it's enough.' She looked at him firmly. 'I can't possibly ask you for any kind of financial compensation for an accident that was partly my fault and partly the fault of the heavens opening up.' In fact, thinking about it, it was probably more her fault than the fault of the weather because she hadn't been looking where she was going. She had stepped out from between two parked cars, intent on getting to that terminal before her arms gave out completely.

'Don't be a fool,' he told her, but sounded more perplexed and irritated than angry.

'I'm not. I don't want any money from you.'

'And what about your holiday?'

Lisa shrugged and pictured herself lying by a pool somewhere with a tinge of regret. 'It was too good to be true anyway,' she said on a sigh. 'I won it, you see.

I entered a competition in a magazine and won it, so it's not really as though I've lost any money or anything.'

'You won it?' He made it sound as though having to enter competitions to get holidays was something utterly unheard of and she said, defensively,

'I can't afford one otherwise!'

She looked at him properly, not at his physical appearance, but at his clothes, his shoes, his watch, and she realised that, although she had no idea what he did for a living, whatever it was paid well because he exuded that air of confidence and power that came to people who had a great deal of wealth. Not the sort of man that she would ever have met under normal circumstances, nor the sort that she would have wanted to meet. A man destined to lead women up garden paths. From the pinnacle of inexperience, she felt sure that she had summed him up correctly.

'Which is all the more reason...'

'On no condition will I accept money from you! I was in the wrong and I would have a guilty conscience if I felt that I had swindled you out of money.'

'I can afford it, for heaven's sake!' He was beginning to look as though she had taken leave of her senses. 'You're not swindling me out of anything!'

'No.'

'Are you always so stubborn?' he asked, with a faintly mystified look. 'I must say it's a new experience to want to give money away only to find it flung back in my face.'

He gave her a long, slow smile that was so full of unintentional charm that she felt her head begin to swim a little. Had she ever met a man as potent as this one was? she wondered. Was that why he was having this heady effect on her? Maybe the fact that she was stuffed full of painkillers had something to do with it. All that medication would have thrown her system out of focus, might be making her responses go awry. She blinked and looked at him and still felt as though something tight was gripping her chest.

'Do you work?' he asked at last, curiously. 'Does it not pay enough for you to have a holiday now and again? When was the last time you had a holiday?'

'I might be stubborn,' Lisa said tartly, 'but at least I'm not nosy.'

'Everyone's nosy,' Angus said, looking at her with a mixture of curiosity and amusement.

'Oh, are they? What a strange world you must live in, where everyone's nosy and willing to accept money wherever it comes from and whatever the circumstances.'

He looked even more vastly amused by that and she felt the colour crawl up into her face, making her hot and addled. For a second she was the fourteen-year-old girl in her party frock again, anxiously waiting at the front door for her first date to arrive, hoping that he wouldn't notice the packing cases, still only half-unpacked in the small living room, assured by her parents that she looked lovely, but knowing deep down that she just looked plain and unexciting. She was only ever exciting in her mind. In reality, she knew that she was shy and reserved and that any self-confidence she had acquired over the years was really only a thin veneer.

'I hope you're not laughing at me,' she said now.

'Laughing at you?' His dark eyebrows shot up. 'Someone with such admirable principles?'

He *was* laughing at her. He was thinking that she was gauche and ingenuous and naïve and heaven only knew what else besides.

'Well,' she said, trying to sound composed, 'in answer to your questions, yes, I have got a job, yes, I suppose I could just afford to go abroad now and again—well, once a year, anyway—but something would suffer, and as a matter of fact I have never been on a holiday.'

'You have never been on a holiday?' He sounded incredulous and she glared at him defensively.

'That's right,' she snapped. 'Is it so unheard of?'

'Largely speaking, yes,' he answered bluntly. He was looking at her as though he had come across a strange species of creature, believed extinct, which, against her better judgement, made her stammer out an explanation of sorts.

'M-my parents travelled around the country a lot... My father didn't...didn't like to be in one place for too long...nor Mum... They—they liked the feeling of being on the move, you see...'

'How thoughtful of them, considering they had a child. Are you an only child? Have you any sisters? Brothers?'

'No. And my parents were wonderful!' she said hotly. True enough, they had been thoughtless—a conclusion she had arrived at for herself a long time ago—but in a vague, generous way. Was it their fault that she had come along? Out of the blue when her parents were already in their early forties?

'And now your one opportunity lands you up in hospital.' He shook his head ruefully, swerving off the subject with such expertise that she was almost taken aback.

'I think fate is trying to tell me something,' she conceded with a little laugh.

Outside, night had fallen, black, cold, starless. The bright, fluorescent overhead bulb threw his face into startling contrast, accentuating his perfectly chiselled features. She wondered how she looked. The doctor had said that she had a few bruises, which probably meant that her face was every colour of the rainbow, and her hair, which had dried, would look straggly and unkempt.

For a moment she felt a burning sense of embarrassment. It was a bit like bouncing into your favourite film star on the one day of the year when you hadn't put on any make-up and were suffering from a bad cold.

She couldn't remember the last time she had been bothered by her looks—or rather her lack of them. She had stopped looking into mirrors and wistfully longing to see a tall, big-busted blonde looking back at her. She had come through that awkward, insecure adolescence and had emerged a sensible, down-to-earth woman who could handle most situations.

Now, though, lying here on the hospital bed, Lisa felt plain. Too pale, too fine-featured ever to be labelled earthy or voluptuous, hair too brown, without any interesting highlights, breasts too small.

'Where exactly do you work?' he asked.

'Are you really interested? You mustn't feel that you've got to be kind or that you've got to stay here with me for an appropriate length of time.'

'Stubborn,' he drawled, leaning back in the chair and folding his hands behind his head, 'and argumentative.'

Argumentative? Her? When was the last time she had argued with anyone? Not for years. She had always been quite happy to leave the arguing to the rest of the world.

'I am neither stubborn nor argumentative,' she defended heatedly, then smiled a little sheepishly because her tone belied the statement. 'I just wouldn't like you to feel that you should stay here and chat to me simply because your driver knocked me over.'

'I never do anything unless I want to,' he said matter-of-factly. 'I certainly do not profess interest in people unless I am genuinely interested in them.'

'In that case, I work at a nursery.'

'Lots of screaming children?' He didn't look as though the idea of that was in the slightest appealing and she wondered again about his lifestyle. She had never even thought to ask herself whether he was married or not. Somehow, he didn't give the impression of being a married man. Too hard, perhaps, too single-minded. Certainly, if his expression was anything to go by, he didn't have much to do with children and he liked it that way.

'Not all children scream,' Lisa pointed out reasonably. 'And when they do there's usually a cause. Anyway, I work at a garden centre—Arden Nurseries, if you must know.'

She would have to ring Paul and tell him what had happened. He would be as disappointed as she was. He had been thrilled when she had won the holiday. He was always telling her that she worked too hard, but in fact she enjoyed it. She loved plants and flowers. If she hadn't left school at seventeen to enter the workforce, she would perhaps have stayed on and studied botany at university.

'And where do you work?' she asked.

'An advertising firm,' he said. 'Hamilton Scott.'

'How interesting.' She smiled politely. 'And what do you do there?'

'Are you really interested?' he asked, mimicking her. 'You needn't feel that you've got to ask.' He laughed and then said, watching her for her reaction, 'You look charming when you blush.'

His vivid blue eyes skimmed over her face and she didn't quite know what to say in response to his observation. This type of lazy, sophisticated flirting—if that was what it was—was beyond her. But then he worked in advertising, the glamour industry, and she worked in a garden centre, spending half her time with her hands covered in soil and compost, wearing dungarees, and with her shoulder-length hair carelessly tied up.

'I own the company,' he said casually. 'My father founded it, ran it down with a handful of spectacularly bad decisions, and since then I have rebuilt it.' He was still smiling, and underneath the smile she could see the glint of ruthlessness, the mark of a man to be feared and respected and courted.

'How nice,' she said, for want of anything better to say, and he laughed aloud at that.

'Isn't it? It doesn't impress you a great deal, though, does it?'

'What doesn't?'

'Me.'

Lisa went bright red and then felt annoyed because there was something deliberately wicked about his teasing, as though she intrigued him, and not because she was sexy, or stimulating, but because she was novel, a type that perhaps he had never encountered before, or at least never to speak to. In short, in his world of twentieth-century glamour and sophistication, she was a dinosaur.

'I am always impressed when people do well,' she said coolly. 'My boss, Paul, started the nursery with a loan from the bank and a desire to work hard, and he made a success of it, and that impresses me as well. But mostly I'm impressed with people for what they are and not what they achieve. A person might have a nice car and live in a grand house and travel in great style, but if he isn't a good person, caring and thoughtful and honest, then what's the point of all the rest?' She meant it, too, although, hearing herself, she realised that she sounded, ever so slightly, as though she was preaching.

'And money means nothing to you?' He lifted his eyebrows fractionally and again she had the impression of being observed with curiosity and interest rather than the magnetic pull of attraction.

'Only in so far as I have enough to get by.'

'And you don't yearn for more?'

'No. I presume, though, that you do?'

'Not more money, no,' he said slowly, as though the question had never been put to him before. 'I have more than enough of that. What I find stimulating is to scale the heights I have imposed on myself.' He paused and then asked, changing the subject, which was a bit of a shame, because she had found herself hanging onto his every word, spellbound by his personality even if the feeling wasn't mutual, 'How long will you be in here?'

'About two weeks,' she answered. 'With any luck, less. I would prefer to convalesce at home.'

'And you have someone there to look after you? A boyfriend perhaps?' The half-closed blue eyes watched her in a way that made her want to fidget.

'Oh, no,' she said airily, 'not at the moment.' Implying that she was sort of resting in between bouts of heavy romance, which was so far from the truth that it was almost laughable.

Robert, her last boyfriend, had worked in a car firm and had wanted marriage, a terraced house, two point four children and steak every Friday. She had been appalled at the prospect and had broken it off, but since stability was what he had been offering and stability was what she had always desperately wanted she had been puzzled at her immediate response when it had been offered. A break, she had thought then, will do me good. That had been two years ago and the break now seemed to be of a more permanent nature than she had originally intended.

'My friend lives just around the corner, but I can manage on my own anyway.'

'Can you?'

'Of course I can,' she said, surprised. 'I always have.'

'Yes.' He looked at her thoughtfully. 'I expect you have.' He stood up and began rolling down his sleeves, before slipping on his jacket and thrusting his hands in the pockets. 'I find that rather sad, though.'

'Don't feel sorry for me,' Lisa said rather more acidly than she had intended. She shrugged. 'It's a fact of life. It's important to know how to stand on your own two feet.'

'Do you really believe that or is that the consolation prize for a life spent on the road?'

She flushed and looked away.

'Not that that's any of my business.' His voice was gentler as he smiled and said, again, how sorry he was about what had happened. He handed her his card, plain white with his name printed on it, and the name of his company, and his fax number as well as three more work numbers, and an intricate abstract design at the bottom which she thought probably meant something, though what she couldn't think.

'Call me if you change your mind about the compensation I'm more than willing to give you,' he said, and stopped her before she could open her mouth and inform him that she wasn't about to change her mind. 'Money might well mean nothing to you, but after this you could do with a good holiday somewhere and I would be happy to pay for it.'

'All right,' she said, propping the card against the glass of water on the table next to her.

'But you have no intention of availing yourself of the offer...'

'None whatsoever,' Lisa agreed, and he shook his head wryly.

He walked over to the door and then paused.

'I'm away for the next ten days,' he said, 'or else I would come and look in, and please don't tell me that there's no need or I'll wring your neck.'

'I don't think I could cope with a sore neck and a fractured leg as well,' she said, smiling. He had only been with her half an hour, if that, but seeing him standing there, with his hand on the doorknob, his body already half turned to leave, she felt a sudden, inexplicable pang which surprised and disoriented her.

She couldn't possibly want him to stay, could she? she wondered. Wouldn't that be altogether pathetic when he had come on what was, essentially, a courtesy visit? She should never have told him all that stuff about her parents. She seldom shared confidences, least of all with a stranger, and now she felt as though he was walking off with a little bit of her tucked away with him, and she didn't like the feeling.

'Goodbye, Lisa Freeman,' he said. 'You're really rather a remarkable girl.'

'Goodbye, Angus Hamilton,' she replied, and when she tried to add a witty comment to that, as he had, nothing came out. She just continued smiling as he closed the door behind him, and then she pictured him striding along the hospital corridor, gathering admiring glances from all the nurses and female patients, walking purposefully towards his car, ready to be chauffeured back to his apartment or house or mansion or wherever it was he lived, because she hadn't the faintest idea.

The mental scenario so overtook the thought of lying by a non-existent pool in the sunshine that, after a while, she shook herself and wondered whether perhaps she was missing the company of a man in her life rather more than she had consciously thought.

She had her little flat, a modern, one-bedroom place on a nicely kept estate a few miles from the nursery, so that travelling to and from work wasn't too hazardous a prospect in her unreliable Mini. She had her friends, most of whom lived locally, and she carefully tended those relationships because in a world with no family friends became your only standby. She especially treasured them because friendships had been so hard to form as she'd roamed with her parents.

She hadn't felt the absence of a boyfriend in her life. Why, then, had she been so stupidly invigorated by *this* man—someone whom she had never met in her life before, a man who lived in an orbit as far removed from hers as Mars was from the planet Earth?

She hadn't thought that she was lonely, but—who knew?—perhaps she was.

Paul, her boss, had been trying for ages to arrange a blind date between her and his cousin, whose credentials seemed to be that he was a nice chap and supported the same football team as Paul did. Maybe, she thought, buzzing the nurse for some more painkillers because her leg, which had been feeling fine, was now throbbing madly, she would give him a go.

That settled in her mind, she eyed Angus Hamilton's business card and then shoved it inside the drawer of the beside cabinet, where it was safely out of sight and safely out of mind.

Then she got down to the overdue business of ringing her closest friends, who sympathised with her bad luck and promised to visit with magazines and flowers and grapes—what else? She also phoned Paul, who soothed and clucked like a mother hen and told her that there was no need to rush back to work until she was ready, but could she tell him where that number for the delivery firm who were supposed to have delivered some shrubs that morning was, because they hadn't and he intended to give them an earful?

Then she settled down, closed her eyes and spent the night dreaming of Angus Hamilton.

CHAPTER TWO

IT WAS two months before her leg was more or less back in working order. She was confined, by Paul, to doing what he called sitting duties, by which he meant tackling all the paperwork.

'All very restful,' he assured her, then proceeded to produce several box files of papers which were in a rampant state of disorder and left her to it.

But she was busy, and for that she was grateful. Only occasionally did she think about the missed holiday, wondering what it would have been like and promising herself that she would get there. Some time. Possibly even during the summer, although Paul didn't like any of his staff, least of all her because he depended on her, to take their holidays during the busiest months of the year.

Rather too often for comfort, she thought about Angus. She must, she thought, have absorbed a lot of detail about him because he still hadn't conveniently faded into a blurry image. She could still recall quite clearly everything about him, even little nuances which she must have unconsciously observed as he had sat there on the hospital chair talking to her, and stored away at the back of her mind.

She hadn't told a soul about him. Not her friends, not Paul. He was a secret, *her* secret. Instinct told her that to talk about him would give even more substance to his memory.

He wasn't about to reappear in her life, was he? What

was the point of inviting curiosity about someone who had appeared and vanished as quickly as a dream?

She was so utterly convinced of this that when, nearly three months after she had last seen him and weeks after she had joyfully relegated her waking stick to the broom cupboard under the stairs of her flat, she found his letter lying on her doormat she was so shocked that she felt her breathing become heavy and her hands begin to perspire.

She knew who the letter was from even before she ripped open the envelope. The writing was firm, in black ink, and the postmark was London. Apart from Angus Hamilton, she knew no one else in London who would send her a letter.

The message was short and to the point. He was going on a cruise with a few friends and would she like to accompany them. 'Of course,' she read, sitting down on the small sofa in her lounge and tucking her feet underneath her, 'you will not even think of refusing this invitation. Consider it an act of charity on your part to ease my guilty conscience over the accident.' As a postscript, he had added, 'I trust you are now back on both feet.'

Of course, she had no intention of accepting, never mind his guilty conscience. She kept the letter in her bag and pulled it out whenever there was no one around, and then told herself why she had no intention of accepting his invitation.

For a start, it just wasn't *her* to rush off and do something like that. Spontaneity was all well and good, but she had spent so many years being swept along on the tide of her parents' spontaneity, like a leaf constantly caught up in a wind storm, that she had come to realise that thinking things through was a much better alternative. Thinking things through gave coherence to the whole disordered business of living.

When her parents had died, she had been just seventeen and craving for what most girls her age would have hated: somewhere to call a home, somewhere safe where she could gaze out through the window and watch the seasons change and the years pass, without any plans for moving on. She never wanted impulsiveness to dictate her actions. Never, never, never. It was dangerous.

Then, reluctantly, she remembered his face. She remembered the pity she had glimpsed there when she had told him that she was used to standing on her own two feet. Pity at what he saw as a sad little thing.

Her parents had felt a little sorry for her as well. How could they have produced such a quiet, timid version of themselves, when they were so exuberant? They had never understood that spending a year or eighteen months in one place before moving on to a different place with different faces and different landmarks was something that she had found increasingly disorienting.

So she found herself accepting his invitation. It was as easy as that. Something stronger than common sense, some powerful emotional urge, tipped the scales, almost when she hadn't been looking.

She called the number on the letter, spoke to an efficient-sounding woman who informed her that she was Mr Hamilton's personal assistant, and threw caution to the winds before she could work out all the pros and cons and ifs and buts.

And here I am now, she thought three weeks later, paying the price for a few moments of recklessness. Feeling nervous and sick and apprehensive and knowing that I'm not going to enjoy a minute of this. It will be an ordeal.

The only saving grace was that there would be lots of people around on the liner so if she found the company of Angus and his friends too uncomfortable she could always lose herself in the crowd. No one would think her odd. Cruise liners were always full of solitary women.

She closed her eyes when the plane took off and for an instant she stopped thinking about what lay ahead of her and thought instead about the dynamics of something as heavy as this being able to travel in the air. She hoped that all the nuts and bolts were firmly screwed together and risked a quick look through the window, open-mouthed at the sight of land fast disappearing beneath her, to be replaced by an infinity of sky and clouds.

She hadn't felt nearly so nervous about Lanzarote. She wondered whether the captain would turn back and let her off at Heathrow if she asked nicely. Failing that, she could hop it back to England when they landed at Barbados and Angus Hamilton, with his far-fetched notions of applying a balm to his guilty conscience, would be none the wiser. He would shrug those powerful shoulders of his and get on with his holiday knowing that he had tried to make amends and she had rudely refused.

He probably would not even miss the money he had spent on her airline ticket.

But since she knew, deep down, that she would obey the instructions kindly laid out for her in the letter from his secretary she didn't feel much better.

She arrived at Barbados feeling rather ragged and, as the unknown secretary had helpfully advised in the letter which had accompanied the airline ticket, made her way to the transit desk and eventually onto the connecting flight to St Vincent.

This time the scenery through the window was rather

more spectacular. She left Barbados looking down at glittering blue sea and strips of white sand and landed in St Vincent to the same staggering view.

The taxi driver was waiting outside the airport for her—just as the secretary had said he would be—when she emerged with her suitcase and her holdall.

She had worn a loose, flowery skirt and a short-sleeved shirt, but nothing had prepared her for the heat that hit her the minute she was in the open. It was the sort of all-enveloping heat which she had never before experienced in England, not even when it got very hot during the best of the summer days.

There was a great deal of activity outside the airport, taxi drivers waiting hopefully by their cars to take tourists to their destinations, but there was nothing frenetic about any of it. No one seemed to be in any kind of rush to get anywhere.

'Where are you taking me?' she asked the driver as he cruised off at one mile per hour.

'Not far.' He looked at her in the rear-view mirror, showing two rows of gleaming white teeth. 'The hotel, it just along the south coast. Very nice place.'

Lisa lapsed into silence to contemplate the scenery, leaning forward slightly in her seat with her hands nervously clutching her bag.

Outside, the marvellous vista unfolded itself. Everything was so lush and green, heavy with the scent of the Tropics. She half wished that it would go on for ever, partly because it was so beautiful and partly because she was beginning to feel sick and nervous all over again.

What on earth was she going to say to him? She wasn't accustomed to mixing in sophisticated circles. She would be completely at a loss for witty, interesting topics of discussion. After one hour, she would no longer be the novelty which had amused him months ago in a hospital ward. She would revert to being just an ordinary young woman without much of a talent for being in the limelight.

The taxi driver pulled up outside the hotel, which appeared to comprise a collection of stone cottages strewn with well thought out randomness amongst the lush vegetation.

He helped her with her luggage and she was almost sorry to see him depart into the distance, driving away as slowly as he had arrived.

She looked around her helplessly, noticing with a sinking heart the other visitors at the hotel who seemed to waft past her, laughing in their elegant attire. Would they all be on the liner? she wondered. Was this hotel one of the stops between ports? She had no idea. She glanced down at her clothes self-consciously, and when she raised her eyes to the reception desk there he was, standing there, just as she remembered him.

He was wearing a pair of light olive-green trousers and a cream shirt and he was, thankfully, alone.

As he approached her, she noticed how the other females strolling through the foyer darted glances at him, as if they couldn't help themselves. 'I thought,' he said, 'that you might back out at the last minute.'

He was taller than she remembered. From a supine position on a hospital bed, it had been difficult to get a good idea of his height, but now she could see that he was over six feet tall, and already bronzed from the sun, so that his eyes looked bluer and more striking than she remembered.

'I take it that your leg has now fully recovered from the experience?' One of the hotel staff hurried up to gather her luggage and she followed him as he checked her in.

'Yes, it has,' she said to his profile, watching as he smiled and then turned to look at her. 'Thank you very much for...this.' She spread her arms vaguely to encompass everything around her. 'It was very kind of you.'

He was watching her as she said this, with a small smile on his mouth, and it was a relief when the porter interrupted them to show her to her room, which wasn't a room at all, but in fact one of the stone cottages with a thatched roof and a marvellous view overlooking the sea. Blue, blue sea and white, white sand.

'Was your trip all right?'

'Oh, yes, thank you very much; it was fine.'

'There's no need to be quite so terrifyingly polite,' he said, amused.

'I'm sorry. Was I?'

'You were.' He folded his arms and looked at her. 'You haven't been invited along to be thrown to the sharks.'

'No, I know that.' She tried a smile.

'That's better.' He smiled back at her. 'You're here to enjoy yourself. That's why you came, isn't it?'

'Yes, of course.' Her replies sounded stilted and she glanced around her for inspiration.

'I'm surprised that you came at all, I don't mind admitting. After what you had told me at the hospital about not accepting charity, I thought that you'd run a mile at the prospect of a holiday at my expense.'

She resisted the temptation to apologize once again, but his remark filled her with dismay. Had he been banking on her not coming? Was that it?

'I...accepted on impulse,' she admitted, looking down

to where her fingers were twined around the handle of her bag.

'I'm glad to hear it. Now,' he continued briskly, 'I expect you're feeling rather tired. He leaned against the doorframe and stared down at her. 'There's absolutely no need for you to emerge for dinner. They will happily bring you some food here if you'd rather just stay in and recover from the trip. Tomorrow morning we're hoping to set sail.'

'Yes, of course. Your secretary did list the itinerary. I have it here in my bag somewhere.' She plunged nervously into the bowels of the tan bag and several bits of paper fluttered to the ground, accompanied by a half-empty packet of travel tissues, several sweets, her traveller's cheques and her book, of which she had read very little on the plane.

They both bent to recover the dropped items at the same time and their heads bumped. Lisa pulled away in embarrassment, red-faced, cursing the bag, which was much too large really and had somehow managed to attract quite a bit of paraphernalia in a way that her normal tiny one never did.

'S-sorry,' she stammered, burning with confusion as he handed her the packet of tissues and the sweets, which she stuffed back into the bag.

'There's no need to be nervous,' he told her gently, kneeling opposite her.

'I'm not nervous!' She was kneeling too, her hands resting lightly on her thighs, her face close to his in the twilight which seemed to have descended abruptly in the space of about ten minutes. She remembered reading that about the Tropics. There was no lingering dusk. Night succeeded day swiftly.

'Of course you are,' he said, as though surprised that

she could deny the obvious. 'You're going on a fortnight's vacation on a yacht with a group of people whom you've never seen in your life before. Of course you're nervous.'

She sprang up as though burnt and looked at him in confusion.

'Yacht? I thought it was a cruise.'

'Yacht, cruise, where's the difference?' He stood up and frowned. 'Are you all right? You look a bit peculiar.'

'Look,' she said steadily, even though she could feel herself shaking, 'please could you clarify what exactly this holiday is? Are we or are we not going on a liner?'

'Liner? What are you talking about?'

'In your letter, you said that we would be cruising... I was under the impression...'

His face cleared and he laughed. 'That we were going on a cruise ship? No. I think there's been a misunderstanding. No cruise ship. As far as I'm concerned, there wouldn't be much point in getting away from the madding crowd only to surround yourself by the same madding crowd, just with a change of faces. In fact, I can't really think of anything worse; don't you agree?'

No, she wanted to shout in frustrated panic, I most certainly do not agree! And I can think, offhand, of one thing that's infinitely worse. It involves a group of friends, on a yacht, none of whom I know, and *me*!

'I—I would never have come...' she stammered in horror.

'If you'd known? You coward.'

'I really don't think that I can... There's been a mistake... It's not your fault... I should have asked, but I didn't think... I'm sorry, but...'

'Don't be foolish.'

'I am not being foolish!' Now she was beginning to feel angry as well as horrified.

'Look at me.'

She did. Reluctantly.

'Do I look like someone who is thoughtless enough to invite you out here, throw you into the deep end and watch you struggle with a smile on my face?'

Pretty much, she thought to herself.

'No, no, I'm sure you're not, but really...I don't relish the thought of... I shall be an intrusion...' Her voice was beginning to fail her under the sheer horror of the enormous misunderstanding that had landed her out here, a million miles away from home, like a stranded fish out of water. She tried to remind herself that she was capable of enormous self-control, a legacy of having spent much of her childhood living in her own world, but something about his commanding, powerful presence made it difficult.

'Nonsense. An intrusion into what?' He didn't give her time to answer. 'Let me have the key. It's ludicrous to be standing out here having a lengthy discussion when we could be inside.'

She handed him the key and barely glanced around her as they entered.

'An intrusion into your privacy,' she explained in a high voice that bordered on the desperate. 'You will be with your friends...'

'What do you think of the cottage?' He turned around from where he had been standing by one of the windows, looking out into the black velvet night, and faced her.

'Super. Wonderful,' she said miserably.

'You've never had a holiday in your life before, Lisa.' His voice was soothing and gentle, the voice of someone dealing with a child, a child whose wits were just a little scrambled, and who needed to be taken by the hand and pointed in the right direction. 'You told me so yourself. When I booked this holiday, I thought about that. Why don't you put aside your reservations for a moment and try and see the next two weeks for what they are? An eye-opener.'

'You invited me along because you felt sorry for me.' She spoke flatly, acknowledging the suspicion which had been there at the back of her mind from the beginning.

He shrugged and stuck his hands into his pockets.

'That's putting it a little strongly.'

'But basically that's it, isn't it?' She could feel tears of anger and humiliation springing to her eyes and she tightened her mouth.

'I felt that I owed you something for having deprived you of a holiday abroad. I wouldn't call that a crime, would you?'

He had a seductive way of talking. Great intelligence and great charm could be a persuasive combination. She sighed and suddenly felt overwhelmingly tired.

'Not a crime, no. But you must understand that...'

'You're apprehensive.'

'I wish you'd stop finishing my sentences for me,' she said crossly. 'I'm quite capable of finishing them myself.'

He smiled, not taking his eyes off her. 'You're scared stiff at the thought of mixing with a group of people you've never met in your life before.'

'Wouldn't *you* be?' she flung at him.

'No.'

'Well, excuse me while I just fetch out my medal for bravery from my bag!' she snapped, and he moved towards her, which she found, inexplicably, so alarming that she had to make an effort not to retreat to the furthest corner of the room.

'That's much better,' he drawled, standing in front of her.

'What's much better?'

'A bit of fire instead of passively assuming the worst before you've even tested the water. Now, tomorrow,' he continued, before she could think that out. 'We normally breakfast in our rooms. Less effort than trying to arrange a time to meet in the restaurant area. We're going to meet at the yacht at twelve-thirty. Shall we come and collect you or would you rather have a look around here and make your way to the boat yourself?'

'How many will there be?' she asked, frowning.

'Just six of us. One of my clients who also happens to be a close personal friend, his wife and their daughter, and a cousin of sorts.'

'A cousin of sorts?'

'We're related somewhere along the line but so distantly that it would take for ever trying to work the link out.'

'Oh.'

'And you still haven't answered my question.'

'Question? What question?'

He grinned with amusement and shook his head slightly. 'My God, woman, will you take me there some time?'

'Take you where?'

'To the world you live in. It certainly isn't Planet Earth.'

'Thank you very much,' Lisa said stiffly, her face burning.

'And that's not meant to be an insult,' he told her,

still grinning. 'I do wonder how you ever manage to stand on your own two feet, though.'

Had he, she thought, remembered every word she had told him all those months ago?

'I'll meet you at the yacht,' she said, ignoring the grin which was now getting on her nerves as much as his fatherly, soothing manner had earlier on.

'Fine.' He gave her directions, told her how to get there, asked her again whether she wouldn't be happier if he came to collect her, so that she wondered whether he thought that she would abscond the minute his back was turned for too long, and then gave her a reassuring smile before strolling out of the cottage.

She sat heavily on the bed and contemplated the suitcase on the ground. Why had she come here? What had possessed her? She had wanted to put to rest, once and for all, the gnawing suspicion she had always had that she was dull, unexciting, too willing to settle for the safe path in life. Her parents, her vibrant, roaming parents who'd somehow landed themselves with a daughter who had never shared their wanderlust, would have smiled at her decision. Was that why she had done it? Yes, she thought wearily, of course it was. Except that a few vital things hadn't been taken into the equation.

Now she was here, the guest of a man whose ability to reduce her to a nervous, self-conscious wreck she had forgotten, a man who felt sorry for her, who saw her, even though he had not said so in so many words, as someone who needed a little excitement, someone whose eyes needed opening. From the fast lane in which he had been travelling, he had seen her standing on the lay-by and had reached out and yanked her towards him.

It was a gesture her parents would have appreciated, but, sitting here, she realised that the fast lane was not for her. Yes, he had been right; she was afraid. It was something which he could never in a million years understand because she sensed that fear of the unknown was not something that ever guided his actions. He was one of those people who saw the unknown as a challenge.

Whereas for her, she thought, running a shower and letting the water race over her skin, the unknown was always equated with anxiousness. The anxiousness of leaving one school for another, of meeting new people, of tentatively forging new bonds only for the whole process to be repeated all over again. And every time it had seemed worse.

How could an accident of fate have thrown her into a situation like this?

The following morning, after she had had her breakfast, which, as he had advised her, had been brought to her in her room, she removed herself in her modest black bikini to the beach, selected a deserted patch and lay in the sun, covered with oil.

She would just have to make the best of things. She had decided that as soon as she had opened her eyes and seen the brilliant blue skies outside.

It was impossible to have too many black thoughts when everything around you was visually so beautiful. The sea was crystal-clear and very calm, the sand was white and dusty and there was a peaceful noiselessness about it all that made you wonder whether the hurried life back in England really existed.

She stretched out on her towel, closed her eyes, and was beginning to drift pleasurably off, safe in the knowledge that she wasn't due to meet the yacht for another four hours, when she heard Angus say drily, 'I thought

I'd find you here. You'll have to be careful, though; the sun out here is a killer, especially for someone as fair-skinned as you are.'

Lisa sat up as though an electric charge had suddenly shot through her body and met his eyes glinting down at her seemingly from a very great height.

He was half-naked, wearing only his bathing trunks, and a towel was slung over his shoulder.

Reddening, she looked away from the powerfully built, bronzed torso and said in as normal a voice as she could muster, 'I know. I've slapped lots of suncream on.'

'Very sensible.'

He stretched out the towel and lowered himself onto it, then turned on his side so that he was looking at her.

'What are you doing here?' she asked, keeping her face averted and her eyes closed behind her sunglasses. He was so close to her that she could feel his breath warm on her cheek when he spoke. It was as heady as breathing in a lungful of incense and she hated the sensation.

'I came to your room and you weren't there. I assumed that you'd be out here. Beautiful, isn't it?' He reached out and removed her sunglasses. 'There. That's better. I like to see people when I'm talking to them.'

'May I have my sunglasses back?'

She looked at him and found that he was grinning at her.

'Don't put them on.'

'Is that an order?' she asked primly, and he laughed.

'Would you obey me if it was?'

'No.'

'I didn't think so,' he commented lazily. 'Which is why I'll hang onto them for the moment, if you don't mind.'

She glared at him and he laughed again, this time a little louder.

'What a range of expressions you have,' he said, with the laughter still in his voice. 'From nervousness to fear, to stubbornness, to anger. How old are you?'

She debated informing him that it was none of his business, reluctantly reminded herself that he was her host and was owed some show of good manners, even if he constantly managed to antagonize her, and said coolly, 'Twenty-four.'

'Caroline is nineteen but she seems decades older than you.'

'I'm sorry, I have no idea who you're talking about.' And frankly, her voice implied, I'm not in the least interested, believe it or not.

'The distant cousin.'

Lisa didn't say anything, but her heart sank. The picture in her head was beginning to take shape. The powerful client with his pretentious wife and their precocious child, Caroline, with her well-bred sophistication, Angus, and herself.

'Why are you here?' she asked politely. 'Don't you need to see to your boat? Make sure that all the sails or ropes or whatever are all in the right place?'

'I do hope that there's no implied snub in that question?' he queried with lazy amusement.

'Nothing could be further from my mind.'

'What a relief.' His voice was exaggeratedly serious and she wondered whether the real reason he made her so nervous was that she loathed him. Intensely.

'Actually,' he said, sitting up with his legs crossed and staring down at her, 'I wanted to find you to make sure that you were all right.'

'Why shouldn't I be?' Lying flat on the towel with

only her bikini for protection against those gleaming, brilliant eyes made her feel so vulnerable that she sat up as well and drew her knees up, clasping her arms around them.

'You seemed shaken by the prospect of enforced captivity with the man-eating cannibals I've invited along as guests on this trip.'

'Very funny.'

'No, not terribly,' he said, very seriously now. 'I wanted to find you so that I could reassure you that they're all very nice, perfectly likeable people before you had to confront them.'

'Thank you,' she replied awkwardly. She kept her eyes firmly fixed on his face, stupidly aware of his animal sex appeal. 'I'm sorry I was so garbled last night; it's just that I was taken aback.'

'I realised,' he said drily. 'And I wish you'd stop apologising.'

'Sorry,' she said automatically, and then she smiled shyly, dipping her eyes and gazing out towards the horizon, where the sharp blue line of the sea met the clear blue sky. It was easy to understand why some people believed that to venture beyond that thin blue strip would be to fall off the edge of the earth.

'Did you tell your boss that you were coming on this holiday?' he asked idly, and she could tell that he was staring at her even though she wasn't looking at him. She couldn't tell, though, what he was thinking. Could anyone do that?

'Not exactly,' Lisa admitted. 'I told him that I needed to have a break, that I was tired. Well,' she continued defensively, 'it was more or less the truth.'

'Rather less than more,' he said blandly. 'Did you think that he wouldn't understand?'

'Something like that.' He would have fallen down in shock, she thought with amusement. He knew how much she liked the safe regularity of her job, of her life; she had told him as much when he had first interviewed her years ago for the position.

'I don't want to take on someone who's going to stick around for six months, get bored, and look for more glamorous horizons,' he had said.

'Not me,' Lisa had replied. 'There will be no urge to hurry away from this job to look for another one. I have my flat, my roots are here and my job will be for as long as you want me.'

Over the years he had come to know her well enough to realise that her most prized possession was her security. She had bought her small flat with the money which had been left to her on her parents' death, from insurance policies which had secured her future, and there she had been happy to stay, content in her cocoon.

'Because you're not given to taking risks?' Angus prompted now, casually, and she threw him a sharp glance before returning her gaze to the infinitely safer horizon.

'I guess,' she said in a guarded voice.

'Have I invaded personal territory here?' His tone was still light and casual, but she knew that he was probing. Probing to find out about her. It was probably second nature to him, and in her case his curiosity was most likely genuine, the curiosity of someone whose life was so far removed from her own that it really was as though she came from another planet.

'Why are you so secretive?' he asked. He reached out and tilted her face towards his and the brief brush of his fingers on her chin was like the sensation of sudden heat against ice. It was a feeling that was so unexpected that she wiped his touch away with the back of her hand.

'I'm not.'

'You should try listening to yourself some time,' he remarked wryly. 'You might change your mind.'

He stood up abruptly, shook the sand out of his towel and slung it back over his shoulder. Mission accomplished, she thought, except there was a vaguely unsettling taste in her mouth, the taste of something begun and not quite finished.

'Sure you know how to get to the yacht?' he asked, and she nodded.

'So, I shall see you around twelve-thirty.'

'Yes,' she murmured obediently, collecting a handful of sand in the palm of her hand and then watching it trail through her fingers.

'And you won't take flight in the interim?' He raised one eyebrow questioningly and then nodded to himself, as though she had answered his question without having spoken. 'No, of course you won't, because, whatever you say, you're as curious now as you are reluctant, aren't you, Lisa?' He stared right down at her and she felt his eyes blazing a way to the core of her. 'This is a new experience for you. You won't regret it. Trust me.'

Then he was gone. She watched him walking slowly away, his lithe body unhurried, and she thought, Are you so sure? Because I'm not.

CHAPTER THREE

WOULD she have been different if she had led a normal kind of life? It was a question Lisa had asked herself over the years and she had never come up with a satisfactory answer.

She was very self-contained, she knew that, just as she knew that most people found her aloof and far too composed for the sort of superficial small talk that made the world go round. Very few had glimpsed the lack of self-confidence behind the composure.

Looking back now, she was old enough and mature enough to realise that this was the real disservice which her parents had unwittingly done her. They had given her variety but her only point of stability had been them, when in fact, at the age of eight or twelve or fourteen, she had needed much more than that. She had needed the stability of a circle of friends, people with whom she could try out her developing personality, learn to laugh without the ridiculous fear of somehow getting it wrong, discover trust without the limits of time cutting it short before it had had time to take root.

When she found herself thinking like that, she never blamed her parents. She accepted it as a *fait accompli*. She had never lacked love; it had not been their fault that she had not been able to fall in with their never-ending travels from one place to another with the same thrill of possible adventure lurking just around the corner.

Her father, a biologist, had been consumed with a

seemingly never-ending supply of curiosity. Nature, in all its shapes and guises, had fascinated him. He would take on a job as gamekeeper to acres of wilderness simply for the satisfaction of exploring the minutiae of the forest life.

Once, for eighteen months, he had worked on the bleak Scottish coastline and had indulged in a brief fling with marine biology, a love which had lived with him until he had died.

That, she thought now, had been the worst time. She could remember having to catch the bus to school in weather that never seemed to brighten. She could remember the smallness of the class, the suspicion of the other children who had treated her with the unconscious cruelty of long-standing village occupants towards the outsider. It had been hard then keeping her chin up but in the end she had made some friends.

Now she could see that it had done nothing for her social self-confidence.

She walked towards the yacht and she could feel the muscles in her stomach tighten just as they had done all those years ago, every time she had walked through the doors of yet another school building.

Everyone else had arrived. She could glimpse the shapes on the boat, the movement, and she hurried a bit more. Someone must have called out something to Angus, because he appeared from nowhere, half-naked, and came down to the jetty to greet her.

The air of restless vitality that seemed to cling to him swept over her and she licked her lips nervously.

'I hope I'm not late,' she began, and he reached out and took the suitcase from her, smiling with that mixture of dry irony and knowing amusement that made her feel so gauche and awkward because it always seemed to imply that he was somehow, somewhere, laughing at her.

'We have a timetable of sorts,' he drawled, 'but we're under no obligation to stick to it. One of the great advantages of a holiday like this. We would have waited for you.'

He turned towards the yacht and she followed him as he threw polite remarks over his shoulder and she made obliging noises in return.

Her legs were feeling heavy and uncooperative, but she took a deep breath and clambered aboard the yacht behind him, allowing him to help her up but then withdrawing her hand as soon as she was there.

From behind the relative protection of her sunglasses, she saw the small circle of people—his guests.

The whole situation inspired the same churning, sinking feeling she had had as a child when she had had to stand up in class, the newcomer, and introduce herself. She made a show of smiling and was swept along on a tide of introductions.

Liz, Gerry, their nine-year-old daughter Sarah, Caroline. They were relaxed, stretched out on loungers on the deck of the yacht, wearing their swimsuits and sipping drinks.

'Now,' Angus said, in that slightly amused, very assured voice of his, 'I shall show Lisa to her cabin.' He turned to her. 'What would you like to drink? We thought we'd have a few drinks here and some lunch before we leave.'

'Anything,' she said obligingly, still smiling, although her jaw was beginning to ache.

'I shouldn't leave the choice open,' Liz said, laughing. 'My husband will simply see that as an invitation to try out one of his lethal homemade cocktails on you and you'll be staggering around before you're halfway finished.'

Gerry laughed and protested at this, and the smile on Lisa's face became a little less forced.

'In that case, I'll have a glass of fruit juice, if I may.'

'Very wise,' Liz said.

'If a little dull.' Caroline hadn't spoken since the introductions had been made. She had stretched out her hand, seen no need to smile and had promptly returned to what she had been doing as soon as the formalities had been concluded: baking under the sun in a turquoise bikini that left very little to the imagination.

Lisa looked at her cautiously, uncertain how to respond to this.

If she was related to Angus, then it was difficult to see the resemblance. Her hair was white-blonde, her eyebrows dark. The only similarity rested on the fact that they were both staggeringly good-looking.

'Don't confuse her,' Angus said amicably, but with an edge of warning in his voice. 'Go back to your sunbathing.'

She removed her huge sunglasses to reveal two very vivid green eyes and glared at him sulkily.

'I'm sure she doesn't need you to look after her,' she said, narrowing her eyes and shifting the direction of their gaze away from Angus and towards Lisa. 'Do you?' She stared assessingly at Lisa.

'I don't need anyone to look after me,' Lisa said politely, feeling embarrassed. 'I've always found that I'm quite capable of doing that myself.'

'Spoken,' Gerry said approvingly from behind her, 'like a true twentieth-century woman.'

Lisa turned towards him with relief.

'All the more surprising, coming as it does from a true eighteenth-century chauvinist,' Liz teased.

They laughed at this shared joke and from behind her adventure book Sarah, without raising her eyes, grinned in the same way an adult would have grinned at the immaturity of two children.

'Now, my dear, what kind of juice would you like?' Gerry, a slightly overweight man in his forties, got up and patted his stomach absent-mindedly.

'Is there a choice?' Lisa asked, surprised.

'Orange, grapefruit, naturally, but also watermelon, mango, pineapple and portugal.'

'The portugal is wonderful,' Liz said helpfully.

'Is it? I'll try that, then. Thank you. I've never had it before.'

'Shall I take her away now?' Angus said from behind her, his voice dry. 'Or is the juice discussion due to continue?'

'Don't be so sarcastic, Angus,' Liz told him, which made him laugh, and Lisa felt his hand on her arm as he escorted her away from the deck and towards her cabin.

The yacht was huge. Immense. And expensively furnished. Lisa looked around her with open curiosity.

'Does it belong to you?' she asked him as he paused in front of a door and pushed it open.

'Yes.' He looked at her. 'Do you like it?'

'Oh, yes, it's wonderful,' she breathed. 'Like a house! I never knew that boats could be as big as this. Not private ones, at any rate.' She flushed, and looked at him. 'You think I'm odd, don't you?' she said with a little laugh, edging round the door and into the room, a difficult manoeuvre because the doorway was very small, and she felt the brush of his body against hers long enough to make her feel a little breathless.

He didn't seem to notice a thing. He walked in, deposited the luggage on the bed and then leaned against the doorframe.

'You were right, anyway,' she continued hurriedly. 'It's all an eye-opener.'

'Good,' he said, sticking his hands into the pockets of his shorts and continuing to look at her. Indolent, amused.

'I'll unpack now, shall I?' The question was supposed to remind him that he had guests above and that she wanted him to leave, but he didn't.

'Was it as bad as you'd feared?'

She was beginning to hate the way he saw her as vulnerable, but she shrugged, and he mimicked the gesture.

'What does that mean?'

'Liz and Gerry seem very nice people,' she said.

'And Caroline?'

'She doesn't look anything like you,' Lisa said, for want of anything else. She hadn't liked Caroline. She hadn't liked the cool condescension she had heard in that precisely manicured voice and she found such perfect looks slightly unsettling.

'You'll have to excuse her,' Angus said, ignoring the remark. 'Caroline is here as a favour to her parents. They find her a bit of a handful.'

'And they think that you might be able to straighten her out?'

'Nothing quite so optimistic, I assure you. Nor am I in the business of straightening people out. Don't let anything she says upset you, though.'

'Thank you for the advice,' Lisa said, coolly, because

he made her sound as though she was a complete walkover and for some reason she was sick of having him treat her like a minor. 'I'll bear it in mind.'

'It's not meant to be an insult,' he said, raising his eyebrows, and she reddened.

'Of course it isn't,' she replied quickly. 'And I'm grateful for it. Thank you.'

'Oh, for God's sake.' He ran his fingers through his dark hair and shot her an impatient glance from under his lashes. 'Will you stop being grateful?'

'But I am.'

'Unpack,' he said, and she impulsively went towards him and rested her hand on his arm for a fraction of a second.

'Don't be angry.'

'Then stop acting as though I've done you the most enormous favour in inviting you here. As I recall, you weren't exactly grateful to me when you found out that this was to be a cruise of six people and not six hundred.'

'I know that,' Lisa admitted. 'But whether it was six or six hundred it was still very kind of you to think of me enough to issue the invitation.'

'I was responsible for ruining your original holiday,' he reminded her. 'Have you forgotten?'

'But most people wouldn't have taken the trouble to recompense me in the way that you've done.'

'Most people haven't got the money to do it,' he murmured, looking at her, watching her, she knew, for her reaction.

'What do you want me to say to that?'

She looked at him and looked away, feeling her breathing thicken and hoping that he was as unaware of it as she was aware. Why did she react to him like this?

Was it just an understandable physical response, or was it an intellectual one?

She was sensible, she knew, so why did her body ignite the minute he came close to her, when common sense told her that he was off limits? Off limits in the way that screen stars were off limits? They lived in different worlds and only a fool would try to unite the two.

It wasn't as though he was attracted to her. When he looked at her, there was no sexual appraisal in his eyes. She wasn't his type. She was just another average face. Her features were regular, except for her lips, which were too full as far as she was concerned. Her figure was neat but not extraordinary. Her hair fell in a clean swoop to her shoulders and that, like the rest of her, was unexceptional. Background material. If her head could tell her this, then why couldn't her body act accordingly?

'Is that why you felt nervous about this? Because you imagine my wealth puts you at a disadvantage? Or was it because you're unsure of yourself?'

'I'm not unsure of myself!' Lisa denied. 'You hardly know me. How can you say that?'

Her heart was beating quickly. She wished that she hadn't tried to detain him. She wished that she had just let him leave and got on with her unpacking, as he had commanded.

He didn't say anything, which was as telling as if he had argued the point.

'This is none of your business,' she muttered, folding her arms and looking away. 'You invited me here and I came, but *I* am none of your business.'

'Do you ever open up to anyone?' he asked, with less amusement in his voice and considerably more impatience. 'Or do you hide yourself away and let the rest of the human race get on with it?'

'Please may I unpack now?'

'Once you've answered my question. I'm interested.'

'You're curious.'

He shrugged and continued looking at her, waiting for her to answer.

'I don't like being an object of curiosity,' she said stubbornly. Nor, for that matter, do I like being an object of pity, she added to herself. 'It doesn't matter to me how much money you have,' she said, prodded into speech by his silence. 'I've already told you that money makes no difference to what a person's worth. But, of course, here...' She paused and flashed him a quick look from under her lashes. 'Here, I am the odd one out. I don't know the responses I'm supposed to make. I've never had to learn them.'

'How about just being yourself?'

'I thought you didn't like that, because being myself means being secretive and reserved?'

Touché.' He grinned at her with appreciation and she blushed. He straightened his long body. 'Now I'll leave you to unpack. Come up when you're ready and wear a swimsuit.'

'I was going to.'

'Not,' he amended, back to his dry amusement, 'that I want you to think I'm trying to give you orders. I don't want you to see me as a dictator.'

Then how would you like me to see you? she asked herself once he had sauntered off. As a benefactor? As a man? She unpacked quickly, not giving much thought to that choice. She didn't want to see him as a man; she didn't want to catch herself thinking too hard about the supple strength of his body or the disarming charm of his conversation.

She emerged a few minutes later to find her juice next

to an empty lounger, inconveniently next to Caroline, and a platter of sandwiches in the middle. They were all eating, making desultory conversation. Liz, who was reading a book, looked up to say something, then returned to the more drowsy pastime of soaking up the sun.

The heat made everyone lazy. It was impossible to be energetic when it was so hot.

Lisa lay back on the lounger with her broad straw hat shielding her face and surreptitiously looked at Angus, who was talking to Gerry in a low murmur, from the looks of it about work because there was a certain amount of animation to their conversation. He was leaning forward slightly, his elbows resting on his knees. She observed the curve of his back and the latent power of his body and had forgotten about Caroline until the other woman said, *sotto voce*, 'You two took rather a long time down there, considering Angus was just supposed to be showing you to your cabin.'

Lisa didn't say anything, but her body tensed and she looked at the fair-haired beauty warily.

'What were you and he up to?' Caroline laughed a little but there was something hostile behind the laughter.

'Up to?' Lisa asked, puzzled. 'Nothing. Why?' Does he get up to things with women the minute he's alone with one for longer than three seconds? she wanted to ask.

Caroline gave an elegant shrug and fixed her expression to one of indifference. 'Just wondered.' She began to apply some more suntan oil with the unhurried thoroughness of someone who knew that her body was worth looking at. 'It's just,' she continued, when Lisa had hoped that the conversation had been terminated, 'that Angus needs protecting.'

That almost made Lisa laugh, but she managed to say, with some incredulity, 'He does? I'm sorry but I hadn't noticed.'

She stretched out with her towel behind her head and her feet crossed at the ankles. Liz and Sarah were chatting in bursts. After a while they got up from their loungers and strolled out of sight and their voices drifted on the breeze, snippets of information which Liz was trying to impart about tropical fish.

'He explained why he invited you here,' Caroline said languidly, in a low voice.

'Did he?'

'Something about George running into you in the Jag at the airport. He felt sorry for you so he asked you here.'

'It was very kind of him,' Lisa said, for want of anything less inflammatory. She had to remind herself that she was a guest and that outbursts of anger were not advisable, but she could feel her fists clenching and she had to take a few deep breaths to steady herself.

'Yes, it was, which is why I wouldn't want you to take advantage of the fact.'

'I wish you'd get to the point,' Lisa said tightly. 'If there *is* a point. I'm not very good at playing games.'

Caroline turned on her side so that she was facing her and propped her sunglasses on her head. The green, feline eyes, when they looked at her, glittered like emeralds.

'The *point* is that Angus is a very desirable catch and I wouldn't like you to get any ideas in that direction.'

The accusation was so bald that for a minute Lisa stared at her speechlessly. Then she said, without any pretense at politeness, 'In that case, let me just set your mind at rest. He's perfectly safe from *me*. I couldn't care less how eligible your cousin is and I find your remarks insulting.'

Caroline's lips thinned and she seemed on the brink of continuing the subject, but with rather more venom now, when Liz and Sarah returned from their stroll around the deck and general conversation took over. The sandwiches were passed around, drinks were topped up, voices grew louder, as did the laughter, and as soon as the anchor was lifted Lisa removed herself from her lounger and went across to where Liz was standing, holding onto the rails of the boat, with the wind blowing her hair back.

Angus and Gerry were sailing it. They were both highly experienced at it; they had learnt together a long time ago. They had known each other for years, Liz told her, even though Gerry was eleven years older than Angus. Her voice was kind as she provided background material which Lisa only partially heard. She was far more absorbed in the spectacle of the ocean slipping past them and in what Caroline had said to her in that cutting, derogatory voice of hers.

The worst thing was that she could see the logic behind the accusations. Angus was, there was no doubt about it, a good catch. It was surprising, really, that he hadn't been netted before, but if what Liz had told her was anything to go by, then he would hardly have had the time to cultivate any sort of family life. Building empires, it appeared, didn't leave much room for a wife and children and winter evenings in front of the fire.

'He's out of the country most of the time,' Liz was confiding, when Angus said from behind them,

'I do hope you're not talking about me. It's very bad

manners, you know, to discuss your host behind his back.'

Liz laughed and turned to him. 'You should be flattered. I've only said good things about you!'

'Is that true?' Angus turned to Lisa with a slow smile. She felt her heart begin to thud and remembered what Caroline had said.

'Yes, it is,' she said lightly, smiling back at him but finding herself quite unable to meet his eyes straight on. 'She says that you're a very hard worker and that you travel a lot.'

'You make me sound like an ant.' He laughed, turning to Liz. There was a warm empathy between the two of them and Lisa felt a brief pang of envy. Her experience of men was limited and she had certainly never had an easy rapport with any of them. On the whole, she was tense in their company, only relaxing slowly, certainly unable to joke in the semi-flirtatious manner that Liz did.

'I think,' Liz said over her shoulder as she sauntered off to be with Gerry, 'I can spot a few basic differences!'

'She's great fun, isn't she?' Lisa said, looking at him.

'We go back a long way.'

'I envy that,' she heard herself say wistfully, and she abruptly turned away so that she was leaning over the rail, staring down at the sea. She hadn't meant to confide in him. It had just emerged, without prior thought, and now she felt a little awkward.

'The fact that she goes back a long way with me?' Angus asked, laughing.

'No, that wasn't what I meant...'

'I know what you meant.' He leaned over the rail alongside her, their arms almost touching.

'How long before we reach land?' she asked, and he

laughed again, as though he had read her mind and knew that she was trying to change the subject.

'Not very long.'

'Do you do this every year?'

'Social *savoir-faire* isn't something you're born with. It's something that's cultivated. As you said, you just never had to learn the art. I don't suppose there's a great deal of it needed if you work in a garden centre.'

'My father worked in Scotland for a while, but the sea was nothing like this.'

'No, I don't imagine it was. What did he do?'

'He was a biologist.'

'And your mother?'

'A biologist's wife.'

'And you were the biologist's child.'

'That's right. There's something very fierce about the sea in Scotland, even when it's calm.'

He shrugged and she could feel his eyes on her. 'The water here is very blue, very inviting, but you'd be stupid to imagine that it doesn't conceal its own dangers.'

'I heard Liz telling Sarah all about it.'

'I'm surprised you weren't sent to a boarding school.'

'I know a bit about tropical fish, from when my father was going through his marine biology phase. He had books on the subject. You think that I had an unhappy life, but I didn't and I would have hated boarding school.'

'Did your interest in plants come from your father?'

'I suppose so. I've never really thought about it. Why are you asking me all these questions? I don't ask you any.'

'Feel free to.' His lazy charm swept over her and she had to steady herself on the rail before she could turn to face him, shielding her eyes from the sun with the palm of her hand.

'I don't want to. I'm not interested.'

She glanced behind him to where Caroline was still basking like a lizard in the sun. Was she asleep? It was difficult to tell although the large, dark sunglasses were turned in their direction.

'Where are Liz and Sarah?' she asked.

'Liz is with Gerry and Sarah is below deck somewhere. There are limits set as to how much time she spends in the sun. Why didn't you go to university?'

Lisa sighed. She wished that he would stop prying, trying to discover what made her tick, treating her like a specimen under a microscope.

'If you must know,' she said shortly, 'my parents died and it was all I could do to climb through my A levels. I couldn't even contemplate university. I just needed to get some sanity back into my life and having a house and a job represented that.'

'Understandable,' he murmured.

She replied, in a tart voice, 'Oh, I'm so glad you see it like that. It makes me feel much better.' She swept her hair away from her face and narrowed her eyes against the glare of the sun to look at him. 'And what makes *you* tick?' she asked angrily. 'You're so keen to point out all my little inadequacies. Does anything make *you* feel inadequate?'

'No,' he said lazily, 'I don't think so.'

'How lucky you are, then. Swanning through life in your chauffeur-driven car, flying from one important meeting to another, jet-setting across the globe. I expect there are lines of beautiful women queuing up for you as well? To complete the picture, so to speak?'

Now that she had worked herself up to self-righteous

indignation, she would have been more than prepared to carry on with the conversation until the cows came home, but the yacht began slowing down. Bequia, their first port of call, was approaching, and she hadn't even noticed, with her back to the sea and her mind seething with anger.

Liz emerged, with Sarah in tow, her face wreathed in delighted smiles as she walked unsteadily towards them, and Angus said to her, under his breath, 'Don't think that this conversation is finished.' He wasn't looking at her when he said this, nor was there any amusement etched on his face.

'Is that a threat?' She wouldn't have said it if she had thought about it.

'A promise.' He pushed himself away from the railing and began preparing the yacht for docking.

Caroline didn't move until the yacht was moored; then she lazily stood up, shaking her hair, which obediently fell back into place, and slung a silk shirt over her swimsuit.

She must, Lisa thought, be quite accustomed to this sort of thing, because she didn't look in the least excited—or perhaps excitement was something that she no longer indulged in at the ripe old age of nineteen.

Two nights in Bequia, Liz was telling her. She was to bring next to nothing from the yacht. If she needed anything, she could always go and get it, but really they would just be sunbathing, swimming and indulging in the odd water sport, if energy levels permitted.

Lisa was glad of the advice. She slipped on a pair of shorts and a halter-neck top and managed to stuff everything she wanted into her holdall, so that she didn't emerge from her cabin five minutes later laden down with three times more than she needed.

They took two taxis to the hotel. She travelled in one with Liz and Sarah, and Angus, Gerry and Caroline took the other. She spent the short journey chatting to Sarah about the plant life, just as her father used to do with her when she was a child. She described what grew where and why and what harboured which sorts of insects. Facts which she had thought she had forgotten sprang back to memory and she surprised herself with the extent of her knowledge.

The taxis disgorged them outside the hotel, a secluded plantation estate, set in rambling orchards of tropical fruit trees.

She looked around her and couldn't imagine that anything, anywhere in the world, could surpass this ageless, discreet magnificence. It was the unspoken epitome of what money could buy. Liz and Gerry had been before, and were pointing out things that had changed, and Caroline, after a quick glance around, stretched gracefully and announced that she was off to the pool.

'Too much sun is bad for you,' Sarah said, holding her mother's hand, and Caroline scowled.

'Bad for *you* maybe, but not me. Oh, no, I intend to return to England with something to show for two weeks in the Tropics!'

'You already have a marvellous tan,' Liz said, and Caroline nodded smugly in agreement, then vanished towards her room.

'And what about you?' Angus turned to Lisa, and she smiled politely.

'I think I shall go to the beach. Why don't you come with me, Sarah?' She looked away from those piercing blue eyes to the little girl.

'Only for half an hour,' Liz warned, and they both nodded.

'Worries too much, I think,' Sarah said as they strolled along the beach, collecting shells.

'Of course she does! She's your mother. Mine used to worry about insect bites and poisonous plants.'

When she delivered Sarah back to the hotel, she found herself, much to her disgust, peering in the direction of the pool to see whether Angus was there. I don't care where he is, she told herself, but if he's by the pool then I shan't feel as though I've got to be on the lookout.

He wasn't there. Then she hated herself for wondering where he was.

She wished that she could block him out of her mind totally; she wished that she could look at him without feeling nervous; she wished that she could converse with him in a natural manner and then relegate everything he said to some compartment at the back of her mind. Somewhere safe and unthreatening.

She set off for the beach, which was virtually isolated, and lay down on her towel with her eyes closed.

When she next opened them, she was staring at the deep blue cloudless sky. She thought that if a painter ever decided to capture this on canvas the painting would be awful. The lines too defined, the colours too vivid and surreal, everything shimmering with an intensity that defied belief.

With a small sigh of contentment, she headed out to the water, which was nearly as warm as bath water, and struck out, swimming far and fast, leaving the beach behind, then turning round and treading water and looking back at the island from her vantage point.

The view was breathtaking. White sand, like powder, clear water lapping lazily up to the shore and falling back. The sound of the breeze and the sea was like a whisper, rising and sinking and never-ending.

She swam back in, slower, lazier, and surfaced to see Angus standing by her beach towel, his arms folded and a scowl on his face.

'What the hell do you think you're doing?' He waited until she was close before saying anything, and his voice was low and sharp.

'Wh-what? What do you mean?' Lisa stammered in confusion. She bent down to scoop up her towel and he pulled it away from her and flung it on the sand.

'Answer me!'

'Swimming!' she said hurriedly, backing away. 'What's the matter? Is something wrong?' She was beginning to feel a little lost. Why was he so angry? Had something happened? Had she done something wrong without realizing it?

'Look around you. What do you see?'

Lisa looked around her and then back at him. 'I don't see anything.'

'Precisely. The beach is empty, isn't it?'

'Yes.' What was he trying to say to her? 'It must be later than I thought. What time is it? I left my watch back at the hotel when I came out here.'

'The time is immaterial. What I want to know is what the hell you think you're doing, swimming when there's no one around.'

'Oh.' She nearly smiled in sheer relief. 'The water is quite safe,' she continued, noticing that his expression was still as black as thunder.

'And what if you had got yourself into trouble out there?'

'Well, I didn't.' She was beginning to feel resentful. 'I'm a strong swimmer.' The sun had left the sky. Twilight was creeping up.

'What kind of answer is that?'

'Look,' she said in a placating voice, 'I'm sorry you were worried, or concerned, or whatever, but I was quite safe.' She took a deep breath and said what she felt ought to be said, because she was tired of being treated like a child. 'My welfare isn't your concern. I'm a big girl now and I can take care of myself.' She sat down on her towel, painstakingly spreading it out so that it was flat, and hoped that he would go away and leave her alone.

To her dismay, he sat down next to her and now she began to feel conscious of her swimsuit.

'Oh, you are, are you?' he said tautly.

'That's right. I am. Now perhaps we should head back in.' She started to get up and he reached out, hardly shifting his position at all, and circled her wrist with his fingers.

'What do you think you're doing?'

'I'm not ready for you to go,' he said, unperturbed. 'You tell me that you're a big girl, that you can look after yourself. Well, Lisa, why don't you prove it?'

CHAPTER FOUR

'PROVE it?' Lisa said. The shadows were gathering around them. The angular lines of his face had softened, but his expression was unreadable, although she could still see the glitter in his eyes and the faint curve of his mouth.

'That's right.' He still hadn't let go of her hand and the warm pressure of his fingers on her skin was sending her into a state of muted panic. She wasn't sure what he wanted from her; her mind just couldn't seem to work its way round what his words had implied.

'I don't know what you mean; I don't know what you're talking about. Please,' she said in a half-whisper. 'I'm really not accustomed to…this…'

'To what?' His voice sounded faintly surprised, but she knew that he wasn't. He had left his hand where it was because he knew that it threw her into a lather and he was enjoying the spectacle of that, like a cat playing with a mouse, not necessarily with a view to a kill, but certainly with a view to having a bit of fun.

'I think we ought to go back inside…'

'Why? I'm your host. Can't you relax enough to have a conversation with me?'

She laughed nervously, but she could feel her heart beating rapidly and the blood rushing round her body, making her hot and tense. She'd had few men in her life, no serious relationships, never a kiss that made her freeze or a hand that inflamed—nothing, nothing that could have prepared her for the surge of sheer yearning that swept through her and left her feeling as though she had been hurled blindly in every direction by a tidal wave.

The vehemence of the emotion left her winded but suddenly strong enough to speak.

'Of course I can, if that's what you want. It's just that I'm beginning to feel a little cold and uncomfortable out here.'

'Cold?' He shot her a disbelieving look. 'I can't possibly understand that. It's still pretty hot out here, and besides...' he paused and allowed his eyes to wander along her body before returning to her face '...your swimsuit covers you up so thoroughly that I doubt you can be feeling even remotely cold.'

It was the first time that he had assessed her physically, and she wondered whether she had imagined it. Had she? She convinced herself nervously that she had, and tried to hang onto her composure.

'You and Caroline seemed to be having a very cosy conversation on the yacht earlier on,' he said lazily. She felt him stroke the soft flesh of her inner wrist, a gesture which to her confused mind seemed shockingly intimate.

'Were we?'

'What was she telling you?'

'I can't remember.' Lisa lowered her eyes. Her body felt as though it was being kept in a state of unnatural stillness; one false move and it would fall apart.

'Of course you can,' he said mildly. 'Tell me.'

'I'd rather not. I'd rather we went back to the hotel. I'd rather you let go of my hand.'

'And I'd rather do neither of those things. So it would appear that we're at a stalemate, wouldn't it? I don't like stalemates.'

The silence thickened around them, and eventually

she said, reluctantly, 'She's concerned about you. If you really want to know, she thinks you need protecting.'

'Does she? Protecting from what? Or should I say... from whom?'

'From me,' Lisa said huskily. She couldn't look at him when she said this and she resented the fact that the information had been torn out of her.

He let go of her hand and looked at her thoughtfully. 'I think that perhaps Caroline and I should have a little talk. Cousin to cousin.'

'No! Please don't.' Lisa looked at him miserably. 'I wouldn't want to land anyone in trouble and anyway, she had your interests in mind. I would probably have done the same thing if I had been in her position.'

'I don't imagine that you would,' Angus said flatly. 'The problem with Caroline is that she can't resist men. She flits from one relationship to another and she assumes that every other woman is motivated in the same way that she is. She's on this cruise recovering from a broken engagement. The third she's called off in the space of under two years.'

'Please don't say anything...'

'You say that you would have done the same thing if you were in her position, but you're nothing like her, are you?'

'No,' Lisa mumbled. Incoherence was beginning to set in. Her mouth felt dry, and she could hardly get the words out without a great deal of effort. 'She's very beautiful.'

'I'm not talking about looks,' he said impatiently. 'Do you flit from one man to another?'

'I suppose not.'

'Have you ever had a lover?'

She could feel his eyes on her, staring at her intently, and the darkness gave them a brooding look.

'That's none of your business.' The thought of her virginity sent a flood of shame coursing through her, making her face burn. What right did he have to ask these questions? What right did he have to assume that he could ferret information out of her simply because he happened to be her host?

'Have you?'

She hesitated for a fraction of a second and knew that the silence had spoken the words she couldn't bring her mouth to formulate.

'I've been meaning to,' she said defensively. 'I take relationships seriously. I've never found anyone... Of course, I've had boyfriends!'

'Naturally.'

She sprang up and began walking away. Her eyes were hurting from tears which she refused to shed, tears of embarrassment and mortification.

'There's more to being an adult than having sexual experience!' she shouted at him, stopping to turn around and surprised to find him on her heels.

'Of course there is.'

'And stop agreeing with me! Do you think I don't realise you're being patronizing? I'm not a fool!'

'No. You're not.'

'There you go again.'

'Would you prefer me to argue with you?'

'It might make a pleasant change! It might make me feel more of a person and less of a charity case!'

He shook his head and then held her by her shoulders and said, enunciating very carefully, 'Stop telling me how sorry I feel for you. How can there be room to feel sorry for you when you're so busy feeling sorry for yourself?'

'That's not true.'

He gave her a little shake, as though it was the only way to make her listen to him, but she was listening, listening with every pore in her body, listening to sounds in her mind and the silences between what he was saying.

'You can't put your past behind you,' he told her. 'It follows you around like an albatross tied to your neck. You came here on a crazy impulse, but now that you're here you can't shed your inhibitions, can you?'

'Why are we talking about this? What has this got to do with anything? I don't want you analysing me.'

'Because you're afraid that I might be more truthful than you'd like?'

'Because it's none of your business—I keep telling you.'

'And I'm telling you that it is.'

They stared at each other and the stillness of the night was like a weight pressing down on her, turning her to fire.

'Why do you think that you're not beautiful?' he asked huskily. His hand moved to the curve of her neck. 'You make a point of saying that money doesn't determine a person's worth. Do you think that appearance does?'

She didn't know what to say. His voice had changed; it was thicker, less controlled, and he was breathing quickly—as quickly as she was. She could see the rise and fall of his chest and she watched, fascinated, unable to move, unable to speak.

His fingers coiled into her hair and he pulled her towards him, bending down slightly so that the features of his face became indistinct. She closed her eyes and thought that she should run away, as fast as she could, but her muscles felt sluggish, and besides, she wanted what was going to happen. She wanted him to kiss her.

Their lips met and she groaned with what was either denial or desire—maybe both. She could feel his hard body pressed against her and his hand moved to mould the small of her back.

His lips, at first gentle and persuasive, moved with a hunger now that sent a shudder through her. His tongue found hers, exploring deeper and harder, and her breasts, pushing against his chest, ached to be touched.

This was the naked face of passion—something she had only ever read about in books. She had never realised the real depth of her innocence until now, when desperate yearning reached out from inside her and spiralled through every vein in her body. It frightened her but at the same time she couldn't stop herself.

Her head fell back as his tongue trailed a burning path along her neck. He was breathing thickly and unevenly and she whimpered as he peeled the shoulder straps of her swimsuit from her shoulders and pulled them down to her waist so that her small breasts were exposed.

She didn't try to pull away. She whimpered in shock and pleasure as his hand cupped one breast, caressing it, while his thumb rotated against the nipple until it hardened to his touch.

She had small breasts but her nipples were large and sensitive and seemed to throb under the impact of his fingers. Her body was trembling, reduced to nothing more than a receptacle for sensations never experienced before.

He bent to take one nipple into his mouth, sucking hard on it while his hands worked her swimsuit still lower. In the process, wrapped around each other, they sank to the sand. Did he let her go for an instant? He must have because now there was a towel beneath her and she had no idea how it had got there. She was so consumed by his lovemaking that she really thought nothing could break through the flaming haze around them, not rain or thunder or even an army of soldiers on the beach.

His fingers played with her breasts as he kissed the bare column of her neck, caressing them, teasing them, squeezing them. She had to feel the wetness of his mouth and she pushed his head lower so that he could take the throbbing peaks into his mouth.

She was prepared to go the whole way; she thought that the intensity of blinding desire would be enough. It was only when she felt his hand move against her thigh, parting her legs, that her thought processes, which had been frozen into inactivity, churned back into life.

She could see herself now and it was like looking down at herself from a great height. Ordinary little Lisa, in pigtails and with her schoolbooks under her arm, ordinary little Lisa in her first party dress, so nervous that she felt sick, ordinary little Lisa lying on a beach with her natural reserve scattered to the four winds, making love with a man who had succumbed to some bizarre, passing whim.

His hand slipped underneath her swimsuit and she wriggled frantically, with all the energy she could muster, pulling away from him.

It's not enough! she thought.

'What's wrong?' His voice sounded slurred and disoriented and seemed to reach her from a long way away.

'I can't do this!' she whispered hoarsely, and he

pinned her back so that she couldn't do what she wanted most to do, which was to spring to her feet and run away.

'You can't stop now,' he grated savagely, and she looked away from him.

'You're hurting me.'

He let her go and she stayed where she was, shivering, as though it had suddenly turned bitterly cold.

'I'm sorry—' she began, but he cut her short with a snarl.

'Forget it.'

'I didn't mean to...I didn't mean for anything like this to happen...'

'I said, forget it.' He stood up and began walking away and she hurried to keep pace with him.

It hurt with a pain that was almost physical to think of their lovemaking. When was it ever going to end? She had come over here on impulse, she had gone against everything she had instilled into herself, and, as if that wasn't bad enough, she had committed the cardinal sin of being attracted to Angus Hamilton.

She had recognized the attraction, but what she had failed to do was acknowledge the power it had over her. Her inexperience had opened doors which should have remained shut. Was that what had turned him on? Her inexperience? The moonlight? A combination of both? It certainly hadn't been a meeting of minds, because in the naked glare of reason it was easy to see that a meeting of minds for them was out of the question.

She glanced across at the dark figure striding back towards the plantation and felt another wave of horror wash over her.

'You're angry, I know,' she said timidly, and was relieved when he didn't jump down her throat, although he hadn't slowed down and didn't appear to be listening to a word she said. 'It's just that I'm not the type of person who...'

'There's no need for a lengthy post-mortem, Lisa,' he said coldly, not looking at her.

'I'm not giving you a lengthy post-mortem, I just want to explain...'

'So that you can feel better about what we did?'

'No.' That's exactly why, she thought miserably. She wanted to explain things so that she could put the incident behind her and justify her behaviour to herself. She wished that he would slow down.

He must have read her mind because he stopped abruptly and looked down at her, his face hard.

'Then do explain why, if it makes you feel better. I'm all ears.'

'Something happened—I don't know what...'

'I think it's called sexual attraction.'

'Whatever.' She couldn't say it; she couldn't allow herself to admit that something as untamed as sexual attraction had turned everything she believed in on its head.

'No, not *whatever*. Sexual attraction. Say it!'

'All right! Sexual attraction. Is that better?' She looked at him defiantly. 'I was caught up in the moment and I'm sorry but I let myself...do something that I would never have done if I'd been thinking straight.'

'How terrible,' he snarled. 'The end of the world.'

'Not the end of the world, no!' she said angrily, hating him for the power he had over her and hating herself for her weakness. 'But a mistake. I just want to say that I made a mistake and if I led you on then I apologise.'

'Apology accepted,' he said tersely. He began walking off again and she had to half run to keep up with the pace of his long legs.

Of course he was still angry. Why shouldn't he be? As far as he was concerned, she had sent out signals only to retreat hurriedly when the moment of decision had come. Women, she thought resentfully, didn't play those sorts of games with him. For him, the step from mutual attraction to lovemaking was a simple one. There were no questions about love, or the rightness or wrongness of what they were doing.

'It won't happen again,' she told him. The hotel lights were up ahead, and with every step closer to civilisation her feeling of stupidity over what she had nearly done grew.

'No, I'm sure it won't.'

She took a deep breath. 'The fact is that you're just not my type.'

He paused outside the hotel and looked down at her. His face was coldly curious.

'And who is? What is your type?'

'I don't know...' Lisa whispered uncomfortably. Not you, she thought. Not someone as good-looking, as clever, as wealthy, as unassailable as you, that's for sure. Not someone who will dally with average little me because the opportunity is there, and then move on to more glamorous types the minute the opportunity arises.

How many women with more convincing credentials had tried to get him to put a ring on their finger? she wondered. Self-confident women with coy smiles and loud voices and perfect faces...

'Come on,' he said, with a humourless, assessing smile. 'Surely you can do better than that?'

She didn't say anything.

'Shall I help you out?' he asked politely. 'You don't jump into the sack with a man simply because you're attracted to him. Oh, no, that would be too easy. What you want is a man who is going to guarantee undying love, and maybe then, if he fulfils the rest of the ridiculous criteria you've laid down in that head of yours, you might consider doing something spontaneous.'

'That's not fair!'

'Except,' he continued, ignoring her outburst, 'there are no guarantees in life.'

'I know that! I don't expect guarantees! You just can't accept the fact that you've been turned down by a woman. I bet it's something that's never happened to you in your life before!'

She could feel the colour burning in her cheeks. 'You've always been able to take what you wanted, and you thought that you would be able to take me as well. You're angry because your pride has been hurt, and you're trying to blame me for it, trying to insinuate that the reason I won't sleep with you, the reason I couldn't, is because of my inadequacies. The simple truth is that I was swept away because, yes, I *am* inexperienced, and, yes, you *are* an attractive man—but I just didn't find you attractive *enough*.'

His eyes narrowed. Had she said too much? Every word had been more or less the truth, but, considering she had been trying to pour oil on troubled waters, she hadn't made a wild success of it, had she? He looked as though he wanted to kill her.

'I'm sorry,' she muttered. 'I shouldn't have said that.'

'Why not? It's always a good idea to clear the air.' He threw her another freezingly polite smile. 'Points us in the right direction, makes sure that things are black and white, with no awkward grey bits in between.'

'Yes,' she said uncertainly. She met his stare briefly and licked her lips.

'So now we can carry on as though nothing has happened.'

'Yes.' She nodded with relief. That, she thought, would be best. To pretend nothing had happened. That way she might be able to shove the memory of his hands on her body, the memory of the way she had felt, into the background, and get on with things in the only way she knew how.

He turned on his heel and stalked off, and after a while she headed back to her room and sank down on the bed with a sigh.

She shut her eyes and saw them together on the beach, her heart racing, her body straining for his. She would never have believed she was capable of anything like that. When she'd been growing up, her life had been controlled to a large extent by her parents, by their constant travelling. When they had died, she had taken control for the first time. She had bought her flat, she had found her job, she had made sure that everything in her life fell into place the way she wanted it to.

She had never really sat down and thought about what sort of man she would end up with, but she had known he would be as unthreatening to her as every other aspect of her life.

She dressed slowly for dinner, and she wondered anxiously whether she would be able to look at him without flinching, without her face telling the world what had happened. She wondered whether her voice would sound normal when she spoke.

But when she joined the others in the dining room, and glanced warily at him as she sat down, their eyes met for the briefest of moments across the table and she realised with relief and a strange sort of disappointment that it would all be easy. Nothing happened, those remarkable blue eyes said icily. You can go back to your hiding hole.

This is life, she told herself, and it is what you wanted. Remember?

Still, it was a shame. She would never have this chance again, this opportunity to see places so beautiful that paradise became reality instead of just a word conjured up on the back of a holiday brochure.

Mustique, which prosaically took its name from the French word for mosquito but had none, small enough to walk around inside a few hours, exclusive to the point of absurdity, flowed into Canouan, with its hidden coves and beaches, which flowed into Mayreau. Then the Tobago Cays, with water so clear that you could see every grain of sand underneath. Lisa snorkelled there, for the first time in her life, and saw underwater scenes that were unimaginable unless seen at first hand.

She saw more islands—beautiful little emerald and sapphire blobs in the middle of the ocean, picture postcards for her to remember from photographs and memories in the years to come.

But as the yacht sailed down the glorious Grenadines everything was so overshadowed by Angus's presence that it all seemed to slip past in a blur.

Not that things didn't carry on as normal, on the surface, because they did. She smiled and laughed and chatted and grew browner under the sun and pretended that Angus's remoteness wasn't affecting her. She watched him from under her lashes and saw everything even when her attention was apparently somewhere else. It was as though her whole body was sensitised to such a degree that everything he said or did, every nuance of every action, was filed away in her mind.

With only a couple of days of the holiday left, she found herself yearning to return to the refreshing normality of her life with its pleasant routines.

Angus intended to dock the yacht off Grenada and they would spend their final night there before flying back to London.

They had breakfast aboard the yacht the following morning, which was lovely. Lisa relaxed on her chair and stared out at the horizon and at the turquoise water. The sun, even at that hour, was already hot. She was as brown as Caroline now and the colour suited her. Her face, she knew, seemed more vibrant, the chocolate-brown of her eyes less uninspiring. She had the sort of colouring which, when its usual pale shade, did not stand out, but which, when tanned, made her look exotic. She half closed her eyes and let the conversation drift around her.

'Super little market...fresh fruit...'

'Must get some souvenirs for the girls at the bridge club...'

'Grand Anse beach is lovely; do you remember it? Shall we meet for lunch at the hotel there? Have a swim...?'

'Darling, have I put on a ghastly amount of weight? Be honest...'

The voices floated over her head. They were making plans but she was too pleasantly lulled by the sun to make any contribution. The sun made everyone too lazy to discuss anything with much vigour, even the planning of the day—their last day.

It was only when she heard Angus mention her name that her mind refocused and she sat up abruptly to find him looking at her.

'I'm sorry,' she said, flustered. 'I missed that.'

Liz made some remark about the sun and its soporific effect, to which Gerry illogically replied that if his financial director hadn't sorted out that tax business for the accountants his head would be on the block, and Lisa repeated, 'What were you saying?' She didn't think that he had addressed her at all for days on end, not directly.

'Caroline is going to spend the day on the beach,' he said casually, and there was an odd look in his eyes, as though he was being very careful not to reveal too much. 'Since it's our last day here and you've never been this way before, I've decided to take you on a tour of the island. You'll be fascinated by the plant life over here.'

'Thank you, but really, I'd rather just laze around.' You've decided? she thought. And so I must fall in? Like the last time?

'I'm sure Lisa would much rather do her own thing than trek around the island with you in this heat.' Caroline's voice, which seemed disembodied because her eyes were hidden, as usual, behind her sunglasses, was sharp.

'I'm sure Lisa is quite capable of making up her own mind, Caroline,' Angus drawled, his eyes on Lisa's face. 'You can't leave the island without seeing the plant life,' he told her blandly. 'Unless, of course, you have other, personal reasons for not coming with me?'

'No, of course not,' she said brightly, with a laugh. There had been a soft challenge in his voice and now he smiled the smile of the victor, knowing that he had trapped her.

'Good. Then that's settled.' And he relaxed back with his hands clasped behind his head, while Liz resumed the conversation, asking interested questions about her job at the garden centre, and Caroline sat stiffly back with a frown on her face.

'My mother is interested in plants as well,' she said, dipping into the conversation and silencing everyone in the process. 'Does a lot for the Chelsea Garden Show. Has a permanent stall there every year. Such a bore. I like flowers but I simply don't see the point of labouring over them, not when you can pay someone else to do it.'

'You don't see the point of labouring over anything, Caroline,' Angus pointed out, looking at his watch.

'Why bother when you don't have to?' she asked, and Angus didn't bother to answer.

Caroline's conversations always seemed to take the same course. She stated, everyone listened, and if none of her statements seemed to provoke lively discussion, then it didn't seem to trouble her because she simply returned to whatever it was she had been doing in the first place. Every now and again she had mentioned her ex-fiancé, with an air of boredom, and Lisa got the impression that very little roused her out of her self-centred little universe, in which she always had the starring part.

Very little except Angus, perhaps. Did she have a crush on him? She did look at him quite a bit when she thought that no one was watching, but then so did most women, she had noticed. He had the sort of dark, arresting face that attracted stares.

The yacht docked and amid the general chatting, clutching of hats and impossible arranging of times when they would meet and where Angus stalked off in search of a car to hire.

'What fun for you,' Liz said, beaming, 'driving around the island with Angus, looking at all those wonderful plants and flowers. What a clever idea of his!'

'Very clever, yes,' Lisa said, trying to look enthusiastic.

She watched wistfully as Liz, Gerry and Sarah bustled off, leaving Caroline behind, elegant in silk shorts and a sleeveless shirt and a large straw hat which shaded all of her face.

'Aren't you going with them?' Lisa asked politely.

'I just wanted a few words,' she said, and Lisa sighed.

'Look...' she began, and then stopped and thought, Why am I apologising for this arrangement? It's hardly as though I engineered the thing.

'No, *you* look. Look at yourself. I suppose you think it's started raining money, being invited along with Angus on a trip round the island. I suppose you imagine that your boat's come in...'

'No, of course—'

'You, in your dowdy little department-store outfits! He's out of your reach.'

'You're getting hold of the wrong end of the stick, Caroline...' she began again, on the brink of apologising and then thinking better of it.

'No, I'm not! It's obvious that you have a crush on him and I'm just doing you a favour by telling you to steer clear.'

'Why should you care?' Lisa asked curiously, and Caroline flushed. 'He's out of your reach as well,' she continued gently. 'I'm not interested in him and I'm certainly not some kind of fortune hunter.' She paused and frowned. 'I understand why you feel protective of him, but Caroline, he just sees you as a child; he—'

'Why don't you mind your own business?' Caroline said, white-faced.

'Liz is waving for you to go.' It was a pointless argument. 'You'll get left behind.'

'You're not in our class.'

'Nor would I want to be,' Lisa informed her with a rush of anger.

'Just so long as we understand one another.' She trounced off, her blonde hair whipping back from under the hat as she half ran, her arms folded.

Lisa waited, and after twenty minutes Angus returned with a bunch of keys. For someone who had pushed her into a corner, he didn't seem terribly thrilled at the prospect that lay ahead. His face was grim.

'We needn't go on this trip,' she said nervously, 'if you've changed your mind. I'm very happy to spend the last day on the beach.'

'I'm sure you are,' he replied tersely, angry with her for reasons which she couldn't begin to fathom but which hardly promised an enjoyable and carefree day. 'I'm sure you'd love nothing better than to be in company instead of condemned to enforced isolation with me, but that's just too bad.' He walked off towards an ageing blue car, opened the passenger door for her and then installed himself in the driver's seat.

'Have you brought a map?' she asked, after a while. 'Honestly, Angus,' she said, when he still hadn't started the engine, 'I don't think this is a good idea.'

'It's a damn good idea,' he contradicted her, in a voice that bordered on aggressive. He looked at her and she fell silent. 'I haven't brought a map, in answer to your question. I've decided we'll just take the inland road and see what happens.'

Lisa didn't say anything. She didn't relish the thought of an aimless drive with him, possibly getting lost somewhere along the line, but she also didn't relish the thought of arguing the point with him.

'Cat got your tongue, Lisa?' he asked, driving off at a leisurely pace which she suspected had more to do with the car than with him. 'Or have you been stunned into silence at the adventure that lies ahead?' He gave a dry laugh and she remained silent. She could cope with nerves, but something about him made her uneasy. What lay ahead? She didn't know and she didn't much want to find out.

CHAPTER FIVE

LISA stared out of the window. There was no air-conditioning in the car and even with the breeze sifting through her hair she still felt hot and sticky and vaguely plastered to the seat with perspiration.

He was, she thought, in a foul mood, and she wondered why he had bothered to invite her along in the first place, especially knowing that she hadn't wanted to come, and why, when she had offered to forget about the whole trip, he had ignored the suggestion. And she had no idea how to break the silence between them. She had never been much good at aimlessly chatting about nothing in particular, and besides, the brooding harshness of his face was putting her off.

At least he seemed to know where he was going, though, even without the help of a map. He had been here before. Who knew? Maybe he had driven this same route with another woman, some poor woman who had now been relegated to the past.

She glanced sideways at him, felt that familiar lurching in her stomach, and hurriedly directed her attention back through the car window.

They had left the coast behind now, heading towards the centre of the island, over mountains and along narrow, uneven and very windy roads.

She stopped thinking about him and started paying attention to the scenery unfolding outside. After a diet of sand and sea, she was unprepared for the savage lushness of the landscape around them. It seemed to engulf them from all sides. She forgot that he was in a bad temper and that she was a bag of nerves, and started talking about the immense variety of plants and flowers.

'My father would have loved this,' she said. 'He would have gone quite mad. He would have been out there, hopping around, dissecting leaves and looking for bugs. He used to bring things home, all kinds of insects and plant life, and show them to me and Mum. Do you know, I could draw a diagram of a cross-section of a leaf before I could read?' She laughed, with her head turned away from him. 'I don't suppose that's proved a very useful talent, mind you.' She laughed again and this time she glanced around to look at him.

He wasn't as grim as he had been when they had first started out, but there was still something unreadable about his expression which was unsettling. She reverted to the less intimidating inspection of the trees.

Town life had already disappeared, to be replaced by village life, and now that too was vanishing as wilderness took over. Trees and forest land rearing up on either side of the road were restrained from making a complete take-over by the bumpy strip of tarmac. Occasionally they passed a house or two, primitive, picturesque dwellings precariously balanced on patches of cleared land. Even less occasionally they passed people, and when they did they were stared at with silent curiosity.

She wished, she said, that she had brought some books with her so that she could identify more.

'It's all so tame at a garden centre,' she explained, not wanting to take her eyes off the roadside in case she missed something. 'All neatly laid out in tubs and boxes. Even the exotic plants like the orchids seem strange and lifeless compared to out here where they grow wild. Am

I boring you?' She shot him an anxious glance and he smiled, a real smile, warm and amused.

'Shall I stop so that you can get out and have a closer look at everything?'

'Would you mind very much?'

So she clambered out and had a look around and picked a few flowers growing wild at the side of the road then scrambled back into the car.

'For me?' he asked drily, eyeing the flowers when she was back inside the car, and he smiled again so that she went pink and felt a little flustered.

'I thought they'd match your shirt,' she joked.

'I'll stick one behind my ear, shall I?' he asked.

'I'm glad you're in a better mood.' She couldn't imagine what prompted her into saying that. Relief, maybe, that he wasn't scowling? She felt light-hearted and carefree. If she'd had anything of a voice, she might even have sung.

'Was I in a bad mood? No,' he continued, glancing at her sideways then concentrating on the road again, 'don't answer that.'

'Was it something I did?' She frowned, thinking back.

'Why do you always blame yourself for everything?'

'Habit, I guess,' she answered, surprising herself again. 'I grew up blaming myself for not being like my parents and I suppose I never really stopped.' She laughed self-consciously and turned away.

They had reached the top of the island now. Everything gave way to the Grand Etang, an extinct volcanic crater, a great yawning mouth of flat, metallic blue water that gave you the creepy feeling of immeasurable depth.

They got out of the car to stretch their legs. Away from the crater, they could plunge into the rainforest and

Lisa looked longingly at it, conjuring up the bamboo trees, the creeping vines, the dark silence broken only by the sounds of birds and wild animals.

For a fleeting second, and for the first time, she felt a vivid empathy with her parents and their constant quest for new things. Then she blinked and the feeling was gone.

There was no one else around. No tourists, no locals.

'We are the first people to discover this,' she announced with her arms outstretched. 'Shall we fly our flag and name it after us?' She laughed, delighted, and he grinned at her.

'You're like a child with a new toy,' he said, amused.

'Can you blame me?' She walked towards him and looked up at him seriously. 'I've never seen anything like this in my life before. My parents may have cultivated the art of travelling, but never outside England, and besides, when you're being dragged along, it's difficult after a while to appreciate new things without feeling a little jaundiced. When you're eleven or twelve or thirteen, moving from one place to another is just disorienting, or at least it was for me. There's no excitement, there's just that horrible tearful feeling of saying goodbye to people whose faces you were just beginning to grow accustomed to.'

'Some might have seen all that constant travel as a way of making hundreds of friends.'

'True,' Lisa said, walking back slowly towards the car, 'but not me. I don't think I was ever extrovert enough for that.' She laughed and said brightly, 'Why are we being so serious when the sun is shining and the birds are singing and it's our last day on this wonderful island?'

'Because,' Angus said softly from beside her, 'I want to get through to you.'

Lisa didn't say anything. For the past hour or so he had been her companion; she had relaxed with him, she had laughed with him, she had forgotten her nerves. Now he was a man again and her nerves were back. The silky intent in his voice, the awareness of his blue eyes on her face were like the touch of something warm and inviting and dangerous.

She slipped into the passenger seat, slammed the door and waited, without looking, for him to get in. She expected him to continue his line of thought, and she could already feel the muscles in her stomach tensing in preparation, but he didn't. He flicked on the engine and began driving away from the crater and out towards the coast on the windward side.

When he spoke, it was about normal things, things she could deal with; he asked her questions about work and whether she was looking forward to getting back, about her plans for the future, about her friends, about what she did in the evenings in Reading. Was there much of a night-life? he asked, and laughed when she told him that the only night-life she seriously considered was a cup of hot chocolate in front of the television, with her legs curled up underneath her and her book on her lap. On weekends she saw friends.

'And no boyfriend,' he stated conversationally, and she ignored him, which made him laugh again, although there was a hard edge to his laughter.

They reached Grand Anse, sticky and tired, and Angus turned to her and said in a dry voice, 'There, back in one piece. Was it as much of an ordeal as you'd expected?'

'Thank you,' she said, looking down so that her hair

fell across her eyes and she had to sweep it aside with her hand. 'It was wonderful.'

And that, she thought later, over supper, should have been that. Except she found herself thinking about what he had said, that one sentence that had sprung out of nothing and led nowhere. He had said that he wanted to get through to her. What had he meant?

She heard herself answering Liz and Gerry's questions, showing the right level of enthusiasm, which really wasn't difficult because it had been a glorious day, but her mind was miles away.

For the first time she contemplated what it was going to be like returning to England and she had a clammy, suffocating feeling of despair. She doubted that she would ever see Angus Hamilton again. Oh, of course, there would be the usual polite parting words about keeping in touch and if she was ever up in London she'd drop by and they could go out for a meal, but she knew that the end of this holiday was the end of it.

Her heart began to beat faster and she stole a glance at him across the table, trying to recapture some of the relief she had felt earlier on at the thought that she would no longer have to be near him and have to cope with the disturbing rollercoaster of emotions which he provoked in her.

I can go back to my life, she told herself unconvincingly. I can get back to reality, because this isn't reality. She wished she could persuade herself that it was a happy prospect, but now, when she thought about it, all she could see was an interminable series of days and weeks and months and years without him around, and she had to struggle to keep a smile on her face when something inside was collapsing. Idiotically.

It was a relief when the meal was finished and the

small talk was done and she no longer had to avoid looking at Angus in case her face revealed too much.

She shut herself in her bedroom, lay on the bed, closed her eyes, opened them, abandoned all hope of sleep, and at a little after midnight slipped into her shorts and T-shirt and made her way to the now totally deserted beach.

She strolled along. There was peace here. The gentle sound of water against coastline, the black sea calm and unruffled. She stood looking out at it and Angus's voice in her ear was such a shock that when she spun around she half expected that it might have been a hallucination.

It wasn't.

'Couldn't sleep either?' he asked, standing next to her but not close.

She couldn't look at him. If she looked at him, she would end up drowning, so she stared out to sea and said calmly, while her fingers curled into a ball at her sides and her head spun, 'I must be nervous about the plane trip tomorrow. I was the same before I flew over.'

'Is that it?' he murmured. He took her arm and guided her away from the shoreline and up the beach. He sat down but she remained hovering. 'Sit. I want to talk to you.'

'Do you? What about?' She sat down, but reluctantly, and he turned to face her.

'Look at me.' He held her chin so that she had to look at him and said, as though continuing a conversation which had already been started, 'I was in a foul temper this morning because I didn't want to take you anywhere but I had to.'

'I'm sorry,' Lisa whispered awkwardly, 'but I'm afraid I don't understand. I think we should go inside; it's terribly late.'

'That's exactly what I mean.'

'What?'

'Hasn't anyone ever told you that the faster you run, the harder you'll be chased?' His voice was curt and she stared up at him, wide-eyed and uncomprehending. 'You act like a startled deer caught in someone's headlights, posed to take flight.'

'I'm sorry—' she began, but he interrupted sharply,

'Will you stop apologising? Can you understand what I'm trying to tell you here? I want you, dammit!'

There was a long silence. She continued to stare at him, and she could hear the sound of her heart beating, the sound of the blood in her veins, the sound of her brain trying to come to terms with what he had just said. She wondered whether she might have imagined it.

'No,' she said finally, in a nervous, placating voice, edging away.

Catching her wrist, he grated, 'Stop running away from me.'

'We've been through this,' she murmured weakly, 'We agreed—'

'Nothing. We agreed nothing. Do you imagine that I like being controlled by something as uncontrollable as desire?' He pulled her towards him so that she half fell, and ended up much closer to him than she wanted.

'I don't know what to say.'

'Then don't talk. Just finish what was started.' He curled his fingers into her hair and kissed her without any pretence at gentleness, with a hunger that stirred the flame within her to fire.

Lisa whimpered and tried to turn away and he said huskily, 'Stop trying to fight this thing.' He made it sound as though 'this thing' was somehow monstrous and overwhelming. It was how she felt as well. She had the sensation of being caught in the grip of something that was too big for whatever small defences she had. Desire. Desire as fierce and as savage and as unrelenting as an animal bent on destruction. Desire was what he called it and he should know because he was so much more experienced than she was.

'Tell me that you don't want me,' he groaned against her mouth, and in that instant the promise of what she might have washed away all the caution that existed in her body. She reached up and pulled him towards her, down to the sand, which was dry and powdery under her, kissing him with the same hunger as he had kissed her, a hunger that frightened and excited her in its intensity.

His mouth burnt against her skin and she knew now just how much she had longed for this. Ever since he had kissed her that first time and maybe even before, something inside her had been simmering, waiting for the match to be lit.

She moaned in abandonment as he kissed her face, her neck, turning her head this way and that so that he could caress every bit of exposed skin. He told her, unevenly, that he wanted to touch every part of her body with his mouth and she trembled.

She was not wearing a bra and her breasts ached under the cotton T-shirt. She held his wrist and guided his hand under it and shivered as his palm covered her breast.

He pulled the T-shirt over her head. The breeze on her skin felt good, cooling, and she lay back with her arms outstretched and her eyes half closed, like someone in a trance.

He bent his head and covered her nipple with his mouth, circling it wetly and hungrily, and she arched herself forward, wanting him to absorb more and more of her, until there was nothing left.

When, with her eyes still shut, she felt his hand unzip her shorts, she didn't resist him. She struggled out of them, impatient to return to their lovemaking, hating any interruption, however slight.

This time there was no sharp awakening to reality. This was reality, the only reality that she needed—the here and now.

She parted her legs to accommodate his enquiring fingers and moved against them, barely able to contain herself. In a minute she would no longer be able to fight off the ultimate climax, but he seemed to sense this because he slowed his hand, and slowly licked and kissed her stomach, then her thighs. And she felt his tongue move delicately into the core of her womanhood.

With one hand he continued to stroke her breast, teasing her nipple which was already large and taut with arousal.

She felt her body flinch as he thrust into her.

'I know,' he murmured hoarsely. 'I know. I won't hurt you.'

When he moved inside her again, it was with infinite gentleness, and after a short while her muscles began to relax and she was no longer tense but moaning as his rhythm gathered momentum.

She watched the flat planes of his torso as he moved against her, propped up by one hand while the other massaged her breast, then she closed her eyes and felt waves of pleasure rushing through her, making her ears sing, making her cry out, a hoarse sound in the still, unbroken night. She felt the warm darkness wrap around them like a protective blanket, and she felt a tremendous sense of freedom, of being as light as air. She could have stayed like that for ever.

'Not the most ideal spot for making love,' he said softly into her ear, and she smiled at him.

I love you, she thought. The feeling was so immense that it seemed to take her over. I love you. When did this happen? She ran her fingers through his hair, liking the feel of it slipping through her fingers.

'Absolutely ideal,' she whispered drowsily. 'All black and silver and empty, with nature around us everywhere.'

He laughed, as though the thought hadn't occurred to him.

'What do we do now?' she asked, looking at him. He was all angles and shadows and his eyes glittered in his face.

'We could go back to your room,' he suggested, and she realised with the first stirrings of reality that they were talking at cross purposes. He leaned over her and stroked the side of her face. 'Or we could stay out here surrounded by black and silver nature.' He laughed softly.

She said in a shaky voice, 'No, I mean, what do we do *now*? Where do we go from here? What happens to us?' The magic and romance were beginning to fade, like mist dissipating, but she had to know.

'What do you want to happen?'

'I don't know.' She did know. She wanted to spend the rest of her life with him but she knew without having to be told that that was not a suggestion to be voiced.

'I'm immensely attracted to you,' he murmured, sounding a little surprised.

She watched his powerful arms. 'And you can't understand why.'

'You're not like any of the other women I've gone out with in the past.'

'What sort of women have you gone out with in the past?' She wanted to sit up now and get dressed. The bubble which had surrounded them in that euphoric moment of lovemaking, when she had whimsically imagined that her dreams were about to come true, had burst.

'If I told you, you'd jump to all the wrong conclusions. You'd think that comparisons were being made.'

'Tell me.'

He shrugged, still smiling, still stroking her hair away from her face. 'Very glamorous, very brittle.'

'Like Caroline?'

'Older, but yes, same model, I suppose.'

She sat up and tried not to appear as though she was about to run away. I get the picture, she wanted to say. You're attracted to me, maybe because I'm a different model from the rest, but I do have one vital thing in common with your queue of glamorous, brittle blondes, haven't I? I'm just passing through.

'I want to see you when we get back to England,' he said softly.

'For how long?' she enquired.

'Who knows? We may get thoroughly sick of each other after a week.' He was teasing her, but she wasn't about to be teased. His words had a chilling element of truth behind them. What he wanted was sex, until she had been weaned out of his system. No talk of commitment, certainly no talk of love.

But I love you, she thought, and I don't know if I can be with you for one week or two or a month or six months, never knowing when the end will come. It was like travelling with her parents all over again. The same insecurity, the same rootlessness. It wasn't what she wanted.

'London's a long way from Reading,' she told him.

'I have a very fast car.'

She slipped on her T-shirt with shaking fingers, feeling the sand against her skin with sudden distaste, then she stood up and began putting on the rest of her clothes.

'What's the matter?' he asked sharply, also standing up and getting dressed, and she shrugged, 'Are you going to tell me or am I going to have to play guessing games with you?'

'Nothing's the matter.'

'You've switched off,' he said, with an edge to his voice. 'One minute you're opening up to me and the next minute you've retreated behind those walls of yours again. Now, are you going to tell me what's wrong or am I going to have to shake it out of you?'

She began walking off. She didn't trust herself to speak. She didn't want to do anything stupid like break down and she certainly wasn't about to confess undying love and risk losing what little was left of her pride.

'Answer me, dammit!' His fingers curled round her wrist and he pulled her round to face him.

She looked at him mutely, which only seemed to sharpen the edge of his anger. Her hand lay limply in the grip of his fingers and she stabbed her toes into the sand, making a little mound like a molehill.

'I can't...' She began helplessly, not looking at him. 'I just can't get involved in a relationship where I'm at the beck and call of someone else. I spent years being at the beck and call of my parents and I can't go through that again.'

'We are not talking about the same thing here.'

'Not the same, no,' she agreed, 'but similar.'

'This is ridiculous.'

Her head snapped up and she glared at him with eyes which were filling up with tears and which would betray her, she knew, if she allowed it.

'For you, maybe, but not for me. That's the way I feel and there's nothing more to be said.'

'And what happened between us?' he asked tightly. 'No more to be said on that either?'

'I enjoyed it...' Lisa muttered. She dashed her hand across her eyes angrily, because he was forcing her to say things that she didn't want to say and which her ears didn't want to hear. She didn't need to be reminded of how much she had wanted him because it would only show her how much she still did.

'But enjoyment is not enough—not without your precious guarantees.'

More silence. The mound at her feet was growing and she flattened it back down.

'Fine,' he said abruptly. 'We'll just write the whole episode off.' He released her and she stumbled away from him without looking back, away from the treacherous night breeze that had felt like a caress against her skin only an hour before but which now felt like ice.

She let herself into her room, had a shower, got into the oversized T-shirt which she slept in. Her movements were automatic. There was only room in her brain for one thing. Angus. He usurped every other thought. His presence filled the room, filled her head, filled her body until she wanted to scream, which of course she couldn't do, so instead she covered herself with the blankets and stuffed her face into the pillow, and was trying to force herself to think of something else, *anything* else, when she felt a touch on her shoulder.

She surfaced from under the layers of bedlinen and

saw a figure sitting on the edge of her bed, and she opened her mouth to scream.

'It's me,' Angus hissed at her. 'Shh...' He put his hand across her mouth and she stared up at him, dumbfounded.

'I've been thinking,' he said accusingly, with his hand still over her mouth, as though now he had calmed her he still didn't want her to say anything.

'Mmm,' Lisa contributed against the palm of his hand. Her fingers curled into the sheet and she had the feeling that if she blinked he would dematerialise.

'I don't care to be blackmailed.'

I was not blackmailing you! she wanted to yell, but again all she could do was mutter something incoherent, and she made another attempt to pull his hand away.

'Not yet.' He paused and raked his hair back in a frustrated gesture. 'I think your attitude is puritanical and misguided.'

Lisa grunted angrily in disagreement.

'But,' he continued, 'since you don't seem prepared to change it, I propose you move in with me.' He removed his hand and for a second she didn't say a word. Not a word. For a second there, when he had said 'I propose', she had insanely jumped to the wrong conclusion. The rest of his suggestion sank in like a stone into cold water. What he proposed was still the same—sex on his terms but with the boundary lines slightly altered. It wasn't commitment.

'I am not,' she said in a deadly calm voice, when her vocal cords finally loosened up enough for her to say anything at all, 'moving in with you. I am not going to be your mistress.'

'Why not?' he asked in a low, furious voice that made her cringe back against the pillow. 'What do you want?'

There was a tense silence, then he said curtly, 'Marriage? Is that it?' And when she didn't answer he carried on relentlessly, 'Marriage is not for me. I've seen the downside of marriage; I've watched my parents stay married, or should I say tied to one another, for no better reason than it was a habit easier to keep than to break.' He leaned over her, dark, threatening, angry, his hands on either side of her body.

'You say that life has no guarantees,' she whispered. 'Does it automatically follow that because your parents' marriage was a bad one, then your marriage, if ever you do decide to marry, would follow the same course? My parents had an extremely close marriage.'

'There is no room for debate on the subject, Lisa.'

'And children?' she flung at him.

'Are for other people and good luck to them. God damn you, woman, I am offering you as much commitment as I've ever offered any woman. Take it!'

'Go,' she said, turning her head so that she didn't have to look at him. 'Leave me alone. I don't want what you're offering.'

She could feel his eyes burning into her but she refused to meet them. As far as she was concerned, there was nothing left to say. He had laid down his terms and they weren't good enough. Sure, he might be handing out the most he was capable of giving in the line of commitment, but it wasn't enough.

Did he expect her to abandon everything so she could spend an indefinite length of time, because she had no idea of where his boredom threshold lay, living on a knife-edge?

He pushed himself off the bed and stood towering above her for a few seconds.

'So be it,' he said, then he walked towards the door

and left, slamming it behind him, and only then did she fall back against the pillows with the sickish feeling of having been put through a wringer. Her head was spinning. She was quite sure that if she tried to climb out of bed she would fall down.

She wished that she had had the sense to lock the bedroom door. If she had he would have had to bang on it to be let in and she would not have answered. She would not have had to listen to what was, in the end, the final insult. However much he was attracted to her, for reasons which she still couldn't pin down, he would never marry her; he would never give her the one thing she needed.

She lay on the bed with her eyes wide open and stared upwards at the ceiling, which she didn't see. Her eyes were blind to everything except what was going on in her mind.

He had told her that he didn't believe in marriage, that it was an institution which had no place in his life. She wondered whether he was being truthful. She wondered whether the real reason why he would never marry her was far more fundamental than that.

She was of a different social background—the most basic difference which Caroline had put her finger on almost immediately, and which she had made no bones about hiding.

She didn't honestly imagine that he would remain a bachelor all his life, but when he did marry it would be to someone with a suitable pedigree.

How dared he call her puritanical and misguided, just because she happened to have a few principles?

It was a shame that her principles hadn't jumped to the rescue earlier, on the beach, she thought, but really, making love with him was something she didn't regret.

If she had turned her back on him and walked away, she would have spent a lifetime wondering.

He had held out his hand and she had taken it; she had willingly let him lead her into a whole new, bright world which she had never known existed.

Somehow, though, she knew that living with him would be a humiliating experience. She would never be able to relax because she would never know how much longer he would be around. And when the time came for her to walk away it would be a shabby, disillusioned parting. No, it made her sick just thinking about it.

Better this way, she told herself. It seems hellish but there are fewer pieces to pick up now than there would be six months down the road.

She closed her eyes and let sleep take over.

CHAPTER SIX

IT WAS cold and dark and raining when the plane landed at Heathrow airport.

Lisa stared out of the window of the taxi and watched the water slide along the glass. She didn't want to think of that trip back, but it was as though her mind had reached an impenetrable barrier and her thoughts could not stretch beyond it.

Angus had not said a word to her for the entire journey. He had barely glanced in her direction. He had sat next to Gerry on the plane, and from behind them she had heard the low murmur of their voices and had miserably fed off the sound of his dark, deep tones, filled with an unspeakable yearning.

The taxi finally cleared the congested airport traffic and began picking up speed on the motorway. The taxi driver's earlier attempts at conversation had met with such blank unresponsiveness that he had eventually given up, but she gathered that it had been raining non-stop more or less for the fortnight that she had been away. Dull grey skies and constant rain that made everyone scurry along the pavements with their umbrellas up and their expressions pinched.

By the time they made it back to her flat, sun and sand and sea seemed like a distant dream. At the time, she had thought the holiday was winding along very slowly. Now she realised that it had shot past like a bullet.

'In a week's time,' Paul told her knowledgeably the

following day when she turned up for work, 'you'll have a look at the photos and it'll seem like a year ago. Ellie keeps telling me that the only way round that is to book another holiday the minute the last one's finished.'

Lisa smiled at him in passing. He had missed her. The paperwork hadn't been done and some of their customers had been asking after her.

She should have felt pleased and relieved to be back among the tubs and plants and dwarf conifers, but she didn't. She had a dreadful feeling of unreality, as though she had stepped back into a life that was now in some way out of kilter.

Two weeks later, when the holiday snapshots arrived through the letterbox, she sat down and looked at them over and over again and realised that what Paul had said was true. The reality of winter had put a stranglehold on her imagination. She found it hard to recapture the memory of blistering sunshine and long, lazy days.

Routine and the humdrum business of living made two weeks of escapism seem like a mirage. If she thought too hard about it, it would all suddenly disappear and she would realise that she had been nowhere at all.

Except, she thought, if that was the case, Angus would have faded into a blurry, distant image as well, a memory neatly stored away at the back of her mind. And he hadn't.

It was so unfair. She was trying so hard to forget, but his image lurked so close to the surface, waiting to spring out at her like an intruder. She could confine every area of her life but she couldn't seem to confine her thoughts at all. One stray memory would creep into her head when she was least expecting it and then it would proliferate until it became a network of memories, strangling the imposed orderliness of her mind like an onslaught of ivy devouring a wall.

The strain of pretending to the world that she was the same person she had been before was so tiring that it was nearly six weeks before some little thought process in her head registered something that made her go cold with fear.

She had missed a period.

She was sitting with her book on her lap and a cup of coffee balanced precariously on her thigh, when everything seemed to shut down inside her. Nearly a month late. She hadn't even thought about it before; she had been too busy trying to get her life back in order.

The following morning she went to the pharmacy, bought herself a kit and watched with a clammy feeling as a thin blue line impersonally informed her that her life was never going to be the same again. She was pregnant.

I can't be, she thought, staring at the little plastic tester as though it were something alien, but she couldn't even begin to pretend to herself that it was wrong, that she had somehow fed it the right ingredients and had been handed back an incorrect answer.

She sat down on the edge of her sofa with her head in her hands and felt ill.

She had never thought that this could happen to her; it hadn't once crossed her mind when she had lain there, on the beach, and made love to a man she was destined never to see again.

She started to laugh hysterically, until the tears came to her eyes, and then, with shock, she realised that she was no longer laughing but crying. How could she have been so stupid? She, of all people? She could remember the talk her parents had given her about the birds and the bees. It had been more of a biological discussion about reproduction and she could remember her mother saying, 'You might not think that it will ever happen to you, but it will and it's as well to be prepared if you don't want an accident to happen.'

Well, the accident had happened, except it was more of a catastrophe than an accident.

She lay down on the sofa with her eyes shut and the enormity of what had happened spread over her until she thought she was being engulfed.

Why me? she asked herself. She was forever reading in the newspapers about couples who couldn't have children, who had had to resort to fertility treatment. It had never crossed her mind that she could fall pregnant as a result of one ill-timed moment of passion.

What was she going to do?

The following morning, dry-eyed, she confronted Paul in his office and told him without any preamble.

'I'm afraid I have some surprising news.' She had to hold onto the edge of his desk because she could feel the ground swaying under her feet. 'I'm going to have a baby.'

There was a thick silence and she didn't dare lift her eyes to his because she could imagine the shock on his face. It wouldn't have been so bad if she hadn't been such an intensely private person, so in control of her life, the sort of person that these kinds of things just didn't happen to.

'You don't look over the moon about it.'

She finally lifted her eyes and saw the surprise still there, unconvincingly camouflaged under a show of cheery *bonhomie*.

when Paul suggested an outing to a flower show. It would be quite an honour to attend because it was the first of its kind. Displays of selected flowers only, rare species, hybrids. Two complimentary tickets had been sent to them.

'I can't go,' he explained, 'because I'll be abroad, but you go and take a friend. You'll enjoy it. It'll make a change from here.'

Lisa looked at his kind, open face with gratitude. He had been marvellous about the whole thing, encouraging her when she seemed low and having her over to dinner at least once a week, ostensibly so that she could see a bit of family life at first hand but really because he felt sorry for her.

'I thought you wanted me here to cover for you while you were in Germany,' she said, and he waved his hand airily.

'I think the place can spare you for a day,' he said. 'Have a day out. It'll do you good.'

So three days later she set off for London under strict instructions to have a damn good time and see if she could sniff out any bargains that they might want to stock for the following summer.

The place, when she arrived, was jammed. The big flower shows, she knew, were always packed, but she had not expected quite such a crowd for what was, after all, an élite event with only certain categories of flowers and plants on display.

At the entrance, she thought that she would never make it, not having to contend with throngs of people pushing against her when all she really felt like doing was having a long sleep, but once she was inside the crowd thinned out and she began to have a proper, thorough look at everything.

There were roses, but peculiarly shaped ones or else unusually coloured ones, and there was any number of foreign flora, with their wild, exotic hues strangely amplified by the ordinary surroundings.

The huge hall was filled with heady, sweet scents and the sounds of people exclaiming over something or other. She had taken a little notebook with her and as she stopped in front of each plant she sized it up with a view to possible stocking, and took the appropriate notes.

She was being swept along on the tide of people moving from one display to the next, when she picked up the well-bred tones of one voice, and as her head snapped around their eyes met through the crowd and Lisa had a swaying feeling, as if she was about to fall.

She heard a woman say, 'Are you all right, dear?'

She nodded distractedly, about to push on, when Caroline's voice said from next to her, 'What a surprise. Lisa something or other, isn't it?'

'Freeman.'

She could feel the blood soaring through her and she had the same giddy feeling she used to have now and again, earlier on in her pregnancy, when she suddenly stood up and felt the ground swaying gently under her feet.

'Yes, of course. I'd forgotten.' Caroline's face was as tanned as it had been when they had returned from the West Indies and she was wearing a glamorous green trouser outfit which seemed far more appropriate to a cocktail party than a garden exhibition, but Lisa could remember that about her choice of clothes. They were never casual. They always seemed just a little too grand for the occasion.

'How are you, Caroline?' she asked faintly. At least

her voice sounded all right, but she knew that her knuckles were white and her hands were tightly balled into fists at her sides.

'Just fine.' The green, feline eyes swept over her, and she said, smiling, but with an unpleasant undertone, 'I see that congratulations are in order.'

Did I really think that she might not notice? Lisa thought. She felt sick as though the air had suddenly become too hot and was pressing down upon her, making her sweat.

'Thank you.'

'And how many months?'

'A little over four.' She tried to smile, as though this were routine stuff for her—a few pleasantries with a passing acquaintance—but she could feel the tension in her body like a rush of freezing water through her veins.

'I see.' Caroline looked at her with those hard, glittering eyes. 'And where is your husband? Here with you?' she asked, and Lisa didn't answer. What was there to say?

'Are you enjoying the display?' she eventually asked, a little wildly.

'Usual dull affair,' Caroline answered. 'Here with Mummy, actually. She's terribly involved in this sort of thing and she dragged me along to help out.'

'Well...I hope you have a nice time.' Good heavens, what pointless small talk, when all I want to do is get away and hope that she doesn't put two and two together, she thought. 'I really must be going...'

'I tried my luck with Angus, you know, but he wasn't interested. I think you were right when you said that he saw me as an underage minor—despite my attempts to persuade him otherwise.' She was smiling, the same repellent, cold smile that frightened Lisa. 'But in a way I'm jolly glad nothing came of it. He said that he was utterly uninterested in any kind of long-term relationship with any woman. He was terribly polite about it. I personally think that that sort of thing would cramp his lifestyle, don't you agree?'

Lisa shrugged.

'Dear Angus moves in the fast lane,' she continued. 'Wouldn't it be a shame if he had to slow down because of some disaster? I mean...' She leaned forward confidentially. Lisa felt the brush of the green silk against her arm. 'Here's a thought... You're a little over four months pregnant. He could be the father, couldn't he? If you two had had a fling... Not that I'm saying you did! But the timing's there, isn't it?

'Do you know, if the Press ever discovered that he had fathered an illegitimate child and not taken responsibility, they would have a field day? He has such a high profile, and some of his largest advertising campaigns are quite morally based. What a thought.

'Still...' she appeared to give this some thought '...I personally would find it very amusing if he was brought down a peg or two. Rejection isn't a word I understand.'

'I'm sure you don't mean that, Caroline,' Lisa said with growing horror at the implications of what the other woman had said. 'I'm sure you're not a vindictive person.'

'Of course I'm not! But there's always something a little sweet about revenge, isn't there? You never said, by the way—are you married?'

Someone jostled her from behind. Lisa had never felt so grateful to an inconsiderate, passing stranger in all her life.

'I really must get on,' she said, bravely meeting Caroline's eyes and not looking away. 'I'm being pushed by people who want to have a look at your mother's display. Do congratulate her from me. It's a beautiful selection of flowers.'

She wouldn't have guessed that she could be so articulate when her mind was whirling around like a spinning top, going faster and faster.

'I will, yes, of course.' Caroline stepped back and offered her profile for inspection. 'And I shall also tell her how glad I am that I was forced into coming here. After all, how else would we have met? And I'm so glad that we did. Aren't you?'

There was no point in even trying to enjoy the flowers now, but she trudged through the rest of the displays, taking notes, even though the blooms had all merged into one great, gaudy mass of colour.

By the time she made it back to her flat, she was spent.

Her mind played and replayed that conversation with Caroline. Every way she looked at it, from whatever angle, she couldn't escape or misread the insinuations behind the words. Caroline wanted her revenge on Angus. She had made a pass at him and had been courteously turned down and rejection, as she had said herself, was not a concept she found easy to swallow. What better revenge now than to see him forced into a fatherhood he didn't want?

She didn't sleep that night. Normally, the minute her head hit the pillow she was out like a light, but not now. She tossed and turned and created a thousand and one scenarios in her mind and then unconvincingly tried to tell herself that she was being foolish, that

Caroline's words had been no more than a vindictive threat.

But it hardly worked. She was, she realised by the end of the week, waiting. Waiting for the phone to ring, standing on the edge of a precipice, waiting to fall.

By the end of two weeks, she was beginning to hope that he had maybe lost her address somewhere, and he would never find her through the phone book because she was ex-directory. She tried desperately to remember if she had mentioned where she worked, but for the life of her she couldn't.

By the end of three weeks, she no longer looked at the telephone with the wariness of someone expecting the worst.

Autumn had now pushed the last vestiges of summer away. The leaves on the trees were beginning to turn red and gold and fall to the ground. She extracted her waterproof jacket and her coat from cold storage, only to realise that they would never last the course of the pregnancy. In fact, not many of her clothes still did fit her. She had had to carefully fold her jeans and put them away and now she began sewing some maternity clothes, which she did without joy, simply with the determined knowledge that she had to. She couldn't afford the luxury of buying an entire wardrobe of maternity wear.

She stopped worrying about Angus because no news was good news. She stopped dwelling obsessively on that conversation with Caroline because if she was going to create trouble then she would have done so by now. She also stopped jumping every time the phone went and then tiptoeing to answer it, as if one false move and it would attack, like something out of a tacky horror movie.

* * *

On a cold, blustery Friday evening, she heard the doorbell ring and went to answer it without a second thought.

Her friend Judy had taken to calling round at the end of the week. Sometimes they went out for a cheap meal, but more often than not they just sat and chatted.

Her shock on seeing Angus standing outside her front door was so profound that she felt her entire body stiffen, as though someone had waved a magic wand and turned her into stone.

She stared at him without saying anything. Shock had not galvanised her into action. It had done the opposite. It had deprived her of her power of speech; it had thickened her mind so that she could hardly think; it had frozen every nerve in her body.

She had been wrong. She had not remembered everything about him. She had forgotten, for a start, how intensely powerful his presence was, how the arrogant sweep of his dark features gave him a brooding, mesmerising look. She had forgotten that peculiar, penetrating clarity of his eyes, the deepest of blues that revealed nothing.

'Surprised, Lisa?'

'What are you doing here?' At least she could speak now, even though it was only in a whisper. At least she could think even though her thoughts were flying around in her head like a swarm of bees unexpectedly released.

'What do you think?' There was no lazy charm in his face. His mouth was a narrow line and he wasn't smiling. She knew that what she was seeing was the cold, hard steel beneath the velvet. 'Aren't you going to ask me inside?'

He didn't wait for an answer. He reached out and

pushed the door back and stepped inside, leaving her to shut the door behind her and stand there, with her hands behind her back. He didn't look around him. He turned and faced her, with his hands in his pockets.

Now that her nightmares had finally materialised, she found that she didn't have a clue what to do, what to say. She stared at him mutely and he gave her a savage, cold smile.

'Haven't you got your little speech ready, Lisa?'

'What little speech? What are you talking about?' Her heart was beating so fast that it felt as though it would burst at any moment.

'Did you think that I wouldn't come around?' he asked, with the same cold, cruel smile on his mouth. 'Were you beginning to worry that your little plan might go astray?'

'What little plan? What are you talking about?'

'Don't play games with me!' he bellowed, and she cringed back against the door, grateful for the support it gave her.

'I've been away in America. Caroline was waiting for me the day after I got back.'

Lisa walked shakily into the living room, across to the sofa and sat down with her hands on her lap. So it hadn't been an empty threat after all. Had she really imagined that it had been? What an optimistic fool. Caroline was not the sort to make empty threats, not when she could taste the honeyed sweetness of revenge.

'I see.'

'I'm sure you do.' His mouth twisted into a cynical sneer. 'And there's really no need to go on acting the innocent with me. Just tell me how much money you want.'

'Money?' She looked up at him with utter bewilderment.

'Yes, money. Or were you hoping that I would skirt round the subject in a more tactful way? When you cut through the waffle, it has such a nasty ring, hasn't it?'

'I don't know what you're talking about. I won't be bullied by you in my own house.'

'When did you devise your little plan, Lisa?' he asked in a dangerously soft voice.

'Angus, please...'

'Angus, please...what?'

'What did Caroline say to you?'

'What did Caroline say to me? What didn't she say to me would be nearer the target. She told me that she was at the flower show, helping her mother, when you confronted her. She said that you couldn't wait to tell her that you were pregnant by me and that you would make sure I paid through the nose for sleeping with you when there was nothing in it for you.'

Lisa's face whitened.

'None of that's true,' she whispered.

'So tell me, when did you decide to play your trump card? Did you lead me on until you knew that making love would result in a pregnancy?' He stepped towards her and she stared at him with wide-eyed horror. 'A bit of a gamble, wasn't it? I suppose you figured that you had nothing to lose, though, didn't you? If it didn't work, if you didn't fall pregnant, then you would slide back into obscurity. If you did, then all you had to do was engineer the right moment to meet Caroline, and that would be the easy part.

'Clever of you to remember that her mother exhibited flowers. All it would have needed was a phone call to see whether she would be there on the same day as you, and if that didn't work, then you could always bump into her somewhere else. Accidentally, of course.'

'No! You're not making any sense!'

'Am I not?'

'I had no idea that Caroline would be there! I didn't phone to find out anything! I don't know how you have the nerve to come into my house and accuse me of things...like that!' Her voice had begun to waver and she had to grit her teeth together so that she didn't break down and start crying. She took a deep breath.

He raked his fingers through his hair and stared at her with a mixture of anger and doubt and sheer frustration. Then he began to pace the room, his movements restless.

'It is mine, I take it?'

'Yes.'

He paused in front of her and said darkly, 'I won't be blackmailed into anything, I can tell you that right now. You say that you didn't engineer a meeting with Caroline...'

'And I didn't confront her either!' Lisa looked at him resentfully. 'She confronted *me*! I wasn't even supposed to be at that flower show but Paul couldn't make it and he wanted me to go along and make notes. By the time I saw her, it was too late to... She guessed at once. She was elated. She said that she had tried to...that she had...'

She couldn't formulate the thought and she couldn't tell whether he understood her meaning or not because he continued to look at her with that opaque, unreadable look that was so frightening.

'She said that she wanted to make you pay for rejecting her.' There, it was out, and she met his stare with bright, stubborn eyes.

'And why should I believe you?' he asked coolly.

'I don't care if you don't!'

There was a thick silence, then he said, with less rage but no more warmth, 'I'm going now, but I promise you I'll be back.' He turned around and walked out, slamming the door behind him, and she collapsed back against the sofa. Now that she was alone, the unshed tears refused to come.

She sat there while the gloom gathered around her and thought about every word he had said. She thought about the savage anger on his face as he had hurled those accusations at her. She knew that she shouldn't be surprised, that Caroline was just the sort of girl who would feel no compunction about twisting the truth into something that she could make into a blunt instrument and use for her own benefit. But it still hurt that he could have accepted her as gold-digger so easily.

How could he have thought she would use him as a passport to money?

She fell asleep on the sofa and awoke with stiff joints the following day. It was just as well that it was the weekend and she didn't have to go to work. Her body ached.

She put her hand on her stomach and thought that the only sensible thing was happening there inside her, and then it occurred to her, with surprise, that over the past few months, while she had been busily saving her money and working out how she was going to cope with a baby, some part of her had slowly become used to the idea and that same part of her now felt more than protective about this child. It had moved from being a catastrophe to something which she now accepted and wanted very badly.

She went and did her shopping and later, just after

she had finished her meal, Paul dropped by. He was literally just passing in front of her house, and wanted to tell her that lunch the following day was off. Timothy had chickenpox and it now looked as though the other two were getting it. Ellie had spotted one sinister red bump on Jenny's stomach and had gloomily predicted that it would have grown into several hundred by morning.

Lisa smiled and listened, cheered up by this mundane conversation when she had spent the whole day in a state of heightened emotional upheaval.

'We don't want you getting ill,' Paul said, smiling and patting her hand. 'Not,' he added with a wicked grin, 'when winter stock is being delivered on Monday and you have to be there to supervise.'

'Oh, I see,' Lisa laughed. 'So much for my welfare.'

'Just joking.'

'I know that!' They continued chatting for a few minutes about their supply of shrubs, quite a few of which had been delivered three days previously and now seemed to be substandard, and he was just getting up to leave when the doorbell went.

Lisa was still smiling when she opened the door. The sight of Angus standing outside drained the smile away from her face and she felt all the familiar apprehension flooding through her again. Every time she saw him, he seemed taller and leaner than she remembered, and more threatening. She remained standing in front of the open doorway, and followed the line of his eyes as they flicked past her to where Paul was slipping on his jacket.

'Come at a bad time, have I?' he asked cynically.

Paul was now standing behind her, and before she could make any introductions Angus said in a cold, tight voice that contained an element of aggression. 'And you are...?'

'Paul Waterman. Lisa works for me.' He extended his hand and Angus looked down at it, ignored it and then raised cool eyes back to Paul's now slightly confused face.

'Really. And calling in here comes under the heading of good staff relations, does it?'

Lisa went bright red and automatically linked her arm through Paul's, an unconscious gesture of protectiveness which didn't escape Angus's attention. His eyes narrowed and he said tightly, 'If you're on your way out, then we won't keep you.'

'I'll decide when my visitors leave, thank you,' she interrupted in a high voice. Her face was flushed and angry.

'I was on my way out, actually,' Paul said stiffly, 'and I'm afraid you still haven't introduced yourself. You are...?'

'Hamilton. Angus Hamilton.' It was the barest of concessions to politeness because his eyes remained hard and glittering.

Paul turned to her and said amiably, 'Sorry about tomorrow, Lisa.'

'Let me know how the children are,' she said with affection, 'and if there's anything at all I can do...'

He smiled, nodded and left, edging past Angus as though he found his presence as alarming as she did, and as soon as he was out of the house Angus turned to her and said icily, 'What a cosy relationship. And what exactly would you do for him? How far do your services extend?'

He brushed past her and she reluctantly shut the door and followed him through. Without the benefit of knowledge, anyone might have said that his reaction to Paul had been the reaction of a jealous man, but she knew the truth, and the truth solidified the little ball of misery sitting in the pit of her stomach.

He didn't care who Paul Waterman was. His caustic question wasn't the fierce interrogation of a jealous lover, it was the caustic enquiry of a man who thought she would do anything for money.

'Well?' he snapped, facing her across the small living room. 'You haven't answered my question. Does that man make a habit of visiting you when you're on your own?'

'*That man*,' Lisa replied, determined not to cower in the face of his formidable presence, 'is my boss and we have a wonderful working relationship. He stopped by to tell me that his invitation for lunch tomorrow has been postponed because his children have come down with chickenpox. There was no need for you to be rude to him.'

She expected him to respond with something cool and cutting but he flushed and turned away, moving to sit down on the sofa.

'Can you blame me?' he asked harshly, but with a look of angry discomfort on his face which she found a little confusing, simply because he was a man whose self-control never slipped. 'You tell me that you didn't fall pregnant on purpose, yet it's an uncanny coincidence that we make love once and it happens. And you blind me with this innocent portrayal of yourself, all girlish blushing and stammering timidity, yet I come here unexpectedly and there's a man in your house, a man whose company you clearly enjoy because you were smiling when you came to the door.'

'Oh, what's the use?' she said with a sigh. 'What's

the good of defending myself? You won't believe me anyway. You've already made up your mind about what sort of person I am, so why don't you just tell me why you've come here?'

'I've come here,' he said, as though challenging her to make something of it, 'to apologise.'

CHAPTER SEVEN

'I WENT to see Caroline,' Angus said evenly, 'and I got the truth out of her. She told me that events hadn't occurred quite as she originally narrated them. Obviously I was way out of line when I accused you of manipulation.

He was leaning forward, his elbows resting on his thighs, his fingers loosely entwined.

'I see,' Lisa said coldly.

'Is that the extent of your reaction?' he asked tautly, and she averted her face.

'How would you like me to react? Would you like me to shout with relief that you no longer see me as the avaricious gold-digger you accused me of being yesterday? Is that what you'd like?' She turned to face him, her eyes flashing. 'Well, I hate to say this but it hardly changes the insult implied when you levelled those accusations at me in the first place.'

'I take your point,' he replied tersely, 'but you have to understand that I'm in the direct firing line for any woman who gets it in her head that her lifestyle needs improving. I'm very good at spotting the danger signs a mile off. Naturally when Caroline ran to me with her tale I wondered whether you had been the one to slip through the net.'

'Fine.' She shrugged and waited for him to continue. She didn't see why she should make things any easier for him and it occurred to her that she would have to develop a bit more backbone as far as he was concerned, if she was to find the strength to fight him on her own ground.

She couldn't continue seeing him through the eyes of a lovestruck girl. This was no longer simply a question of her. There was the baby to consider now, too.

'Would you care to offer me a cup of coffee?' he asked eventually, and she glanced across at him suspiciously, as though suspecting there might be some further, carefully concealed attack lurking behind the perfectly ordinary request. She wasn't about to fall into the trap of trusting him. She had seen the depths of his rage beneath the civilised veneer, and that, she thought, would be a constant reminder to her that the real man beneath the sophisticated, urbane glamour was as ruthless and dangerous as a jungle animal.

'I would have,' she said politely, standing up, 'but I didn't realise that you intended to stay long enough to drink it.'

He followed her into the kitchen and said to her averted back, 'We have to talk.'

'I suppose so,' she answered reluctantly. She poured the hot water into the mugs and her hand was trembling. So much, she thought, for that passing bravado. She wasn't looking at him, but she could feel his presence in the kitchen and it made her nervous and jumpy. She had to force herself to control her face so that when she turned round to proffer the mug to him her expression was blank and composed.

She followed him back into the living room, took the chair facing his and eyed him silently over the rim of her mug.

'Would you ever have told me?' He crossed his legs, ankle resting on knee, and regarded her.

'I don't know. Maybe one day.' She frowned. 'No,

probably not,' she admitted. 'I can't see that there would ever have been the need to.'

He very slowly rested the mug on the table in front of him and then said coldly, 'No need? No need to inform a child of the identity of its father?'

'No,' she said, nervously aware that she wasn't saying the right things. 'Look, I have no intention of upsetting your life.' She paused and tried to think how to proceed from here without treading on any mines.

'Let's move on from there, shall we?' he countered in a hard voice. 'Let's begin with the assumption that my life is already, as you put it, upset.'

'In that case, there's no need for it to be upset further. I just want you to know that I'm not going to try and force you into taking any responsibility for this. It was a mistake. I wasn't thinking straight; I never imagined I would get pregnant.'

'So, ideally, I should just walk right out of that door and not look back, is that it?'

'Yes. That would be for the best, I think.'

'Oh, it would, would it?' There was cold cynicism in his voice, making her hot and nervous.

'I think so, don't you? I mean, this is my responsibility. It doesn't have anything to do with you.'

'*Your* responsibility!' he bellowed furiously. 'Nothing to do with me!'

'Of course,' Lisa said hurriedly, 'I know that you're *responsible*. Technically, that is. But what I'm trying to tell you is that I have no intention of making any demands on you or having this interfere with your life.'

'How thoughtful of you.' His mouth curled derisively.

'Yes, I think so!' she snapped with hostility. 'I can't win, can I? First I'm accused of getting pregnant so that

I can blackmail you, then I'm accused of doing just the opposite!'

'You're being deliberately obtuse.'

'I am not!'

'You're avoiding the truth of the situation because it suits you to do so and you expect me to fall into line.'

'And what *is* the truth of the situation?' She was perched on the edge of the chair, and now she sat back and tried to get a grip on her emotions. This sort of arguing couldn't be good for the baby. She placed her hand on her stomach and felt it kicking. Was it her imagination or was it kicking more than usual? Was it picking up vibes, or responding to all the high voices and the surge of feeling running through her blood?

She wished that she had never laid eyes on him again. In fact, she wished that he had never entered her uncluttered, uncomplicated life. Why couldn't he accept that she was doing him a favour by not disrupting his life with an unwanted baby? He lived his life at breakneck speed. There was no room in that sort of life for any relationship other than the most transient and babies were not transient creatures. They were demanding, voracious human beings who didn't need occasional, disruptive appearances from a man who was technically a father but in reality more of a stranger.

'The truth is that you bitterly regret what happened between us and you expect me to vanish conveniently off the face of the earth so that you can put the whole unfortunate episode behind you. Sadly for you, I'm not about to oblige. This isn't about you. I happen to have some stakes here too. Just a few. About fifty per cent.'

'I'm going to be bringing up this baby,' she said stiffly. 'I know that you mean well...'

'But...?' he asked cynically. 'You can manage quite happily on your own?'

Lisa didn't say anything. She looked down stubbornly at her fingers, her mouth set. There didn't seem to be much point in arguing with him. Whichever way she turned, he found a door and slammed it in her face.

'Well?' he persisted, and she shrugged and muttered, 'That's right.'

'How much money do you earn?'

'Money has nothing to do with it!' she told him hotly. 'What difference does it make how much money I earn? Does it follow that if I lived in a big house with a big garden and took expensive holidays every year I would somehow make a better mother? Do you think that money buys everything? If you do, then I feel sorry for you!'

'How much?' The hard blue eyes looked at her steadily and she grudgingly told him what he wanted to know. It didn't matter anyway. She was in the right on this.

'And you honestly don't believe that it would make the slightest difference if I accepted responsibility and allowed this baby to benefit from my wealth?'

'I don't want any of your money.'

'We're not talking about you.'

'All right, then. In answer to your question, no! Swanning in here once a year laden with expensive presents wouldn't do anything to improve this child's quality of life. You might think that that's the answer, but it isn't. In the end, it just disorients a child. I spent my childhood moving from pillar to post and it was upsetting. I know we're not talking about me, but my experiences are enough to tell me that what you're offering will be the same sort of thing. I won't have any child of mine subjected to that.'

'But why can't we stay in one place?' she could remember asking her mother. Over and over, until she realised that it was a futile question. She wasn't going to put up with her own child asking, 'Why can't Daddy be here with us like everyone else's?'

And anyway, long-distance relationships like that never lasted. They couldn't. After the initial burst of good intentions, things would begin to wane. The visits would become fewer and further between. They would be replaced by presents sent through the post at appropriate times, and then even those would inevitably dry up. It just wouldn't work out and it would be better if the whole thing did not begin.

And then, she thought, ashamed, there's the question of me, isn't there?

Angus Hamilton might find it easy enough to breeze into her life now and again because he was indifferent to her, but how was she going to feel? How would she ever be able to loosen the stranglehold that her love for him had on her, if she couldn't rely on his absence giving her the strength she needed?

She couldn't conceive how unsettling it would be, living in between his visits, desperately trying to break free but with the knowledge that he might appear, at any given moment, and send her hurtling back to square one. How would she ever begin to get her life back into order? It would be beyond her. Like Sisyphus pushing his rock up that hill only to find it slipping away from him before he could reach the top. Over and over again. A never-ending task of recurring pain.

'I have no intention of "swanning in here", as you call it, once a year, with presents to compensate for my not being around for the other three hundred and sixty-four days. I don't see that as accepting responsibility for my child any more than you do.' He stood up and went across to the window, which, prosaically, overlooked a small neat car park, and beyond that a tiny park hemmed in by row upon row of small, neat, doll's-house-type houses, all very tidy and characterless. 'No, that's not what I had in mind at all.'

'And what exactly did you have in mind?'

He didn't answer immediately. He stuck his hands into the pockets of his trousers and continued to stare outside, seemingly riveted by the lack of inspiring scenery.

His silence, for some odd reason, began to make her feel more nervous. She didn't like it. It was more ominous than his biting sarcasm and anger. What was he thinking? Had she thrown him? Had she put him in a spot with her flat refusal to accept money so that now he was forced to think on his feet and come up with an alternative? Was that it?

'I propose that we get married.' He slowly turned around so that he was facing her, and she stared at him in shock. After the first wild surge of colour, her face had gone white. 'You seem surprised,' he said laconically, moving away from the window to sit back down on the sofa.

'You must be joking.'

'It's not that surprising a proposition, is it?'

'Are you mad?'

'We get married and our child can grow up in a normal family environment. There won't be any part-time parenting, no lavish gifts to make up for unavoidable absences when I can't make a certain Saturday or a certain Wednesday afternoon. And it will have all the material advantages which I am in more than a good position to offer. You're right when you say that money doesn't make a good parent—or a happy child for that matter—but if the opportunity is there, then how can you sensibly deprive our child of it?'

'You're not listening to me!'

'You're alone in the world, Lisa. No family network that you can fall back on. Do you really feel comfortable with the thought of bringing up a baby with no support at all?'

'Of course it's frightening,' she answered unsteadily. 'I know it isn't going to be a bed of roses. I know there will be times when I wish there was someone there to take over, to help out, but...'

'But...?'

'But that's no reason to marry you. Can't you see that? There would be no love involved...' She dropped her eyes and stared down at her lap. 'Your lifestyle isn't suited to a family. It would be a terrible mistake.'

'Stop being naïve,' he said curtly, and she bristled at the note of command in his voice.

'I am not being naïve. I don't want to marry you.'

'I thought that marriage was high on your list of priorities,' he told her coolly, and she flushed. 'I thought that relationships with men were not to be contemplated unless a wedding ring was waiting just around the corner.'

'I never said that...'

'Of course you did. You just choose to forget.' He moved to where she was sitting and loomed over her, bending down so that the impact of his words wouldn't be lost across the distance of the room, so that she could feel his breath on her face. It brought back confusing memories of his body against hers, his fingers exploring her, his hands caressing her. She flinched at the unwanted images, averting her head, and his eyes narrowed.

'Do you regret what happened between us so much?' he asked, and although his voice wasn't raised there was no gentleness there. 'Do you now loathe me so much that you can't stand the thought of being in the same house as me?'

'It would be a mistake,' she repeated wearily, turning to look at him. 'It would be wrong. You say that marrying you would provide a normal life for our child, but it wouldn't, would it? What's normal about a marriage between two reluctant people, forced to live together for the sake of a child? What kind of environment would that be? A happy one?

'At least…' her voice had dropped to a whisper '…my parents loved each other. I might have hated all the travel, all the upheavals, but when I was inside the house with them, wherever that might have been, there was warmth and love there. What do you imagine it would be like without that?'

'I see,' he said, straightening up. He had removed his jacket earlier on. Now he slipped it back on and looked at her. 'I never imagined that I would find myself proposing marriage to a woman who would rather cope with a difficult situation in complete isolation than get tied up with me. What does that say about me, I wonder?' He laughed humourlessly.

'I'm sorry,' Lisa said.

'Don't apologise. Why should you?'

'It's just that I wouldn't want you to think that I don't consider your offer very generous…'

'But all in all the job just doesn't suit you.'

'That's it.'

'Which still leaves us with the problem of arranging

some sort of visiting rights. And can we do that in an informal manner or would that not suit either?'

'We can work it out ourselves,' she replied, depressed because suddenly everything seemed to be not quite the right way up. After their heated confrontation, after his astounding proposal, his calm acceptance now was something of an anticlimax. Then she told herself that she was being utterly stupid. He would have to have access to their child, whether it disrupted her life or not, so wasn't it preferable that any such access was achieved with the least acrimony possible?

But at the back of her mind there was the niggling thought that he had surrendered awfully quickly once she had informed him that she wouldn't marry him. No protestations, no attempts to persuade her to change her mind. He must be relieved, she thought, with a stab of bitterness. Relieved that she had not taken him up on his offer, relieved that he had squared it with his conscience, had been seen in his own eyes to have done the right thing, so that now he could carry on with his life knowing that he had tried his best.

'Good,' he said abruptly. 'I'll be in touch.' And he turned away, letting himself out of the flat without a backward glance.

It was only when he had gone that she realised how drained she was. She switched on the television set and pretended to watch something but she was too fraught to concentrate.

Now that he had come and she knew that he would be back again, if only to sort out things, she was back on that tightrope of suspended animation. Doing normal things, like reading her book, washing the dirty mugs in the kitchen sink, carrying on except that her mind had been frozen in some dreadful time warp, dwelling obsessively on him, desperately looking forward to the next encounter. She would have to fight very hard if she wasn't to go through the next few months or years leaping from one emotional encounter to the next and only managing to exist in between.

If only she could do the sensible thing and dislike him. There were, after all, a million reasons why she should. If only, even, she could put him in some sort of perspective, but she couldn't. He overwhelmed her. Even when they were arguing, even when bitterness filled her mouth and her head and her thoughts, even when he alarmed her in a way no one ever had before, he still excited her. She found it hard to tear her gaze away from him, and when she did she could still see his face reflected in her mind.

On Monday, Paul, surprisingly because he normally respected her need for privacy, asked her about him. He didn't ask whether Angus was the man responsible for the pregnancy, but she told him anyway since there seemed little point in hiding it.

'And is he going to support the baby?' he asked casually. They were sitting in his office, going through the books, with a plate full of sandwiches between them and two cups of coffee. He was busy poring over the figures, frowning because his mind, which was so tuned in to anything to do with plants, found it almost impossible to piece together anything that involved numbers, and she hesitated, wondering whether to change the subject tactfully or not.

'He wants to contribute,' she said honestly. 'He wants to take some responsibility.'

'And you find that surprising?'

'No, not really,' she answered, thinking about it.

'In that case, why didn't you approach him from the start?'

'Because...' she said, faltering. He looked up at her thoughtfully. 'Because I didn't want him to feel obliged to...'

'But he is; of course he is.' He was looking at her and his pleasant, open face was speculative. 'He struck me as a very aggressive type. The sort of man who wouldn't do anything in half-measures.'

'He has a very fast, very high-profile lifestyle. There's no room in it for anyone else.'

'And you resent that.'

'Of course I don't!' Lisa exclaimed.

'I don't mean to pry, Lisa,' he said a little tentatively, because her personal life was an area into which he had rarely ventured in the past, 'but if you were indifferent to him it wouldn't matter a jot to you whether you disturbed his lifestyle or not. Your only thoughts would be for the baby and you would probably find it easy to accept that he was duty-bound to share the responsibility.'

She didn't say anything. She knew what he was getting at but she couldn't put it into words; she couldn't come right out and admit that she was frantically in love with Angus Hamilton. To voice it would make it more real; it would be as though there was no turning back, no more hiding from the truth. She would have to don the public face of her private life, and, however much she had opened up with Paul recently, she still wasn't prepared to go that far.

'If you ever need somewhere to go,' he said, after a while, 'to think things over, the cottage is empty and you're welcome to it.'

He owned a two-bedroomed cottage in the Lake

District. Lisa had been there once for a long weekend and she had rather enjoyed it, even though it was in a fairly sad state of repair, despite Ellie's brave attempts to hide it with new curtains and scatter cushions on the sofas. Paul had been given it by his father and apparently it had been in his family for years and years and years, and since each successive inheritor had done minimal work on it the task of now overhauling it would cost a fair penny.

She didn't think she would be needing to think anything over. She wouldn't need the cottage. There was, really, not much thinking over to be done. The fact was that Angus Hamilton would see his child and her only protection lay in her ability to forge ahead with her life and close her eyes to the effect he had on her. Time had a way of sorting things out, of putting things into focus.

'Thanks, Paul,' she said obediently, then she lowered her eyes and steered the subject back to work and he accepted the change without batting an eyelid. It was one of the things that she had liked about him from the very start. He had never allowed curiosity to dictate to him. He had left her to her privacy, the way she had liked it. Once. Sometimes, now, she wasn't entirely sure.

If she hadn't clung so tenaciously to her security, would she have been better prepared for the earthquake that had turned her tidy, ordered world upside down when Angus Hamilton had entered it? Brick by brick she had built the fortifications around her to protect her from life's slings and arrows, yet when he had come along it had taken only a puff to blow them all away.

If she had never tried to cling to the illusion that stability was somehow a controllable commodity, then wouldn't she have been less vulnerable in the end? Better prepared to cope with a man like Angus

Hamilton? If, if, if. She could drown thinking about all the ifs in her life.

Still, she would have to learn to cope with her emotions, learn not to give herself away when she was with him, however infrequently that might be.

It was a week before she next saw him and this time when the doorbell rang she knew it was going to be him before she even got there. She composed her face suitably and opened the door, quite prepared to talk through the visiting rights issue in a dispassionate manner.

It was not quite seven and he had obviously come straight from work. He was still wearing his suit, which was dark grey, with his coat, which was black, and she looked at him politely, expecting him to get straight down to business, but when she invited him inside, in a voice which neither wavered nor stumbled, he asked instead whether she had eaten yet.

'I...was about to,' Lisa said hesitatingly.

'Get your coat. I'll take you out for a meal.'

'Why?' she asked, and he smiled at her with the speculative, amused charm that reminded her of how he used to be months ago on that holiday.

'That's not a very gracious response,' he murmured.

'I'm sorry, but I just thought that we might as well discuss whatever terms of visiting that you'd like right here. There's no need to take me out.'

'No, you're right, there's none, but the way I look at it is that we're going to be seeing one another on a regular basis for an indefinite length of time, even if it is only in passing. We might as well get accustomed to some sort of relaxed, amicable relationship.' He was still smiling, though the temperature in his voice had dropped by a few degrees. 'Or is that asking too much?'

'No, of course not.' He was right, and maybe a politely friendly arrangement was the way to go, after all. She smiled and said, 'I'll get my coat; I won't be a minute.'

They went to an Italian restaurant, which was lovely because she hadn't eaten out in a restaurant for ages, and over the meal he showed her photos of the Caribbean islands they had visited, which Liz had sent to him because, he explained, he never remembered to carry a camera anywhere.

'I think the problem,' he said lazily, 'is that the damn thing's just too complicated. It was my mother's. She used to take impressive shots of flowers. My problem is that I'm fairly useless when it comes to gadgets like that. Too many dials to twist.'

When he chatted like that, easily and without any of that cold cynicism which he was capable of, she could feel her guard dropping. She had to remind herself that charm was a commodity at his disposal, something he pulled out at will.

It was only when they were standing outside her flat that she said, with surprise, 'What about arrangements to see the baby? We haven't discussed it at all.'

'Oh, no, we haven't, have we?' he answered, as though startled himself by the omission. 'Perhaps I could call by next week and we can discuss it then. What about next Saturday?'

'I don't know,' Lisa said uncertainly. 'I'm not sure.'

'Why?' He looked at her with a slight frown. 'Are you going somewhere? We could make it another day if you'd prefer.'

'No.' Her face cleared. 'Saturday will be fine.' She decided that she was being foolish, that they had just spent a perfectly enjoyable evening together with no angry exchanges or bitter accusations.

'Right, then, I'll call for you around seven-thirty?'

She nodded, and watched him as he walked to his car, gave her a wave and then drove off.

She didn't quite know why but she felt unsettled by the evening. It didn't make any sense because when she sat down and thought about it she had nothing to feel unsettled *about*. He had been pleasant and charming in a totally unthreatening way. He had displayed the same polite, almost brotherly concern that he had shown towards her at the very start of that holiday, when he had been at pains to make her feel at ease.

It was a good thing, she told herself over the next few days, that they could relate to each other in a civil, adult fashion. What kind of life would it be for a child to be torn between two warring parents? And she would never be able to conduct her life in a state of constant emotional upheaval; she would end up having a nervous breakdown.

He had been angry and upset, she realised, when he had first found out about the pregnancy, but now he had had time to think things over and in his usual firm, calculating way he had taken the reins and was steering them in the most sensible direction.

He had offered marriage, but had not tried to fight her objections. No, he had wanted marriage as little as she had and now that that idea had been squashed he intended to conduct a courteous, occasional-dinners-out type of relationship with her so that when they met they would at least be able to exchange conversation without arguing.

She couldn't find fault with that, could she?

She was now nearly eight months pregnant. She didn't need to cope with unnecessary strain. Very shortly, she would be stopping work, and counting down the days on the calendar. She had already had a tour of the maternity section of the hospital where she would be having the baby, and it had had quite an impact on her. She needed to feel reasonably relaxed and it would help if she didn't have to do battle with a man whose presence was enough to throw her time and again.

So when she next saw him she was prepared to make an effort and she did.

They went out for a meal, this time at another restaurant where the music was a bit louder and the atmosphere a little more hectic, and when he asked her questions about what she had been doing for the past week she didn't frown and wonder whether there was anything more meaningful behind the questions; she just answered with a smile.

She told him that she only had a little over a week to go before she gave up working, but that she would be back again almost as soon as she'd had the baby because she needed the money, and it only occurred to her much later, when she was in bed, that he had not argued the point.

He had not informed her that she would have no need to return to work if she listened to him and accepted the money he wanted to give her. He had not pointed out that she had chosen not to marry him, that instead she had picked the harder of the paths to follow. There had been no recriminations and none of the terse, vaguely threatening accusations with which he had initially confronted her.

Instead he had nodded understandingly, moved on to discuss the maternity benefits in his company, which he was hoping to upgrade within the next year, while she ate and listened and was hardly aware of how fundamental his change in attitude towards her appeared to be.

Now, with the lights in her bedroom off, lying on her side with a pillow angled by her stomach, she realised that what was now missing between them was that spark which had manifested itself in passion when they had been on holiday and which had still glowed when they had argued heatedly over the fate of the baby.

They had reached some kind of even keel and she said to herself that nothing could be better. She even wondered whether her violent attraction towards him was beginning to ebb away. She had certainly relaxed enough in his company not to feel permanently on edge every time he looked at her. She could meet those blue eyes evenly and she had even stopped apologising in that automatic way of hers which appeared to have been a habit cultivated over a lifetime.

She also realised that they had discussed nothing practical, which had supposedly been the object of the exercise.

She decided that the next time she saw him she would insist that they reach some sort of agreement as to how often he would want to see the baby. She would do that before they went anywhere or did anything. She couldn't continue to see him as though they were friends.

She wouldn't allow herself to be lulled into some kind of false security. He didn't love her and he had nothing to lose, but she couldn't afford to become too dependent on his kind, solicitous visits because there would come a time when she would find that she couldn't do without them.

The next time she saw him, she would lay the cards on the table.

CHAPTER EIGHT

LISA had, stupidly, she now realised, left almost everything till the last minute. Her friends had given her bits and pieces over the months, which she had stored away in a cupboard, out of sight, but she had bought hardly anything herself. The cot, the pram, and all the other things which she vaguely assumed a baby might need, she had left to the very end.

At first, because she had not wanted to think about things like that, and anyway nine months seemed such a long time, she had kept telling herself that there would be more than enough time.

Later, when she had found herself unconsciously growing more and more attached to the baby inside her, she had held back because of some irrational fear of pre-empting fate by going out and buying things.

Then she had told herself that she would do it all when she gave up work, except that she had never really anticipated staying at work for quite as long as she had. Keeping busy had seemed so much more preferable to staying inside her house, day after day, preparing for the baby, being constantly reminded of how lonely it was going to be giving birth, then looking after a baby, all on her own.

The only thing she hadn't quite foreseen was how tired she would be in the latter stages of pregnancy.

But it's got to be done, she told herself after she had picked off some breakfast on the Saturday morning. The thought depressed her for no reason that she could put her finger on.

It wasn't as though she had no money in the bank because she had. She had been diligently saving every month. She could easily afford the cot and the pram and she hardly needed to buy any clothes at all because her friends had bought quite a few for her, though she hadn't looked at them for so long that she could hardly remember what exactly they were. All she could remember was holding them up, exclaiming with the right degree of pleasure in her voice, and then stuffing them away because the sight of them had made her feel like bursting into tears.

She cleared away her plate and cup slowly. Her pregnancy had been an easy one, with no complications. For the first few months she had felt sick occasionally, but then that had cleared and almost up until a couple of weeks ago she had felt perfectly fine.

Now it irritated her that she had to move so lethargically. Everything took three times longer than it normally would have. She never complained to anyone, though. She felt that she had no one to blame for getting herself in this situation and there was no way that she was going to moan about anything at all.

She brushed her hair, looked at herself in the mirror and decided that, all told, she didn't look too bad. Apart from her stomach, everything had remained more or less the same size.

She could remember Ellie telling her proudly that she had swollen to the size of a barrage balloon with each of her pregnancies, because she just couldn't stop eating and putting on weight.

Lisa's arms and legs had remained thin and her face looked healthy but that was all.

She sighed, gathered up her bag and slung it over her shoulder, then went to the front door and pulled it open.

Angus was standing outside and because she had had absolutely no warning that he would be there she very nearly yelped in shock.

'How long have you been here?' she asked. She hadn't spoken to him since she had made the decision to get this visiting business sorted out and to stop meandering into some kind of frightful, dangerous friendship with him.

She only wished that her body could be as pragmatic as her mind. She looked up at him and her heart fluttered at the dark sexiness of his face and the taut lines of his body.

It was cold and windy outside and the wind had tousled his dark hair, which somehow made him look less intimidating but rather more dangerous.

'I was about to ring the doorbell.'

'Oh.' Lisa stepped outside firmly and shut the door behind her. 'As you can see, I'm on my way out. I'm afraid you'll have to call back. It might be an idea if you phoned me in advance.' She hoped, with something approaching nausea, that his visiting times weren't going to be along these lines. Just showing up when it suited him and not giving her any advance warning. She had to brace herself for him. She didn't think that she could cope with surprise calls. She would have to make sure that he understood that when they discussed arrangements.

She began walking laboriously towards her car and he fell into step with her.

'Where are you going?' His questions never seemed to emerge as questions, she thought, more like politely phrased commands. All part and parcel of a man who had no time for uncertainties, who was accustomed to taking the lead and being followed.

'Shopping,' Lisa said, not looking at him. Her thick coat seemed to weigh ten times what it should and was pressing down on her, making her movements even more sluggish. The wind was blowing against her as well, so that it felt as though she had to do battle with it. At this rate she doubted that she would make it further than a few shops. 'There are some things I have to get,' she added vaguely.

'I'll come with you.'

He took her arm and steered her away from her car and towards his, which was a gleaming, high-powered anachronism among the other run-of-the-mill cars.

She tried to pull away and opened her mouth to tell him that she intended going on her own, but before she could say anything he told her, with silky authority in his voice, 'And don't even think of being stubborn and arguing with me. You've finally realised that you need to buy a few things for this baby, like something to sleep in, and I'm coming with you whether you want me there or not.'

'How did you know...?' she asked, blushing, surprised.

He said drily, 'I looked. No nursery. Nothing but a small spare room hastily cleared away and half-empty.'

'You nosed around my house!'

'Hardly. Your house is so small that I could sit in one spot and have a pretty good view of every room in it.'

He held the passenger door open for her and she settled herself inside, tucking her coat around her.

His appearance had thrown her. She now felt as though she had lost command over her own day but she was too stunned and taken aback to feel angry.

'Where to?' he asked, slipping in beside her.

She said stiffly, 'Reading, please. There are some children's shops there.'

'We'll go to Harrods,' he told her, and she bristled and twisted to face him.

'We will *not* go to Harrods! I can't afford anything from Harrods!'

'But I can,' he said smoothly. He drove off, heading out towards London.

'You can't take control like this,' she spluttered.

'Of course I can. We're going to Harrods and I shall be paying for whatever we get and there's no point in getting in a state over it.'

'You're impossible,' she muttered under her breath, staring out of the window and watching the built-up countryside of Berkshire give way to the busy network of roads leading into London.

After a while, he said, with a hint of amusement in his voice which made her even crosser, 'I can feel you simmering there next to me, ready to explode. Very bad for a woman in your condition. We don't want you going into premature labour, do we?'

'I'll make sure I spare you the experience,' Lisa snapped sarcastically, which left him unperturbed.

'I told you I intended taking responsibility. I have no idea why you're so surprised that I'm buying a few necessities for you.'

'Because I can buy them myself!'

'Now listen to me,' he said, with an edge of steel in his voice. 'I don't intend to go round in circles every time this business of money comes up. You just have to accept that I have a lot of it and I'm going to make sure that our child gets the best, whether you like it or not.'

She tried to think of something suitably cutting as a

rejoinder to this high-handedness, but she couldn't, so she lapsed into sulky silence until they were in Central London, when she said, sweetly, 'And where do you intend to park?'

He laughed, not looking at her. 'I don't.' He reached for his car phone, spoke into it and replaced the receiver. 'There. All done. George will meet us outside Harrods and take the car.' He flashed her a quick, sidelong glance, then returned his attention to the packed roads.

'How convenient, having a chauffeur at your beck and call,' she said under her breath.

'Isn't it?' He was smiling, and she shot him a look full of resentment. How was it that he could be so cheerfully immune to anything she had to say, when what she wanted most at the moment was to pick an argument with him?

She had come to the conclusion that if loving him was bad, then liking him was almost equally so, and she had caught herself doing both in the past few weeks. She would have to be frosty and polite and the only way she could achieve this would be to set him at a distance, to shift him out of this 'be kind to Lisa' approach which he appeared to have adopted recently. She didn't want him to be kind to her. She preferred his coldness to that.

George was faithfully waiting at the agreed spot for them, rubbing his gloved hands together, hurrying to the car as soon as it pulled over so that he could drive away with the least possible delay, and she allowed herself to be guided up to the Children's floor of Harrods, her body stiff with hostility.

If he noticed a thing, then he made no comment, just held her elbow and cleared a path through the crowds with seemingly very little effort.

'Now,' he said, 'where do we start?'

Lisa, who had perversely made up her mind to be as unhelpful as she could possibly get away with being, told him what she needed, and they proceeded to look at every cot, from every angle, until reluctantly she felt some of the coldness beginning to thaw.

She had had no idea that such a variety of cots existed. Some of them were works of art. She ran her hands along the smooth, dark wood and shyly began to relax.

He had told her that she was not to look at the prices of anything, had forbidden her to, but she still did and she flushed guiltily at the cost of some of the various bits they were looking at.

From their joint positions of inexperience, they amicably discussed the merits of this or that over something else, and it was only after a while that she discovered she was enjoying herself, that this was the first time her eyes had been opened to what it must be like to be pregnant and involved with someone and that she liked it.

Why couldn't it have been different? she asked herself sadly. Why did I have to fall in love with a man as out of reach as Angus Hamilton? Why did I have to get pregnant? Why couldn't it have been Mr Ordinary from next door, so that we could have lived happily ever after like two people in a fairy tale? Why, why, why?

She looked up to find him watching her narrowly, and she forced herself to smile and carry on.

The cot they decided on wasn't the most expensive one, but it was getting there, and then they moved on to other things, other things which she had had no idea she might need, but which looked so wonderful, so tempting that she let herself be swayed by him, so that by lunchtime she was exhausted and uncomfortably aware that the money he had spent made her paltry savings look like bits of copper.

They had lunch at the café in Harrods, and she dabbled about with her sandwiches, so that he said wryly, 'I thought pregnant women were supposed to eat enough for two?'

Lisa laughed and looked at him briefly before lowering her eyes. It hurt too much to keep them on his dear face. It raised too many if onlys and whys in her mind, which made her feel tearful.

'Difficult when you're at this stage of the pregnancy,' she said, concentrating on another bite of sandwich. 'There's nowhere much for the food to go. I find it easier to pick.'

'And how's your conscience getting along?' he asked, pushing his plate aside and then leaning back in his chair to look at her. 'I watched you while we were up there, like a tiny little orphan who's suddenly found herself transported into the biggest toy shop in the world and can't quite believe that she's really there.'

'I'm not used to such extravagance,' Lisa told him with a small smile. 'I kept trying to tot up the cost of everything we were buying, but after a while my head couldn't hold such big sums and I had to give up.'

'I told you not to do that,' he drawled, but with amusement in his voice, and she felt the same pleasure she had felt earlier on when they had been looking at everything together—a feeling of absolute unity—so that she had to pull back and remind herself that any such feeling was an illusion.

'So you did,' she agreed, and he laughed and continued to look at her.

'Did you enjoy yourself?' he asked abruptly, sitting forward and resting his elbows on the table, his blue eyes intent on her face.

The place was humming with activity, people coming

and going, tables being cleared, but when he looked at her like that it was as if there was no one around them; it was as if the whole universe had narrowed down to just the two of them. She could feel her heart pounding.

'Did you?' he pressed softly, and she nodded and pushed her plate aside as well.

'It's easier with two, isn't it?' he asked her, though he didn't wait for a reply to a question which she would have found virtually unanswerable without giving herself away. 'Easier not having to cope on your own, easier not having to look at things which aren't meant to be looked at alone. Isn't it?'

This time he waited, his head tilted slightly to one side, his dark, powerful features revealing nothing.

'I don't suppose I would have browsed so much,' Lisa answered, hedging the question the best she could.

'Easier not to have complete and total responsibility on your own.'

'What are you trying to say, Angus?' she asked at last, raising troubled eyes to his. 'It's always easier sharing responsibilities; of course it is. But sometimes it's just not possible.'

'Yes, it is.' His voice was low and urgent. 'Marry me, Lisa.'

She licked her lips and shifted in her chair. She felt like a rabbit which had been run to ground and was cornered. She was no longer even on her own home patch.

Was that why he had been so nice to her recently? Because he had been trying to warm her up to the thought of marrying him? But in a way that would not make her suspicious and have her running off in the opposite direction like a frightened deer?

She wished that she could explain to him how much

she would have wanted to marry him, but not like this, not under these circumstances. It was the cruellest of tricks that she should find herself with everything she wanted so nearly within her reach and yet so far.

'I can't,' she whispered, and he flushed darkly, with anger.

'Why not? Haven't I proved to you that we can coexist? That I'm not some kind of monster?'

'I never said you were,' she protested. It was easy for him to speak of coexisting, she thought. From where he was sitting, she must appear stubborn and stupid, because as far as he was concerned they could rub along well enough together, well enough for their child to grow up in the presence of both parents, where a harmony of sorts existed.

If he could see deep into her mind, he would soon realise why any such situation was out of the question.

He would be able to give her the security of a house, with all the trappings, and that kind of security, she knew, was important. For a long time, she had thought that it was the only security she needed. But then she had met him and she had realised that there was a greater security than that. The security of being emotionally bonded to someone else, of having your love returned, of being anchored.

It had never occurred to her before, but in a blinding flash she could understand why her parents had never considered their nomadic lifestyle destabilising. Quite simply, it hadn't been. Their stability had lain in one another; it had transcended such things as geography. At night, they'd lain in one another's arms, and the fact that they were in a different bed, in a different house, in a different county had been immaterial.

'You're wasting your time, Angus,' she said, more

sharply than she might otherwise have done, and he brought his closed fist down hard on the table, so that the people sitting around them glanced across briefly, before looking away. 'And you can't threaten me or blackmail me or persuade me into seeing your point of view.'

'If you could give me just one good, coherent reason why you won't marry me, then I would understand,' he said harshly, in a low voice, leaning towards her so that his presence filled her head and made her feel a little dizzy.

'I already have!'

'You've told me that if we got married our child would grow up in an unhappy, inhibiting atmosphere. But when we're together, in case it's escaped you, you can enjoy yourself.'

'You don't understand.' He made it sound so easy. To make him understand seemed like a tortuous, uphill struggle. 'It's not as simple as that.'

'It's as simple or as complicated as you want to make it.'

'I don't know why you're so keen to...to get married,' Lisa said in a low voice. She had only made the observation with a view to buying time until she could work out some plausible line of defence, but when she looked at him she was surprised to see a dark flush of discomfiture cross his face, and vanish as quickly as it had appeared. Too quickly for her to try and work out what it meant, if anything.

'I mean,' she persevered, 'marriage and children were never part of your long-range plans.' Or maybe they were, she thought to herself, but just not with me. I was only ever good enough to fool around with. Isn't that how these upper-class types think? They might have their dalliances with any number of women but in the end they marry the ones who are suitable, whether or not love and attraction come into it.

Part of her told her that this didn't quite tie up with the Angus Hamilton that she knew, but then that was an emotional reaction to him.

'No,' he conceded abruptly.

'Well, then.'

'Well, then, what?'

'You can begin to understand how I must feel, Angus.' She took a deep breath and decided to lay as much of her hand on the table as she possibly could. 'We had a fling, not even an affair. A fling, for heaven's sake! Something that would have fizzled out after a few weeks under normal circumstances. Except that the unexpected happened. The unthinkable.' She lowered her eyes and stirred her now ice-cold coffee with the teaspoon, swirling the liquid round and round so that it formed ripples like the surface of a dirty pond.

'Something that can't be ignored, or locked away in a cupboard somewhere,' he pointed out curtly, which kind of made her want to cry because they had had such a wonderful morning and she didn't want it all to end on a sour note.

'I know that. But marriage is going from one extreme to the other, isn't it?'

'It's a solution to a fairly extreme situation, wouldn't you say?'

'Do you want to marry me because you're an important person in an important, high-profile job and an illegitimate baby would discredit you?' She looked at him evenly and saw something like the ghost of a smile cross his face.

'And where did that line of reasoning suddenly spring from?'

'Well...now that you mention it, Caroline...'

'Ah, yes, it had something of a Caroline ring about it,' he said grimly. 'Caroline lives her life playing to an audience. I don't. I really don't give a hang what the rest of the world thinks of me because I don't live my life for the rest of the world.'

'Then why...?'

'Because this is my child. I never considered marriage or a family, at least not in the foreseeable future. I also never considered what I would feel when fatherhood presented itself to me.'

She knew what he meant. Children, before, had been other people's problems. Now he looked at her, only a couple of weeks away from giving birth, to *his* child, and he wanted this child with a fierceness which he had never foreseen. That was why he didn't want to be a part-time father. That was why he wanted to marry her.

Chances were that even if she had continued their relationship, even if their relationship had stretched beyond a few weeks, he would never have married her because there would never have been a need to marry her. There was a need now, as far as he was concerned, except that *she* was playing only a secondary role in the whole proceedings.

'Yes, I see that, but...'

'But you can't have marriage without the trimmings. Without the declarations of love, without the magic and stardust.' His voice, when he spoke, was impatient and he made the whole concept of romantic dreams sound like the whimsical imaginings of a fool, which was probably how he saw them. 'Fine.' He looked straight at her. 'Marry me, Lisa. I love you.'

For just a second, time stood still. She had a second of intense, perfect happiness, then the bubble burst and reasoning reasserted itself and told her that those were empty words. They didn't mean a thing.

'I think we should go, Angus. I'm beginning to feel a little tired.'

He didn't say anything. He pulled his mobile phone out of his pocket, called George and then said that he would be there by the time they made their way down to the street.

He didn't mention another word about marriage until they were in the back seat of the car, when he turned to her and informed her that he was still waiting for her answer.

'I won't give up,' he said smoothly, when she didn't reply. 'I never give up on anything I want.'

'And you want this child.'

'That's right.' He folded his arms and she looked at his profile, clean and strong, with worried eyes.

She began to wonder why she was bothering to fight. Wasn't it going to be a losing battle? She had laid her cards on the table and so had he. He wanted her for the sake of his child and he was going to get what he wanted because he always did. Whether she liked it or not, he would insinuate himself into her life and erode her until she gave in.

'And what if you fall in love with someone else when we're married? What if I do?'

'You can't conduct your life based on some hypothetical speculation. What if this car goes over the edge of a cliff with us in it? What if the Third World War breaks out and the whole world goes up in smoke? When you start thinking like that, you can carry on ad infinitum.'

'Those things aren't likely to happen. It's far more likely that—'

'You'll marry me and then fall in love with another man, only to find yourself unhappily trapped in a situation of my making?' His voice was hard.

Lisa didn't answer. There was no possibility of that, she knew. The Third World War scenario was far more likely.

They had cleared the traffic of central London, and now they were picking up speed along the motorway. They would be back at her place in no time at all, and for the first time since he had voiced his preposterous suggestion that they get married she just wasn't sure. She just didn't know whether it *was* a preposterous suggestion. Hadn't they strolled through Harrods if not entwined like a loving couple anticipating the birth of their first child, then at least like friends, sharing a single dream?

And hadn't it been easier? She imagined what it would have been like trudging wearily through baby shops in Reading, choosing things happily enough but never escaping that edge of sadness, knowing that she should be sharing things like that with the father of her child.

She thought about all the months and years that lay ahead, the decisions that would have to be taken, the childhood illnesses that she would have to face on her own.

What, she thought a little desperately, am I to do? Which path do I go down? She could actually see her life in front of her. Her life was a wilderness and the paths forked in opposite directions.

So, he didn't love her. Well, he must at least *like* her. He surely wouldn't have proposed if he hated her, would he? She might not be his first choice as a partner for life, she might not even be his second or third, but, as he'd said, these were exceptional circumstances.

And would it be so awful? She had so much love in her heart—enough for the two of them. And maybe one day, when he was least expecting it, he might turn around and realise that he did in fact love her, that time had nourished something which didn't presently exist into fruition.

'And what if *you* stray?' she asked timidly.

'Then you can divorce me and have full custody of our child and I'll abide by whatever rules you want.'

'I never imagined...that things would turn out like this for me.'

'You imagined that you had learnt lessons from your childhood and that you could arrange your life in such a way that it fitted in with what you wanted?'

'Yes.' Except now it was difficult to remember what those lessons were. Falling in love with Angus Hamilton had turned those preconceived ideas on their head and whenever she tried to grasp the things that had kept her going all this time she found that they were not quite within her reach.

'I know I'm not your type...'

'You know less than you think,' he answered ambiguously.

'I'm not a social butterfly. I'm no good at arranging dinners for twenty. I don't glitter and sparkle.' She knew that she sounded as though she was apologising, but she couldn't help it.

They had reached the outskirts of Reading now. Angus pressed a button so that the glass partition separating them from George in front slid aside, and he gave brief directions to the driver, then leaned back in his seat and looked at her.

'Will you let me think about it?' she asked, and he nodded. 'I'll call you.'

'No. I'll call *you*.'

'Don't you trust me?' she enquired with a faint smile, which he returned.

'Not when it comes to this. I'll drop by on Wednesday.'

The car pulled up outside her flat and now that they had arrived she felt a desperate urge to get inside, where she could be alone with her thoughts and decide for herself what she should do, without Angus's handsome, clever face swaying her every thought.

'Yes, OK.'

She pushed open the car door and Angus got out and said wryly, 'The bags in the boot?'

'Oh, yes, right.' She had forgotten about those. The big items were due to be delivered on Monday, but they had also bought an assortment of smaller things which had, in the mood of the moment, fallen into the category of cute, unnecessary and utterly irresistible.

He helped her with them into the flat, deposited them on the sofa, and before he left he turned to her and said, 'No more wriggling, Lisa.' He looked at her for a long time, then he did something completely unexpected. He reached out and laid both his hands on her stomach, caressing it, and she felt a spring of desire gush into life.

'No,' she agreed faintly, her body tensing, against her will, in expectation of his hands sliding upwards to her breasts. They didn't. He let them fall to his sides then turned around and let himself out of the flat.

She went across to the window, from where she could see his car, and watched as he slid into the back seat, leaning forward to say something to George, and she continued watching until she could no longer see it. Even after it had disappeared, she remained by the window and imagined the car heading back towards London, towards his place. Where was it? What was it like? There was so much, she realised, that she didn't know.

Then she spent the afternoon, and the rest of the weekend, unpacking all the assorted bits and pieces which she had collected over the months.

On Monday morning, she telephoned Paul as soon as she got up and asked him whether his offer of the loan of the cottage was still on.

'Isn't it too far for you to travel,' he asked dubiously, 'in your condition?'

'I'd really like it, Paul. I need to sort myself out; I need to get away from the house, just for a couple of days.' She didn't really know whether it would help being in a different place, but she thought that it might. She might be able to think clearly and lucidly without her familiar walls around her, and the familiar sights of those baby things lurking in the spare room, waiting in readiness as time ticked by and the day that had seemed so far away crawled nearer and nearer.

'It'll be cold. It'll take a little while to warm up.'

'No matter. I shall be back by Wednesday afternoon.'

She could sense him thinking, worrying about her, but he finally said that she could. He said he would make sure that Ellie stayed in so that she could get the key, and that he would also have her prepare some food—no arguments, please, or else no cottage—which made Lisa smile.

At a little after ten, after she had thrown a few things together in her case, she dropped by his house and collected the key along with enough food to last the duration of her stay and waged a friendly war with Ellie about the sanity of going somewhere so far when the baby was just around the corner and she should, really, be putting her feet up and taking it easy.

'I'll take it very easy,' Lisa promised. 'As soon as I get there. Feet up and all that stuff. And I won't have to cook. Thank you so much, Ellie.' But when she looked in the rear-view mirror as she drove off she could still see Ellie's face as she stood on the pavement outside their house, looking concerned and worried.

It was going to be a long drive, but at the end of it she would find peace—peace in which to decide what she should do with her life.

And, she thought, it was a fine day for driving. Cold and clear and blue. A good day to start a trip, as her father used to say every time they left one place and headed towards another. A good day to make the biggest decision of her life.

Look at me, Mum and Dad, she said to herself, no more that frightened little thing. Wherever you are, I know you'd be proud! She smiled.

CHAPTER NINE

IT WAS a good drive up. Lisa stopped at every service station she passed, so that she could stretch her legs, and she switched on her stereo for the entire drive. The various disc jockeys' voices boomed through the small car and it felt as though she had company.

Halfway through the journey, she pulled off the motorway, took a side road, parked the car in a lay-by and ate some of the sandwiches which Ellie had prepared. They tasted wonderful. She could already feel her head getting clearer. As she put distance between her and her house, the cobwebs began falling away and quite a bit of that worried agonising which she had done the previous night, alone in bed, began to recede.

By half past three, she was at the cottage. It was just as she remembered it. Small, clean, with minimum mod cons. A typical holiday home, Paul was always telling her, begging for attention except that no one could be bothered because it was never used enough to warrant a great deal of money being spent on it.

The ground floor was all open-plan, with the sitting room flowing into the kitchen, separated from it only by the width of a counter.

In the sitting room, there was a large, open fireplace and a stack of logs next to it, neatly contained in a basket which had seen better days but which comfortably matched the rest of the place.

Before she even unpacked, Lisa switched on the central heating, which cranked into life. It had been a fairly mild winter so far, so although it was very cold in the cottage there wasn't that deep-frozen feeling which tended to attack unused places in the depths of winter.

By the time she had hauled her bag upstairs and unpacked her few possessions, then laid out the food in the kitchen, it had warmed up enough for her to remove her coat, and, an hour later, her thick cardigan.

Ellie had prepared a generous hamper of milk, eggs, bread, several cans of several things, coffee, juice, butter—everything that Lisa could possibly need—and she made a mental note to buy her a huge bunch of flowers on the way back.

It was already dark by the time five o'clock rolled round—dark and warm and cosy—and she settled onto the sofa with her feet up and lay there with a cushion behind her head and her hand on her stomach and let herself think.

Her mind drifted into the past. She remembered bits of her childhood days, happy memories that filled the cottage like warm companions.

She remembered how she had longed for a life of security, but here, with no sounds around, just the silence of the darkness outside pressing against the windowpanes, she couldn't recapture the passion with which she had longed for it.

Fate had thrown her into an impossible situation where that placid, settled contentment which she had envisaged for herself would simply never materialise. Fate had thrown her Angus Hamilton and now, because she already knew what her decision was going to be, she began to enumerate the reasons why marrying him was what she intended to do, why it was the right thing to do, the only thing, in many ways.

It wasn't, she argued to herself, as if she could turn

her back on him and walk away. It wasn't as though she could ever find again any sort of happiness in the monotonous tenor of her life. Even if she never laid eyes on him again, which was out of the question because of this child inside her, things would never be the same. He had filled her with the sort of wild, uncontainable passion that made a mockery of everything that was ordered and neat and safe.

It was as though she had lived her life like a two-dimensional cardboard cut-out, and he had taken her and given her shape and form, made her into a three-dimensional human being, with all the attendant problems.

And that, she knew, was her greatest problem. Whatever lay before her, she would never again be that cardboard cut-out. He had changed her and she would remain changed until the day she died, whether he stayed as a part of her life or not.

I can't be wary any more, she thought to herself. I have to meet this challenge even if it leaves me broken in the end.

And anyway, maybe it wouldn't. Hope would give her the impetus to carry on and who knew? Who could see into the future? She might get to like dinner parties for twenty. She might just find that it wasn't as bad as she'd imagined. She might find that laughter came easily after a while. She might well discover that she could shed the defensive caution that had sat on her shoulders from as far back as she could remember.

In a strange way, he had made her into the sort of person she had never thought she could be. She had discovered deep within her some spark of impulse, some stirring of recklessness, something of her parents, and nothing had extinguished it and nothing, she now knew, ever would.

Later, at a little after seven, she made herself some food, opening one of the cans which Ellie had thoughtfully provided and helping herself to some pasta which was already in the cottage. Basic provisions, Ellie had told her, were always kept in the cupboards because they did use the place at least once every five weeks or so and they planned it so that they only had to bring perishables with them when they came to stay.

Then she settled down to read her book. There was no television. They had been adamant about not having one installed, despite pleas from the children, because they'd decided that there was already too much television at their house without it taking over their lives at the cottage as well.

Lisa didn't miss it. In the car, it had been fine listening to the voices talking at her out of the radio, but here it would have been intrusive.

It was only when she found herself drifting into sleep that she went upstairs, had a bath and then settled into bed.

There were only three small bedrooms in the cottage, but they were very pretty bedrooms, oddly shaped with sloping roofs. This one had a skylight and from where she lay she could look up and see the black, starry sky. She fell asleep thinking that out there, in another part of the country, the same black, starry sky was looking down on Angus, wherever he was. Working probably. It wasn't yet eight-thirty. Would he stop working such long hours when she married him? When he had this baby to come home to?

When she next woke up, it was black and silent outside and she had a brief moment of woolly disorientation which threw her into a panic as she wondered where she was. Then, sleepily, she remembered, and closed her eyes and felt it. The twinge that had awakened her, a cramping feeling. A contraction.

Oh, no—oh, my God, no! she thought. In real panic, she reached out to switch on the bedside lamp and in the process sent her alarm clock skittering across the darkened room. The noise, intruding into the silence, was piercing and nerve-racking.

She lumbered out of bed, her movements clumsy, and another contraction made her bend over double, grunting with pain. The blackness and the isolation, which had been comforting earlier on, were now a hostile force that brought home the seriousness of her situation in a way that nothing else could.

She was in labour, much earlier than her expected date, and contrary to what her doctor had confidently told her at her last antenatal appointment three days previously. At that point the baby had not yet engaged and he'd predicted that it would be late. Very few babies were born on their due date, he had told her. Some arrived early but most arrived late and he had assured her that she fell into the latter category.

She headed for the stairs, very slowly, and she was trembling by the time she made it to the telephone.

When she picked up the receiver and heard nothing at the end of it, she began to shake. She felt ill and lost and terrified.

She hadn't even bothered to check to make sure that the phone was working when she had arrived. She had just assumed that it would be. She had assumed that Paul and Ellie would have known if it had been disconnected for whatever reason.

Another contraction and now the dreadful pump of

adrenaline through her made her act quickly, switching on lights to ward off the frightful darkness, hunting for her bag containing her car keys, which she located just when she had more or less given up in desperation.

She slung her coat on over her nightdress, made it to the car, and had actually driven it partially down the track, with the trees pressing down on either side, when she realised, with horror, that she wouldn't be able to go the distance. She wouldn't even be able to make it to the main road, never mind that she had no idea where the hospital was even if she did. The contractions were coming stronger and harder, making her grit her teeth together in pain, turning her stomach into a hard rock that made her cry out.

She couldn't even begin to think of what she could do next. The pain made thinking too difficult. She switched off the engine, made her way to the back seat, and she had no idea how long she had lain there, with the pain getting more and more unbearable, when she heard the roar of a car and the screech of brakes as it scudded to a halt behind her.

She didn't care who the hell it was. It was help. She didn't care whether it was a car-load of robbers on their way to ransack the cottage. By God, she would collar them and make them take her to the hospital, or at least to the nearest house where she could use a phone and call for help.

Her eyes were squeezed shut and in between her cries of agony she was panting. She heard the door being yanked open and then a muttered exclamation before someone reached inside the car and she felt herself being lifted out.

She opened her eyes and saw, in a haze, that it was

Angus. Carrying her to the house, opening the door with her key and then kicking it wide open.

'How long?' he demanded, putting her down on the sofa, and she tried to answer but only a long groan emerged. 'Have you telephoned the ambulance?'

'Not working,' Lisa panted. The sweat had cooled on her. She felt slippery and incoherent.

'Dammit! Don't move. I'll be back.'

'Don't move'? Where did he imagine that she was going to move *to*? Did he think that she might go for a quick jog through the woods? Or lumber towards the kitchen to politely fix him a cup of coffee?

It occurred to her that she didn't have any idea what he was doing here, at the cottage, and it also occurred to her that she didn't care. His presence had taken the sharp edge off her terror, though not the tremendous pain. That was still there and getting worse.

She had been to her antenatal classes, and they had all sat around in a civilised group discussing pain-killers. What a joke! To think that she was here now and the only pain-killer in sight was the cushion, which she was biting hard on for all her worth.

'The ambulance is on its way. I've called them from my car phone.' She heard his voice from a long way off and raised her frightened eyes to his, while he stroked her hair back from her forehead and reached out to take her hand in his.

'My darling,' he whispered. 'Hold on. They won't be long. Hold on, my darling. Half an hour at the outside. This place is in the middle of nowhere.'

Had he called her *darling*? She couldn't think. She could hardly breathe and she could hear the high sounds of her cries, torn out of her body, wild and primitive. She squeezed his hand tighter.

'Angus, I've decided...'

'Not now.'

'Angus...!'

'Later, my love, later.'

'Listen to me!' she yelled at the top of her voice. 'The baby! The baby's coming.'

And then things started happening with such speed that she forgot where she was, even forgot *who* she was. She wondered whether he was feeling the same numbing terror that was spreading through her, but when she looked at him as he laid her on the rug in front of the fire he was calm, a deep, reassuring calm that was as soothing on her nerves as any pain-killer could have been.

His voice, ebbing and falling continually, was deep and comforting.

How could she ever have wondered, at those antenatal classes, how she would know that she had gone into labour?

Then her mind went completely blank and nature took over. A strong, driving force that made her body do what it should, when it should. She heard Angus say, 'You're doing beautifully, darling.' Then, almost on top of that, he said, with an emotion that made his voice break and which was as primitive as any emotion she herself had felt, 'I can see the head.'

And the baby was delivered just as the ambulance wailed up to the cottage, sirens going, people everywhere. Lisa's eyes met Angus's, the question formed on her lips, and he answered it before it could be asked.

'We have a girl.'

They were bundled into the ambulance and driven with immense speed along the deserted roads towards the hospital, with Angus pelting along behind them in his car. They had wrapped the baby in a cream-coloured blanket and Lisa stared at her for the duration of the drive.

She couldn't believe it. She had to keep stroking the tiny head with its mass of dark hair; she wanted to smother the little, crumpled face with a million kisses. She wanted to collapse with happiness. She couldn't even remember the pain and terror. That all seemed like a long time ago.

'We'll have to take her from you,' one of the uniformed men said, bending over her. 'Just for a short while!' He held up his hand, smiling at the protest that was already forming on her lips. 'To check her over, make sure that everything's all right. It's not every day that we arrive to find that the baby's already been delivered.'

She nodded obediently, then there was yet more activity as they got to the hospital, and lots of smiling faces and 'Well done's' from seemingly everyone they bumped into.

She was carried in on a stretcher and was told that she would have to be thoroughly checked over, to make sure that everything was in order, and she nodded obediently again.

'We won't be long with you, my dear,' the doctor said—another smiling face. They were all making her feel like a national heroine instead of a complete idiot who had done the most foolish thing in the world by going to stay in that cottage in the middle of nowhere when her baby was imminent.

She wondered, for the millionth time, where Angus was. Now that she could actually think, she wondered whether she had imagined those words of endearment back at the cottage.

'Where's Angus?' she asked.

'Is that your young man? Outside. He wanted to come with you in the ambulance, but there wasn't enough room. He can come in as soon as I'm finished with you.'

During the brief but thorough examination, the doctor made complimentary, slightly awestruck remarks about Angus's coolness, his capability.

'Seemed far less nervous than I was when I delivered my first baby!'

Then, at long last, he left her alone, and when Angus walked in she felt just as shy and tongue-tied at his presence as she had felt all those many, many months ago, when he had walked into a different hospital room to see her after her accident.

He was as dishevelled as she had ever seen him. His hair looked as though he had raked his fingers through it several hundred times and there was darkish stubble on his face. And she didn't know what to say. She just knew that she adored this man, no matter whether the feeling was returned or not.

'You look as though you've had a rough night,' she said weakly, lying back on the pillows, and he pulled a chair over to the bed and sat next to her.

'I have had a rough night, now that you mention it. I'll tell you about it some time. How are you feeling?'

'Wonderful,' she answered truthfully. 'On cloud nine, as a matter of fact. They've taken her away to do a few tests, just make sure that everything's where it should be.'

'I know. I saw her.' He looked a little overwhelmed. 'And now that I've got you to myself there are just one or two things that I want to ask you.'

'You're going to ask me why I went up there.'

'Why did you?'

'I needed to think. I had no idea that I would end up doing more than thinking.' She couldn't seem to stop herself from grinning. She wanted so much to tell him how much she loved him, and it was only the thought of seeing him turn away, unable to reciprocate the emotion, that made her hold back.

She didn't want this one day to be marred by anything. It was the most wonderful day of her whole life and she wanted to keep it that way.

'How on earth did you find me?' she asked.

'I got a phone call from Harrods.'

'Harrods?' She frowned, puzzled, and he shook his head woefully, as though he was talking to something not quite all there.

'You remember that large department store where we went to buy a few bits and pieces? They tried to deliver the furniture to you and there was no reply, so they telephoned me at work. I knew that something didn't quite make sense because you had been quite sure that you would be at your house, ready and waiting for them when they called. So I telephoned your boss, because, quite frankly, he was the only person I could think of.'

'And Paul told you.' She nodded.

'I needn't tell you that I let him have an earful for sending you on your way to that cottage in your condition. I dropped what I was doing and headed up here immediately.'

'Oh, dear.' Lisa giggled and reddened. 'I'm glad you came, though.' She paused and then said in a rush, 'I can't begin to thank you enough. I don't know what I would have done—' Her thoughts were interrupted by a knock on the door, which as a gesture of politeness was hardly worth it, because a nurse entered almost immediately with a transparent carry-cot which she mounted by the bed, and another nurse followed with the baby. Her baby. *Their baby.*

She was absolutely perfect, the senior nurse told them, which Lisa thought was a little irrelevant since she could have told them that herself; she weighed a little over seven pounds and she could sleep for another hour or so, but then would need a feed. Lisa was to call if help was needed. The nurse then offered her congratulations to both of them, adding, 'Won't this be one to tell the grandchildren?'

Then both nurses left and Lisa and Angus stared at the baby. When she looked at him, she saw, with a burst of pride and elation, that he was looking at the little over seven pounds scrap of humanity as though he had never seen a baby in his life before.

Let me savour this moment of perfection for just a little longer, Lisa thought to herself. She decided not to mention anything about marriage just yet because that would be like coming back to earth with a bump. She had already relegated his whispers of tenderness to the realms of imagination induced by circumstance. Her mind must have been playing tricks on her because, although he was being kind enough now, there certainly hadn't been any repetition of 'darling' or anything of the sort.

So she said, looking at the sleeping baby in the cot, 'She's still an "it". We must think of a name.'

'What do you like?' He was still looking at the baby, couldn't take his eyes off her.

Lisa thought and said finally, 'Emily. Emily was my mother's name.' And this baby, she thought, is going to be free like my mother was, free from all those hang-ups that plagued me, free and happy and secure, whatever her surroundings. She's never going to be scared of taking life into both her hands and living it to the fullest.'

'Emily Natasha.'

'Why Natasha?'

'My grandmother's name.'

Which was lovely, Lisa thought, and just left the surname.

'Angus,' she said hesitantly, 'I know we're going to have to discuss this, so we might as well do it now. The reason I went up to Paul and Ellie's cottage, like I said, was to think. I had to get away and I had to get myself sorted out.'

He didn't say anything. Just strolled across to the window and stared out, and she wished that he had remained back where he had been, instead of moving away, putting a barrier between them.

'I've been so confused. I can't begin to tell you what it was like when I found out that I was pregnant.' She looked down at Emily, Emily Natasha, lying in the hospital cot, on her back with both her arms stretched above her, her fists tightly closed, her legs bent at the knees. She couldn't believe that this beautiful creature had started its life as an unwanted pregnancy.

Angus was looking at her in silence, a silence which was neither encouraging nor off-putting, merely waiting to hear whatever she had to say. What was she going to tell him? Enough, she thought, but not too much.

'I was so shocked and horrified and lost I felt as though I had suddenly found myself trapped in a box, with nowhere to turn and no one to turn to.'

'You could have done the most obvious thing and turned to me,' he said roughly, and she smiled.

'But I couldn't, could I?' she asked sadly. 'We hardly knew each other.'

'Some would say that we knew each other very well.'

'When I thought of you, all I could see was an immense gulf, with me on one side and you on the other side. I'm not a fool, Angus. I might not have all the polish and finesse of the other women you've been out with, but I'm not a fool. I know that when we slept together all we were doing was giving in to impulse.'

She laughed to herself. How strange to think that she had once been an inhibited creature. Impulse was something that she'd associated with unhappiness. She'd never known that she would discover it was also what made the vital difference between living and existing.

'I never expected anything to come of our...' She sighed. I never expected it, she thought, but, like a fool, I hoped. 'I always knew that we were too different for anything between us to last.' She risked a glance at him but his face was unreadable and she dropped her eyes, back to the sleeping miracle in the cot.

'You ran away,' Angus said, without any hint of accusation in his voice, merely stating a fact, and she nodded.

'Yes, I ran away. I ran away because you invited me to become your mistress and all I could see was an invitation to be hurt because it would be a relationship with no conclusion.' She waited a bit to see whether he would dispute that, and when he didn't she swallowed down the lump of regret and carried on. 'Then I found out that I was carrying your child. I know you think that I should have told you, but I couldn't. I knew what kind of life you led. I knew that if I turned up on your doorstep and dropped this bombshell on you your life would be wrecked.'

He didn't answer but a look of dark impatience crossed his face.

'Of course, I hadn't banked on bumping into Caroline.'

'Who informed you in no uncertain terms, just as she had on the yacht, no doubt, that whatever you thought you were spot on.'

'I didn't need Caroline to support my views,' she told him with heat in her voice, but then she looked back down at Emily and felt calm and in control again. 'I would have arrived at the same conclusions with or without her. No, I bumped into Caroline and I knew that it would get back to you that I was pregnant.'

Another accident of fate, she thought. Ever since she had met him, she had been destined to have accidents of this nature, or so it appeared.

'And when you asked me to marry you...'

'It was your worst nightmare come true.' He strolled across to the bed and perched on the side of it.

'How do you imagine a woman feels when she's proposed to by a man out of a sense of obligation?' She wanted to dislike him when she said this, but she found that she couldn't. She wondered whether she really ever had. Maybe a little voice in her head had told her that she needed to dislike him, and she had listened to that little voice and assumed that it was how she felt. 'I always imagined that a proposal of marriage would be a wonderfully romantic moment...'

She found that she couldn't continue because her eyes were filling up with tears and her voice was beginning to waver. She had to make an effort to go on.

'My father proposed to my mother on bended knee. She told me. They were only eighteen at the time, and then they waited until he'd finished his university course before they got married. When he proposed, he gave her a bunch of flowers, then he spent half an hour discussing the leaves…can you believe that? Mum said that she was enchanted.'

'It certainly sounds like a magical moment,' Angus said drily, which made her laugh a bit. 'How did they die?'

'In a car accident.'

It was something that she had never talked about. At the time, there had been no one close enough to her in whom she could confide, and then, later, she had not wanted to; she'd preferred to keep their memory stored away inside her, carefully preserved like the pressed flowers she used to collect as a child.

'They were going into town to get some stuff—food—preparing for yet another leap into the unknown. I was at home, studying madly. It was very rainy and there was a collision with a lorry that lost control and swerved across the central reservation. They both died instantly.'

She took a deep breath. 'The fact is, my parents were a romantic couple, and although I don't think I ever appreciated that at the time, something must have embedded itself in my head, because I always assumed that I would find romance. Instead what I found was a fling with a man and a baby on the way.'

It could have been romantic, she thought; it could have been everything she'd ever wanted and more, except that romance had to involve both people and there was no love from him, and, whatever hopes she'd had, she had to face the fact that there probably never would be.

'Anyway, I don't suppose any of this is relevant. I just wanted you to know the reasons why I had to think very hard about this marriage thing.'

There was movement in the cot and Emily's eyelids

began to flicker and then her eyes opened. Blue eyes. She had Angus's bright blue eyes and his dark hair. Lisa instantly pressed the buzzer for the nurse.

She needs feeding, she thought, panic-stricken. What do I do? What if I drop her?

She was relieved, though, that there was this intrusion, because the conversation had been so intense, and she was very much afraid that if she had carried on much longer she would have ended up telling him everything, telling him how she felt.

She would never tell him how she felt. She had made that decision. She would marry him but she would never trap him in a situation where he felt constrained by the fact that she loved him and he didn't return the love.

The nurse bustled in as she was lifting Emily out of the cot, and Lisa looked at Angus, embarrassingly aware that she was about to breast-feed and willing him to go away, but he didn't move. He remained sitting where he was, and she felt her face growing redder and hotter as the baby fumbled by her nipple before finding it and beginning to suck.

He is the father, she thought, but when she raised her eyes to him she still felt hot.

'And...?' he asked.

'And my answer is yes.' She looked down at the tiny thing at her breast and prayed that she had made the right decision.

CHAPTER TEN

LISA didn't quite know what she had expected Angus to say. It was a scenario which she hadn't worked out in her mind. What she hadn't expected was the complete lack of response. Total silence. And she didn't dare lift her eyes to meet his because now a dreadful uneasiness began to sweep over her.

What if he had changed his mind? She concentrated very hard on Emily's mouth, working vigorously at her breast. A strong feeder, the nurse had said, despite being a little early.

All the while, she was wondering why he hadn't said a word. Perhaps the reality of a child had only now sunk in. It worked that way with some people. They imagined parenthood as a cosy little picture with a forever smiling child who never screamed its head off and went to bed when it was told.

Had delivering his own baby opened his eyes to how much his life would change if she married him and he found himself a husband and father? She had thought that it had been an intensely emotional moment for him, and perhaps it had been, but maybe now that that brief excitement was over he was already thinking ahead and not liking the look of what he was seeing.

Was that it?

Her hair hung down across her face, shielding her from eyes which she didn't want to meet, eyes that would gently tell her that he had changed his mind, that she had her freedom. Eyes that wouldn't see the bald truth, which was that she no longer wanted her freedom. It was a commodity which was no longer hers to enjoy, not if he wasn't around.

She had thought, when he had first proposed to her, that to accept would be to condemn herself to a prison in which she lived with the man she adored, but was forever trapped in the hopeless situation of one whose love was not returned.

She realised now that the real prison would be her flat in Reading, her job at the garden centre and a life without focus. The misery of living with him would be infinitely preferable to the misery of living without him.

She had so resigned herself to what she assumed was going through his head that she finally said, breaking the silence between them, 'Of course, if you've changed your mind...then it's not a problem.' She looked at him. 'We can easily work out arrangements.' Emily appeared to be dropping back off to sleep and she removed her from her comfortable position at the breast, drew her robe together, and held her over her shoulder, supporting her with both her hands.

'I—I'm sorry,' she stammered. 'I've been a bit silly. I never thought that you might change your mind. I...'

'I haven't.'

Lisa looked at him, confused. 'Then you still want me to marry you?'

Emily had fallen asleep. Lisa could tell from the slow, rhythmic breathing and she gently lowered her back into the cot and then folded her arms.

'Will you tell me why *you* changed your mind?'

Because I just can't live without you.

'I just thought it over. I realised that it was the most practical thing to do.'

'And what about love?'

'As you said, a successful marriage... Lots of people have stars in their eyes when they get married, and then everything goes wrong... This is more of an arrangement, I know...'

Why did she feel so unhappy? she wondered. Was it because all this talk about arrangements and practicalities was such an anticlimax after Emily's arrival? She told herself that Emily's birth had transported her to another planet, a planet where worries couldn't intrude, but now she was back down to earth and what else could she expect?

How could I ever have thought myself to be a sensible, controlled person? she thought. I'm little more than a hopelessly romantic, incurably impulsive fool.

Angus moved closer to her, sitting so near now that she could have touched his thigh with her hand.

'There are certain conditions,' he began. 'I'm not sure that you'll find them at all acceptable.'

She was feeling more unhappy by the minute. She wondered whether it could be a symptom of postnatal depression. They had spent an entire class devoted to postnatal depression. Maybe that was why she was feeling so tearful. She wished that he hadn't mentioned conditions. That was so cold and clinical. Would he want her to sign something as well? Some legally drawn up contract laying out the terms of their marriage, like a job contract?

She smiled bravely and said, 'Of course, I understand. I know I shall be expected to mingle with your friends. I'm not used to things like that, cocktail parties and business dinners, but I know that that will be a condition of my marrying you. I hope I won't let you down. I hope I won't prove to be an embarrassment.'

She stopped talking. Something had crossed her mind.

What if, by 'conditions', he meant that he should be allowed to have affairs outside marriage? She hadn't thought of that before but she was no great beauty and he mixed in a world of glamorous, tempting women, women for whom married men were not out of bounds, but fair prey. A solitary tear trickled down her cheek and she hurriedly brushed it away.

'Of course, I'm not a great cook. I may have to take lessons...' She didn't want to think about other women in his life. She didn't want to think of him loving anyone or making love to anyone.

'You silly little fool...' he said, catching her hands in his.

'I know,' Lisa said in a small voice. 'I know I'm not very sophisticated. I realise that—'

'Stop talking and listen to me.'

Except he didn't say anything, which made her think that he was trying to work out in his mind how to phrase what he wanted to say, what he *needed* to say, trying to find the right words to tell her that he could never love her, that he was no longer even attracted to her, that she would merely be around because of his daughter.

'I'm not sure how to say this...' he began, and she took a deep, calming breath and braced herself. 'I haven't got many conditions, but they're important ones, and if you don't feel that you can meet them, then you're free, Lisa. Condition number one is that you give up your job at the garden centre.'

'Of course.'

'We could live in London, but only until we find somewhere out in the country. I don't want my daughter being brought up in London. London is no place to raise a child.'

'No,' she said.

'We can start looking for somewhere just as soon as you feel able to. It will have to be within commuting distance of London. Condition number two is that...' He paused and she waited for the bomb to detonate. 'Condition number two is that you start trying to like me.'

'I do like you, Angus.'

'No.' He shook his head and tilted her chin up with his finger. 'No, I mean... I never thought that I would say this to anyone; I never thought that I would have to... Friendship is all well and good... The fact of the matter is...'

A long silence followed and eventually she said, 'What is the fact of the matter?'

Angus sighed heavily and raked his fingers through his already tousled hair. Did he know what an endearing gesture that was? she wondered.

'I'll start at the beginning, shall I?' he asked, and she replied, with a stab at humour,

'OK. I never realised I would be settling down to a story, though.' She waited for him to return her weak smile but he didn't. He looked very serious.

'Do you remember the last time I visited you in a hospital?'

Lisa nodded. Remember? How could she ever forget? Hadn't it changed the entire course of her life? Changed *her*? Released some wild, free bird inside her which she had never thought even existed?

'Well, I never thought that I was opening a door inside me which I would then find impossible to shut.'

A little flare of hope rose inside her. Had he felt that way as well? Because that was exactly how she had felt! She tried to stifle the rising hope. She was deeply in love with him but he had never once said that he loved her, not even in their moment of passion when declarations of love should have been uttered with abandoned ease.

'You intrigued me.' He shot her a brooding, accusatory look.

'Is this a story or a fairy tale, Angus?' she asked, looking at him intently, trying to read the meaning behind his words.

'No interruptions. It's hard enough for me to say these words without interruptions. The fact is that I had never met a woman like you in my life before. You were such a confused mixture of contradictions. Intelligent, amusing, apologetic, without a shred of vanity. I left that hospital never expecting that I wouldn't be able to put you out of my mind, but I couldn't.

'Heaven only knows what I would have done if you had turned down that holiday. Hounded you to your lair, I expect. And I think now, that at the back of my mind I arranged the holiday with you in mind.'

It was an effort not to let every word send her higher and higher. There was a sheepish huskiness in his voice that made her head swim with a thousand possibilities.

'I really thought that I would get you out of my system if I saw you for more than a few hours. I really imagined that all that holiday would entail would be my showing you a good time. You were ripe for being shown a good time, Lisa. You probably don't realise how much. Those timid eyes, that defensive, vulnerable face...you were begging to see things you'd never seen before and I hadn't admitted it to myself, but I wanted to be the one to show you sights that would make your head spin. I had no idea that in the process I would also end up wanting to show you more. Much, much more.'

Lisa felt a quiver of excitement. What was he telling

her, though? Just that he had been attracted to her. Then. Once. No more than that.

'I don't know whether I told myself that you were a challenge. I only knew that I was fiercely attracted to you.' He looked at her very directly when he said this and she met his eyes without blinking.

'Yes, I know,' she said quietly. They had both been burning up with a desire that had taken them by surprise. She looked across to the cot and wondered whether he would have turned his back on that particular challenge if he had only known what the outcome of yielding to it would be.

'I noticed everything about you on that cruise. My eyes followed you; they saw everything you did, every move you made. I wanted to get inside your head so that I could see what you were thinking as well. But that wasn't easy. One step forward, two steps backwards. You have no idea what a frustrating person you can be without even trying! You would reveal so much but then no more and I thought I was going to go mad trying to get to the bottom of you. Then we made love and you informed me that you wanted nothing more to do with me.'

'I explained why,' Lisa said defensively, and he smiled at her.

'Yes, you did. I thought you were a fool. I was offering you what I had never offered any other woman in my life before, and you wanted no part of it. I could have strangled you, but in the end pride won out and I let you run away. I told myself that it wouldn't have lasted. I told myself that it would be better if you weren't around anyway, that my head would be clearer, that all I wanted from life was the satisfaction derived from work. That women, in the end, demanded complicated things which I had no intention of giving them. I knew that you were after marriage and marriage was just not on the agenda as far as I was concerned.'

'Then you found out that I was pregnant.'

'Then I found out that you were pregnant.'

'You weren't very happy.'

'I wasn't unhappy about the pregnancy. In fact, I was amazed at how calmly I accepted that. No, I was furious with you. Furious that you hadn't thought to get in touch with me.'

'Even though, if I had, you would have immediately accused me of being a gold-digger.'

'Being near you does nothing for my sanity,' he said ruefully, with a crooked smile. 'Then you had the nerve to inform me that you weren't going to marry me. I produced the most infallible arguments in the world and you turned your back and told me that I was wasting my time.'

'I changed my mind,' Lisa said, looking at him. 'I went to the cottage because I told myself that I needed to think things over, but I had already made up my mind to accept your proposal.'

'Which brings me to my last condition.'

Lisa was no longer feeling nervous. She didn't know what this last condition was, and her emotions were in a complete muddle, but there was something in his eyes, something in the set of his features that made her feel wonderfully reckless, even if she couldn't quite analyse what that something was.

'You know what I'm telling you, don't you?' He leaned a little over her. 'I'm in love with you, Lisa, and it's no good marrying me for practical reasons if you can't see your way to returning my love at some point in time.'

She smiled. A smile that grew until it reflected the happiness spreading through every tiny niche in her soul.

'About time,' she said, flinging her arms around his neck. 'It's about time this love of mine was returned.'

Lisa and Angus stood outside the black and white house. They had left Emily in London, with the girl who came in from time to time to help out.

The garden was a mass of weeds, which appeared to be winning the battle for supremacy over the rose bushes and various other plants which had not been tended, according to the estate agent, for a year and a half.

'Well, Mrs. Hamilton?' Angus slipped his arm round her shoulders and she felt a thrill of pleasure, contentment, possession. They had been married now for six months and she still loved the way he looked at her, the way he excited her.

They let themselves into the cottage. It was musty, but not dirty. Sunlight filtered through the uncurtained windows, great shafts of it, like arrows striking the floor and the walls.

'It has character,' Lisa said, looking around her.

'As well as all the necessary physical credentials.'

'In need of a face-lift, though.'

'Minor cosmetic surgery.'

They went upstairs and explored the bedrooms—all seven of them. The master bedroom overlooked an expanse of trees and garden and beyond that fields.

'Could you put down roots here?' he asked as she perched on the window-ledge and he placed his hands on either side of her. She never doubted his love for her, but in some tiny part of her she continued to be amazed that a man as sexy and as accomplished as he was could find her so utterly bewitching.

'I think I could,' Lisa said slowly. Putting down roots. With the man she loved and their child. The stuff that dreams were made of. She wrapped her arms around him and lifted her face to his, closing her eyes as his mouth parted her lips and explored wetly and hungrily.

When he slipped his hand under her shirt and caressed the swell of her breast, without the constraint of a bra because it was so warm a day, she giggled and protested half-heartedly and he grinned and buried his head into her neck, nipping with his teeth, rousing her with his fingers, which stroked and teased her swollen nipple.

He unbuttoned the shirt and drew it aside, then bent to suckle at her breasts, and then, on his knees, he lowered her jeans and she stepped out of them. His mouth trailed along her stomach, down to the furry patch of her womanhood. He nuzzled against it, and she groaned as his tongue began a delicate, leisurely exploration. She sat on the ledge of the bay window, parted her legs to accommodate his questing tongue and looked down hungrily at the dark head moving there.

How sweet the memory was of that first time, on that beach a thousand years ago. They had been back there, on their honeymoon, and had taken Emily to the same spot, and had felt the same wonder at the life they had created there.

She drew him up to her and said, with a flushed smile, 'I need you.'

'I should think so.' He unbuckled his belt and removed his trousers then pulled her onto him, and, with her legs wrapped round him, their bodies fused in wild passion. Her breasts pressed against his chest, her head was flung back and his mouth caressed her flesh—hot kisses that made her dizzy with desire and need.

As the roar in her veins gradually subsided, he said,

half joking, half serious, 'Now this house is ours. We've christened it.'

'You're a corrupting influence, Angus Hamilton,' she said, laughing, slipping back into her clothes.

'Only with you, my darling.' He took her hand and they went down the stairs and out into the sunshine. 'I was made just for you and no one else.'

'Good.' Her voice was teasing, satisfied.

They stood outside and looked back at the house. Their house. The house of her dreams, even though, as she now knew, it mattered not in the least where they were, because wherever he was would be home.

Modern Romance™
...seduction and
passion guaranteed

Tender Romance™
...love affairs that
last a lifetime

Sensual Romance™
...sassy, sexy and
seductive

Blaze
...sultry days and
steamy nights

Medical Romance™
...medical drama on
the pulse

Historical Romance™
...rich, vivid and
passionate

27 new titles every month.

With all kinds of Romance for every kind of mood...

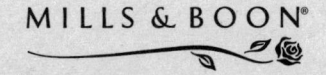

MILLS & BOON®

MILLS & BOON

FOREIGN AFFAIRS

*A captivating 12 book collection of sun-kissed seductions.
Enjoy romance around the world.*

DON'T MISS BOOK 11

mediterranean moments–
Gorgeous Greeks...

Available from 2nd August

Available at most branches of WH Smith, Tesco, Martins, Borders, Eason, Sainsbury's and most good paperback bookshops.

Women & Love

Three women...
looking for their perfect match

PENNY JORDAN

Published 19th July 2002

Available at most branches of WH Smith, Tesco, Martins, Borders, Eason, Sainsbury's and most good paperback bookshops.

MILLS & BOON

STEEP/RTL/16

The STEEPWOOD Scandal

REGENCY DRAMA, INTRIGUE, MISCHIEF... AND MARRIAGE

A new collection of 16 linked Regency Romances, set in the villages surrounding Steepwood Abbey.

Book 16
The Missing Marchioness
by Paula Marshall

Available 2nd August

Available at most branches of WH Smith, Tesco, Martins, Borders, Eason, Sainsbury's, Woolworths and most good paperback bookshops.

'Ellie will help out, you know that...' he said gently, and she didn't answer. Ellie, his wife, was a dear. She had three children of her own, but like Paul she would be shocked at the news, shocked that the unimaginable had happened. As would everyone she worked with. They would all find out in due course. She would become a topic of conversation and, even if it wasn't malicious conversation, the private part of her was dismayed at the prospect.

But it eased her mind to know that her job was safe, and over the next three months she added a few more tenuous silver linings to the cloud. She had a roof over her head, and she had a few good friends.

They had all been sympathetic, they had all hidden their curiosity about the paternity of the baby with a great deal of compassionate understanding, and they were all quite excited on her behalf.

She needed it because she felt next to no excitement at all. She just felt sick most of the time and tired the rest, and anxious.

She was beginning to show and occasionally she would glance down at her growing stomach with a certain amount of wonder at what was happening inside there, out of sight. When she did that, she did feel protective, but there was no counting of days on the calendar or strolling through baby shops excitedly planning what to buy. That, she thought, was more appropriate for women with partners, both sharing the joy of a new life in the making.

It wasn't for her. She just continued feeling vulnerable. In due course, when the time came nearer, she would buy things for the baby, but not yet.

Summer was beginning to fade, with the blue skies becoming rarer every day and the nights drawing in,

'You're a dark horse, Lisa,' he said. 'I didn't even think there was a man in your life.'

'There isn't,' she replied shortly, then she regretted the abruptness of her answer because she could understand how he was feeling. Over the years they had developed a closeness of sorts and it would be as though he had misread her personality altogether.

'It just happened,' she said wearily, sitting down, 'and I'm not sure what I'm going to do.'

'Nothing rash, I hope.' He looked at her sympathetically, which made her feel like crying, and reached out and squeezed her hand. 'It's not the end of the world, you know,' he said awkwardly, but with feeling. 'Your job here's safe. Is there any chance that the father...?'

'No.' Her head shot up. 'He doesn't know and he won't. This is my problem.' She remembered Angus telling her that children were for other people and good luck to them. Unnecessary clutter, his voice had implied and he had swiftly moved on. It was a subject on which he had probably never dwelled and had no intention of doing so.

'Thanks for, you know, reassuring me about the job,' she said, clearing her head of unwanted thoughts.

'Is there anyone you can tell? Any family at all?'

'No one.' It sounded forlorn, said like that, but it was true. There was no one, and the loneliness of her situation forced its way on her with a great wave of despair. Friends would rally round, she knew, but it would never be the same as having family support. In the end, she would be on her own. On her own with a pregnancy she didn't want, on her own with a baby, on her own with every imaginable responsibility, although she told herself that she wasn't the only person to have found herself in this kind of situation.

MILLS & BOON

heat of the night

**LORI FOSTER
GINA WILKINS
VICKI LEWIS THOMPSON**

3 SIZZLING SUMMER NOVELS IN ONE

On sale 17th May 2002

*Available at most branches of WH Smith,
Tesco, Martins, Borders, Eason, Sainsbury's
and most good paperback bookshops.*

Modern Romance™

Eight brand new titles each month

...seduction and passion guaranteed

Available at most branches of WH Smith, Tesco, Martins, Borders, Eason, Sainsbury's, and most good paperback bookshops.

GEN/01/RTL5

Tender Romance™

Four brand new titles each month

...love affairs that last a lifetime.

Available at most branches of WH Smith, Tesco, Martins, Borders, Eason, Sainsbury's, and most good paperback bookshops.

GEN/02/RTL5

Medical Romance™

Six brand new titles each month

...medical drama on the pulse.

Available at most branches of WH Smith, Tesco, Martins, Borders, Eason, Sainsbury's, and most good paperback bookshops.

GEN/03/RTL5